SENIOR'S
HIGH

A NOVEL BY DAVE GOOSSEN

Mary SD,
Enjoy!
DAVE

Also by Dave Goossen
The Living End
12 Cups of Coffee

Trade Paperback ISBN: 978-0-9878917-4-7

Published by David Goossen

www.davegoossen.com

For Shana
You are the one who inspires me to let my imagination soar.

To all the amazing grandmothers who have been part of my life:
Beda & Maria
Marion & Bea
Kirsten & Evelyn

Special thanks to Mike Gobbi, Amy Hinrichs,
Pat Pattison and Malcolm McCallum for their honest opinions and
for helping me make this as good as it could be.

Gratitude and appreciations to Ginny Glass and Tracey
Tannenbaum from Book Helpline and Maylon Gardner for their
editing skills and for turning what I thought was great into
properly punctuated great.

SENIOR'S HIGH

Prologue

"I'll give you twenty-five bucks for the lot."

Paul Carter stared at the guy who spoke—the guy standing in front of him with a handful of fishing rods and reels in his hands. Paul stared at him with a slight squint, a squint that made the steel in his blue eyes glitter menacingly. His wife, God bless her, had known that squint, his children certainly knew it, and those who served under him back in the Army were terrified of it. Only his grandson hadn't experienced it. So far.

Sitting in a crappy old Adirondack chair in front of his garage for the whole morning had done a number on his 'new and improved' hip. It didn't help that his teenaged grandson, Devon, was supposed to be helping, but had gone off with his friends shortly after the sale started. He winced at another hip twinge and slowly rose to his feet to face the ruddy-complexioned middle-aged man who failed to hide his age with a rock band t-shirt and a backwards trucker cap.

"Those, my friend, are Temple Fork fly rods with Orvis reels. Originals. You don't even want to know what I originally paid for them."

The guy rubbed his gut and chewed his gum for a moment before saying, "All right, all right. Fifty bucks for the lot."

Paul scowled, something he also did quite well, and then gave up.

"Fine. Fifty bucks."

With a grin, the guy passed over two rumpled twenties and a ten and rushed back to his Lexus with his haul. Paul pocketed the cash and looked around the garage at the half-full tables. *Eighty years on the planet and I'm selling it off for pennies on the dollar,* he thought cynically. *And for what? Pocket change for where I'm going next.*

A half an hour later, the sun had started to set behind the towering row of trees he'd helped plant as a child. He still remembered his father rolling up with the farm truck bed full of skinny saplings. As his oldest brother worked away from the farm, Paul received the honor of pacing out where each tree would go along the edge of their property. Then came a long day of digging, but, by dinnertime, they'd done it and the trees were planted. He remembered clearly, picking at his new blisters, how uninspiring the trees looked.

From the front porch, it had looked as if a row of tall sticks had been shoved into the dirt along the road that ran past their farm. He'd said so to his father, who simply brushed some rich prairie dirt off his work pants and told him to be patient. But being patient was nearly impossible for a ten-year-old boy and it seemed like a thousand winters before those spindly sticks were a huge wall of glorious trees — with only one gap where his youngest brother had tipped the tractor that he shouldn't have been driving and spilled a barrel of weed killer.

That one tree had greyed and died within a week and, despite a couple of attempts, they couldn't get another tree to grow in the space. Behind those trees there was nothing but prairies until the Rocky Mountains in Idaho.

Beside him was the house he had built with his father. At the time, building the main floor up high enough to be above the winter snows seemed pretty smart—nothing much worse than being snowed in—but since he fell on the front stairs and broke his hip, that long-ago decision had made Paul's life miserable. But now, everyone involved in that long-ago tree planting was gone, dead and buried, except for him.

Brothers, sisters, parents—all gone. *Not much keeping me on this plot of land anymore,* Paul thought.

A clattering at the back of the garage brought him back to the present. He watched as an old guy—not that he should be calling someone in their sixties old, but this guy did look old, early old—poked around at the table covered in his perfectly-cared-for tools. In the distance, a light cloud of dust heralded someone new to his fire sale. *I'm sick and tired of this,* he thought. Haggling over pennies, what a waste of time. Not that he had any place he needed to be, or anything he needed to do, except sit in an uncomfortable chair and fake smile at strangers picking over his bones.

A Nissan pickup pulled up in a cloud of dust and a blare of music. His teenaged grandson, Devon, hopped out, fist-bumped the driver, then started a casual, cool, and slow stroll across the lawn towards him. The driver honked the horn a couple of times, and Paul waved as the truck cruised back down the driveway. *Let's see how long he waits before pushing the pedal to the floor,* Paul thought.

"Hey, Gramps."

Paul gave him a nod as he continued watching Devon's friend stop at the end of the driveway, blatantly checking both ways for the benefit of Paul, before turning away from the farm and taking off in a squeal of tires. Paul shook his head at the transparency of youth and turned to his grandson.

Devon was tall like his mother, wiry strong like his dad, with a mop of sun-faded brown hair that defied gravity even with the help of some industrial-strength hair product.

"How's it going?" Devon asked, glancing around.

"A pain in my… hip. Vultures, all of them."

Devon laughed as the guy at the tools held up a router in pristine condition and called out, "How much for this?"

"What does it say on the tag?" Paul called back.

The guy looked and then said, "Ten bucks."

"Then it's ten bucks."

The guy frowned in confusion. "I'll give you five."

"Why I'll give you..." Paul muttered but Devon stepped in between the two and said, brightly, "Ten, and we'll throw in the jig and the bits."

"Deal!"

Another hour and another fifty dollars earned later, they watched as the last car full of looky-loos started down the long driveway. *Enough of giving away my hard-earned possessions,* Paul thought, before asking Devon to pull down the garage door. Whatever's left is a problem for the new owners. Paul fumbled with the cell phone his daughter, Natalie, had insisted he carry with him since the accident. At all times. *Like an irresponsible teenager,* he thought. Meanwhile, you couldn't keep Devon off his phone—he was always playing some silly game. He poked at the keys for a bit before turning the phone back off and turned to his grandson, "Tell your mom we're ready to be picked up."

Devon didn't look up from his phone to reply, engrossed in some game. "Already did."

"You ready to leave this place?" Paul asked, glancing around at the aging buildings and acres of early wheat rustling gently in the evening breeze. It hurt that he hadn't been able to keep up with the maintenance on the farm structures. That had always been a point of pride for him. Luckily, his neighbor rented the fields so they weren't being left unploughed.

"Sure," Devon said with a shrug.

"That's all? 'Sure'? We're not going to be back here for a long time. No more Montana sunsets."

Devon paused his game and looked at his grandfather, saying, "No more hiking down that driveway to get the school bus through three feet of Montana snow."

"Fair enough."

Devon really only had a decade of memories here, Paul thought, *but I've got a lifetime. Years of school, chores, play, and making do. Growing up and getting old right here. My wife, buried beside the willow at the back of the property.* He'd miss walking back to sit at her grave to tell her about his day. He'd miss a lot, but that was life. There was always something, or someone, to miss by the time you got as old as he was.

With a groan, Paul leaned down to the Igloo cooler beside his chair and poked around inside.

"Devon, my hip's acting up; could you run inside and grab me one of those non-alcoholic beers from the fridge? There's a Pepsi here for you."

"Ok."

Paul watched until Devon entered the back door of the farmhouse and then he furiously shook up the can of pop, returning it to the cooler before Devon came back out. As he crossed the yard with the can of beer, Devon called out, "Hey, how much of the money from the garage sale do I get?"

"How about I give you ten bucks for each hour you were physically here?"

"But that's barely worth it," Devon said, handing him the can.

"You should have stuck around," Paul said with a smile, innocently taking the Pepsi out of the cooler again.

Paul leaned back in the chair as Devon popped his drink open. Foaming liquid shot out, drenching him completely.

"Damnit, Gramps!"

Paul laughed and said, "You gotta watch them cans, you never know..." and opened his beer only to get equally drenched.

"You little—"

Devon laughed uproariously, wiping his face while enjoying his grandfather's dilemma.

While the two were concentrating on cleaning themselves up, a minivan pulled up and honked.

The two stopped laughing quickly and looked at each other.

"An accident. Don't tell your mom we were joking around, or else."

"Have I ever told her? C'mon."

Devon winked, and Paul winked back. As the driver climbed out of the van, Devon called out, "Hey Mom!"

"What on earth happened here?" Paul's daughter, Natalie, called out as she came around the front of the van.

Paul shrugged, and, with a quick glance to Devon, said, "I guess the cooler sat in the sun too long."

Natalie shook her head, taking in her soaked father and son.

"What am I going to do with you?"

Paul smiled, "Me? He's the one with the drinking problem."

One

The light was different. Rich, lush, diffused through the canopy of ancient trees along the road. The air was different, too, so unlike where he'd lived his life up until then—humid, thick, and full of life.

Paul wasn't sure he liked either of them.

Paul watched the streets and houses pass. The dark canopy of branches overhead brought back memories of his Army training at Fort Bennington—which was just a few hundred miles to the south—of parade squares, barracks, and running under similar trees, sweating like dogs, a fifty-pound pack on their shoulders. He preferred the open sky of the prairies to being hemmed in by the expansive cover of the trees. At least back home he knew what was coming, especially the weather—thunder clouds building on the horizon, portents of an incoming storm, or, even better, nothing but clear blue skies as far as you could see in all directions.

He leaned forward, looking at the trees sliding by overhead; here you couldn't see a damn thing. With a barely audible snort, Paul eased himself back, made some slight adjustments to how he sat, and returned to gazing impassively out the window. It may have been called North Carolina, but he was back in the South, a place he would have bet good money or bad cards that he wouldn't be returning to again.

•

Natalie hadn't noticed the light or the air; she'd been concentrating on the road and the GPS. On the screen, a blue arrow patiently and confidently moved the three of them closer and closer to their new life.

Natalie maneuvered her minivan through the calm streets of Cloverton, North Carolina. On both sides of her, children were playing in the front yards of immaculate old houses and well-dressed people walked their polite and attentive dogs on the sidewalks, most clutching a tied-off plastic bag in their free hand.

Another block was taken up entirely with a stately southern plantation, barely visible back from the street across a pristine front yard larger than what had remained of the family farm they'd left five days ago.

She glanced up at the rearview mirror at her teenaged son slouched in the back seat, crowded by their luggage, and deeply engrossed in some video game on his phone.

Stoic, that's how her son took her decision. She would have preferred a little drama from him, a bit of youthful outrage, a bit of railing against the system, even some stomping and door slamming. Instead, she had gotten a couple of sighs, exactly like the ones from her dad. Both knew how hard the decision was for her, knew how much effort it was. Of course, she was pretty sure neither of them was particularly happy, but stoic had won out. Before they knew it, the farm had been sold, the minivan loaded with their luggage, the U-Haul trailer filled with furniture rattling behind them, and they were on the one road out of the town they had grown up in.

She flicked her eyes over the road, ensuring no errant kids on bikes were about to shoot out into traffic and looked over at her father in the passenger seat. She had no idea what was going on in his mind; his face was as neutral as it had been for most of her upbringing, with only the occasional frightening moments of emotion that she knew meant something awful had happened or was about to happen.

Like when she crashed the tractor into the irrigation ditch at age ten when she wasn't supposed to even to know how to drive it. Then she had seen that neutral face turn to anger and, worse, disappointment. Much harder to take was what she saw on his face after her mother had passed after suffering through four years of lung cancer.

Now she had taken them both off to the other side of the country to start a new life. Three new lives.

•

"Devon, look! Devon!" Natalie called back over the seat at him, "Devon!"

With a quick flick of his head, the bulky Dr. Dre headphones slid back off his ears and settled around his neck. Devon paused his game— the same one he'd been playing since he'd downloaded it at a Holiday Inn with free WiFi in Kansas City.

"Uh-huh?"

Devon assumed either his mom or grandfather would point out some historical monument or roadside attraction, as they had been doing annoyingly regularly for the entire trip. Who cared when some wagon train passed some boring hill in the middle of nowhere? He grew up in the middle of nowhere. He knew the middle of nowhere. What they should have been pointing out was some place interesting in the middle of somewhere interesting.

His mom slowed the van and pulled over the side of the street. Devon glanced out his window. Houses. Old houses with yards. More big old trees. Cars in driveways. Big whoop.

"Yeah—houses, cars, trees. I've seen them before, Mom." He started to pull his headphones back up onto his ears and return to shooting at zombies.

"She means this side, Devon," said Paul, with a bit of a smirk.

Devon leaned over the luggage piled up around him and saw a vast, old, three-story brick building at the far side of a perfectly mowed front lawn. Four white pillars rose in front of the center doors. Across the top of the doors, carved in the massive stone lintel were the words: General Sherman Cavanaugh High School, established 1755.

Natalie said, "That's your new high school."

Devon shrugged and leaned back, pulling on his headphones. "Whatever."

In the front seat, Paul looked over at Natalie and said, "He's thrilled."

"Yeah, I can tell."

With the briefest of smiles, she checked the rearview mirror and pulled back out into the street.

What had she expected? He'd be thrilled seeing his new school? Was any teenager ever excited to see their new school? Would she have been excited to move across the country only to find a school ten times larger than the one she had left? Paul watched his daughter while she took in a deep calming breath as she put the van into gear and pulled out into traffic.

"So, are we going to drive up and down every street in this town, Natalie? I understand getting a feel for the place, and I'm all for it, but I'd surely love to climb off this damned seat for a while."

"Ok, Dad. One more stop and then we'll grab some lunch."

With the ever-present help of the GPS, she made a couple of turns and figured out where to go. How would we have ever made it here without the Tom-Tom on the dash? She gave it a pat like a faithful dog that had brought her slippers. Without it, it would have been three thousand miles with her father as navigator, keeper, and the folder of the maps, debating and re-debating their options at all highway interchanges.

They would have killed each other five times over. She gave the GPS another appreciative pat and looked out the window.

Across a parking lot stood a modern two-story building clad in blue-tinted glass. After the streets of antebellum mansions, it was a startling change. The trees around the parking lot were tiny in comparison, three or four years old, giving away the age of the building.

Devon leaned forward between the seats, asking, "Is this where we're having lunch?"

Paul glanced over at him, the kid had ears like a barn owl when someone mentioned food; otherwise, he tuned out everything he wasn't interested in as effectively as if his head were sealed in amber. Exactly like his mom had been at that age.

"Well, I'll be having lunch here."

"Mom! What about us? I'm totally starving!"

Natalie laughed and pointed out the window. "Devon, that's where I'll be working. Enviro-Dyne. The whole building is theirs. Twenty-two thousand square feet."

Devon waited out the silence for as long as he could—more than twenty-seconds, he figured—then sighed, "Ok, we've seen it, super-amazing. Now what about lunch?"

Paul ruffled Devon's hair and pushed him back into his seat.

"Lunch sounds about right, Natalie."

Natalie nodded and started up the van.

"Ok, you two. I guess I'd better feed you before you both pass out on me."

She had seen pictures of the building before. They were on the Enviro-Dyne website, as part of her contract package, and she'd even used Google Maps Street View to virtually drive right along this same street and paused right where she had just parked. But despite knowing what the building looked like, she now knew that being there in front of it was different.

This building would be the core of her new life. It would pretty much be the anchor for her and her family. If she made this work, their life would be good. If she didn't make it work, then they'd be even worse off than when she piled them into the minivan and started off across the country. *Please, let this job, this town, work for us, ok? I'm not asking a lot here; it doesn't have to be perfect, but it must work. For me and for us.*

Two

After failing to find a local restaurant the three of them could agree on, Natalie gave up and pulled into a Denny's on the outskirts of town, smack in the middle of a mile of big-box stores like Walmart, car dealerships, and fast food restaurants. Devon settled in the middle of one side of the booth, leaving Paul and Nat to slide in on the other side. Quickly Devon ordered his favorites: a double cheeseburger, fries, and chocolate milkshake. Natalie hadn't even opened the menu yet. Paul kept his closed like his grandson, ordering what he always had also.

"Two easy; toast, brown; bacon, crispy; coffee black."

The middle-aged waitress nodded and turned to Natalie. She flicked through the dozen pages of the menu, looking for something to draw her eye. "I'll have a BLT, on brown, side salad with a vinaigrette and a Diet Coke to drink, please." She shut the menu and passed it the waitress who disappeared in a flash only to return with the coffee and a smile for her dad.

"Ooh, Gramps is making friends already."

"Maybe she has a granddaughter for you, Devon."

Devon and Paul shared quick smirks across the table.

"And a son for you, Mom."

Natalie laughed and said, "Let's settle here before we start planning three weddings, okay?"

An hour later, they were back in the van. Natalie typed some coordinates into the GPS while Paul scanned the slightly more open skies above the parking lots.

"Where to now?" Devon asked before firing up his latest game on his phone.

"We'll settle your grandfather and then we'll find our new place."

"Don't know why I'm not living with you two," Paul muttered.

Natalie put the van back into park, sighed, and looked over at her father. She knew that going from living in the house he'd built to having a room in the assisted living center she'd found for him would be a difficult transition. Once, a while after she'd brought it up back in Montana, he'd said that going into the home would make him old.

She understood that. She didn't want to be putting him in a home either, that made her feel both old and like a bad daughter. But the semi-furnished apartment the company had found for her had only two bedrooms. Hard enough for her and Devon to live in a quarter of the space they'd left behind, but to add her dad would have made it unbearable. But Paul's hip, a memento from the Vietnam War, sealed the deal. The two flights of stairs up to the apartment would be too difficult and potentially dangerous for Paul to try and manage over and over every day.

Twenty minutes later, after driving through the bustling historic center of the town, Natalie turned off the heavily treed two-lane road that wound a short distance along a meandering river and into the spacious grounds of a fully restored antebellum plantation mansion. Shining white against the blue of the sky and the bright green of the grounds that lay before it, the building looked ready for the arrival of Scarlett O'Hara for some cotillion. Mature trees graced the lawn, providing gentle shade.

Natalie pulled the van over to the side of the white gravel drive as soon as she entered the estate through the impressive stone archway.

Devon leaned forward between the seats, his headphones around his neck, the faint sounds of music seeping out of them. "Wow, you could fight the Civil War on the front lawn of this place."

"They probably did," Paul replied.

"So, what do you think, dad?"

"You sure you have the right place? 'Cause I forgot to pack my tuxedo."

Devon laughed; Natalie smiled and rolled the van slowly forward to stop under the massive porte-cochere along the side of the main house. As she and Paul climbed out of the van, Natalie could that see a recent three-story addition had been skillfully added behind the main structure. It looked like a medium sized hotel had cuddled up behind the mansion. *Those must be the rooms,* Natalie thought, seeing the individual balconies, each with a view of the lawn sloping away into a well-tended forest ending at the ancient stone walls that marked the edge of the property.

Maybe there's a room for us to live here too, she thought as she leaned back into the van.

"You going to come in with us and see where Gramps will be living, or are you just going to hide here in the dark and play that pointless game on your phone?"

Devon laughed, popped his headphones back on, and slouched back in his seat in reply.

Shaking her head, Natalie looked across the front of the van at her father. Paul grudgingly pulled his aluminum cane out of the back of the van and started struggling to shut the sliding door.

She started to ask if he needed help when she saw a manager-type person stride out the wide front doors of the mansion towards them. A well-kept, nearly handsome man around her age—mid-forties—dressed and groomed to be somewhere above a four-star hotel manager and slightly below a mid-level corporate executive.

"Ah, you must be the Carters. Excellent. Excellent. Kevin Wright, owner, manager, chief cook, and bottle washer."

It might have been a joke, or he might have been serious. Kevin's neutral face didn't show any sign either way. Natalie decided a laugh might be the right response and was rewarded with a well-groomed smile, showing off perfect teeth. He might be the same age as her, but he sounded like he'd stepped out of a Masterpiece Theatre production. She put on her best business smile and arched out her hand. "Hello, I'm Natalie Skaarsgard. And this is my father, Paul Carter. My son, Devon, is hiding in the van."

After shaking Natalie's hand, Kevin held out his hand to Paul. Paul took Kevin's smooth, clearly manicured hand into his own scarred, calloused, weathered one and gave it a firm shake. Years of running a farm hadn't softened his grip, and he leaned into it, out of sheer amusement. To his surprise, Kevin met his grip.

"Quite the place you've got here," Paul commented, not letting go of Kevin's hand.

"Been in the family for over two hundred years," Kevin replied, not breaking eye contact.

Paul suddenly realized that this wasn't the man to make an enemy of, not on his first day. First day. The first day of school, the first day in the Army, first day on the ground in Vietnam. The first day was pretty much the worst day to piss anyone off. Paul smiled and let go of Kevin's hand, strategically faking a wince. Kevin smiled slightly, the victor, and turned towards Natalie.

"Why don't we show you around, then we'll tidy up the paperwork before Paul joins everyone for dinner. Marcus will take Mr. Carter's bags to his room."

And, without waiting for their reply, Kevin strode into the mansion.

Paul and Natalie turned around to find a large, solid man standing behind them. He wore an immaculate black suit with a crimson vest over a crisp white shirt. His skin was the color of dark chocolate and his bald head shone in the afternoon light. Inside, Kevin paused in the grand rotunda foyer and adjusted the flower arrangement on an ornate round table placed perfectly in the center of the parquet floor. Paul flexed his hand, recovering from his handshake with Kevin.

"I see you're going to be like that, then, aren't you, Mister Paul?"

"Like what, Mister Marcus?" Paul grinned up at the huge man.

"'Like what?' he says… You and I both know like what."

As Natalie opened the back of the van and reached in to grab Paul's suitcases, Marcus frowned at Paul, then turned to her. "No ma'am, I'll be taking those for you. That's my job around here. Getting things and taking them places. Then making sure them things stay in their places."

Natalie stepped back as Marcus reached into the van and pulled out the suitcases she indicated. He easily handled the four bulky cases as if they were pillows.

Paul watched as Marcus shut the van hatch and headed into the mansion. *I'll have to keep an eye out for him,* he thought, *especially since he's already got my number. Not good, picking fights with the boss and antagonizing the toughest-looking guy I've seen in years within five minutes of climbing out of the vehicle. For Nat's sake, I'd better be quiet and—what does she always say?— 'go with the flow' for a bit.* He smiled at his daughter, who watched Marcus saunter across the rotunda and down a corridor heading towards the guest rooms. Taking her hand in his, Paul moved her into the mansion. "Quite the place for an old codger like me."

"Dad, you're not old… but you sure are a codger sometimes."

With that, they crossed to where Kevin waited for them.

As they strolled down the immaculate hallway, Paul glanced at the perfectly framed and mounted prints and paintings on the walls. Displayed on both sides of their walk, it was a cavalcade of history going back in time to the beginning of photographs. The last two portraits, immediately outside of Kevin's office, were of a proud, noble-looking man and a radiantly beautiful woman. Paul paused and glanced at the brass titles attached to the frames.

The man was clearly Kevin's father—they shared the last name—who, according to the plaque, passed away some twenty-five years ago only in his early fifties. *Pretty young,* Paul thought. *Looked healthy when he died, lots more years left in him. Wonder what happened?* He turned to the other portrait, aligned on the wall respectably close to the image of Kevin's father. *I wonder who she is and why she's on the wall?* Before Paul considered anything more than 'she sure must have been the belle of the ball...' a substantial jolt to his shoulder sent him stumbling.

Paul quickly reached out and grabbed the back of a delicate chair before he fell to the carpet. Regaining his balance, he turned around and looked up into the chest of an eighty-year-old quarterback, still wearing his letterman's sweater.

Christ, not one of these guys, Paul thought as he pulled himself upright. Glancing around, Paul noticed that Natalie and Kevin had already gone into Kevin's office. Like high school: alone in the hallway with the king of the school.

"I'm gonna have to assume that was an accident, ok?" Paul said, rubbing his shoulder.

"Now why would you think that?" Quarterback said, leaning in, attempting to be menacing. Paul sighed. Menacing was an enraged steer pawing at the ground in front of you, or the North Vietnamese shelling your position when you had no way out. Menacing was your teenaged daughter needing to use the car on a Friday night and you saying no. This guy? Nothing. Nothing but soft.

"Because you wouldn't have been stupid enough to do it on purpose."

"I would. And I will again if I catch you making googly eyes at my girl."

Paul leaned back; then pointed at the photograph on the wall.

"That's your girl?"

Quarterback nodded.

"Oh, I'm sorry, I didn't understand. My fault."

Quarterback took a step back, adjusting his sweater where it stretched across his ample belly. A quick wipe with his hand ensured his rapidly thinning, and obviously colored hair, remained in place.

"Don't do it again."

Paul reached out, and they shook hands. Paul glanced back at the picture. Quarterback started swaggering down the hall.

Paul called after him, "See, I thought that was your mother."

As Quarterback swung around, another man stepped into the fray.

"Gentlemen, gentlemen," the new man said, hands up in front of both Paul and Quarterback. "He means nothing by it, Chuck, nothing at all. He's new here, ok? First day jitters, I reckon. That's all, Chuck."

"I'm not jittery at—"

The new man turned to Paul and said, "Son, at this point, jittery is what you are. I've been on this earth long enough to know jittery when I see it."

Paul caught the wink the new man gave him and sighed. "It has been a long trip, I will admit that."

The new man lowered his arms and turned to Chuck, saying, "See? A long trip is all. Jittery after a long trip. You'll acknowledge everyone gets a mite jittery after a long trip, won't you, Chuck?"

With a scowl, Chuck nodded and, with a huff of air to prove himself the better man, turned and continued strutting down the hallway and out of sight.

The new man watched him go and once Chuck disappeared turned back to Paul.

"Good Lord, clearly you took one too many kicks to the head as a child to come into a new place and start out kicking the meanest animal in the stable..."

Paul smiled. "Daddy said it was my greatest weakness."

"Your daddy was truly right." The new man stuck out his hand, "Jim Lyons."

"Paul Carter."

The two shook hands. Paul felt faint tremors in Jim's palm as they shook.

"You been in here long?"

"Lord, it's not a prison. Five years."

"And?"

"Could be worse."

Paul glanced down the hall the direction Chuck had gone.

"That as bad as it gets?"

Jim nodded. Paul shrugged.

"Then that's not so bad."

Jim smiled. "Nope, not so bad at all."

Jim glanced at Kevin's office door.

"You'd best be joining them in there. Mr. Wright doesn't take kindly to being kept waiting."

Paul looked at the door, then at the photo of the woman beside the door.

"My daughter is in with him, telling him all about me and my 'issues.' I'm good waiting out in the hall. Done that enough in my life."

Jim looked at him sharply, then sighed before responding, "A wait-in-the-hall kind of man. You haven't even settled in, and I'm already mediating on your behalf. Mercifully, I don't have a practice anymore or I could leave your first invoice on your pillow."

"Pleasure to meet you, Jim."

"Likewise, Paul."

They shook hands again. Paul sat down in the chair under the woman's picture. He stared resolutely across the hall at a heroic painting of a noble Civil War battle as Jim made his way down the corridor, the same direction Chuck had gone. But while Chuck had strutted, Jim moved slowly, gracefully, and, despite being supported by his cane, a bit cautiously.

Damnit, being old sucks, Paul thought as he returned to staring at the Civil War painting across from him, pondering what he would have done to Chuck if he had been his commanding officer in the Army. KP duty, or maybe a nice midnight run with a full pack. In the rain. The thought made Paul smile. That would knock him down a few notches, definitely.

Paul had nearly tuned out the quiet noises of the building—the occasional hum of some machine turning on or turning off; whispered conversations in rooms along the hallway; quickly answered telephones—when the door beside him swung open, and Kevin bounded out with Natalie coming up behind him.

"Right! Let's show you both around the facilities and then we'll show you to your new room!"

Without waiting for Paul to get up from the chair, Kevin started off down the hallway. Natalie gave her father a weak smile and offered a hand to help him up from the chair.

Paul scowled at her. "I'll look after myself."

She dropped her arm to her side like she had been slapped. "I know that, Dad. I know."

Paul pushed himself up from the chair. *I should have taken the hand,* he thought briefly as a sharp jolt of pain twinged in his hip. They headed down the hall to where Kevin waited for them, only partially able to mask his impatience.

"What kind of a man runs a nursing home if he's impatient with old people walking slowly?" Paul muttered to Natalie.

"He's not impatient; he's busy. He has a lot to do."

"Like get into your pants."

"Dad!" Natalie stopped and turned to face Paul. "He does not want to—" she dropped her voice to a whisper, "get into my pants!"

"If you say so," Paul said and continued down the hall to join Kevin.

Natalie took a deep breath and watched Paul walk away from her.

Paul and Kevin waited for Natalie in an uncomfortable silence. When she joined them, Kevin opened the double doors in front of him with a well-practiced flourish.

"And here is our dining hall."

Without pausing for their reactions, he stepped inside and started pointing out different areas and items. Natalie took up the slack in Paul's continued silence and commented appropriately as Kevin aimed his arm at seating areas, self-service coffee and tea stations, and French doors that opened to an outdoor patio.

Paul simply glanced around the room quickly, took in the items of most importance—an industrial-sized coffee urn—ignored the rest, then spent the rest of the time casually watching Kevin.

A smooth operator, that's what he is, Paul thought. Kevin's eyes were always watching Natalie, even if his hand pointed to some place in the room. And Kevin listened to her reactions and then tailored his next comment to fit with them.

A salesman, Paul thought. *Never did like salesmen. They're always trying to sell you something. Always with a smile.*

Suddenly Kevin turned and strode back out into the hallway. Natalie and Paul followed, Paul taking one last glance at the tables placed evenly around the large room. In one corner, he saw Chuck lounging in a comfortable chair surrounded by a couple of other fading members of the football team. Before stepping out the door, he saw Chuck finish his joke. There was a pause before his buddies clued in to laugh, and then they laughed weakly.

What fun this place will be, Paul thought darkly, before he turned to catch up with his daughter.

Three

They spent the rest of the afternoon moving from place to place with Paul always last to arrive wherever Kevin took them, and last to leave. He saw the outdoor walkways through massive old trees that had apparently been planted by Kevin's great-grandfather. Probably by Kevin's great-grandfather's slaves—but Paul kept his mouth shut with that one, noticing Natalie give him another one of her many glances.

They paused at the tennis courts—where no one played; the lawn bowling courts—where no one bowled; and even strolled down to the riverside dock—where no one fished.

"It certainly is a wonderful place you have here, Kevin," Natalie said with a smile as they began walking back up to the mansion. Kevin smiled a proud smile.

"We try our best, and have for four generations now, to run the best establishment possible."

"And what about the next generation? Have you any children?"

"We have one child. A daughter, Dawn. She goes to the high school."

Paul piped in, "That will be nice for Devon, to know someone at school already."

"Yes, of course," Kevin said with an utterly neutral face.

Paul thought of a few choice words, but another look from Natalie kept his mouth shut. They walked on, passing the occasional resident or two. Kevin would nod his head and wish them a pleasant 'good afternoon' as they strolled along. For all his smiles, to Paul it looked like Kevin simply went through the motions, not interested in a conversation with anyone, merely stating a fact that it was a good afternoon.

"What's through there?" Paul asked, looking at a pair of sturdy hospital doors at the end of a short corridor.

"That's the secure wing of Shady Acres," Kevin replied.

"Secure in what way?"

"The third floor is our Memory Care residents—those with Alzheimer's and dementia. The second floor is for Assisted Living and then the ground floor for Extended Care."

"And after that, they go right into the ground," Paul quipped.

No one laughed and Kevin continued down the hallway. Paul sighed and followed, ignoring his daughter's reproachful gaze.

As they passed through the massive foyer, Marcus leaned out from his desk and informed Kevin that Paul's belongings had been placed in his room. With a polite nod of acknowledgment, Kevin took the plastic key card from Marcus and passed it over to Paul.

"Now, I'm sure your grandson is eager to get to his new home, so we'll say goodbye for now to Natalie and then you retire to your room, settle in, and freshen up for dinner," Kevin said, again not offering any space for disagreement.

"Oh, I thought—" Natalie said, clearly expecting a visit to her father's new room.

Paul smiled and turned the key card over in his palm, saying, "It's peachy, honey. Come back and I'll give you the grand tour of my room some other time."

Kevin slipped back a couple of steps to give them some privacy. Natalie gave her father a long hug and a kiss on the cheek; Paul resisted pulling away from the rather public display of affection, but instead took a breath and let her hug until she finished. Just because he didn't like getting hugged didn't mean she didn't like hugging. The things you do for family.

Natalie stepped back and looked at him before asking, "You going to be okay?"

Paul gave her the largest smile he could. "Of course. I'll be fine. I'll be grand. Like the first day in the Army, but with better food, lodging, and women."

Natalie wiped a tear from the corner of her eye and gave him a smile. "Come say goodbye to Devon. Then we'll go find our new place."

With Marcus watching impassively and Kevin watching with barely veiled impatience, Natalie and Paul walked out to the minivan. Paul rapped hard on the window by Devon's head, but he didn't notice, engrossed in his video game. Paul sighed and turned to Natalie, saying, "You gotta wean him off that thing, occasionally. It'll ruin his head."

"I know, Dad. Once school starts he'll have homework and new friends and won't use it at all."

She clicked the car keys to unlock the doors. Paul pulled open Devon's door, finally startling him away from the game. "Ah! I nearly got killed!" he yelled, pulling his massive headphones off his ears.

"I would have caught you, Devon."

"In my game!"

Natalie and Paul laughed.

"Say bye to your grandfather, he needs his nap before dinner."

"I'm not having a nap. I'm not a baby."

"You had a nap every day we were driving here."

"No, I didn't."

Devon looked up. "Well, then you shut your eyes and snored so loud we couldn't hear the radio for a couple of hours every day."

"That's different," Paul said gruffly, "That's the rhythm of the road. Lulls you to sleep."

Natalie smiled and gave Paul another hug, "If you say so, Dad."

As Natalie started around the van to the driver's seat, Devon reached out a fist and Paul gave him a fist bump. *No handshakes for this generation,* he thought. No hugs, either, and he wasn't sure if he was fine with that or not.

"Help your mom ready your new place, ok? No sitting in an empty room playing whatever game you're playing."

"It sucks you're not going to be living with us."

"It'll be fine, Devon. And you tell your mom that I'm happy here, and you're happy in your apartment, even if you're not. She's under a lot of stress, and doesn't need complaining from us right now."

"Ok, ok…"

"This is between you and me, right?" he said, eyeing Natalie as she opened the door to enter the van.

Devon rolled his eyes, "Yes, Gramps."

"Good, now you two get out of here."

Paul stepped back and waved as Natalie pulled out of the parking lot. Devon already had his headphones back on and had disappeared into his game. Paul stood in the parking lot while they drove back along the driveway and turned onto the road back to town, disappearing behind the thick trees. With a final wave, he turned and headed back inside.

Kevin slipped his smart phone into his jacket pocket and turned back on his bright smile as soon as Paul entered the foyer.

"Everyone on their way?"

Paul nodded, and Kevin clapped his hands.

"Excellent. I'm sure they're going to love their new place as well. Now, I have some items I need to deal with before the work day ends, so I'm going to have Marcus show you up to your room."

Paul looked over at Marcus. Marcus looked back at Paul and gave the briefest of nods.

Kevin looked at them both. "Marcus, he's all yours."

Then, with a final wave, Kevin strode off down the hallway, back to his office. Paul glanced over at Marcus. "What are chances of stopping by a bar before you show me to my cell?"

"Always going to be the funny man, Mister Paul?"

"Always going to try, Mister Marcus."

Paul had to be happy with the briefest twinkles in Marcus's eyes on his otherwise impassive face. *That's a start,* he thought. *A start.*

Paul followed Marcus over to the elevator and, in silence—other than some languid Muzak playing through hidden speakers—they rode up one level, exited, and strolled along to Paul's room. The hallway was nicely appointed in light shades of brown, with fancy crown molding and occasional delicate chairs and tables in seating areas along the way. *Resting spots for us infirm,* he thought, angry they were there, and also grudgingly grateful.

On the walls were more framed paintings of glorious bygone eras: antebellum estates, horses, and carriages, interspersed incongruously with more Civil War battles. After a few minutes of strolling down the pantheon of history, they arrived outside Paul's new room.

Marcus stepped aside and let Paul try out the keycard.

"So far so good," Paul said as the door unlocked. "My daughter's first check didn't bounce."

"That is certainly a reassuring start," Marcus said, holding the door open for Paul to enter.

So, he did.

The room looked like something you'd find at a business Hyatt or Marriott by an international airport. High quality indestructible wall-to-wall carpeting with a pattern designed to hide stains, beige paint throughout, and unassuming furniture in more shades of beige and light wood. *Much better than a Motel 6 off a mid-west interstate with trucks rumbling by at all hours and the smell of old smoke even in a non-smoking room,* Paul thought, glancing around the suite.

Marcus let him look around for a moment, then pointed out the main features.

"Full bathroom over there, with a security alarm in case you fall, hurt yourself, you know?"

Paul sighed, rubbed his hip, and nodded. He knew.

"There's a nice balcony with a pretty decent view of the river. Better than a view of the parking lot. TV remote is on the bedside table, right beside the security alarm."

"In case I need my pillows fluffed?"

"Don't joke about it, Mr. Carter. The medical attendants don't take kindly to it."

"Got it. No using it to call for room service."

Paul sat down on the end of the bed and bounced up and down a bit. "Bed seems nice."

"All new ones last year. A huge outlay of capital. Now, in that drawer there, you'll find a copy of the rules and regulations of the facility. I highly recommend you read it thoroughly so that we won't be having any... confusion."

Paul opened the top drawer of the bedside table and pulled out a thick, bound book. He flipped it open and read, out loud, the first line he saw, "Thou shall not covet thy neighbor's wife..."

Shutting the Bible, Paul looked up at Marcus with a smirk. "Quite the rulebook, Mister Marcus. I might have come across a few of those rules already."

"No doubt you have, sir."

They looked at each other for a moment while Paul continued bouncing lightly on his bed. Finally, Marcus sighed and turned to the door. "I will see you at dinner."

"I suppose you will."

Marcus left the room, then paused and leaned back inside. "Read the rules, please?"

Paul nodded, and Marcus shut the door behind him. Putting the Bible back in the drawer, Paul pushed it closed without taking out the leather bound Shady Acres rulebook. *I know all about rules*, he thought. *It'll be like the Army: do what you're told, don't make waves, don't have fun.*

He looked around his room at his four cases sitting on the floor in front of a broad, low chest of drawers. On the wall above was another huge framed painting of young men charging over some hill to their deaths. With a frown, Paul stood up, crossed to the painting, and looked at it closely.

'The Battle of Averasboro, fought March 16, 1865.'

"Sorry, boys, I've seen enough death for my liking."

With a grunt, Paul lifted the painting off its hooks and lowered it behind the chest of drawers. Once on the floor, only the top inch of the frame could be seen.

Maybe I'll find an Elvis painting on velvet to put there instead, he thought. He glanced down at his luggage and sighed. Might as well put everything away now. He tipped the first suitcase over and was fiddling with the locks when a gentle chime rang out. With a frown, Paul looked at the clock on the wall.

6 pm.

The chime rang again.

Ah, the dinner bell. Paul stood up, slowly, rubbed his left knee and his right hip, took one last look at his unpacked life, grabbed his keycard, and headed out the door.

Paul nodded politely at a couple of old people entering the dining room at the same time as he was. *Whoops, better not call them old*, he thought, *they could be younger than me.*

He stepped off to the side and scanned the room for a moment. Most of the chairs were still empty, with only a few early eaters scattered about. A couple staff members moved around the room, checking on those patrons. Off to one side, by the entrance to the kitchen, a half-dozen staff milled about, apparently preparing for the incoming horde.

Paul wandered through the room and settled in at a round table with a beautiful view out of the open French doors to the sunlit patio. *From here, I get the view and air conditioning,* he thought. *Perfect.* It would be a while before he'd be interested in sitting out in the heat and humidity to eat. *Bugs, too. Must be lots of bugs, what with that slow-moving river up against the property.*

"Good evening, sir," a female voice said behind him as he pondered bugs and rivers. "I take it you're new here."

He turned around and smiled up at the middle-aged woman standing beside his chair. Her hair was professionally pulled back in a bun and her black and white uniform—with a red bow tie for accent—was perfectly clean and pressed. Of course, at the beginning of dinner, she hadn't yet had the chance to work up a sweat or spill anything on herself. A gleaming name-tag said her name was Grace.

"You're pretty sharp, and you're right. First day, first meal. So, what's good?"

Grace listed off some specials; each sounded excellent to him. Hopefully they tasted as good as they were described. But he noticed that she glanced at the main doors of the hall quite often, and would then look back at him, with concern.

Paul finally stopped her and ordered the first special she had mentioned—meatloaf, mashed potatoes, vegetables, and a garden salad to start.

"And a glass of ice tea would be grand on a hot one like this."

Grace smiled thinly, took another quick look across at the entranceway, and then headed off to order his meal.

While he waited, Paul glanced around the room. He smiled at the few people seated, all of whom were looking at, and obviously discussing, him. *The joys of being the new kid,* he thought. *The bringer of a little excitement and a little something to talk about. Not like they're coming over to introduce themselves to me, are they?* Not that he was the most social of creatures by any means, having grown up on a farm, and then having run that same farm since he mustered out of the service.

There hadn't been much time for socializing, especially once you had finished everything a farm required to keep running, and then had a thirty-minute drive on dirt roads to get anywhere to find anyone to socialize with. Of course, he didn't stroll over and introduce himself to them, either.

A different waiter slid up and placed his iced tea beside him and then disappeared before Paul had a chance even to say thanks. *That was certainly fast,* he thought. *One of the benefits of eating early.* He'd only had a quick sip of his drink before Grace placed his meal in front of him.

"Will there be anything else?"

"A bottle of beer would be nice, Grace."

"It certainly would," she said, and then smiled, "but, as you know from the rulebook, this entire facility is dry."

"Ah, well, then you'll have to keep me topped up with this lovely iced tea then."

She nodded and walked over to a couple seated at the next table and asked them how their meal tasted. Paul listened to them chat away, while Benny Goodman played at an appropriate volume through the hidden ceiling speakers.

Paul started in on the best meatloaf he'd had in twenty years—especially after two weeks on the interstate eating only at cheap roadside diners and fast food joints—savoring each bite. He had made good progress through his meal when he noticed he was surrounded by blue. Light blue, frilly blue, blue rinsed hair, blue.

Five women, in blue, were standing around him, frowning at him. And, directly across the table from him, in the center of the group, was the woman from the picture outside Kevin's office.

"You'll need to find another chair if you'd like to join me," Paul said, gesturing to the remaining four chairs around the table.

A couple of the women stifled shocked gasps, but Paul calmly returned to his meal. He forked some more meatloaf into his mouth, then glanced up again. The woman from the hall photo looked down at him. She had curly white hair, but bright blue eyes—there's some Swede or Dane in her, he thought. Those eyes were quite alive, and clearly not happy with him.

One of the other women spoke up, "You may be new to our home, but you're enjoying your meal at our table."

Paul paused cutting, finished chewing, and placed his cutlery down on the plate in front of him. Then he leaned forward and looked around at the table, observing the salt and pepper shakers, cream and sugar, and the compact flower arrangement in the middle.

"Huh, I don't see any sort of reserved sign anywhere."

The woman who spoke leaned back, apparently unaccustomed to being replied to like that.

"But it's our table."

"Oh, I doubt you five lovely ladies would bother with owning a table this ordinary."

After a bit more stuttering and fluttering, another of the ladies turned to the woman from the photo and said, imploringly, "Joanne…"

Joanne took a moment before replying, "You'd be surprised at who owns what around here."

Paul smiled and parried back, "You receive your own table when your picture goes up on the wall, now, do you?"

"The two are absolutely unrelated."

"I sincerely doubt that, Joanne," Paul returned to eating his meal. "But when you find yourself a 'reserved' sign, put it on this here table and I'll never sit here again. Unless I'm invited."

After some more fluttering, the oldest of the women huffed, "I'm going to call the manager." She headed off across the now-filling hall, cutting through the crowd like a battleship in a sea full of rowboats.

"Am I in trouble now?" Paul asked as he finished up his meal. As soon as he put his cutlery down on the now-empty plate, a server slipped in under his elbow and whisked it away. He raised his coffee cup and gestured to the server as he tried to leave.

"Coffee would be grand, thank you."

Joanne continued to scowl down at him. "Well, now that you've finished your meal and have moved on to coffee and dessert, possibly could you possibly move to a different table?"

"I don't know, Joanne. This table does have a wonderfully nice view."

Then Paul winked at her.

Joanne took a breath and bit her lip. *What kind of man is this?* She wondered. *Arrogant, for sure; self-centered, absolutely. He had the tan of someone who had worked outside with his hands for most of his life, which was nice, and he did look healthy—she liked healthy—but that attitude. Rough. Yes, that's what it was, rough. And an accent right off the prairies. Nebraska or North Dakota.*

The server slid back in, poured Paul a cup of coffee, and placed the dessert menu in front of him. Paul glanced down at the menu then back up at the women.

"What do you recommend?"

The woman to the right of Joanne, already running with a full head of righteous indignation under a hat that wouldn't be out of place at the Kentucky Derby, sputtered, "We recommend you get up out of that chair before I—"

"And how is everyone this fine evening?"

Everyone turned, and Jim Lyons smiled at them. He had put on a suit jacket that hung loosely on him. *We're all getting shorter and thinner,* Paul realized as he thought about how his jackets were starting to fit the same way. The women politely said good evening to Jim. He then leaned against the back of the chair beside Paul and shook his head, slowly.

"You certainly do have yourself a way of being noticed, Paul."

"One of my best features, Jim."

"Ah, but being noticed isn't always the best thing, is it?"

"Oh, I don't know…"

"I'm sure you thought otherwise while in a foxhole."

Paul paused and looked at Jim. Yup, Jim had served in the forces, he thought. *I see it in his eyes.* "Is that where I am now?"

Jim glanced around at the five women staring at Paul; their arms crossed tightly, purses hanging from wrists, ready to be swung or flung.

"It most certainly is, Paul. Most certainly."

Paul shifted his eyes from Jim over to Joanne. *My, oh my, she must have been the belle of the ball, if not the whole county when she was younger,* he thought. *Not that she isn't the best-looking girl in this place right now.* Paul sighed and looked back at Jim.

"I've always found it prudent to retreat in the face of overwhelming odds."

He could sense the tension simmer down around the table and even around the room. Paul took a final sip of his coffee, put down the cup, and slid his chair back.

"Ladies, I hope you find your meals as pleasant as I did."

As the rest of the ladies quickly seated themselves, in case he changed his mind and sat back down, Joanne replied, "I have no doubt we will; my son runs an excellent establishment."

"Your son?" Paul questioned. "Is he the chef?"

With a sharp laugh, Jim grabbed Paul's arm and turned him away from the table.

"You'd best join me before you find yourself Missing-In-Action."

Paul glanced back at the ladies, now seated around the table in deep, animated conversation, surely about him. Actually, he glanced back at Joanne, ignoring the other ladies completely. Joanne caught his glance and made fiery eye contact before returning to lead the conversation that flurried around her. *Quite the woman,* he thought. *That is quite the woman...*

Four

Paul followed Jim back to a table on the other side of the dining room. Jim's now cold meal waited for him when they arrived at the compact table for two up against the wall.

Paul sighed as he sat down. "Looks like I've ruined your meal."

Jim sat down, even more slowly than Paul. "Ah, it was my choice to come over and save your bacon. I could have sat here, enjoyed my meatloaf, and watched the floor show."

Jim pushed his plate away and flipped over his upside-down coffee cup. Paul did the same. A different waiter came by and poured them coffee. They both thanked him, and Jim asked, "What's the best dessert tonight, Michael?"

"That would have to be the strawberry-clementine pie, Mister Jim."

Jim rolled his eyes in pleasure. "Two slices of that, if you please." Michael nodded and headed for the kitchen.

Jim took a sip of his steaming coffee and looked across the table at Paul. "Oh, did you want a piece for yourself?" He smiled. "Joking. Just joking. But it is that good. Joanne's recipe, if you must know."

Jim laughed and took another sip of his coffee as Paul tried mightily not to react to the sound of Joanne's name.

•

An hour of chatting later, after a couple more cups of excellent coffee and a slice of the best pie he'd ever tasted, Jim and Paul strolled back to their rooms. It turned out Jim lived in the next one down the hall from his.

"Well, try your best not to find yourself any more situations without me until the morning," Jim said with a smile. "Granted, I am an early riser so if you start causing a ruckus any time after 6:30, I'll be ready for you."

"I appreciate you watching my back," Paul replied.

And with that, they both entered their rooms.

Paul let the door shut behind him and glanced around the room. His luggage still wasn't unpacked; the bags were still sitting in front of the chest of drawers. Paul checked his wristwatch and saw it was only 7:00p.m. back in Montana. He fumbled with the old mobile phone Natalie had insisted he have once he was alone on the farm. 'I can't have you falling and breaking your other hip in the barn, or falling off a tractor, without some way of letting me know.' she had said, pushing the flip phone into his hand. 'I'm paying the bill, so you don't have to even worry about that. Make sure you charge it, and keep it with you all the time.'

Paul had agreed and, after a pretty steep learning curve and some humiliating lessons from Devon, he had mastered the art of making telephone calls. No listening to music, watching videos, surfing the Internet, or playing games on this phone. It had a calendar program, but he hadn't bothered opening it. What events did he have to keep track of now?

He scrolled through his address book and dialed a number. Sitting down on the end of the bed, he waited for someone to answer. After five rings, the phone clicked, and a gruff voice said, "Legion Hall."

"Stevey, Paul calling. Any of the boys around?"

"Pauly! Good Lord! How was the drive? You enjoying the East?"

Paul laughed, "The East is good, thanks. The drive was the drive, if you know what I mean."

Stevey, who had spent a couple of decades as a long-haul trucker before retiring to run the bar at the Legion in Paul's hometown, laughed and said he knew exactly what Paul meant. Then he put the phone down on the bar and headed off to find one of the boys.

Paul shut his eyes and listened to the background sound of the bar—the pool table where someone had just broke; the jukebox pumping out one of those new country singers... Keith Urban or someone like that; the whine of the bar dishwasher; the murmur of conversations. He could see it all, right down to the beer coasters, and, damnit, he missed it all.

A sudden thump as someone picked up the phone, then, "Paul? That you?"

"That it is, Sal, that it is. Live from fifteen miles before you bump into the Atlantic Ocean."

"Ah, it's good to hear yer voice, Pauly. When ya comin' home to visit?"

Paul laughed and wished he had a beer. "I only got here, Sal, and haven't had time to be tired of the place yet."

"Cute ladies there, Pauly?"

Paul thought about Joanne glaring at him across the dining room, "Well, there might be one or two."

"Excellent, that's what you need, you know?"

Before Paul could reply, the background murmur increased on the phone. "Ah hell, Pauly, gotta go. My turn to call the Meat Draw! You call again, anytime, yeah? You know we're always here!"

"You bet, Sal, you bet." But Sal had already hung up, and Paul was left talking to dead air. He clicked shut the flip phone and tossed it behind him on the bed. Silence. *I'm ten years old and been sent to my room*, he thought. With a sigh and a groan, he pulled himself up off the bed and crossed to his luggage. He dug around and pulled up a silver cigar case.

Opening it up, he pulled out a thin cigar and, from another compartment in the case, a couple of wooden matches.

Looking around the room, he saw the large 'no smoking' sign on the back of the door. *Balcony it'll have to be then,* he thought, opening the sliding door and stepping outside, closing it behind him. The evening sun still brightened in the western sky, lighting up the massive trees that edged the property. Smooth green grass filled the space from the building to the river.

Standing at the railing, he took in the view. Fragrant flowers nearby filled the air with their perfume, reminding Paul of going to a department store in Wichita in an attempt to buy some *eau de parfum* for his wife's 50ᵗʰ birthday many years ago. He'd walked into a mist of perfume and when he'd returned home, he'd spent a couple of hours explaining why he smelled like a whorehouse. And he had gotten so flustered at the perfume counter that he hadn't actually bought her anything. The memory brought a smile to his face while he absently lit his cigar.

Paul took a couple of puffs and leaned against the balcony railing. Certainly not a view he was familiar with—he missed the miles and miles of Montana grassland stretching off in all directions, blocked only by his barn and out-buildings and that windbreak he'd planted with his siblings.

"The third page of the rulebook states pretty clearly that no smoking, of any sorts, will occur in the buildings or on the grounds of Shady Acres." Paul looked over and saw Jim leaning against the railing of his balcony. "Surely Marcus mentioned the hallowed rulebook to you."

Paul looked down at his cigar then back at Jim, "He surely did."

Jim nodded and looked out at the view.

"You're not going to turn me in, are you?"

"I pondered it, rules being rules and society requiring rules to operate in an orderly fashion and all that," then Jim pulled a cigar out of his inside coat pocket. "But I'd rather have someone to smoke with."

Paul smiled and took another puff while Jim lit up. Together they looked out at the trees in the twilight and smoked their cigars.

"So," Paul said, without looking over at Jim, "what's the story with Joanne?"

Jim shook his head and laughed. "I wondered how long it was going to take you to ease around to asking that. You always been this open of a book?"

"That's why I stalled out as an NCO."

"I thought as much."

"You?" Paul asked.

"Major. In the JAGs."

"Should I be standing at attention, sir?"

"At ease, soldier," Jim said, sternly. They both smiled at each other and returned to smoking for a bit.

"Now, about Joanne..."

"Good Lord. Like a dog with a bone, you are."

"Another reason you don't have to salute me," Paul said.

"I'll give you the basic facts, since once a lawyer always a lawyer. She's been seeing the captain of the football team—who you met in the hall earlier—"

"Chuck."

"Yep, Chuck. Not much else to say about him other than he's been like that since I met him in first grade. Always had to be king of the class, king of the hill, king of the home."

"He came on awful strong in the hallway. He have some dementia going on to be acting like that to someone he just met?"

"He might. You can't really know until it's too late with something like that. You weren't exactly the paragon of friendliness yourself."

"Ah, he started it," Paul said with a smile.

"That your default excuse?" Jim asked.

Paul waved the question away then took a puff before asking, "He serve?"

Jim looked at him, "What's your guess?"

Paul shook his head, and Jim nodded in agreement, "Some 'medical issue' got him exempted. Didn't hurt that his father was the congressman for the district."

"Certainly didn't meet a lot of congressmen's sons in the trenches."

"Nope. Me neither. So, Chuck's been in here about as long as I have, give or take. Five years now. It took him three years to wear Joanne down, and now they're a couple. It means more to him than to her. He puts on a good show as a boyfriend, and she likes that."

"And what about her gang of harpies?"

Jim laughed. "Never heard them called that before. Best you never call them that to their faces or they'll peck your eyes out. They're 'The Bees.'"

"Come again?"

"They're the Queen Bees of the place. And Joanne is *the* queen bee of the Queen Bees."

"This place is sounding more and more juvenile," Paul said, and Jim laughed.

"I've never heard it called that. As you've hopefully figured out, The Bees have their table in the dining room and from there they rule the home—magnanimously, of course. It helps that Joanne's son runs the place."

"Kevin Wright is her son?"

Jim nodded. Paul sighed. The only interesting woman in the place and she's related to the boss and attached to the bully.

And I've made enemies of them both.

Five

Two days later, Paul stood in the foyer, arms crossed, scowling at Marcus. The large man sat at his desk, an array of signup forms and brochures in front of him. Marcus took a frustrated breath, wiped a hand across his shaven head, and started again. "You need to find something to do here, Mister Paul. No point moping around all day. Not healthy, for you or the other guests."

Paul gestured at the forms in front of him with disgust. "Bocce? Bridge? Knitting?"

Marcus calmly took the Knitting Club signup form off his desk and returned it to the credenza behind him. "Slipped that one in to check if you were actually reading them."

"What about a shop? I'd be interested in something like that. Mechanical repair, I'm good at that. You must have some place to fix the machinery around here."

"We do. And we have employees who do it."

"There you go, hire me to work in that shop. Better than me learning to knit."

Marcus looked across at him, "Knitting's been taken off the table. I'm pretty sure The Bees wouldn't let you into that club even if you wanted to join."

"The Bees?" Paul looked at Marcus with interest, "Maybe I want to learn to knit. I'll make socks in my rocking chair during my last fading days."

Shaking his head, Marcus gestured to the full desk of brochures and forms. "Please find something to fill your time, Mister Paul."

Paul looked at Marcus for a moment, ignoring the brochures, then said, "Why do you insist on calling me 'Mister Paul?' 'Cause I gotta tell you, it sounds pretty old-fashioned to me."

Marcus sighed and said, with a broad Al Jolson accent, "A little too pre-Civil War for your likin', Massuh Paul?"

Paul nodded and Marcus continued, "Consider it being polite. 'Mr. Carter' is too formal and 'Paul' is too familiar. 'Mister Paul' carries an element of respect and the Southern gentility we strive for here at Shady Acres."

"Sure isn't the way we talk out in Montana."

"Surely is not, Mister Paul."

"Glad we got that sorted." Paul picked up a brochure on pottery making.

Marcus gestured to the brochure, "That would be a good choice. Anything would be a good choice, Mister Paul. Management does not look kindly upon those who fritter away their days."

"Fritter?" Paul repeated, in amazement. "You're worried about me frittering away my-"

"Gramps!"

Marcus and Paul turned to see Devon striding into the foyer, removing a battered black bike helmet.

"Devon!" Paul exclaimed before he turned back to Marcus, tossing the pottery information back onto his desk, "We'll chat about this tomorrow."

"But Mister Paul…"

Paul had already turned around and walked over to give his grandson a fist bump and then impulsively gave him a quick hug, much to both of their surprise.

"What are you doing here?"

Devon shrugged, attaching his helmet to his overloaded backpack. "Thought I'd cruise by on my way home from school."

Paul gestured to the backpack, "Looks like they've got you working. Let's grab a drink and you tell me about it. I need to sit down anyway."

With Devon remembering to walk slowly so his grandfather could keep up, the two strolled down to the dining hall, leaving Marcus to clean up the paperwork on his desk. Marcus called after Paul, "You will be choosing an activity tomorrow, Mister Paul." Paul waved back over his shoulder; it wasn't a question, but a clear statement.

"Totally huge, crazy huge!" Devon said as Paul nodded and sipped his coffee. "I thought when we saw the high school from the street it wasn't any big deal, but that old building is only one of four huge buildings! There are like over fifteen hundred students, you know? Two football fields; one of them's nearly a stadium! I figure it's gotta be as huge as the one in Bozeman!"

They were sitting on the patio outside the home dining room under an umbrella. A refreshing breeze off the river kept the heat and humidity slightly at bay. *Like being at some resort,* Paul thought, *and I'm not sure if that's a good thing or not.*

Devon continued, "And there are these different groups, you know? Different cliques?" He sighed and brushed his hands back through his hair, "At my old school, we all sorta hung out—the jocks and the nerds and the rest."

"I went to that school, too, Devon. There never were enough people going there to break into groups. There's no such thing as a clique of one."

Devon took a gulp of his iced tea and then played with the rings of condensation on the glass table. "I'm the new kid, and everyone knows it. Like there's a spotlight on me, everywhere. I don't know if I like it, but I can't tell Mom that. She'd freak and start worrying if the whole move had been a bad idea."

"You know what, Devon?"

Devon stopped playing with his glass and looked up at his grandfather. "What?"

"I'm in exactly the same situation."

"Yeah?"

"You been in trouble with your principal yet?"

"Gramps, c'mon. We've only been here three days."

Paul sighed. "Three days is a long time around here. A lot can happen in three days."

•

Kevin pulled into the long drive at the house his great-grandfather had built a few short miles from Shady Acres. Mature trees graced both sides of the immaculate lawn, and the house gleamed white in the early evening light. He stopped on the crushed gravel by the side door to the house and turned off the car.

Sitting for a moment, he tried to slow down the million thoughts and items he needed to remember at the end of each day, ensuring those thoughts were ready to be recalled on demand first thing in the next morning when he woke up. Despite a skilled and well-meaning staff at the home, Kevin knew it was really up to him to keep every piece of the machine called Shady Acres perfectly tuned and operating at peak efficiency. This he had learned at his father's side from pretty much the first day of the first summer he had worked at the home as a teenager. 'Control not constraint,' his father had said sitting at the same desk Kevin used now. 'Manage things before they manage you. It wasn't the easy way, but it worked, and that's what mattered most.'

After a few minutes of mental filing and collating, Kevin climbed out of his BMW and stretched; it wasn't the length of the drive which made his back and shoulders tighten up—one day's crises tended to flow into the next, never giving him a chance to slow down.

Hopefully tonight will be calm, and I won't have any phone calls, he thought, immediately realizing wishing for some peace had worsened his chances of making it through the night.

He entered the pristine mudroom and put his briefcase in its place and gave it a brief pat, like telling a faithful dog to stay, then entered the kitchen. Beth, his wife, was finishing preparations for dinner. He paused at the doorway and watched her move gracefully and with complete focus around the kitchen island, pulling plates from the warmer; garnishing the meat course; opening a bottle of red wine and pouring it into their crystal decanter. She was tall, just shorter than himself, and as shapely as when they married. And she still carried herself what that innate grace she'd had in school. He was a lucky man.

Behind her, through a wide archway, he could see their gleaming dining room table set for dinner. They were more comfortable sitting at their modern kitchen table than at the antiques that came with the house—more legacies of his great-grandparents—but Beth liked using the dining room for dinner. Otherwise, she said, when would they use it?

"Dawn!" Beth called into the hallway, "Your father will be home any moment. Wash your hands and come to the table, please."

Beth turned around and saw Kevin smiling in the doorway. She gave him a smile back, brushed her hands off on her white apron, slipped an errant strand of her long auburn hair behind her ear, and crossed the kitchen to give him a quick hug and peck on the cheek.

"Any value in asking how your day was?"

"Better than most, I guess. How was yours?"

"The same, I guess. The wine is open if you want to pour."

Kevin shrugged out of his suit coat and loosened his tie as he walked to the table. After draping his coat on the back of his chair, he poured a full glass of wine for himself and a half a glass for Beth. As he put the wine decanter back on their stainless-steel trivet, their teenaged daughter Dawn came into the room via the old servant's staircase from the second floor. She pulled her ear buds out, tucked her phone into the edge of her bra, and gave Kevin a hug.

"Hey, Dad. How's Grandma J?"

"She's good, button."

"And the rest of The Bees?"

"Good. You should come by for tea this weekend, they'd love it."

"All right, everyone," Beth said, moving past them with tonight's dinner on a large platter. "Sit, sit. Dinner is ready."

Dawn and Kevin jumped and quickly sat down, hands crossed on the edge of the table the way Joanne had taught both Kevin and Dawn when they were a children. Beth laughed and took her place to Kevin's right, across from Dawn. Then she reached out her hands, one to each of them, and Beth said Grace.

"In a world where so many are hungry,

may we eat this food with humble hearts,

in a world where so many are lonely,

may we share this friendship with joyful hearts.

For this and all we are about to receive,

make us truly grateful, Lord.

Through Christ we pray. Amen."

They started their meal in companionable silence until Beth asked Dawn how her school day was.

"Well, there's some drama with the cheerleaders, again. Pretty much the same drama as last year, but way worse. Because I didn't rejoin the squad, it's like I'm a bad person now, and have been dumped as a friend. I told them I needed the time to get good grades for university, but they don't even care. Now I'm so glad I didn't join them. Was there much drama when you were a cheerleader, Mom?"

Beth laughed, "Drama about what? Boys? Of course, there was. But I knew who I liked, so I didn't need to bother with any of the drama."

Kevin put down his wine glass, "Who was it, again, that you liked, Beth?"

"Yeah, Mom, come on. Spill..." Dawn said, eagerly.

Beth blushed, "Oh well, so long ago. His name was Joey Clarkson. He was the captain of the football team. There wasn't a girl on the squad who didn't have the hots for him. But your dad here was a solid second place."

"Thanks, I think." Kevin said.

Dawn always wanted more and more details about what her parents had been like in high school—did they go on dates, did they make out, how much did they make out?

Beth attempted to weave a fine line between coming across like some 1950's virginal Daughter of the Confederacy and one of the trashy sluts from the wrong side of town. It wasn't easy, that fine line of how to be honest with a teenager—but not too honest.

"There's a new boy at school from Montana!"

Kevin knew full well who she was talking about. The grandson of his latest problem at the home, Paul Carter. Rather than speak, he picked up his wine glass and took a sip. "Oh?"

Beth, God bless her, asked what Kevin wanted to find out, "What's he like?"

"He's different, I guess," Dawn said, picking at her steamed vegetables. "He doesn't fit in, that's for sure, but he doesn't stick out either. He's trying to be not quite here, but he's here anyway."

"Do you have any classes with him? Maybe you could be a good girl and show him around the school," Beth said.

Kevin wanted to speak out in complete disagreement—the last thing he wanted was his only daughter befriending the kin of a troublemaker. If a family had one, there would be more, that much he knew.

Dawn rolled her eyes, "Yuck, Mom. That would be totally embarrassing. There are student advisors to do that."

Beth looked at Kevin questioningly. "Hon, that must be the grandson of the new tenant you told me about. You said he's from Montana, and she's at Enviro-Dyne, right? Goodness, such a long way to move for work, especially as a single mother."

Kevin filled his mouth with mashed potatoes and nodded.

"We should have them over for dinner some night. Show them some Southern hospitality!"

"Mom!" Dawn said, horrified.

Kevin swallowed, took another sip of wine, and said, "Honey, I'm not sure it would be right to mix business with pleasure. We don't want to set the wrong example at the home, now."

Dawn quickly nodded in agreement. They looked at Beth until she sighed. "Well, I thought it would have been a nice gesture."

"It certainly would have been, but…"

"Mom, I promise to be nice to him at school, ok? And I'll warn him if he's hanging around with the 'wrong' kids. Ok?"

Beth started clearing the table, halfway between relieved she wouldn't have to make dinner for new people and disappointed she wouldn't have a chance to meet someone who might be a new friend for her. She called back to the dining room as she rinsed off the dinner plates, "Who's up for some dessert? I have one of your grandmother's pies."

When no one answered, she turned around and saw the table empty. Both Dawn and Kevin had left the room. She heard Dawn stomping up the stairs, followed by the slamming of her bedroom door. From Kevin's office down the front hall, she heard him talking on his phone—checking in on the night staff at the home.

Beth sighed and returned to the empty dining room to take the rest of the plates from the table, pausing only to top up her half glass of wine.

•

Natalie took another sip of her wine and continued digging around in one of the half-unpacked boxes which were stacked up in the corner of the kitchen. *I'm sure I labeled these boxes when I packed them; did someone tear off the labels as a prank?* As soon as she thought it, she realized either her son or her father—or both—probably did do exactly that.

"Devon?"

Silence, except for the sounds of thumbs and fingers clicking away on the buttons and knobs of the Xbox in the next room. Natalie gritted her teeth trying to come to a decision between finding the stupid spatula by herself before the pork chops needed turning on the stovetop and dragging Devon off that stupid video game to help—which would probably take far longer. Maybe both would be the answer.

"Devon!"

The clicking silenced, "Yeah?"

"Could you come and help me in here?"

I actually hear him rolling his eyes, she thought before he sauntered through the doorway into the compact kitchen.

"I'm trying to find the spatula. Do you remember which box it was put into? The labels seem to be mixed up."

Devon, doing his best keep a straight face, said, "That's weird, mom. Maybe try the box that says 'linen.'"

Natalie stared at him, but he looked away and put a box up on the kitchen table.

"It better be in here, or we're eating hockey pucks instead of pork chops for dinner. And then you'd be totally grounded."

At that, Devon finally couldn't hold his impassive face any longer and burst out laughing. "Grounded for accidentally hiding a spatula, Mom. Awesome! When I have kids, they'd love that story about their mean grandma!"

Natalie pulled the spatula out of the box and attempted to swat him with it, but Devon nimbly hopped clear, grinning.

"You are such trouble!"

"But that's why you love me, right?"

Natalie shook her head as Devon headed back to his game. "Oh, no you don't. Bring your butt back here, the table needs to be set."

"Aw, Mom…"

Natalie smiled to herself, turned back to the stove, and flipped the pork chops—just in the nick of time.

Six

"Are you kidding me?" Paul said, leaning back in the lounge chair.

"Sir, that is the program which is to be watched at this time." The dowdy matron who ran the television room replied, with an indulging smile. "It says so here in the book."

She held up a large, bound book as if it were the Gospel. *Which it mostly was,* Paul thought. He had found out, much to his dismay, he couldn't wander into the lounge, pick up the remote, and find a show for watching. Oh, no, not here at Stalag 13 Acres. He had to go to the activities office and request—in writing!—the show he thought would be worth watching and, if there were no conflicts in The Book, then he and anyone else in the room could watch it.

His comment about trading cigarettes for TV time hadn't gone over well, so Paul had shut his trap and put in his request to view a particular History Channel show on the Bismarck. But now that had settled in, ready to enjoy some naval battles, here was the matron to rain on his parade.

"This is the book where you wrote down my request, this morning, for this show at this time, right?"

The matron nodded and opened the book to the day's page. She skimmed a fat finger down to seven pm. She nodded to herself in confirmation of what she saw and looked down at Paul, saying, "Management, based on a concern lodged by one of the other residents, has decided the show you requested was inappropriate."

"Inappropriate? It's the History Channel!"

The matron read on from the book, "The show in question might cause grief and possible trauma to those residents who were active in the Second World War."

"Oh for God's sake…" Paul muttered, "The war ended seventy years ago. How many veterans of the North Atlantic you see in this room?"

They both looked around, Paul to confirm there weren't any ninety-year-old Navy vets in the room and the matron to verify that there might possibly be a ninety-year-old Navy vet hidden away in a corner.

The only others in the room were Chuck and a couple of his soft-bellied hangers-on snickering to themselves on the other side of the lounge and a scattering of other residents.

"I'm sorry, the concern has been noted by management and they have decided to decline your request for your show. Perhaps you would rather watch it in your room?"

"If I wanted to watch it in my room, I'd be in my room watching it. I want to be in here, which is one of the many perks of now living in this home. It's in the rulebook. A mightier book than yours, I do believe," Paul said.

The matron was taken aback for a moment, and then recovered and slammed her book shut with solemn finality. She raised the remote—attached to her belt by a retractable wire—and turned the TV channel to an insipid game show populated with idiots who didn't know the first thing about anything. Chuck and his buddies cheered as the theme music blared out.

"Speak to management in the morning if you're unhappy with their decision, Mister Paul." With that, the matron returned to her office, settled into her desk chair, and started enjoying the show along with everyone else in the lounge.

Paul scowled. He had spent the past couple nights chatting with Jim instead of coming down to the lounge, but Jim had some correspondence to work on. Despite being retired, Jim still helped out his son—who had taken over his law practice—with some of the more complex paperwork.

This is what happens when I finally decide to come out and join the other inmates, Paul thought darkly as he watched Chuck and his buddies trying to guess the missing letters on the game show.

With a grunt, Paul used his cane to push himself up out of the chair and started towards the hallway.

"Don't leave on our account, Pauly."

Paul stopped, turned around, and saw Chuck smiling at him.

"Excuse me?"

"Wouldn't you rather watch a fun game show instead of some dismal black and white footage of the Battle of the North Atlantic? I surely know I would."

Chuck's buddies snickered, and Paul took a step forward, then paused and took a breath. He glanced over and saw the matron watching him and everything he did. In fact, everyone in the lounge watched everything he and Chuck were doing.

"I guess that's true, Chuck. Once you start dodging war, you'd better keep on dodging war."

"I never did such a thing!" Chuck exclaimed, pushing himself up off his chair, immediately followed by his followers.

"You keep telling yourself that," Paul said, "but unless you've been in battle—and I have most certainly been in battle, my friend—you weren't in a war, and if you weren't in a war, then shut up about those of us who were."

Paul turned and started for the exit, leaving Chuck, his followers, and the rest of the room with their jaws agape. As he arrived at the door he smiled politely at the matron, who had stepped out of her office—probably eager to use her Taser on him—and said, "I do believe you were right, and I will retire to my room to enjoy my show lest I upset the delicate constitutions of those present."

He turned back for one final glare across the room at Chuck and then left, as calmly as he could manage.

Paul steamed as he walked down the hallway to his room.

Damn bastard must have submitted that complaint himself to irk me, he thought. *No other reason I see except that. Damn those soft bullies with their golf tans and their entitled attitudes!* They'd been trouble his whole life, and no matter where he went, there was always at least one of them to piss him off.

The door across the hall opened and a woman his age, wearing only a house robe with her hair mussed up, stepped out. "Oh!" she said in surprise, then blushed.

"Good evening," Paul said, politely. She grinned at him, "Yes, it certainly was." Then, after giving a lingering kiss to the man now in the doorway, she rushed down the hall.

"Hey, new guy. If you need some blue pills, let me know. I've got a connection. Reasonably priced."

Paul looked at him, confused. The guy saw his confusion, patted down his thinning hair and laughed. "Viagra. You're gonna love it here. For each of us old men, there're five women craving 'attention.' Without the blue pills, this would be an unhappy place."

The man grinned and shut his door. Paul shook his head and let himself into his room.

His suitcases were still leaning against the dresser, still unpacked. He grabbed the remote, turned on the TV, and scrolled through the channels trying to find the show he wanted. He stopped at the History Channel, but the screen had a large warning saying this channel wasn't available. With disgust, he turned off the TV and flung the remote onto the bed.

They're even controlling the stations I watch! It's worse than a damn kindergarten.

He dug into his suitcase and pulled out a CD. With a bit of work, he turned on the miniature stereo on top of the dresser, put the CD into it, and finally started some music playing.

Art Blakey began cutting up some jazz and spreading it around the room, filling the corners with exuberance. Paul hadn't started out liking jazz, but a fellow grunt had turned him onto it while in the service.

'Damn sight better to listen to this than the crap rock 'n' roll them other kids are listening to,' his second gunner had said while they were sharing a blisteringly hot tent outside Saigon. It had taken a few months, but slowly Paul had realized the beauty of the music and the creativity of the musicians.

Letting the sound flow over him, Paul sat down in the one comfortable chair in the room and shut his eyes. For a moment, he could let the heat and the home slip away; let the trip across the country disappear into some other not-chosen path. He could believe that he was back in his living room on the farm in Montana, that the wind through the trees outside was the wind through the trees he had planted with his sister and brother many long years ago. Believe, for a moment, his hip and knee didn't hurt as much as they did, that the aches and pains were temporary—from a long day's work instead of from a long life.

A knocking on his door whipped him back from Montana to North Carolina. With a groan, Paul rose out of the chair he'd barely gotten settled in and made his way to the door. He pulled it open and looked up at Marcus.

"Mister Marcus, how can I help you on this fine evening?"

Marcus looked a bit embarrassed, although the discomfort was barely visible on his face, "I'm afraid I'll need you to turn off your music, Mister Paul."

Paul sighed and walked across his room to the stereo and turned down the music a bit.

"Art Blakey too much for this wing, eh?" he said as he started back to the door.

"Not turn it down. Turn it off."

Paul stopped and stared at Marcus. "I'd say, 'Are you serious?', but I know the answer. Another rule in the blessed book that we are supposed to be as quiet as church mice after the witching hour of—" Paul looked at his watch, "of 7:45?"

Marcus looked at him dispassionately, "Unless you have yourself a pair of headphones, yes, sir."

Paul scowled, "I most certainly don't have a pair of headphones." He returned to the stereo, but stumbled and reached out for balance. His hand landed on the volume knob, and accidentally twisted it hard as he righted himself. After a beat, Paul turned off the blaring music and sheepishly apologized to Marcus.

"A respectful volume in our rooms, Mister Paul, at all times."

"Of course, Mister Marcus. At all times."

Marcus locked eyes with Paul for a moment, and then pulled the door shut behind him.

Paul gritted his teeth then flipped the door the bird. It didn't help. He thought about turning up the stereo again, out of spite, when another knock rattled on his door.

Marcus returning to apologize, he thought and crossed to the door. *Serves him right, that's no kind of a rule, not letting me listen to music the way I want to.*

Paul swung the door open and said, "No need to apologize, Mar—" Instead of Marcus, Jim stood in the hallway.

"Art Blakey?"

"Come on in."

Jim stepped inside and put his polished wooden cane in the stand next to Paul's aluminum one as Paul shut the door behind him.

"You won't believe—"

Jim interrupted him, "Oh, I believe, Paul. But before you build up a full head of righteous indignation, how's about we step out to your deck and light these up?"

He held out a couple of fine looking cigars.

"They'd be better with a shot of whiskey," Paul muttered, with half a head of righteous indignation.

"That they would, but they'll have to work their magic on their own tonight. Come on."

Paul followed Jim outside, and they lit up while looking out at the trees in the twilight.

After a couple of leisurely puffs, Paul finally couldn't take it anymore and turned to Jim, saying, "So what exactly is the deal here? My daughter is paying good money for me to be here, but each damn day the screws are turned tighter, the small pleasures suppressed a bit more."

"Now I've been here a tad over five years now, and I don't believe it's as bad as you imagine."

"I bet when you arrived here you thought exactly like I did."

"I doubt anyone sees the world exactly like you do," Jim said with a tight smile.

Paul brushed off the joke, and said, bitterly, "I'm in a prisoner of war camp, but with nicer curtains."

Jim started to make a joke but stopped himself, "Were you?"

Paul shook his head, "Nearly trapped once, but the gunships arrived at our position north of Da-Nang with minutes to spare. I got lucky. What kind of law did you do when you were in?"

Jim shook his head. "I worked in Saigon HQ for two tours, then Guam, working myself back to the mainland. But Indochina was by far the worst I ever experienced."

"Yes. Yes, it was." Paul took another draw on his cigar.

Jim said, mostly to himself, "It's pretty good here."

"You have your own stash of blue pills, too?"

Jim looked over at him. "I see you met Bob." Paul nodded, and Jim continued, "Look, it's easy to be a hound here if you want to be. I don't choose to do that. Of course, if you decide to go down that 'path,' make sure you use protection."

"I'm not going anywhere near that 'path,' but if I did I'm not worried about any of the woman here getting pregnant."

"Not pregnant, there's been an outbreak of chlamydia. Again."

Paul stared at Jim. Jim shrugged as if to say, 'What can you do?' Paul shook his head in amazement.

"This isn't high school; it's college."

"Ah, it's a nice place. Sometimes people need to let off some steam, that's all."

Paul turned and looked at him, "How long are you going keep telling yourself that?"

Seven

As the sun rose on another glorious day in the Grand Old South, Paul dressed in comfortable clothes, grabbed his cane, and left his room before the day became too hot. He had barely made it twenty feet down the hallway when he heard another door slam behind him.

"That you, Paul?"

He stopped and turned around and saw Jim coming out of his room.

"Surely is."

"Good, I'm looking for some conversation over breakfast. Care to join me? Pick the topic, other than some arcane sub-subject of farming in Montana or any of the mid-western states."

Paul laughed then waited for Jim to slowly catch up with him. The two of them sauntered down to the elevator, their canes silent on the industrial carpeting.

"Well, Jim, I figured on making my way into town for a good Sunday morning meal with all the fixin's. Sort of a habit of mine back home. I saw what looks like a good place right there on the main street when we came through."

Jim paused at the elevator and didn't push the button. Paul looked at him quizzically, "There a problem?"

Turning to him, Jim said, with a sigh, "You didn't read any of that rule book they so kindly bound and placed on your bedside table, now, did you?"

"I only read it when I'm having trouble sleeping. And I haven't had any trouble sleeping, so—"

Jim shook his head and rolled his eyes, an impressive feat that must have gone over well on juries, and said, "You want me to wait here for you while you go and read yourself Section 7 and 8, or shall I enlighten you from memory?"

Paul frowned, looked back down the hallway towards his room, then back at Jim. "Ah, you'd best fill me in. I haven't had any coffee yet today, and I've made it all this way."

"I'm not in the habit of directly quoting from rulebooks, but Army is what Army does, so I'll make an exception for you. Section 7 states that no resident of Shady Acres is permitted to leave the grounds of Shady Acres without a management approved chaperone and the express written permission of said Shady Acres management."

Paul stared at him, aghast.

Jim looked at him sympathetically, "I surely wish you would read that book so's I don't always have to be the one who is breaking the bad news to you. My self-esteem is taking a beating."

"Dammit, now I can't even leave if I want to?"

Jim sighed and pushed the down button on the elevator, "Yup, maximum security without the barbed wire and attack dogs. But the coffee is better."

Paul continued ranting when they came out of the elevator.

"I would make my way into town every week—every damn week—to have a good breakfast, not that granola and yogurt crap my daughter filled my house with. You ever been in a Montana blizzard, Jim?"

"Can't rightly say that I have."

"Well, I have, many a time—and I still didn't miss my damn breakfast."

"You're like a dog with a bone, aren't you?"

"Ornery like a dog, but this ain't no bone. This is about having some semblance of life in this damn mortuary. We're stacked up in here, not allowed to do anything, and they're waiting until we kick the bucket and then they'll rent out our room to the next old bastard."

"Christ, you're pretty hard on this place. They've been doing good work for a long time. You should see some of the other homes out there. I don't know about Montana, but everywhere else I've read about, the places make this look like the Presidential Suite at the Waldorf-Astoria."

"That doesn't make it right to clamp us down like this; we're not kids."

Jim stopped and looked at Paul, "You're right, we're not kids. We're old men. Old men with bad hips and dodgy tickers who can't climb stairs without having to stop to go to the toilet on each flight. Who should be watched over. At least a bit."

Paul was taken aback by the vehemence of Jim's words. He was an independent old coot who had always hated giving up anything, to anyone. And despite the attempts of the school system, the Army, and a firm yet loving wife, he still had that independent streak—one as long as the Missouri River.

"Ah hell, I'm not having an easy time being old. And I don't like being told what I can't do."

Jim placated him with a wave and chuckled. "Army must have loved you."

Paul laughed. "They weren't sad when I left, I'll tell you that much."

They had arrived outside the dining hall. Jim put his hand on Paul's arm and stopped him. They let a few people enter before them. Then Jim looked at Paul and said, in complete seriousness, "I've been musing. Since today's Sunday, we should probably go through this door instead."

Then he pushed open a single unmarked door. With a gesture, he started down the long plain hallway and Paul followed, slightly confused and utterly curious.

Eight

Sunday brunch always had the largest turnout of the week at Shady Acres as most families came to visit their relatives and enjoy an affordable meal at the same time. The kitchen ran at full tilt, sending out plate after plate of eggs Benedict; bagels with lox and cream cheese; and waffles with strawberries and whipped cream. The waiters were moving efficiently through the room pouring champagne glass after champagne glass of virgin mimosas.

The Bees were at their table, with the notable exception of Joanne. Subsequently, the conversation was a bit subdued compared to their average meal.

"Something is off about this hollandaise," Frances said, frowning and tasting another fingertip of sauce.

"The only thing off is your taste buds, Franny," Lillian said with a laugh.

"Yes, you say that again and again, and we know they haven't changed the recipe in over ten years," piped in Helen.

"But if there is something off with the sauce, we could come down with listeria," Hazel said, worried.

"The hollandaise is fine, Hazel. You're fretting about nothing again," Lillian said.

It was clear Hazel wasn't convinced, but she remained quiet, scraping the sauce off her eggs Benedict instead.

It was the same dynamic they had been playing out since sitting in their high school cafeteria all those years ago: Hazel worrying about the mayonnaise in the egg salad, Frances stirring her up, Lillian shutting her down, Helen tossing in smart aleck comments, and Joanne playing peacemaker. A lifetime together, and yet all that had changed was their wardrobes and their bodies.

Frances resigned herself with a harrumph and started delicately cutting up her meal. After a pause to see if there would be any continued discussion of the state of the hollandaise, the rest of The Bees returned to eating.

•

On the other side of the hall, Chuck and his boys were munching their way through plates of turkey sausages, egg white omelets, and decaf coffee. It wasn't what they would have chosen, but it was the most indulgent their doctors would allow. One of the guys, John, went on about some show he'd seen on TV the previous night, but Chuck wasn't listening. He rarely listened to any story they would spin. He told the best stories; the stories that were rewarded the loudest laughs or the largest shocks.

While John rambled on and on, pausing only to put more food in his mouth, Chuck looked across at The Bees table, focusing on Joanne's empty seat. They were rarely able to eat together as The Bees were fiercely possessive of Joanne and especially of whom she ate with. Best he could get was the occasional afternoon stroll or watch some TV with Joanne a couple of times a week. His attempts to woo her into the sack had, so far, failed. Not that he hadn't told the guys he was getting some on a regular basis. But simply separating Joanne from The Bees was such a damn struggle. *A bunch of old busybodies,* he thought, and turned back to the table as John finished his story to lackluster laughter.

"Let's finish up here and go," Chuck said, ever the leader of his pack.

•

Marcus looked across the dining hall at the sound of Chuck and his gang laughing. Even across the room, he could see Chuck dominating the table, speaking whenever he felt like and overriding whoever tried to talk. *Men like that were born bullies,* Marcus thought to himself. *Born to lean in and sweat those who considered themselves stronger than him, even if they weren't—* Marcus didn't even finish his thought as some motion outside at the far edge of the estate caught his eye.

A couple of figures, moving slowly, made their way along the shaded edge of the property line. The distance and the French doors in-between made it impossible to recognize who it was, but Marcus clearly made out the red coat of one and the white baseball cap on the other. *Won't be hard to find you two when the time comes,* he thought. *But now's the time to be patient and rest. Hunting is much easier when the prey comes to you. You pop up and bag them, easy as pie.*

He smiled to himself, turned, poured himself a coffee, and continued observing the dining room, the diners, and the staff.

•

The single lane road they walked on wove through ancient trees along the side of a smooth flowing river. In places, the road shifted left, then right, to go around an unusually massive tree. Nature held sway; the constructions of man took second seat. The sun shone through the leaves and made the river glisten. Except for the pavement they strolled on, they could have been early explorers marking out the original Indian trail beside the river.

Paul and Jim walked along in quiet contentment—Paul from being out of the home and Jim from letting Paul convince him to get out of the home. Occasionally a car would cruise so slowly past that it was as if even the traffic had to move at the pace of the river and the two men.

"This is much better. And after a pleasant stroll, I'll be right and ready for a huge breakfast," Paul said with a smile.

Jim nodded and winced a bit, leaning a bit more on his cane. His knees and lower back were hurting, but not enough to mention. *Probably because I haven't walked any distance in months,* he thought. *Maybe this could become a regular occurrence and help build up some strength...*

"You know, I fished this river, further upstream, with my grandfather when I was a kid. A few years ago."

"Good fishing?"

Jim nodded and continued, "He fished it with his grandfather. I reckon eight generations of my family have pulled bass and trout out of this river, if you count my grandkids."

"You ever fish with your dad?"

Jim shook his head. "He was always too busy, and that's why my granddad took me. By the time my father had time, I was out the door and into the welcoming bosom of the Air Force."

Paul agreed, "Pretty much the same story for me. My grandpa was an ornery old coot, but he liked me for some reason. We drove my old man crazy. My grandpa knew which buttons to push on my dad, and he got me helping him from time to time," Paul laughed in recollection. "My grandpa loved practical jokes."

"And you?"

"I've been known to partake in the occasional joke or two," Paul admitted.

Jim shook his head. "You're gonna make me rue the day I saved you from Chuck, aren't you?"

Paul thought about that for a moment, and then nodded. Jim laughed, and they continued along the road.

As they came to the edge of downtown, Paul stopped and looked out on the river. Half to look at the river, and half to rest his body a bit.

"There's something to that, you know…"

"Something to what?"

Paul frowned. "Grandfathers and grandsons. Like my grandpa and I were united against my dad. His son. I never got in trouble from my grandpa, but constantly butted heads with my dad."

"A generational thing, I reckon," Jim offered.

"It is that. And I find myself siding with my grandson against my own daughter. Like we have to stick together or something."

"Probably been going on since the dawn of civilization."

"Probably," Paul sighed. "Doesn't make it easier for my Natalie."

"Or my sons," Jim admitted. "When my grandkids were little, I'd always have a candy bar for them when they'd visit. They probably bounced around the back seat of the car the whole way home."

They both laughed at that image.

Paul turned from the river to regard the start of the old downtown.

"If I remember correctly, the diner we're looking for is within a block of the town square."

Jim put up his hand to stop Paul. "Hold your horses, Cowboy. This here is my town, and I'll take you to the one and only place for the kind of breakfast you're looking for. It's the least I can do for the man who persuaded me to go AWOL and who will probably get me locked in the brig."

Paul laughed. "The Army don't have brigs. That's the Navy, flyboy."

"Then you pay for breakfast, wise guy."

With a grin, Jim crossed the street and Paul followed him.

Nine

"Could you make sure that Gwen and her family get settled in on the patio, Marcus? I can't see Evangeline anywhere, and that's her section today. You know how Gwen is," Kevin said as he rushed into the server's area off the dining room.

Marcus slipped his cup of coffee behind his back and nodded, "I'll get right on it."

Kevin checked the coffee machines, grabbed a pot, and handed it to Marcus. "May as well fill them up while you're out there."

Marcus took a breath, smiled, and started across the room toward the patio doors. *If I didn't need this damn job,* he thought, *there'd be some trouble right now. Serving old folks coffee…that's not why I've been going to night school for five years.*

•

Back in the servers' area, Kevin scanned the room quickly, making sure the servers were in motion or working their tables. Then he straightened his tie—one of his father's favorites: navy blue with a slight pattern of red—and, with a combination of smoothness and speed, crossed the room to the entrance in time to greet two more families.

"You're right on time, as always," Kevin said with a smile, shaking hands with everyone except a couple of sullen teenagers engrossed in their cell phones. "Follow me."

With the two families in tow, he crossed the room and settled them in at a couple of round tables, each with an elderly resident waiting.

"Marjorie will be your server this morning, and she will be right with you," Kevin said as the families sat down, and then he made his way back to the entrance. By this time, Marcus had returned from the patio, and they met up at the tiny maître d' stand.

"You get them seated?" Kevin asked Marcus. Marcus nodded, and Kevin crossed a name off the sheet on the stand. Then he turned and scanned the room again.

"Looking pretty good to me, sir."

"It looks pretty good, but it's not, Marcus. You see Grace over there?" he pointed across at a statuesque black woman at a table by the patio doors. "She's been chatting with that table for far too long. When the servers are chatty, then our residents and their guests receive slow service. Remember that."

Marcus nodded. Kevin continued, "What's paramount is for everyone here to see that management—that's you and me—are here and on top of everything. We have to show them we care, and that we are entirely responsible for their well-being."

"I understand, sir, and I'll be here, keeping on top of it all, as you've laid it out for me. I know how important this is for you."

Kevin nodded, distracted by the action of the room around him.

Marcus continued, "And I'll talk to Grace, sir. We have it covered if you want to leave now."

"I should, Marcus," Kevin said. "I should do a lot of things, like not go rushing off to church; hiring a maître d' so you and I don't have to do this on Sundays; getting out to play golf at least once this year…"

"Those would be nice things, sir," Marcus said. Kevin nodded, still scanning the room for anything amiss. Still watching the servers as they rushed in and out of the kitchen.

Kevin said, "But I need to get the Catholics settled in, and then the Baptists, so you have the door."

And then Kevin was gone. Marcus sighed and watched him move down the hallway toward the two sanctuaries. Once Kevin turned the corner, Marcus pulled out his Care Home Management textbook hoping to get a little studying in before tomorrow night's test. But then he saw Grace heading for the kitchen, sighed, put his book away, and followed to speak to her about being 'all chatty' at her tables.

Kevin walked through the foyer and down the corridor in the East wing of the building. Past the TV and games rooms were the two sanctuaries—non-denominational spaces that were in full use on Sundays, and one of them on Saturday for the Jewish residents.

The Baptists were settling into the Oak Room with the Roman Catholics across the hallway in the Cedar Room. He couldn't remember it ever being different—which religion in which room had been set in stone as if written in the Old Testament. And ninety minutes later, the Protestants and the Episcopalians would shuffle in for their turn. Only the two Hindu residents were picked up and taken into town for a service for their faith.

Only once Kevin had made sure everyone was in their respective places could he finally relax. Then he double-checked his phone, realized he was late, and rushed out to the parking lot.

Ten

"How long exactly has this town been here?" Paul asked as they made their way down the pristine Main Street toward the town square. On each side of the street were perfectly kept historic buildings, each with an antique brass plaque stating when it had been built and its original purpose. Massive, perfectly spaced and groomed trees surrounded the town square and shaded the sidewalks and pathways.

"First settled in 1675," Jim said, proudly.

"Probably by your ancestors, right?"

Jim laughed. "They came along a bit later. The first few years were pretty tough; my folks waited until the settlement got their feet under them, then started farming up river a ways."

Paul looked around at the perfect buildings on the perfect street. If someone magically removed the cars and covered the pavement with dirt, he'd believe he was back in time at least 100 years. Except the buildings would probably have had been coated in the dust and grime from the industrial factories along the river, not to mention the filth from a civilization run on horses.

"And the Civil War bypassed it?"

"We simply weren't strategic enough to be fought over, although enough boys were sent off and died elsewhere to have an impact. Like pretty much every town in the South."

"And then again for the Great War, and WW2."

"And the non-wars."

"Yup."

They walked past the town square with its gray granite statue of some general seated proudly on his horse. On the next block, across from the courthouse—another imposing classical building transported directly from Athens or Rome to rural Carolina—was The Main Street Diner. Straight out of the 1950s with a half dozen large glass windows on each side of the door, planter boxes with perfect geraniums under each window, and an immaculate neon sign sticking out from the building above the door.

"That, my friend, is what I was looking for," Paul said with a smile.

"Best in town! I should know, came here for lunch most days. My office—my son's office now—is right around the corner."

"Handy to the courthouse, too," Paul said as they climbed the stairs and into the diner. A soft ring of a bell greeted them as they pushed the door open.

"Location, location, location," Jim said.

Paul looked around the diner.

On both sides of the door were booths against the windows, each with shiny red benches and glistening chrome and white tables. Black and white tile angled 45 degrees to the walls covered the floor. A gleaming stainless steel bar covered the entire back of the diner, and behind it was an array of coffee machines, classic milkshake blenders, ice cream freezers, and a pass-through to the kitchen. It was every 1950s diner Paul had ever been in—straight out of *American Graffiti* or some Annette Funicello musical. The place was about half full, but the staff worked the room efficiently like they'd been doing it for years.

A powerful woman in her mid-fifties turned around from the kitchen pass-through and clapped her hands to her cheeks when she spotted Jim and Paul. She rushed around the end of the bar, tugging her unruly graying hair back into her bun.

"Jim! Jim Lyons! What a wonderful surprise!"

Jim let her embrace him, then said, "Good seeing you, too, Marge."

Then she stepped back and gave him a slap on the arm, "I said not to be a stranger when you stopped practicing, but I haven't seen you since! That's not the neighborly way; you know that."

Jim tried to placate her. "I know, I know, what with Shady Acres being so far out of town…"

Marge wasn't taking his excuses at all, "But you've made it here today, and, looking at the two of you, you didn't have yourself a ride in either."

Jim shook his head and raised his hands. "I withdraw, your honor. The defendant would like to change his plea to guilty and throw himself on the mercy of the court."

Marge grinned and gave him another quick hug. "That's better."

Jim pointed at Paul and said, "Marge, this is the new resident of the home, Paul Carter."

Marge gave Paul a quick scan. He felt like a suspicious policewoman was giving him the once-over.

"He looks like trouble; you defending him?"

"Not yet. But it wouldn't surprise me."

"Hey, don't I get a chance to defend myself?" Paul chimed in.

"Let your lawyer speak for you," Jim responded.

Marge gave a laugh and, after wiping her hand on her apron, held it out.

"Nice to meet you, Paul."

"Nice to meet you, Marge."

She gave Paul a firm, quick three-shake handshake then turned to Jim.

"Go on back to your table and I'll bring over coffees and menus."

She turned and quickly slipped behind the bar, grabbing a couple of plates of food to take them out to a table. Paul followed Jim toward a booth on the left side of the diner.

"Your table?" Paul asked as they were seated.

"I told you I was a regular."

Paul nodded and leaned back. Before he had a chance to say anything, two steaming hot cups of coffee and one laminated menu were slipped down in front of them. Then Marge disappeared before either had a chance to thank her. Jim slid the menu over to Paul, took a sip of his coffee, and sighed.

"Nice place," Paul said, picking up the menu.

Jim nodded. "Finest kind. Marge started working here bussing tables for her parents when she was still in elementary school, back when you could have a ten-year-old kid working in a family business. Now she runs it."

Paul watched Marge rush around. "She certainly does run it."

Jim laughed. Paul looked over the menu. He saw everything he expected to see: clubhouse sandwich on white, grilled cheese, prime rib meal on Sunday evenings. And no fancy coffees or eggs Benedict to be seen. It even had a senior's section with reduced meal sizes.

Paul put down the menu. "You know what you want?"

"Ah, they'll bring me what I'll eat without even asking unless I say otherwise. I told you, I was a regular here."

"Then how come you haven't been coming? It's not like it's that far from Shady Acres."

Jim shrugged. "When I worked around the corner, popping in to have a meeting or a quick lunch before going back to a trial was easy. Once I left, all the effort to get here didn't seem worthwhile…"

"You could meet your son here. He's working at the office, right? Have a nice lunch with him occasionally."

Jim shook his head. "Michael doesn't eat this kind of food. High blood pressure troubles, and this place doesn't have a lot of salads or even vegetables on the menu."

"I saw cream of cauliflower soup."

"They make it with whole cream. A week's worth of fat in one bowl."

"Must be good."

"Fantastic."

They laughed. Marge arrived at the edge of the booth in a burst of energy. "Jim, your usual?"

"I'd best not confuse you, or me, so yes please."

Marge turned to Paul, saying, "And for you?"

Paul looked at the menu again then asked, "His usual isn't egg whites on gluten free toast is it?"

Marge and Jim laughed, and Marge said, "Far from it. Two eggs, over easy; local breakfast sausage; baked beans—house special—and brown toast. With some of my mommy's red mulberry jam."

"Sold! Make it two," Paul said, and Marge zipped away to the kitchen.

"I haven't even had the food yet and I like this place. I hope we turn this into a regular escape."

Jim started to say something, but some recognizable laughter coming from the far corner booth behind Paul interrupted him. Cautiously Paul looked at Jim. "Is that who I think it is?"

Jim leaned to his left, looking over Paul's shoulder, then leaned back, took a sip of coffee, sighed, and nodded.

Eleven

Kevin's white BMW rolled slowly down the tree-shaded street, as he tried to find a parking spot, preferably near the church on the corner. But he was a good five minutes late, and promptness was certainly a virtue, which meant the good parking spots had already been taken. He frowned, letting frustration slip onto his face for a moment, then took a deep breath and pulled into half a spot near a fire hydrant a block away from the church. Climbing out of his car, Kevin chirped the key to lock it and started down the sidewalk, straightening his tie as he went.

Three quick steps up and then he slipped through the heavy doors into the tiny church. He nodded to the congregant standing by the doorway, took a program, and looked down the aisle for his family.

The room was on its feet and was finishing a hymn. Dappled sunlight flowed through the simple stained-glass windows above the pews. At the far end of the aisle, the pastor stood at the pulpit, singing along with the choir and the congregants. The pastor was a formerly powerful man, clearly someone who once had great strength both of body and soul. But now, in his late eighties, the departure of his body strength had left him stooped and frail. But his eyes were still bright, his voice firm, and his thinning gray hair immaculate.

As the hymn came to an end with a final long 'Amen,' and everyone began seating themselves again, Kevin slipped down the aisle and into the pew beside his wife and daughter. He gave them both a smile then turned forward and saw the pastor looking at him. Kevin gave Pastor Alistair a weak smile, and the pastor tapped his old wristwatch in admonition before returning to his sermon notes on the pulpit in front of him.

•

Beth tried not to show her astonishment at Kevin joining them at church; Sundays were usually such a busy day at the home, and he was always up and out the door before either she or Dawn came downstairs for breakfast. Not that she wasn't happy to have him beside her. She was a bit surprised, that's all. *Surprised in a good way,* she thought. *Maybe he was going to actually, finally, let go of some of his work responsibilities and have a bit of a life—both for himself and for us.*

On the other side of her mom, Dawn carefully folded an intricate origami crane out of a crisp square piece of paper. She'd finally learned how to make the cranes at school as part of a section they'd been doing on Japan, and she found it a reasonable way to pass the time when she wasn't allowed to have her phone to play games, listen to music, or text her friends. Making cranes was an ok alternative. Her mom had loved the one she'd made for her with her best piece of Japanese silver paper and had placed it on the mantle between their family portrait and her great-great grandmother's silver candleholders.

Beth gave Kevin a quick peck on the cheek and whispered, "I'm glad you made it; what a lovely surprise."

Dawn put the crane away before her father could see it. "Hi Dad, how's the home?"

Kevin turned and looked at the two of them. "Where's Grandma?"

Beth shrugged and whispered back, "I haven't seen her yet, why?" Dawn looked down at her hymnal intently.

"No reason," Kevin said with a thin smile.

The pastor started his sermon in his still-thunderous voice, abruptly silencing any more conversation.

"Many times, you see children who are rebellious troublemakers, and it is an indication of their 'raising.' In many cases, you trace their actions directly back to a lack of discipline and lack of proper training. When you see someone living a wretched, sinful lifestyle, you may be quick to blame the parents. But that's too easy, too simple. Sometimes you may be right, and at the same time, what about personal responsibility for one's own actions? Troublemaking doesn't spring to life from untended soil."

Kevin sighed, my life's full of troublemakers. *If it wasn't my daughter acting up, it was my mother,* he thought. *At least Beth doesn't act up. If she did, I'd have to commit myself.* He shuddered at the thought and tried to return his focus to the voice from the pulpit.

•

When Marge brought out Jim and Paul's food, she found Jim's personal booth empty and the two men seated in the corner booth. She smiled and continued over and put the meals down in front of them. "I wondered if you all would join up."

Joanne quickly said, "This isn't a double date or anything, Marge."

"Not a date, no," Paul quickly said in agreement.

Marge laughed. "I didn't say it was. You two did." She smirked and left the table.

Paul looked at Jim. "Is she always like that?"

Jim nodded, and Joanne said, "For better or worse, she treats us like family."

Jim looked down at his huge plate of food and smiled. "I'd offer you ladies some, but I'm planning on finishing this all off myself."

"We'll fend for ourselves, thank you so much," Joanne's friend, Ruth, said. As Paul started eating, he glanced across the booth at the woman sitting beside Joanne. Ruth was a tiny lady the same age as the rest of the table. She had sharp eyes, quick fingers, and her thin silver hair had been dyed a bright pink. She claimed it was pink so everyone would remember her when she was out and about. It was hard to argue with her logic, as her hair lit up the room.

Paul hadn't wanted to join the two women, but Jim insisted saying it was the way things were done in the South. So, Paul had bit his tongue and followed Jim over to the other booth. Joanne's smile at seeing Jim fell off her face as Paul stepped into view beside him. They hadn't talked since that first night in the dining room, and suddenly they were uncomfortably seated across from each other. With nothing to say to the other, Paul felt like a kid on his first blind date. *Which is stupid,* he thought. *I'm a grown man, not a nervous teenager.* But that wasn't enough to get any words out of his tongue-tied mouth.

Across the table, Joanne snuck glances at Paul as he silently listened to Ruth and Jim pass town gossip back and forth. She'd known of Jim—he'd been a couple years ahead of her at school—and Ruth had gone out with at least one of his brothers. *But why would such a polite and upstanding man like Jim Lyons be associating with this roughneck from out West?* she wondered. She still had a bad taste in her mouth from their encounter on Paul's first night, so she wasn't going to even attempt to engage him in conversation. *That will teach him,* she thought and sipped her tea.

Luckily, Jim and Ruth kept chatting until the food arrived so the table wasn't enveloped in an uncomfortable silence.

Between bites of his breakfast, Jim asked Joanne, "So how did you make your escape from the home? You're too clean for it to be through a tunnel, so did you sneak out in the laundry truck?"

Ruth piped in, "I clipped the wires on the fence on the far side and distracted the dogs. I had a motorcycle with a sidecar waiting in the forest with fake German uniforms."

Everyone laughed. "Shady Acres is much better than that, Ruth," Joanne said, slightly defensively.

"Right, that's why you've broken curfew and are here," Ruth said smugly. "You won't see me in one of those places. It'd be the death of me."

Joanne turned to Paul and explained, "Ruth is still in her house, about two blocks away from here. She doesn't let me forget that. Honestly, the best thing about her place is it has no stairs."

As Ruth proudly nodded, the other three touched their replaced hips lightly. No stairs... how sweet a life that would that be...

"So how do you really sneak out?" Jim asked Joanne after a bite of toast.

Joanne sighed guiltily. "My granddaughter picks me up for church, but drops me off at Ruth's."

"But aren't you then expected at church?"

Joanne smiled. "Dawn then tells her mom I didn't sleep well, so stayed behind."

"Why not get Ruth to pick you up and drop you off? Why the subterfuge?"

"Because her baby boy doesn't like me," Ruth said. "Says I'm trouble and doesn't like her visiting me. So, the joke's on him."

Paul nodded, "Smart. So Shady Acres and your son figure you're at church, your daughter-in-law is sure you're at the home, and you're here with us."

Joanne nodded, appreciating Paul's recognition of her plan's complexity. "I only get away with it once a month. I don't want Dawn to be in trouble, either."

Jim looked over at Paul. "Your theory about grandfathers and grandsons can now be expanded to include grandmothers and granddaughters."

Joanne looked quizzically at Paul. "What theory is this?"

"Ah, something I've been pondering about," Paul said, slightly embarrassed, "on the long trip driving here." Paul saw he wasn't going escape explaining that easily, as the two women were still staring at him. "Well, I've been pondering about how my grandson and I like to joke around and bug his mother, my daughter. And when he's had troubles at school with the other kids, he'd come and talk to me, instead of her."

Ruth piped in, "Oh that's simply a boy-girl thing. No boy would talk to his mom about girls."

"Oh, no, about that he does talk to her. We kind of conspire against his mom with our secrets, I guess. Like you have with your granddaughter."

Paul noticed everyone staring at him. "Ah, I'm flapping my jaw now." He shrugged and sipped some coffee.

"No, you might be on to something," Joanne said with a smile. "Centuries ago, I'd bet the frail grandparents did most of the child-rearing while the healthy parents ventured out and found food."

Paul said, "Of course, those grandparents were in their thirties with a life expectancy in the low forties."

Ruth said, "That's quite the brain you've got in that noggin of yours, Paul."

"Thanks, maybe," Paul replied, and Ruth laughed.

Twelve

"Why do we gotta be here?" Devon whispered to his mother as he fidgeted in the pew beside her.

"Because this is a good way to become part of this community," she whispered back, hoping no one heard them. "And I want us to be part of this town since we're living here now."

Devon muttered something inaudible under his breath and loosened his tie. Natalie suppressed a dramatic sigh and looked forward.

They sat at the back of the quaint church. The old preacher was up to full steam in his sermon. Natalie slowly glanced around at the rest of congregants. They looked like nice people. Lots of families; multi-generational. But predominantly white. *Not that I'm too surprised by that,* she thought. *I am in a Protestant church after all. But it would have been nice for it to have a bit more color.*

Beside her, Devon alternated between staring at the wooden floor beneath his feet and the arched wooden ceiling above his head. If someone asked him at gun point, he wouldn't have been able to repeat one thing the old guy at the front had said. *I hope this finishes quickly,* he thought and picked up a hymnal then put it right back down. The old lady in front of him leaned forward to get a tissue from her purse, and Devon spotted, through the churchgoers, a cute brunette girl sitting up at the front of the church.

Finally, something interesting! he thought, and leaned forward onto the back of the pew in front of him to get a better view. She had shiny brown hair, long and straight—like most the girls at the high school. He could see a bit of her face, but she looked down into her lap instead of at the pulpit. *She's as interested in being here as I am,* he thought. *Maybe if we hang around for the tea and stale cookies, I'll see who she is.* He smiled to himself.

•

Dawn glanced over her shoulder, sure someone was looking at her, but she couldn't see anyone. All she saw were old people and tired parents trying to keep their children from causing a fuss. She leaned to her side, away from her parents, and slipped her phone out of her purse.

I'd better let Grandma know Dad is here at church so she'll change her story... she thought.

Kevin shifted in his seat, and Dawn slipped the phone under her skirt to hide it. And that's when she received the text. She had turned off her phone ringer, but not the vibrate alert, so the phone buzzed loudly on the hardwood of the pew. People around her turned, looking for the noise's origin. Dawn's cheeks flushed crimson as she tried to stop it from buzzing unobtrusively.

Devon watched the girl try silencing her phone and shook his head in dismay. The girl's parents were looking at her with scowls on their faces. *She's so going to be in trouble after church,* he thought. He quickly took his phone out and made sure it was in airplane mode—not that anyone in town knew his cell number other than his mom, and she sat beside him.

"Dawn! Give that over. Now!" Kevin hissed, reaching across Beth's lap and angrily taking the phone.

"Dad..."

"You'll have it back after church, if you're lucky," Kevin whispered to her as the phone finally stopped buzzing.

He looked up at the front of the church to where Pastor Alistair stood behind the pulpit, a stern look on his face. Kevin felt exactly like he had as a child when his father had been angry with him. No, not angry; disappointed. A look of supreme disappointment. It was all he could do not to shrink down in his seat to hide and that feeling made him even guiltier.

Instead, he mouthed, 'sorry' and looked downward, shamefully. He flicked Dawn's phone to off and put it in his suit jacket pocket, then subtly pulled out his BlackBerry and confirmed he had turned off the ringer.

The silence continued for a long, drawn-out moment; then the pastor resumed his sermon without digressing to speaking about the evils of technology, much to Kevin's relief.

Natalie leaned over and whispered in Devon's ear, "Your phone is off, right?"

"Mom, come on, of course," he whispered back, defensively.

"Do you know her? I bet she's in trouble."

"I don't know anybody here," Devon said sulkily.

Natalie started to say something about not knowing anyone here either, but stopped herself. It wasn't the time, and it certainly wasn't the place to have that conversation again. Besides, it had to be easier to meet new friends at a school with fifteen hundred students in it rather than finding a friend in the dozen people she worked with in her division at the office. *Comparably, he's got it easy,* she thought with a sigh.

Thirteen

"You'd better let us out here," Jim said. "We'd best not arrive together."

"You sure?" Joanne asked as she turned around in the front seat of Ruth's car.

"You may have a weak excuse why you're gone from this prison, but Jim and I don't. We're AWOL. It would be the brig for us."

"Thought you boys were Army?" Ruth said. Paul grinned at Jim who rolled his eyes.

"The stockade. We'd be tossed in the stockade." Paul said.

"Then in the brig," Jim said, dryly.

Ruth nodded and pulled her massive, old, gas-guzzling 1974 Mercury Montego over to the side of the road at the far edge of the home's property. Paul and Jim climbed out of the back seat and shut their doors. Ruth pulled out onto the road. Ruth and Joanne waved, and the men waved back. Silence descended as her car rounded a curve in the road and they started sauntering along the road.

"That was fun," Paul said, neutrally.

"Except when you switched the salt and sugar on me and I nearly ended up in the hospital."

Paul chuckled, remembering his practical joke. "At least Marge didn't kick us out what with the racket you were making."

"She may not have kicked us out, but she did add ten percent to the bill for the ruckus we caused."

Paul stopped and stared at Jim. "You're kidding. I didn't even notice when I paid."

"She does the same with the unruly teens."

"She's a strict woman."

Jim looked back at him. "You don't mess with Marge."

Paul started walking and caught up to Jim, saying, "Now it's official: I like that place."

"I knew you would."

"You're a smart man, for a retired lawyer."

Jim laughed and passed Paul a cigar. They lit up and continued along the road, beside the lazy river, underneath the canopy of ancient trees.

•

Joanne checked her cell phone once more as Ruth continued towards to the home.

"I don't understand it. Dawn said to text her when I wanted to be picked up, but she hasn't replied. I hope something hasn't happened."

Ruth dismissed Joanne's concerns with a wave of her hand, sending the car wobbling across the centerline of the road. "She's a teenager. I remember being a teenager, barely, and I ran the opposite direction from any responsibility."

"I remember, barely, too," Joanne said and sighed. It had been one of the nicer breakfasts she'd ever had with Ruth, especially once the boys joined them. Well, maybe 'boys' wasn't the right word, but calling them 'men' seemed so formal.

"That was fun," she said, filling the air. Ruth hooted, sending the car across the centerline again.

Joanne looked at her. "What are you laughing about?"

"Oh, say you've got the hots for him, won't you? Don't be demure and delicate about it for once."

"I don't know what you're talking about."

Ruth laughed again, before saying, "Ok, sure. If you want to play it that way, I'll play along. But you've got the hots for him whether you're willing to admit it or not."

"For goodness sake, Ruth, I don't have the hots for him."

They turned into the driveway toward the home.

"Keep telling yourself that, sweetie."

Joanne huffed exasperatedly and looked out her window while Ruth laughed again.

As they drew closer to the Shady Acres portico, they both spotted Kevin standing outside; his arms crossed tightly.

"Oh, oh," Ruth said. "Want me to turn around and drive away? We could make it to Florida in ten hours."

"Too late," Joanne sighed. "He's seen us."

"Well, then dive out of the car so I don't have to stop and talk to him, the little dictator."

"Ruth! He's not a dictator!"

"Fine, but he's still little."

Ruth pulled under the portico and stopped her car. Kevin stepped over and opened the passenger door to let his mother out. He leaned down and said a polite, if terse, hello to Ruth. She said an equally terse hello back. And that ended their conversation like every other time they had to speak to each other.

"I appreciate the ride, Ruth," Joanne said as she climbed out of the car. "I'll give you a ring tomorrow."

"If you still have phone privileges."

"You be quiet," Joanne hissed at Ruth.

Kevin shut the car door, and Ruth quickly drove off.

Joanne started toward the front door quickly while Kevin watched Ruth drive away. He turned back and saw his mother going inside. He followed her, catching up in the middle of the foyer, and took her arm to stop her.

"You were supposed to be at church. You were expected; I expected you to be there. You can't wander off like that. And why did Ruth drop you off when you left with Dawn?"

Joanne paused, her mind racing, then turned to face her son. "Ruth called to say she felt under the weather so I had Dawn drop me off so I could care for her. We lost track of time, that's all, Kevin. Ruth bounced back over a cup of tea and we got to chattering and the morning slipped away," she shrugged. "You know how us old ladies are. Besides, I tried to call Dawn, but her phone must have been off. Ruth offered to drive me back. Is Dawn okay?"

Kevin ignored his mother's question, realizing he'd been the one to turn off Dawn's phone at church.

"Mom, you have an example to hold up here! You can't go off with your friends, not without permission! People look up to you!"

Joanne could see that Kevin was growing upset. But it wasn't her fault; she needed to escape from Shady Acres occasionally, like everyone else. Now he expected even more from her.

Kevin continued, "Unacceptable, Mom. Not acceptable, and it won't happen again, understand?"

"Darling, I'm your mother. I said those same words to you when you were a kid. When you stayed out late playing on a school night..."

"That's the past. I'm the adult now."

As if I wasn't an adult anymore, she thought. *That's what he was saying.* Joanne started to point out that she was also an adult, but before she could open her mouth, The Bees burst into the foyer, crowding around her, chattering about macramé and tea cozies, then pulled her off to their table for lunch.

Kevin stood alone in the foyer, full of exasperation. *Teenagers and parents, the banes of my life,* he thought, and then stormed back to his office.

The Bees laughed as they sat down at their table in the dining room.

"Oh my, the look on your son's face..." Lillian said, chuckling.

"Fit to burn, and we whisked you out of the fire in the nick of time."

Joanne smiled and said, "I could have handled myself, and he is my son after all..."

"Oh, it's better we handle him, keep you innocent in his eyes," Frances said.

"But what if Kevin were to find out, he would be so angry with you," Hazel said, fretting.

Joanne rolled her eyes, "Goodness, girls. I met Ruth and—I merely met Ruth for breakfast. I don't need you covering for me."

"Joanne, you asked us to cover for you, remember?"

Joanne sighed as the table burst out laughing. "Well, clearly I've forgotten my entire cunning plan."

The laughing continued even as their afternoon tea was served.

•

Chuck stood out on the patio, half-listening to his gang arguing about college football—despite living in North Carolina for nearly all their lives, they'd each gone away to school and were still defiantly loyal to whatever college they'd gone to—and half-listening to The Bees and Joanne chattering away inside.

With the cooling breeze off the river, it was a perfect day to relax on the patio, but Chuck was anything but relaxed. He was pissed off, and he didn't even know why. *Listening to these idiots go on about Ole Miss vs. South Texas could drive him inside to join The Bees conversation about the last Oprah show,* he thought darkly.

A couple of the older guys were playing bocce underneath the willows on the far edge of the property. It looked like they were having fun and Chuck thought about joining them and beating their sorry asses, until he noticed a couple of figures off in the distance.

Someone's snuck off, and now they're sneaking back, he thought. *That'll make for some excellent entertainment if I catch them before they slip inside.*

"Come on you idiots, we've got some rule breakers to catch!" Chuck said and stood. The gang quickly followed.

Chuck handed out instructions as they trooped into the foyer. "I'll find Kevin, y'all go outside and be on the lookout for two guys coming back in from the woods. One's wearing a bright white ball cap."

"Who cares, Chuck? They were probably out sneakin' a cig."

"I care because I'm pretty sure it's that damn smug lawyer and his buddy. Understand?"

The gang nodded quickly, but didn't move. Chuck glared at them, fury in his eyes, until they finally caught his meaning and rushed off.

Chuck headed down the hallway to Kevin's office. *I hope that new guy is out there,* the thought bringing a smile to his face. *How fitting for him to be caught.*

•

As they slipped out of the forest, Paul noticed Chuck's gang coming out the front doors of Shady Acres a little too quickly for his liking.

"Turn around, look at the river!" he said, urgently.

Jim did, as Paul reached over and grabbed the fedora off Jim's head.

"Hey! That's my lucky hat!" Jim said, trying to take it back. Paul put his hand on Jim's arm, pulled off his own white cap, then tossed the two hats into the bushes in front of them.

"I think Chuck's band of fools spotted us coming out of the woods. So, we're going to stand here and look out at the pretty river for a while. Which is what we've been doing since breakfast, if anyone asks."

"That's a staggeringly weak alibi, Paul."

"Simple is better; I'm sure you've counseled that."

Jim passed Paul one of the mints from the diner, and he popped it into his mouth to hide some of the smell of the cigar.

"You'd best slip off that jacket. It's a glowing red target," Paul said.

As Jim slowly removed his coat, Paul gazed over Jim's shoulder until the gang looked the other way.

"Good, now we will turn, like we're bored with the bucolic view, and saunter back to the patio."

"I've been wanting a cup of coffee, and this seems as good a time as any."

Together they turned and strolled across the green grass towards the patio. Over by the entrance, Chuck's gang looked around, squinting in the bright sunlight.

"You're not going to stop until we're both in trouble, are you?" Jim asked.

Paul laughed. "I'm not going to stop until this place is fun."

Jim sighed. "Then we'll be in the stockade."

"You always such a pessimist?"

"Surely isn't any value in being both a lawyer and an optimist."

They were at the steps to the patio when Chuck came out the front doors of the home with Kevin at his side. Chuck started pointing off to where Jim and Paul had slipped back onto the grounds. While Kevin looked along the distant edge of the property, Chuck turned and spotted them at the corner. Paul gave him a bright wave. Chuck turned to get Kevin's attention, but it was too late—Paul and Jim stepped out of sight around the corner of the building. Paul laughed as he and Jim sat down on a pair of shaded chairs.

Jim said, "Why'd you wave at him? You're going to rile him up."

"I'm not particularly worried about him being riled up, Jim."

Jim frowned as the waiter came over to their table. "I'd advise you to be worried, but I know you're not likely to be taking any of my advice. Lord, I pity the lawyer you'll have if you're ever in a genuine predicament."

"I thought we had a gentlemen's agreement you'd come out of retirement and represent me in that unlikely circumstance."

"I'm old, but I'm not an old fool," Jim said and ordered a coffee and a piece of pie. With a grin, Paul did the same.

•

"Did you see them coming onto the property?"

"Well, I guess, no sir, we didn't."

Kevin frowned and looked at the group around him. They were up to something for sure.

"Did you see who it was?" he asked Chuck.

Chuck shook his head; as much as he wanted to claim he saw Paul, he'd forgotten his glasses so his long-distance vision was suspect, and he was smart enough not to make accusations without proof.

"Damnit, if someone is breaking the rules, I want to know about it. If you see anything out of the ordinary, you let me know, got it? You come and tell me, or you tell Marcus."

With that, Kevin turned and walked back inside. Chuck watched him go then turned to his gang. "I'm sure I saw that new guy, Paul Whatever-His-Name, out there, coming back from somewhere he shouldn't have been."

"If you saw him, why didn't you tell Kevin?" one of the guys asked.

"Because I couldn't prove it, you idiot. They were like a football field away. But mark my words, Paul's gonna get what's coming to him.

First flirting with my girl, then sneaking off property; who knows what's next? Everybody keep an eye out, and we'll catch him, for sure."

With the gang nodding in agreement, Chuck stormed back into the home.

Fourteen

"I have to say I certainly enjoyed today, Paul."

Paul and Jim were out on their respective balconies, enjoying post-dinner cigars. Twilight was coming on, and the setting sun backlit the trees to the west in oranges and reds. The heat of the day was diminishing, and, with it, so was the humidity—much to Paul's relief. He still hadn't made the shift from the dryness of the prairies to the moist swampland of North Carolina.

Paul nodded in agreement. "We will do it again."

They continued to smoke and look out at the trees moving languidly in the warm breeze.

I'm actually feeling at home, Paul thought, much to his surprise. *I figured those ridiculous rules were going to keep me hating each day here, but now with a buddy to break rules with, it's not too bad. Not that Joanne doesn't make it pretty nice on her own.* Her feisty attitude reminded him of his wife, Sharon. Not exactly but close enough.

The four long, miserable years after Sharon had her cancer diagnosis, he'd struggled daily to keep his memories of her from when she was healthy and alive, not fading and sinking under with the disease.

He took another puff, looked out at the trees, and then finally said, "When Sharon was diagnosed, we were sure it was a mistake."

"Which one did she have?" Jim asked quietly.

"Lung. She hadn't smoked a day in her life. Hated the smell. Tolerated me with these, but only a couple times a year. But that's the one she got. It came on strong, like a runaway train, and then settled in to grind her down for more than four damn years."

"How'd it happen, if she didn't smoke?"

Paul laughed sharply, bitterly. "The way they eventually figured it out, her and her brother had a summer job when they were kids—ten-eleven years old—shoveling a load of asbestos out of a barn. It wasn't heavy; perfect for kids to make a couple of bucks doing. They spent more than three weeks on that job."

Jim looked over at Paul. "Jesus. And her brother?"

"A year older than me, in perfect shape. He gets checked out yearly. Nothing."

Jim shook his head; there was nothing to say.

Paul continued, "This morning was probably the longest time I've gone without dwelling on her since her diagnosis. So—" Paul raised his cigar in a toast to Jim, and Jim raised his back.

They both looked back out at the waning light on the trees and smoked.

"Evening, sirs."

Paul and Jim both quickly hid their cigars behind the wide railings of their balconies. Below, Marcus stood, looking up at them, impassively.

"Evening, Marcus," Paul said, holding in a lung full of smoke.

Jim did the same, nodded, but didn't dare speak.

"Now I'm sure you gents are fully aware of the rules of this home, so I wouldn't presume to remind you about any regarding unapproved departures from the grounds, correct?"

They both nodded their heads, slowly.

Marcus continued, "Because I know if someone were to sneak off and if those someones were to be caught, those someones might end up being kicked out of Shady Acres, if you get my meaning."

They nodded again. Paul was exceptionally close to coughing up a cloud of smoke, but held it together. Jim looked the same.

"So you will be pleased to know about a new curfew here at Shady Acres, from seven in the evening until ten in the morning, to ensure you stay nice and safe."

Marcus stared up at the two of them. They stared back down at him. After what felt like an hour, Marcus nodded his head and walked on around the corner and out of site.

Instantly, both Paul and Jim exhaled huge clouds of smoke and gulped in deep breaths of fresh air.

"Lord, I haven't held in a lungful of smoke for that long since high school," Jim said, coughing.

"In the toilet?"

Jim nodded, looked at the still smoking cigar in his hand. He butted it out in disgust. "Could be a few days before I want to have another one of them."

"You were caught smoking in the boy's room?"

"Got the strap from Mr. Hennigar, the mean old cuss of a principal, too," Jim said, reliving the memory.

"Tough luck. I climbed out the window and escaped."

They both were silent for a moment then Paul remembered what Marcus had said. "A damn curfew! This place is unbelievable. Worse than high school! Why, I bet if I combed my hair into a rat-tail, Kevin would be wanting to give me the strap."

Jim tried to calm him down. "It's no big deal…"

Paul turned and stared at Jim. "Do you believe that bull you're spreading? No big deal?"

Jim raised his hands in appeasement and said, "I really liked it here, you know, once my sons settled me in. Oh sure, I didn't like not being in my home, but it didn't take too long before I was happier here with my books and my secret cigars instead of an old house far too sprawling for proper looking after," Jim sighed and continued, "I didn't notice the little rules here, mostly because they didn't concern me. I guess I became content. But—"

"But what?" Paul said.

"But now, I reckon those little rules are starting to weigh on me. Like they weigh on you. Kevin would trot me out as the model resident because I go along to get along."

"And now?"

Jim paused, then relit his cigar and took a large puff. "I never rebelled in school, nor in the Army, but I reckon now I might have missed out on something."

Paul lit his cigar and turned towards Jim. "You know, you might be right. And I remember being taught, a long time ago, it's never too late to start."

The two of them looked out at the darkening trees for a while, and then Paul said, "You know where we could find matching monogrammed leather jackets for this gang of ours?"

Jim burst out laughing, and Paul joined in, neither of them caring if laughing after curfew was against the rules or not.

Fifteen

After midnight, Paul's room door slowly, quietly eased open. Paul slipped out into the dim light of the hallway, but only after scanning up and down its length for anyone out for a nocturnal stroll. Grateful for the quality of the home's doors, he silently shut his behind him. In his sock feet, Paul tiptoed down to Jim's door and waited, watching the corridor. After a moment, Jim's door opened and he slipped out, shutting it behind him as quietly as Paul.

"Ready?" Paul whispered, and Jim nodded with a grin.

Paul continued, "You know which room is his?" Jim nodded again and tapped his index finger against the side of his nose. Paul looked at him quizzically. Jim sighed and said, "That means yes, so we don't have to talk out loud."

"Look who's been watching old spy movies without me..."

Jim grinned and crept down the hallway as lightly as his arthritis and bad hip would let him. Paul suppressed a chuckle and sauntered after him.

Other than the nocturnal sounds of lightly sleeping senior citizens, the home was silent. The occasional table lamp and red exit signs above the fire staircases dimly lit the hallways. Jim arrived at the elevator and went to push the up button when Paul pushed Jim's hand way with his cane, stopping him.

"Too noisy!" Paul whispered, and pointed at the fire stairs beside the elevator. Jim tapped the side of his nose and sighed. It took them an extra-long time to climb the one flight of stairs, not counting the two fire doors to sneak through silently. On the final landing, Jim turned to Paul and muttered, "I need to confirm we won't be causing any bodily harm this evening, soldier. I won't be part of that, understand?"

Paul nodded. "No bodily harm. Agreed. Though with Chuck, it would be a bonus…"

Jim glared at Paul, then Paul shrugged. "Call it wishful thinking on my part."

"Keep it wishful, my heart can't stand the strain otherwise."

Once out in the third-floor hallway, identical to theirs below, Paul followed Jim down the East Wing and around the corner to the last few rooms on that floor.

Jim stopped and pointed at the second to last door.

"That's it."

"Good. Excellent."

The two stood in the hall, looking at the door in front of them. Finally, Jim turned to Paul and whispered, "Now what?"

"Oh, right. Where's the janitor's room?"

Jim sighed and looked at him, "By the elevator."

Paul shook his head in amusement. "Cat burglars we ain't. You wait over there in that alcove, and I'll be right back."

Jim slipped into the shadows at the end of the hall, beside a window looking out into the darkness. Paul snuck back along the hallway, around the corner, and down to the janitor's room across from the elevator. *Please don't be locked*, he thought, shaking his head. *I'm becoming rusty, or I'm getting dementia because I should have checked this out in advance. Making it up as we go will end up with us caught.*

He tried the door to the janitor's room and, to his relief, it swung open. Not larger than a laundry closet, with shelves full of cleaning supplies and toilet paper on one side, a couple of brooms leaning in the back corner, and a rolling pail full of foul water with a mop in it.

Paul smiled, grabbed the mop and gave it a light squeeze to wring most of the water out of it. Then he took one of the large gallon jugs of cleanser, shut the door quietly, and returned to Jim.

"What's the jug for?" Jim whispered, meeting him back in front of the door.

Paul grinned, feeling younger than he had in years, handed the mop to Jim and put the cleanser jug on the floor at the base of the door, directly under the knob.

"The trick," Paul whispered to Jim as he stood back up, wincing from the pain in his lower back, "is to know where the head will be when the door opens."

Jim looked down at the tub on the floor in confusion. Paul took back the mop, turned it upside down, and, balancing the tip of the handle on the top of the full jug, leaned the wet mop head against the door. After a quick adjustment to ensure the mop didn't slide over, Paul stepped back and grinned at Jim, "Voila!"

"Now, let's book it back to our rooms. We'll hear about it in the morning."

Paul started down the hallway, but paused at the corner when he realized Jim wasn't behind him. Turning around, he saw Jim still at the door, looking at the mop. Paul gestured for Jim to come and Jim nodded back, tapping the side of his nose. Paul turned the corner, heard the sound of someone pounding on a door, and looked back around the corner and saw Jim shuffling as quickly as he could towards him, a huge grin on his face, despite the ache of his arthritis.

Paul pulled him around the corner and hissed, "You're crazy!" Then they both leaned out as Chuck opened his door and received a dirty, wet mop right in the face.

Yelling in alarm, Chuck flung the mop away, sending it clattering across the hall, banging into the wall across from his door. "What the hell!" he yelled, frantically wiping muck out of his eyes and mouth.

"Come on! We're gonna get caught if we stay here!" Paul hissed and pulled Jim into the fire exit. They made their way quickly down to their floor. All was still quiet, and they arrived at their rooms without seeing anyone.

"Good Lord, the look on his face..." Jim whispered, trying to keep from laughing out loud.

Paul chuckled along. "I thought he was going to cry for his mommy."

"I wonder if my son has a video camera we could borrow."

"Forget that. Better to enjoy it live, and have no incriminating evidence, understand?"

Jim opened his door and turned to Paul, saying, "Keeping a straight face at breakfast is gonna be tough."

"What? A seasoned lawyer like you?" Paul whispered. Jim started to answer when they both heard the elevator arrive on their floor with a ding.

With one last grin at each other, they both tapped the sides of their noses and retired to bed.

Sixteen

Sitting in the back of the Shady Acres shuttle bus, Paul watched houses go past as he waited for his drop-off at Natalie's apartment building—his first visit to her and Devon's new place. Because of the additional rules, Natalie had been forced to fill out an official form giving Paul permission to be delivered to her home for dinner. She had also had to confirm that she would have him back at Shady Acres before the evening curfew.

Despite his initial dislike of the rules of the home, Paul was coming to like his days more than he had expected to. His mind was full of practical joke ideas, some he hadn't thought of in seventy years or more. It had also dawned on him that he hadn't felt the impulse to phone back to the Legion in Montana and chat with his friends. *Looks like I'm putting down some new roots,* he thought. *I didn't think that would happen but it looks like it has.*

As the bus rolled through town, Paul reminisced about the ruckus at the home at breakfast with a smile on his face.

By the time Paul and Jim had made their way down to the dining room for breakfast, the word was out and it was clear the dining room was talking about nothing else. The two had paused at The Bees table to say good morning and heard the news.

"—whoever it was swung the mop and hit him full in the face!" Hazel said, worrying the edge of her napkin in concern.

"No!" Jim said, conveying, to Paul's relief, a perfectly innocent blend of interest and shock.

"Oh, yes!" Hazel continued, "I heard they rushed him to the hospital! What is the world coming to, if we're not safe here?"

Jim looked at Paul, a bit of concern flickering across his face. "That is terrible!"

Everyone at the table nodded in agreement. But as they walked off to their table, Paul felt like Joanne's eyes were watching him a little too closely.

Once they were at their table and had coffee, Paul murmured, "Chuck is playing this up more than I thought. I wouldn't be surprised if he's brought in for breakfast in a wheelchair."

"He's always been like that, trying to make the most out of any situation."

Then Jim put his coffee cup up to his mouth and said, "But the look on his face…"

Paul quickly covered his mouth and coughed to cover his laugh. From across the room, The Bees, including Joanne, looked over at him. He took out his handkerchief, coughed again, and shook his head in what he hoped looked like concern for Chuck.

Jim continued to chuckle behind his coffee cup.

Paul muttered, "Oh, grow up." But he smiled behind his handkerchief.

The shuttle bus stopped outside a 1970s three-story apartment building that was surrounded by other three-story apartment buildings of the same vintage. Someone had thought to put four white columns along the front of the building in an attempt to have them fit in with the general theme of the town. Whoever that was had failed miserably.

The trees along the street were as old as everything else. *Some farm had become the suburb,* Paul thought as he climbed out of the homes shuttle bus. The bus pulled away from the curb behind him as he double-checked the address. *Hopefully this is the right place, or I'm in for a long walk home,* he thought and walked up to the front door of the building.

He pushed the intercom button for apartment 303-the only button without a name beside it.

"Hello?" came a crackling voice from behind the metal grille beside the buttons.

"Natalie?" Paul said, unsure of the voice at the other end.

"It's Devon! Jeez, I can't believe you thought I was Mom!"

"Lemme in, all right? I'll apologize once I'm inside," Paul said, making a mental note never to guess who talked to him on the intercom ever again.

The door buzzed, and Paul grabbed the handle before the buzzing stopped.

"Got it!" he called out.

"I'll come down and help you up," Devon said and hung up before Paul could stop him.

Paul crossed the bland lobby, passing the mailboxes and a couple of nailed-to-the-wall paintings of Civil War battles. *What is it about this town and its compulsion with history?* he wondered as he opened the doorway he assumed led to the elevator. He doubted there was more than one historical picture on display in the entire town he grew up in. Of course, it hadn't been a town, if you want to call it that, until the late 1800s. On the other side of the door he stopped and looked up at three flights climbing off into the distance with only two landings to break up the entire staircase.

Paul leaned into the lobby and looked around for an elevator or a door leading to an elevator. The only other door said 'Laundry' on it. Turning back, he looked up to see Devon appear at the top of the stairs.

Paul waved up at him, and Devon started down the stairs quickly, lightly skipping every second stair as if floating.

Paul absentmindedly rubbed his hip as Devon leaped the last five stairs and landed beside him. They had a quick fist bump, then Devon said, "Come on, dinner's ready, and you know what Mom's like if we're not sitting down with our hands in our laps when the plates hit the table."

With that he turned and started up the stairs, again skipping every second stair effortlessly.

"No elevator, huh?" Paul said as he took a tight hold of the banister and started up after his grandson, putting his full weight on his cane for each step.

"Nope. Sure sucks to be a moving guy here."

Paul's hip and leg held out for the first flight of stairs, but they started whining at him as he started the second. He slowed down and concentrated on using his arm on the banister to pull himself up from stair to stair. Devon arrived at the top and turned around, "You need a hand?"

"Of course not! Just a bunch of stairs," Paul growled and pulled himself up another stair.

"You sure? I mean, not that you can't, but I could help."

Paul waved a hand at Devon, dismissively, and then paused, rubbing his hip. *Stupid hip,* he thought. *Stupid building without an elevator. Stupid—*

"Gramps, please, let me help you, ok?"

Still looking down, Paul said, angrily, "I said I don't need any help—"

He looked up and saw the look of concern on his grandson's face. Sighing, resignedly, he nodded, and Devon hopped down the stairs, took his arm, and together the two started up the rest of the stairs.

"Don't tell your mom you helped me, understand? She'll worry I'm getting old."

Devon smiled. "You are getting old, Gramps."

Paul would have swatted him, but he thought he might topple over and tumble down the stairs, so he didn't.

"I still beat you at checkers."

Devon laughed and shook his head.

•

In the kitchen, Natalie pulled the broccoli off the steamer and tossed it into a bowl. She started to yell for Devon to bring himself to the table, but paused as she heard her father and her son coming in from the stairs. As always, the two of them were joking away, ribbing each other in a way that Natalie couldn't with either of them. Not with her son because she was his mother and made the rules; and not with her father because he had made the rules, but now they were in a sort of limbo as she started to make the rules.

"Good timing, dinner's ready," she called out. "Sorry I couldn't come and get you, but work is crazy right now."

"It's all good, the home delivered me right to your front door."

Natalie opened the oven to pull the roast out as her father and son entered the kitchen.

"You want me to take that for you?" Paul asked.

"I'm good, Dad, thanks. Devon, get your grandfather a beer."

Devon grabbed three beers out of the fridge, put them on the counter, and then looked around for the opener. Paul stared at him, "Oh, you're old enough to drink now?"

Devon replied, deadpan, "Gramps, the drinking age in North Carolina is fifteen. So, yeah, I drink beer now. Everyone does."

"That's ridiculous! Why, you can't even drive and you can drink-"

Paul stopped talking when he saw Natalie giggling. Devon shook his head in amusement. "Gotcha!"

Then he handed Paul a bottle of non-alcoholic beer. "Cheers."

"Wise ass," Paul muttered and took the beer from him.

"Language!" Natalie said as she took the platter with the roast and potatoes over to the table. Devon grabbed the broccoli and brought it over.

"Do I have to ask if you've washed your hands, or can we sit down and eat?"

Both Devon and Paul looked at their hands, checked their fingernails, gave their palms a quick sniff, and then gave her a thumbs up. Rolling her eyes, Natalie sat down and took a sip of her non-alcoholic beer, wishing it was red wine.

"I appreciate your attention to personal hygiene. Sit down and dish up."

•

Nice to be out of Shady Acres for a meal, Paul thought as he ate. *After spending all that time driving here from Montana, stuck in the same car and the same hotel room with these two, how odd that I'd miss being with them. I guess that's what family is all about—driving each other crazy when you're together, but missing each other when you're apart.*

•

Across the table, Natalie picked at her food, as it was a much heavier meal than she would have made for her and Devon. The heat and humidity in North Carolina had her leaning towards lighter meals—more salads instead of slabs of beef. But when she finally arranged for her father to come over to the apartment, she knew he'd like a proper home cooked meal, so she'd gotten everything ready last night and then had literally paid Devon to come right home from school and put it in the oven so it would be ready in time.

It's a shame they couldn't have found a three-bedroom place, maybe a proper house, for the three of them to live in, she thought for the thousandth time. But Paul's insurance wouldn't pay her as his landlord; they'd only pay an approved and registered assisted care facility. Then the HR department at her new employer had found her this place, close to Devon's school and a quick drive to her office, and had even negotiated an excellent deal on the rent. But she still worried it wasn't going to work out for the three of them. So far it was, but it wasn't like either her son or her dad would go out of their way to talk about their emotions with her.

Dinner proceeded smoothly until Paul asked Devon how he liked school. Devon stopped smiling, but continued eating.

"Fine," he said, through a mouthful of broccoli.

After an uncomfortable pause, Natalie turned to Paul, "And how's life at Shady Acres?"

Paul slowly put a forkful of potato in his mouth, then said, "Fine."

Natalie took a sip of her beer and said, "Well that was totally insightful, thanks to the both of you. I know so much about your lives now. Would you like me to share with you what work has been like? Because it's been fine. Totally, utterly fine."

She waited, staring first at her son, then at her father, until Devon finally cracked and snickered. "TMI, Mom. TMI."

Natalie laughed, and Paul joined in for a moment before asking, "What's Team-Eye?"

Natalie nearly snorted beer out her nose, which set off Devon, which set off Paul.

After they had settled down, Paul asked Devon again about school.

"Why don't you tell us about Shady Acres, ok? I don't want to talk about school, it sucks."

"Devon, mind your manners!" Natalie said, angrily.

Paul wasn't fazed by his grandson's outburst. "Fine, you want to know about the home? OK. It sucks. It's a bunch of old people with nothing in their lives who are taking up space on the planet waiting to die. Every day they add new rules trying to suck the last morsels of fun out of the entire place."

"Oh, yeah?" Devon said. "They've put me in an Advanced Chem class, even though I said I didn't want to be in Chem at all, so now I'm the dumb one in the class and word's getting around that I'm the 'Prairie Idiot.'"

"Woo," Paul countered. "I'm not even allowed to pick my TV shows. I have to ask the attendant, and if they imagine someone—anyone—might not like it, they say no and I'm stuck."

"Whatever. My teacher advisor expects me to join a sports team. He's a complete dick!"

Natalie slammed her hand down on the table, rattling the plates, "Enough!"

Paul and Devon looked at her in shocked silence. "Enough," she repeated, quieter. "Stop it, both of you. You're not the only ones with a tough life!"

Devon and Paul both quietly picked up their cutlery and started eating again. Natalie fidgeted with her fork for a bit, then stood up from the table, entered the kitchen, and poured herself a large glass of red wine. She returned to the table, sat down, and took a deep gulp of her wine. Neither Paul nor Devon said anything, but glanced quickly at each other, concerned.

After a couple of minutes of silent eating, Devon finished his meal, placed his cutlery correctly across his plate, wiped his mouth with his napkin, and said, "May I be excused?"

Natalie merely nodded. Devon took his plate to the kitchen and put it in the sink.

"Mom, some of the guys from school are going to toss a ball around at the park, I thought maybe I'd go and... uh, hang with them."

Paul looked up, "They good kids?"

"I guess. I don't really know them yet. They're nice."

Natalie sighed. "Take your phone and don't be later than 9. Tonight's a school night."

"Ok. Thanks, Mom," Devon quickly grabbed his coat and headed for the door. At the last minute, he stopped and leaned back into the kitchen, "Excellent dinner." And then the door slammed, and he was gone.

Paul and Natalie listened to him thumping down the three flights of stairs.

Wiping up the last of his gravy with a piece of bread, Paul cleaned off his plate and leaned back in his chair. He looked across the table at his daughter. *What brought that display on?* he wondered and sipped his non-alcoholic beer. Natalie wasn't eating the food still on her plate, but she drank from her large glass of wine. She didn't make eye contact with him either.

"It's not that bad," he said.

Natalie forcefully put down her wine glass, sloshing a bit onto the table. "Not that bad means not that good either. He hates school, you hate the home, and I hate—"

"You hate what?"

Natalie looked down at the table. It wasn't that she didn't want to talk about what was going on with her, but did she want to talk about it with her father? She was pretty sure he'd tell her to buck up and push through like he had all her life—but that wasn't the advice she wanted right now.

What she wanted right now was her best friend back in Montana—Eileen—and another bottle of wine. Then they could chatter about when they were in elementary school together, and the fun they had in the years before they both became wives, and then mothers, and then single, divorced mothers.

The thought of Eileen started her eyes watering. *Great, now I'm going to cry in front of my dad because that's what I do,* she thought, and wiped at her eyes.

"Honey? What's going on?"

"Nothing, Dad. Nothing's going on. I'm having a stressful time at work, with meeting everyone and figuring out how to manage a team of software engineers, and with settling into this apartment—which is a lot tinier than it looked on the internet—and trying to transfer Devon out of that Advanced Chem class..."

Paul leaned back and took a breath. "That's tough."

"Yeah, Dad. Truth. Really tough, and with Martin not making his payments, this month is even tighter. One of the girls at work is pregnant, and now it looks like HR isn't going to replace her when she goes on maternity leave. So we're going to be short for at least six mo—"

"Wait. Martin's not paying his child support?"

That had slipped out, and Natalie immediately regretted it, "Dad, it doesn't matter—"

Paul banged his non-alcoholic beer bottle down on the tabletop. "Of course it matters, Natalie! A man has to fulfill his responsibilities! Have you talked to him about it?"

"Dad," Natalie said forcefully, "if he was the kind of guy who met his responsibilities, we'd still be together! And besides, you're changing the subject."

"No, I'm not."

Natalie sighed and looked at her dad, "Yes, you are. You're trying to shift the conversation to what a jerk my ex is instead of why Devon is having trouble fitting in at school. And why you're having trouble fitting in at the home. Are you getting in trouble there too?"

"Devon will figure it out; he's a smart kid."

"Dad, smart isn't what he wants to be. He's smart in the classroom, but he doesn't want that to be all he's known for in the halls.

Did you ever have to change schools to one where you didn't know anyone?"

Paul shook his head; he'd grown up on the outskirts of a prairie town with one elementary school and then had to take the school bus to the high school one town over.

"Going off to McAllister for high school wasn't anything easy, you remember that, right?"

Natalie nodded. She'd gone to the same elementary school as her father, and had taken the same old school bus to the same high school the same town over.

"But we had our entire grade with us on that bus and at that new school. We had older siblings there to help us out. Devon? He has nobody. Here, his oldest friend is someone he's known for less than two weeks."

Paul responded, defensively, "When I drafted into the Army, I didn't—"

"You chose to join the Army, Dad. Devon didn't have any choice moving here. Shit, you didn't have any choice, really. But I didn't have any choice either. This is where my work is; this is where I have a chance to make something—" she sighed and searched for the right word. "Something better for myself, for us."

"I know, honey, I know," Paul said, gently. "You know me, I'll be upset and want to bitch and moan and gripe about it for a while. Look, Shady Acres is great; my neighbor is a good guy—other than being a former lawyer. So, you forget about your old man spouting off, would you?"

Before she could say anything more, Paul pushed himself up from the table, wincing a bit, and shuffled into the kitchen with his plate.

"You finished with that?" he asked when he returned, pointing to her meal, and she nodded. Paul took her plate into the kitchen and started washing the dishes. Natalie watched him rooting around for a dishcloth and sipped her wine. Then she realized he'd done it again—changed the subject, blew off any concerns, and diverted her attention by cleaning up.

"Thanks for a grand meal, honey. Next time, you two come to my place for dinner. They do up a nice fish on Fridays," Paul said from the kitchen.

He's a tricky old guy, she thought. *I wonder how the home actually is, and I wonder if he's ever going to tell me if it isn't going well. And what am I going to do if it's not?*

She sighed, realizing that he and Devon had been telling her of their troubles earlier, but she had told them to shut up and stop whining. Exactly like her father had said to her when she had complained as a kid.

Seventeen

Lillian, the most senior of The Bees, wandered out of her bathroom rubbing at the edges of the thin mask of Pond's cold cream she had applied to her face. She'd just gotten to her room after sneaking upstairs for a quick roll in the hay up on the third floor. *Thank goodness for those wonderful blue pills,* she thought naughtily, *and Astro-Lube.*

Removing the crocheted throw pillows she always placed in the center of her bed, she pulled back the covers, sat down, kicked off her slippers—even in the late spring she needed those slippers—and put her legs under the covers. Except they didn't go under the covers, they were caught up because her top sheet had been folded back on itself! She struggled and removed her feet from the mess under her comforter and stood up. She yanked the covers back and saw that her bed had indeed been short-sheeted.

Furious, she grabbed the phone off her side table and called the attendant. "You have someone come up here and fix my bed! What kind of a place are you running here? Short sheet an old woman's bed! I could have fallen out and hurt myself! And you'll be sure I'll be giving Kevin a stern talking to in the morning!"

With that she hung up the phone, sat down on the edge of the bed, but then quickly stood up as if touching the shorted sheets would rub the practical joke off on her. She sat down in her one comfortable chair and glared at her bed, not trusting to take her eyes off it.

•

Paul and Jim leaned out of their doors, along with most of the people on their floor, and watched the tired housekeeper roll her cart down to Lillian's room. From across the hall, Bob asked them, "What's going on? I barely fell asleep when I heard this unladylike yelling."

Jim shrugged, and, in his best steady, lawyerly voice, replied, "Don't rightly know, Bob. I do hope she's okay."

Paul said, "If she weren't okay, we'd be seeing a stretcher rolling down the hall, not a laundry cart."

"I reckon we will hear about it in the morning," Jim said, unconcernedly.

Bob gave a last look down the hall and then returned to his room, muttering, "I'd better be able to go back to sleep. Barbara screwed me something fierce this afternoon, and I figure I pulled a muscle."

After Bob had shut his door, Paul and Jim looked at each other, tapped their noses, and headed back to bed.

•

Devon walked through the crowded hallway of his new high school toward the cafeteria. A mass of students urgently trying to be somewhere else filled the hall. The sounds of a hundred conversations, lockers banging shut, and the occasional scream of laughter filled the air.

Luckily, I haven't been singled out for any 'welcoming/hazing', Devon thought, but he was still wary—well, wary-ish. After two weeks of school, his uniqueness—whatever uniqueness he had had—was fading. Since teenagers had the attention spans of newborn kittens, the students had moved on from pointing at him to pretty much ignoring him. And that was perfect, as far as he was concerned.

Devon had found himself in three classes with four other guys, a couple of whom had recently joined the school at the start of the year, so they knew what he'd been going through and took pity on him. That's who he would meet up with for lunch.

Stepping into the huge cafeteria was like entering the prototypical Hollywood movie high school lunchroom. The long counter with an array of food to help yourself to; the old ladies in dirty white aprons and hairnets behind the line who took orders for hot food; a salad bar surrounded by girls; and a frozen yogurt dispenser with the longest line up. Devon took his place in line and started shuffling forward. One of his new friends, JC, slipped in beside him to the dismay of the rest of the line behind him. He waved his hand back at the line, "Come on, I'm helping out the new guy, okay?" The line grumbled, but let him cut in.

JC turned back to Devon with a grin. "Thanks, man. I'm starving."

"No sweat," Devon said, grabbing a couple pieces of pepperoni pizza and an empty paper cup to fill at the fountain pop machine. It would be a while before he started saying 'soda' instead of 'pop,' another strange difference from Montana. JC reached past him to grab some pizza and a large chocolate milk. They shuffled forward toward the cashier. After paying, they made their way, carefully, through aisles clogged with backpacks and out-stretched legs to join the others. Eric, his lab partner in Advanced Chem and who also had a grandfather in Shady Acres, shifted over so Devon could sit down.

As they started eating, Devon began explaining, "The way I see it, there are two kinds of practical jokes. With the first, you need to set the joke up and then be somewhere else with an alibi."

"Like committing the perfect murder!"

They laughed. "Exactly," Devon said, then continued, "The second is as tricky, but in a different way, because you've gotta be a magician."

"What the what?" JC said, confused.

"Sleight of hand, man. You've gotta do the joke yourself, be there when it happens, and still get away with it."

Eric muttered, "Better to not do any jokes and not have to worry about getting caught..."

Devon fired back, "Where's the fun in that?"

The table laughed.

Eric said, "I mean, is it worth the risk just to play some sort of joke on someone?"

Devon looked at him, incredulously. "Of course it's worth it, Eric. It's the thrill of the hunt only with whoopee cush-"

"Oh, no effing way..." Ben, a quiet Asian guy muttered, stopping Devon's comment cold.

"What?"

Ben pointed across the cafeteria to where a group of jocks huddled together. The three watched as, one by one, the jocks would glance over at a group of cute, cool girls, then turn back into their huddle.

"Something's about to go down, I know it," Allan said, sadly.

Lunches forgotten, they watched as a jock crossed to the soda machine, refilled his cup—making sure he had no ice in it—and started back, still glancing around casually.

"That's Adrian Cavanaugh. Quarterback. This building is named after his family. King of the school."

"He's always been king of the school. Even back in daycare," Ben said, bitterly.

His jock friends were watching carefully as Adrian absently tugged his ear. One by one, the jocks subtly tugged their ears.

"Wonder who their victim is?"

"It was me back in September; effing sucked. They put spaghetti all down the back of my shirt..." JC said, and then Devon saw the perfectly placed victim. She stood in the aisle, facing away from everyone. She was part of the group of cute girls, who were busy in the middle of telling a story. Even worse, lots of people were moving in the aisle, so there'd be tons of distractions.

Adrian started his approach. Full paper cup of soda in his right hand, nothing in his left, with a vacant look on his face—but his eyes were totally focused on the girl. A stumble, a splash, and then he'd be gone past her before she knew what happened.

As he walked, Devon saw a black bag on the floor a bit behind the victim, perfectly placed for Adrian to pretend to trip over. Then the talking girl turned slightly, and Devon saw it was the cute brunette from the church—he was pretty sure her name was Dawn—and she was about to get totally pranked. Without any thought, he stood up and started toward the group of girls.

"Devon, whoa, what are you doing?" Eric called after him, but he gave the table a reassuring wave he didn't feel and sped up to get closer to the jock.

Five paces away, the jock started moving his soda-carrying hand into position.

Four paces away, the soda hand started forward. To all intents and purposes, looking like he was about to bring the cup to his mouth for an innocent sip.

Three paces, he started speeding up the soda hand. Inside the cup, momentum built.

At two paces away, Devon could see everything was exactly where it needed to be—no students were looking at the jock, Dawn looking away, a couple of students getting up from their table on the left covering the approach, and the soda cup in motion.

And then, at one and a half paces away, Devon called out, "Hey Dawn!"

With the jock's cup of soda in forward motion, aimed at her head, Dawn turned around. *She's even prettier up close*, Devon thought, then lunged past the jock to change the direction of the open cup, now held horizontally—the liquid being kept inside by forward momentum. Devon's outstretched hand connected with the moving cup, sending it away from her face.

She reacted in sudden shock, as she hadn't expected someone to be right behind her. She recognized the new guy staring at her with an alarmed look on his face, and in the next instant completed her turn as a full cup of soda flew from some jock's hand and connected perfectly with a teacher's face.

The teacher's bellow brought the entire cafeteria to a complete halt.

Devon and Dawn—and the whole student body—froze. The boys PE teacher, Mr. Monds, stood beside them, dark soda dripping down his face, soaking his white shirt and brown tie. On either side of him, students started wiping themselves off and shifting back away from the teacher and the guilty ones. Adrian slipped into the crowd behind Devon, free and clear.

Mr. Monds looked down at his ruined shirt, then up at Devon and Dawn, standing together in front of him.

"I—" Dawn started to say.

Mr. Monds held up his hand. She stopped talking.

"Both of you, to the office."

Devon said, "But—" and the hand raised a notch higher. Given his options, Devon chose to shut up.

A student offered the teacher a napkin, but he ignored her, continuing to glare at the two.

"The Principal's office. Right. Now."

Dawn turned and glared at Devon, then pulled her pack onto her shoulders and walked off. Students cleared a path for her the entire way across the cafeteria like she was being led through the villagers up to the guillotine. As Devon looked over at his friends, Allan raised Devon's pack to say he'd take care of it. *Well, now I've certainly cemented my school reputation as an idiot and a loser,* Devon thought, sighing as he followed Dawn across the cafeteria to his doom.

•

The high school principal, Mr. Russell, studiously ignored the two students sitting, silently, in front of him. He had enough paperwork to keep him busy twelve hours a day, so spending any time not grinding through the piles on his desk was wasted time. And what was it about schools and paper? Didn't they know the digital revolution had happened? At least half of what he had to read and file could have been sent by email...

He sighed and continued skimming a Department of Education report on intramural badminton regulations for North Carolina. Out of the corner of his eye, he could see the students on the other side of his desk react to his sigh. Good. Let's let that guilt build up inside them for a while; it makes wringing a confession out of them so much easier.

•

Devon and Dawn sat beside each other facing the principal. It had been an excruciatingly long half hour of silence after receiving an initial stern lecture from Mr. Russell. Both looked down at their laps. That last sigh was brutal. The expressed level of disappointment was over the top, even for a principal. Devon took a deep breath and tried to calm himself.

Okay, we're not going to be in trouble for an accident, right? he wondered. And that's what it was: an unfortunate accident. *But accident or not, Mr. Monds will surely give me hell in gym class for the rest of my high school life,* he thought sadly. Then his thoughts shifted as he realized she had nice knees.

•

Dawn squirmed in her seat. *How is he so calm? Even if it was an accident, my dad's going to be so mad when he finds out. Hopefully, they phone Mom first... Wait, is he looking at my legs?*

A knock at the principal's door brought them both out of their leg-focused thoughts.

"Come on in," Mr. Russell called out, not looking up from his paperwork.

The door opened to reveal Natalie and Kevin, both looking gravely concerned with more than a bit of anger. Mr. Russell stood up and waved the two parents into his office. Behind them, his secretary shut the door.

"Ah, the parents. It would have been nice to meet you under better circumstances, but here we are." He motioned toward the two remaining seats, one on each side of Devon and Dawn. Natalie and Kevin sat down beside their children. The principal continued, looking at Kevin, "How's the home, Kevin?"

"Just fine, thanks, Wally. Your mother's doing well, you'll be glad to hear. And her sister, too."

"Good, good. Good to know."

He then turned to Natalie and reached his hand across the table towards her. "I'm Wally Russell. You're the new folks from out west, one of the Dakotas?"

Natalie reached out and shook his hand. "Montana actually. Natalie Skaarsgard."

She watched Mr. Russell update his mental file, replacing Dakota with Montana, as he sat back down. He paused, looked at the kids, and then at the parents, before finally speaking, "So here we are. Your children were involved in a bit of fracas in the cafeteria at lunchtime."

Natalie spoke up, concerned, "What kind of a... fracas, exactly?"

"One of the teachers had a full cup of soda thrown in his face and—"

"—it was an accident, I swear!" Dawn said, urgently.

Mr. Russell held up his hand to stop her as Kevin reached down and gripped Dawn's knee.

"And some students have come forward saying this 'accident' looked to be intentional."

Silence. The kids looked at their laps. The parents looked at their kids. The Principal looked at the four of them. Finally, Natalie said to Devon, "Well?"

Devon looked up with the most serious face he could and said, "I tripped."

Kevin leaned forward and stared at him, "You tripped..."

Devon nodded. "On purpose?" Kevin asked, sarcastically.

"No!"

"Dad, it was an accident."

Kevin turned, looking at Dawn, barely containing his anger and embarrassment. "Oh, and how do you know it was an accident?"

Dawn started to speak then shut her mouth. How did she know it was an accident? Or that Devon tripped? Obviously, he didn't trip. She tried to recall what she remembered of that moment in the cafeteria.

Hang on. One of those moron jocks, Adrian, walking with the open soda, a stupid grin on his face. God, he was pranking me, and Devon must have been trying to stop him. The new guy and he's already in trouble. But he is kind of cute, and he did save me from getting soaked...

Dawn looked up and took a breath, "Because I turned around and hit his arm."

Devon looked up in alarm. "No! I was—"

"I knocked the cup onto Mr. Monds. It was me," Dawn said, decisively.

Silence. Mr. Russell rubbed his hand on his chin. *An unexpected surprise*, he thought. *I didn't see Dawn Wright, of all people, to stand up for the new kid from Montana.* He thought it through for a moment while looking at the four people seated in front of him. He checked his watch, leaving the four hanging for a moment longer.

"Here's what we're going to do," Mr. Russell said, stating his verdict from upon high. "What happened may have looked a lot like a coordinated effort to play a practical joke on a teacher, but was most likely an unfortunate accident."

He watched the tension leak out of the four and continued, "If these two are willing to pay, out of their own pockets, to have Mr. Monds shirt and tie dry cleaned, this entire matter can be closed without any notes in their permanent records."

Everyone exhaled sighs of relief and nodded.

"Good. I'll have the secretary inform you two of the cleaning costs, and you will reimburse her."

"Yes, sir," Devon said, weakly. Dawn simply nodded.

Mr. Russell stood up, indicating the meeting was finished. "Now, you two get notes and return to your classes. Nice seeing you, Kevin. And meeting you, Natalie."

Kevin and Natalie shook his hand and the four left as the secretary came in with another half dozen full folders of paperwork.

•

While their children waited to receive their absentee notes from the school secretary, Natalie and Kevin both fumed in the hallway outside the office. Kevin pecked furiously at his smart phone while Natalie worried about having to leave work early—because her son was in the principal's office! *I've only been on the job less than two weeks and this already? I better not get fired because of this,* she thought pessimistically. *I can't uproot these two and drag them off to some other city—if I could find another company that'd take me. Jesus… what a mess.*

She scowled through the glass wall at her son, leaning against the counter beside that girl. She didn't take in what she was looking at for a moment, instead experiencing the frustration, anger, and fear. But then she suddenly noticed how Devon stood—taller, shoulders back, not slouching. *Oh dear,* she realized in a flash, *he likes her.* She did her best to hide a smile that even her fear and anger couldn't suppress. *My goodness, he likes her a lot.*

•

Trouble, Kevin thought as he pounded out another message on his phone. *The father is trouble, and now the son is trouble too. What the hell is with this family?* He glanced over at Natalie, but she stared at the two still in the office. He looked in at his daughter. *What am I going to do? This isn't like Dawn, having 'accidents.'*

He was sure Devon had lied, but with Dawn backing up his story, even taking some of the blame, he knew he couldn't convince her to tell him the truth. *Maybe her mother could,* he mused. *They still talk, but we haven't really since Dawn left elementary school.* Not since she stopped looking up to her father as her idol in fifth grade when he'd had to ground her for not telling them about forgetting to do a major school project on Stonehenge.

The secretary finished giving them notes and buzzed them out of the office foyer.

Dawn and Devon shuffled over to their parents.

"I—" Dawn started, but Kevin cut her off.

"Not here, not now. This will be discussed tonight."

Dawn slumped her shoulders and nodded. Kevin continued as his phone rang, "I'm disappointed in you, Dawn. Tonight." Then he turned and walked down the hall, phone to his ear.

Natalie continued looking at her son while he avoided her gaze. "I took the afternoon off because I didn't know what had happened, so I'll be outside the front doors at three."

"I'll take the bus, Mom."

"Yes, but you won't. I'll be there, waiting for you."

Devon nodded. The bell rang, and the hall started filling with students rushing to their next classes. Dawn gave Devon a weak wave and disappeared into the flowing mass of students.

Natalie leaned over to Devon and said, quietly, "I'm infuriated with you, but I still love you, ok?"

Devon nodded slightly. "I know."

Natalie stepped back out of the way of the football team carrying a huge stuffed mascot bear. "Get to class. I'll see you at three."

Devon nodded and slipped out of sight behind the mascot.

Natalie leaned against the glass wall of the office and struggled not to let the noise and confusion overwhelm her. *What I want is a simple life... is that too much to ask for?* she thought, before pushing off into the river of students.

•

"God, Devon! Sure, you're in a new school and you want to fit in, but playing practical jokes on teachers? That's insane! And totally the wrong way to fit in," Natalie said as they drove back to their apartment.

"I swear it was an accident," Devon said, remembering the amazement of his friends when he finally arrived in class—he'd saved one of the prettiest girls in school from getting pranked. They were sure he'd be able to ask Dawn out, especially after he told her the truth. And, they continued, with Dawn taking the blame for him, he'd better ask her out.

Natalie laughed sharply. "Oh please. This is not my first time at this rodeo. And don't give me that innocent look."

She'd had the whole afternoon to forget how to be calm and instead built up a pile of worry. Sure, she had phoned her office and checked on any messages, and she'd gone through her emails while eating a late lunch in a McDonald's parking lot. But trying to keep on top of everything at work exhausted her and having to deal with a practical joke-playing son was the limit.

"I don't know why that girl stood up for you. She's crazy to do that unless she likes you…"

"You think so?" Devon said, trying—and failing—to be indifferent. "But, I mean, it really was an accident."

"You keep singing that same song. I know you're not telling the truth, and you got away with it, but don't do it again, you hear me? If you get kicked out of this school, I'll put you in a military academy."

Devon flicked his long hair out of his eyes and looked at her with shock. Natalie shook her head and said, "And that long hair will be the first thing to go after I drop you off, sonny."

"Mom," Devon said, sincerely, "I don't do jokes, promise."

"Good. Act like your grandfather, please? You don't see him in trouble or goofing around, do you?" Devon shook his head. Natalie nodded and continued, "There you go. You're not a kid anymore. There's a time and a place for that kind of joking. You're in high school; time to grow up."

They drove on in silence for a while, Natalie realizing that if she put in a few hours of work after dinner, she should be able to catch up on her missed afternoon and maybe be a bit ahead on a couple of projects which had been dropped on her desk that morning. She shifted her thoughts to figuring out what to have for dinner and if they needed to stop at the grocery store before arriving at home when Devon said, quietly, "You really think she likes me?"

•

Kevin pulled into his driveway and parked outside the garage. He turned off the engine but let the stereo play through to the end of 'American Girl' by Tom Petty, remembering a time before marriage when he and his college buddies had made the road trip over to Raleigh for an outdoor concert with Tom Petty headlining. The smile on his face faded as the song ended and he considered when he'd last gone to a concert of any kind other than one of Dawn's school performances or the Christmas and Easter shows at their church. *Too long,* he thought, dragging his mind back to the present. But there was no time for fun anymore.

Dinner sat on the table when he entered. After plugging in his phone to charge in the kitchen, he joined Beth and Dawn at the table. A glass of red waited for him. Beth gave him a weak smile, and he nodded back. Dawn avoided his eye altogether. After Beth said a quick Grace, they dished up and ate—in silence.

Dawn knew better than to try explaining her actions to her father at the dinner table. She'd given her mom a truncated version of the 'accident' when she'd gotten home from school. They had both agreed to let Kevin bring it up when he was ready. Beth expected there to be a conversation after Dawn headed to bed when she'd have to do some diffusing. She'd been with Kevin long enough to know how upset he became when he felt embarrassed.

Having his only daughter caught in an accident which looked, to everyone who'd witnessed it, exactly like a practical joke—on a teacher, no less!—was exactly the kind of embarrassment Kevin hated most. Shame on the family brought shame on him, personally.

Luckily for Dawn, Beth thought, looking across the table at her husband as he carefully cut up his baked salmon, *it really was an accident, or else there'd be hell to pay.*

Eighteen

Abe realized he was late for breakfast. It had been another long night, what with a late-night booty call from one of The Bees, and then someone setting off a damn air horn around two AM. He shrugged himself into his cardigan and started toward his door.

As he opened the door, he checked his pockets for his room key, and stepped out into the hall only to walk into a wall of Saran Wrap stretched tightly across his doorway. His whole body bounced back, and he stumbled across his room and sat down sharply on his couch.

"I don't want to be part of this! I'm a goddamn Veteran!" he yelled. After yelling for a while more, he stormed back over to the door and kicked at the thin film. His foot bounced back but the film didn't break.

•

As Paul and Jim sauntered into the dining room and waited at the maître d' stand, Paul noticed Chuck over at The Bees table. He frowned as Chuck handed a delicate bouquet of flowers to Joanne then received a kiss on the cheek in return. As Chuck turned away from the table, he spotted Paul, smiled smugly, then scratched his nose with his index finger. Paul gripped his cane tightly, considering how nice it would be to swing it hard against Chuck's thick head. But before he could finish the thought, Marcus stepped up to the stand and blocked his view of Chuck returning to his boys.

As Marcus showed them to their usual seats, they were aware of Abe commanding the center of attention. Surrounded by a half-dozen people, he was recounting his morning adventure.

"Wonder what's up with Abe?" Jim asked.

"Someone covered his door in cling wrap. He says he took a tumble when he walked into it, but he's fine, only a bit shook up," Marcus said and stared inscrutably at the two of them.

"That's a damn shame," Paul replied as they arrived at their table.

Marcus looked at him for a moment before saying, "Yes, Mister Paul, it is a shame. But we'll catch whoever is doing these jokes."

"I have no doubt you will, Mister Marcus, no doubt at all," Jim said and sat down. Paul sat at the same time, and the two of them tumbled to the floor as the back legs of their chairs collapsed.

"Son of a bitch!" Jim yelled as he hit the floor.

Marcus pulled Jim to his feet and said, "Is it your hip? Is everything ok?"

Jim angrily pushed Marcus away, saying, "I'm fine, damnit. I'm fine."

Around them, people were up on their feet watching the commotion, shocked looks on their faces. While Paul slowly pulled himself up off the floor, Marcus turned to the room and said, clearly, "Everything's all right over here, thanks. They're both a bit shaken up. Some work for maintenance on these chairs here is all, y'all go back to your meals."

But most people continued watching as Marcus pulled a couple of chairs over from the next table, checked the legs to ensure they hadn't been tampered with, then offered them to Jim and Paul. Across the room Chuck and his gang stayed on their feet, watching them.

After the two had sat down, Marcus frowned and said, "We'll find whoever did this. Hell, I'll find them myself."

And with that, he turned and stalked across the room to the maître d' stand.

Their waiter quickly brought them coffee, took their order—the same as each morning—and left. Paul groaned and leaned back in his chair cautiously. Jim continued muttering angrily about being pranked.

Paul leaned over to him and said, quietly, "I'm the one to be angry with."

"Why you? You ended up on your ass like me. The sons of bitches that did this? I want to find them and take out my revenge. Do you figure Chuck did this? It's pretty complicated for him; he's more of a 'push you down a flight of stairs' practical joke guy."

"It wasn't Chuck, trust me."

Jim stopped staring angrily across the room at Chuck and turned to Paul, "You know who did it?"

Paul nodded and sipped his coffee. Jim leaned over, took Paul's hand and made him lower it to the table, then said intently, "Who?"

Paul removed Jim's hand from his wrist, raised his cup to his lips and said, with his mouth covered by the raised cup, "You're looking right at him."

Jim's mouth dropped open. He was speechless. His mouth opened and closed a couple of times before he whispered, "But why?"

"Why? Because now we're off the hook as suspects. Because we were number one and two on everyone's list. Now we're a couple of poor old guys who were pranked, exactly like the others."

Paul stifled a grin behind his hand and faked a cough.

Jim continued to stare at him before shaking his head in amazement.

"Good Lord, you're good at this, aren't you?" He rubbed his hip and continued, "I'd hate to be on your bad side."

"Now that we're out of the spotlight, we'll have some serious fun."

"You have a different definition of fun than most people."

"Ah Jim, you're having fun, aren't you?"

Jim nodded, grudgingly. "So, who's next? What about Herbert over there? The guy to Chuck's left, with the sad comb over."

Paul looked over at Chuck's table. The gang talked quietly, sneaking curious glances across at the two of them. Paul shook his head slightly and said, "Herb? No, Herb has a more important role in this."

"Oh? What role is that?" Jim asked, confused.

"We aren't going to prank old Herbie at all. He's going to be our own Lee Harvey Oswald," Paul said with a smirk.

Jim thought for a moment, then looked across at Herb and smiled. "Nice to have a patsy, isn't it?"

Paul nodded and took another sip of coffee.

They stopped talking while their food arrived in front of them. After thanking the waiter and waiting for him to leave the table, Jim sighed. "One request, though. The next time you need to divert attention away from us, could you do something a bit gentler?"

Paul grinned and started eating his breakfast. Jim grinned quickly, then started eating also.

Nineteen

The home settled down for a couple of days because everyone walked around constantly watching everyone else. Paul and Jim kept to themselves, for the most part, realizing it was better to let everyone start to relax again before pulling any more pranks. Not that it wasn't fun observing the residents double-check every chair, door, window, and handle, always expecting some joke to explode in their faces.

"Can't we get back to the program? I'm getting bored," Jim muttered as they sat in the garden, half watching the Bocce players.

"Soon, my friend, soon," Paul replied. "I've an idea for an exploding bocce ball that could be a lot of fun."

"Exploding like shrapnel?"

"Na, like one of those joke golf balls. It disintegrates when hit."

Jim looked over at him, impressed. "Let me reiterate: I'm glad I'm not your enemy."

That evening, while Paul and Jim were having dinner with The Bees-including Joanne-Chuck stormed into the dining room, bypassed Marcus at the maître d' stand and made a straight line through the tables to stand in front of them, steaming mad.

"Why, Chuck," Hazel said, concerned, "You're looking rather upset. What is the matter? Are you coming down with something? Is it contagious?"

He looked down at the table, wild-eyed, his usually perfect hair askew.

"You have no idea why I might be upset?" he said in amazement.

"Chuck, I dare say you should lower your voice," Frances said.

Chuck ignored her, "Maybe you should look closer. Like at my eyebrows!"

He leaned down and swiveled his head back and forth so everyone at the table could see that he, in fact, was completely missing one eyebrow. The Bees gasped and leaned back as if Chuck had begun to vomit over the table.

"Razor slip while shaving, Chuck?" Paul asked, and Chuck swung around to glare at him.

"You did this. I don't know how, but you did! I woke up from my afternoon nap, go to get ready for dinner, and my eyebrow was gone!"

Jim leaned over, concerned. "Did you check under your pillow?"

The Bees tittered at Jim's joke, except for Hazel who still looked quite concerned.

Chuck glared even harder at the two of them. "I know you did it."

Paul looked up at him calmly, "I don't know how since we've been either in here or out on the patio for the past two hours."

Jim added, "More like three hours. And there are certainly many people who will attest to that."

"Maybe it was one of your gang," Paul offered. "Maybe you insulted Herb one too many times, and he couldn't take it anymore."

"They're not *my* gang, and they didn't do it. I don't know how, but you did this to me."

Paul took another bite of his dinner, enjoying the mashed potatoes, before saying, "Maybe you sleepwalk." Paul stared up at Chuck with a concerned look on his face. "You should have that checked out; it might be something serious."

Chuck stared at the table, at Jim, and then leaned down beside Paul. Without a word, he scooped some mashed potatoes with his finger and stood back up. As everyone watched, Chuck made to eat the potatoes, but instead flicked them at Paul. They spattered across Paul's shirt and neck.

After the shocked gasp of The Bees subsided, Paul glanced at Jim, and then slowly turned to face Chuck. With a calm intensity, he whispered, "You shouldn't have done that."

Chuck looked down at the remaining potatoes on his fingers and flicked them at Paul as well, a couple of dabs landing on Paul's face. Then Chuck proudly turned and started walking away.

"Oh my," Joanne said, "that wasn't particularly nice." The Bees agreed, Lillian offering a napkin to Paul. Ignoring the napkin, Paul took a deep breath, and then another.

Jim muttered, "Leave it be, Paul, leave it…"

"You know I can't do that, my friend."

Paul grabbed a handful of potatoes and stood up. "Hey!" he called, and Chuck turned around. The ball of potatoes hit him right on the side of the face, splattering the tables and people around Chuck. The entire room gasped as one. Sitting back down, Paul said, over his shoulder, "I told you not to do that."

Enraged, Chuck reached down to the table directly beside him, grabbed a full handful of creamed corn from in front of one of the residents and flung it back at Paul. Quickly and calmly, Paul leaned to the side and let the poorly thrown corn spatter the back of the man sitting at the next table.

Clearly, old Chuck wasn't the best quarterback, Paul thought as he eyed the remaining food on the table in front of him. *He has a terrible throwing arm.* Reaching across to Jim's plate, Paul grabbed a pork cutlet. Jim said, warningly, "Don't do it, Paul. This isn't the Middle Ages. He didn't slap you with his glove. There's no dishonor in avoiding a fight, soldier."

Before Paul could reply, a white roll bounced off of Jim's head. Jim paused, brushed his hair back into place, and stared Paul in the eyes. "Death before dishonor."

"Semper Fi."

Someone on the other side of the room yelled out, "Food fight!" and the dining hall exploded into anarchy.

Marcus ducked down behind the maître d' stand. *What the hell was wrong with these old folks?* he wondered as a bowl of Jell-O smashed off the wall beside him, showering him with jiggling red cubes. Taking a deep breath, he flicked some Jell-O off his shoulder, then peeked around the side of the stand.

Food was flying everywhere. One group had tipped their round table over and were hiding behind it, popping up to fling buns and pork cutlets. The Bees had opened their parasols and were backing towards the patio like a Roman Legion in retreat when a salvo of steamed vegetables showered down on them. Undaunted, they pushed on through the overturned walkers and chairs toward the French doors.

In the middle of the room, fifteen feet apart, Chuck and Paul faced each other, oblivious to the carnage around them. Chuck frantically looked around for more food to defend himself with, but Paul stood calmly, a leader of men in battle. Beside him, hidden behind another tipped chair crouched Jim, patiently handing ammo up to Paul. But Chuck wouldn't back down and continued being battered by the never-ending onslaught coming at him.

"Running low, gunny," Jim called out through the screaming, handing up one of the last few buns.

Without looking down, Paul grabbed the hard roll, then said, "Then I'd better make this one count."

As Chuck leaned over to reach for a plate of food, Paul wound up, ignored a spray of corn bouncing off his head, and threw the multigrain roll with all his might. The throw was perfect, missing a piece of cherry pie in mid-flight, hitting Chuck right in the back of the head. Chuck toppled forward landing face down in the amazingly pristine dinner he had been reaching towards. Corn, mashed potatoes, and gravy covered his head. He didn't move.

Marcus took advantage of the kill shot to stand up and yell in his most impressive and frightening voice, "Goddammit! Everybody freeze! Now!"

Everybody froze. The last of the flying food landed with either a thud or a splat. Outside the closed patio doors, The Bees watched, mouths open, but their hair still perfect.

Out from the kitchen, like a SWAT team breaching a hostage situation, came the restaurant staff, only to come to a full stop as they surveyed the destruction. Paul reached down and helped Jim up from the floor. Jim looked around at the mess, and then said, "You'll be needing my representation any moment now."

"He started it," Paul muttered.

Before Jim had a chance to reply, Kevin came through the dining room doors, slipped on a pile of mashed potatoes and lost his balance. Luckily, Marcus grabbed his arm before he dropped. Kevin regained his balance and shook off the help. Mouth agape, he surveyed the room, taking in the tipped tables, toppled chairs, and food-coated residents. In the middle, standing proudly despite being covered in food, were Paul and Jim.

Kevin's jaw tightened, and he struggled to refrain from saying the words he wanted to say—wanted to yell. Instead, he pointed at the two in the middle of the room, "You two, in my office. Now."

Then Kevin turned and walked out, stepping carefully until safely out of the spatter zone. He called back over his shoulder to Marcus, "I want this cleaned up before I return."

Twenty

Paul stood by the side of Kevin's desk, staring at a framed portrait on the wall of Joanne and her husband. It was an expensive print of what had to have been an expensive photo shoot. After studying her husband's eyes for a while, Paul turned to stare at Joanne's bright, smiling face. *I appreciate that smile,* he thought with a bit of a grin.

Behind him, still covered in spatters of tonight's dinner, Jim sat calmly in one of the two chairs in front of Kevin's desk.

"I can't believe, after what we've successfully pulled off, we're going to be sent up the river for a food fight," Jim muttered, wiping some corn off his arm.

Without turning around, Paul repeated, "He started it."

"That defense surely ain't gonna cut it with the judge, son."

"He started it," Paul said seriously, turning around to face Jim, "and we finished it."

Jim shook his head and said, "At least you finished it well."

They both snickered as they remembered Chuck toppling into the full plate of food.

"You ever play any baseball when you were young, Paul? That was a hell of a—"

The office door swung open, and Kevin stormed in, barely containing his anger. Behind him were Natalie—looking worried—and a stern man Natalie's age who was clearly Jim's son. Upon seeing his son, Jim stood and tried to straighten himself up, "Michael, what are you doing here?"

Michael stared at him, "You're kidding, right, Dad?" Jim closed his mouth and sat back down in the chair. Kevin moved around to sit down at his desk, shifting into his corporate power position. Paul moved over to stand behind Natalie, who'd taken the other chair in front of the desk. After squeezing her shoulder and receiving a shrug from his daughter to not touch her, Paul dropped his hands to his sides and stood at ease.

As Kevin tried to calm down enough to speak, Paul spoke up, "I'd like to say that it was an accident."

Both Kevin and Natalie swung their heads up looking at him in unison. Both angry.

Through clenched teeth, Kevin said, "What did you say to me?"

"Nothing," Paul said, backing down quickly. "Nothing at all."

"You keep drawing the fire for me, gunny, and I might get out of here safely," Jim muttered, and Paul stifled a snicker.

Of course, Kevin caught the snicker, but not the comment, and glared at Paul. "Nothing funny here, Mr. Carter." Everyone in the room noticed Kevin's use of Paul's last name—not a good sign. "There was considerable damage done to the dining room this evening, and you were right in the middle of it all."

"Only because that's where I was sitting," Paul said.

"Smart comments won't help you out of this."

Jim pulled himself to his feet and stood beside Paul, saying, "I'm not sure what you've heard about the events of this evening, but I assure you, we in no way started that fracas. And if you've taken the time to speak with any of the ladies who were dining with us this evening, including your lovely mother, you'll know we were merely defending ourselves against the aggressive behavior of another resident."

Having completed his opening remarks, Jim nodded to Natalie, Michael, and Kevin and then sat back down.

After a pause, Kevin stood up behind his desk, attempting to loom over them like an angry judge. "Defending yourselves against mashed potatoes? Against Jell-O? I don't know what you did to rile 'another resident' up, but I'm sure you did it!"

"Excuse me," Natalie said, aware of the power Kevin held over her father, and over herself. "My father doesn't lie, and he doesn't rile people up for fun. That's not the kind of man he is, and that's not the kind of man he's ever been. Have you talked to anyone else about what happened?"

Behind her, Paul felt a wave of guilt over his daughter's heartfelt defense, particularly since he'd been actively riling Chuck up since the moment they'd met in the hallway right outside this office on his first day. But now wasn't the time to confess anything like that.

"I don't care what kind of men your fathers are, frankly, either of you. This establishment has been in continuous operation for over one hundred and fifty years, and there has never, ever, been an episode like what happened here tonight. I'm going to have staff in there working most of the night cleaning. Again, something that has never happened before. Would you like for me to work out the overtime costs, so you have a better idea of what this little joke is costing?"

Everyone in the room shook their heads. Kevin scowled at them.

"Dammit, you're supposed to be adults! This is a seniors assisted living facility. You two are senior citizens. So, start acting like it. This isn't high school, where you'll fill my office up with balloons on the last day of the year, ha, ha, ha."

Paul harrumphed at the idea of filling Paul's office with balloons. That's a stupid prank because of the noise the balloons make when they rub together. Better to fill his office with something that started out compressed and expanded quickly—

The door opened, and Paul lost track of his planning. He joined everyone in turning around as Marcus came into the office with Chuck in front of him. Chuck's hair was slicked back with gravy, and there were hardening mashed potatoes in his collar. He growled at Paul, but Marcus moved him off to Jim's side of the room before anything could happen. Kevin stepped back from his desk in exasperation, "Now what?"

Marcus gave Chuck another aggressive look, then turned to Kevin. "I took a moment to speak to your mother and the rest of The Bees, and they told me what they saw tonight."

Kevin struggled to contain his aggravation at his mother getting dragged into this mess. The last thing he wanted was his mother's involvement in starting the food fight. Because then he'd have to reprimand her, and he couldn't play favorites at the home, even if he wanted to.

Kevin realized everyone was waiting for him to say something, so he said something. "Well?"

Marcus continued, unfazed by Kevin's behavior, "The ladies say the same thing. It wasn't an accident."

Kevin turned to scowl at Paul and Jim. "I know it wasn't an accident and you started it." He shook his head and continued before either Paul or Jim could protest, "I don't have words for how disappointed I am in the two of you. Especially you, Jim. You've been an upstanding and contributing member of our family here at Shady Acres for more than five years—"

Marcus coughed to get Kevin's attention. "Sir, your mother— Joanne—clearly said it wasn't an accident and that Chuck initiated the fight."

Chuck looked up, "She said that?"

Marcus nodded. "That's why you're here. And they also confirmed that one of Chuck's friends, Herb, called out 'food fight.' So, who started what is pretty clear."

Kevin looked at each of the three food-covered old men, and then said, "I will not allow this kind of childish, dangerous behavior in my facility, that's to be sure." Kevin sat down and leaned back in his chair, as powerful a position as he could muster, and continued, "Any more 'events' like tonight—any more shenanigans of any kind—and I will have no choice but to request that your children move you to another facility. I cannot have the lives and health of the other residents endangered."

And with the end of his pronouncement, Kevin slapped his hands on the desktop and pointed to the door to his office.

"Paul, Jim, you've been warned. And Chuck, what the hell happened to your eyebrow?"

Chuck didn't say anything, so Marcus turned him around and aimed him at the office door. Jim tried to avoid looking at Paul as he stood up but caught the smirk on the side of Paul's mouth and stifled one of his own. Chuck did look pretty ridiculous with only one eyebrow. Jim avoided eye contact with his son as he came around the chair.

Paul continued looking at Kevin, wondering if he should say anything—defend himself—or, more importantly, explain Jim's lack of involvement in his personal grudge with Chuck. But now was the time to keep silent before the judge, so Paul kept his mouth shut. Finally Kevin growled, "Go clean up, you're filthy."

Paul nodded once to Kevin then Natalie stood up, planning to say something, but failing. Giving up, she followed the old men out of the office.

In the hallway outside Kevin's office, Joanne sat in a chair, waiting nervously. Chuck came first out into the hall, and he scowled at her. "How could you blame me?"

"Because you started it, Chuck. You threw the mashed potatoes at Paul," she said gently.

Chuck waved her answer away. "You should have stood up for me; I thought we had something."

"So did I. But I suspect we don't anymore," she said sadly.

Chuck stared at her for a moment and then said, "I'm breaking up with you. You don't break up with me. I'm a catch, especially here. Both my goddamn hips, and original knees."

Marcus stepped up beside him. "You need help returning to your room, Mr. Chuck?"

Chuck waved Marcus off and stomped down the hallway. Marcus sighed and walked back to his desk in the foyer. Joanne stood up as the four came out of the office.

"Well?" she asked, concerned.

Paul looked at Jim then said, "We're on probation."

"What does that mean?"

Jim spoke up, "It means we now have marks on our permanent record and if anything like this happens again, we're out on our keisters."

"Oh my," Joanne said, alarmed.

"It'll be fine," Paul said, calmly and reassuringly. "This'll blow over."

And that was it for Natalie. She grabbed her father's arm and pulled him away from the group.

"Whoa! Honey, careful I'm not as young I once was."

"Don't you 'honey' me, Dad," Natalie said once she'd gotten a few paces down the hallway from the rest. Over her father's shoulder, she could see Michael talking expressively with Jim. *Probably starting the same conversation I'm about to begin,* she thought. Joanne had gotten up and gone into her son's office, shutting the door behind her. Natalie took a breath and continued, "Swear to me you had nothing to do with starting that fight. Swear! Because there is no other place nearby for you to live, and I can't have you stuck in my apartment, moping about, trapped on the third floor all day long."

"Hon—Natalie, I did not start that fight. I swear. Besides, how bad could it be, me living with you and Devon? I could cook and clean up."

Natalie laughed sharply through her exasperation. "You'd burn the place down with your cooking, and I cleaned up your house before we left Montana. You have to stay at Shady Acres; you can't even climb the stairs to my place without help!"

"Ah, your building's not that bad, I was kind of tired when I came over for dinner."

"Dad! I can't—I really can't—deal with this shit right now. I've got eight major software projects I'm supposed to be managing."

"Natalie, I-"

"No! You need to be a good boy and not fuck this up. I mean it."

Paul stepped back, unaccustomed to his little girl swearing at him. Natalie wiped a tear away from the corner of her eye, angry with her father and with herself for starting to cry—but, damnit, he made her so angry sometimes. Then she turned away before more tears could come and walked down the hallway, leaving her father alone, silently watching her go.

•

Joanne sat on one of the chairs in front of her son. Every time she had to talk to him in his office, she had faint but unsettling recollections of going into her father's study as a child to be reprimanded. Her father would be seated behind his massive oak desk, his pipe simmering, and a rough-cut glass half full of whiskey on the blotter in front of him.

She would sit down, meekly, hands clasped in her lap and await her punishment, handed out only after a terse and truncated reprimand. The worst was the time she and Ruth had been caught in the town's Lovers Lane with a couple boys by her father's best friend and chief of police. Not only had the riot act been read to her, her father had also brought up the Bible, the Constitution and, worst of all, their family honor.

Once more, she pushed that shameful memory away and looked across a different desk at a different adult male disappointed in her.

"I know you like Paul Carter, Mom," Kevin said, angrily, staring at her intently. "Are you covering for him, too?"

"I don't lie," Joanne said, hearing her voice as if she was that eight-year-old girl again. "You know Chuck and his temper. He doesn't like his authority questioned. That's why you like him so."

"Dad liked him, too."

"Yes," Joanne sighed, "they were the best of friends for many years. He gave the toast at our wedding and the eulogy at your father's funeral."

Kevin sipped from a highball glass half full of amber liquid. *He must have poured it after everyone left,* Joanne thought. *There is absolutely no way he would be willing to let residents or their families see him with a drink.* Any weaknesses were to be kept hidden from the public at all times.

"Dad didn't have these kinds of problems with the residents," Kevin finally said.

Joanne paused before speaking, knowing she had to be careful. "There were always problems with residents, Kevin. Just different problems." *Like when her husband let the first Jewish resident live there,* she thought. *How absurd, looking back and remembering the uproar over timid Mr. Siegel, who'd been born and raised in the town, exactly like the rest of them.* Or when Marcus' father had come to the home. They'd fully expected burning crosses in the front yard for over a year. In comparison, some harmless flinging of mashed potatoes and Jell-O was inconsequential.

"Don't take them personally."

"But I do, Mom. I have to. If I don't, who will?"

He took another sip of his drink and grimaced. "If I'm not the responsible one around here, and make sure everyone obeys the rules, then you know what's going to happen? One huge mess."

"Darling, you're not responsible for everything. That's too much of a burden to put on your shoulders."

"But I am responsible, don't you see? After Dad died," Kevin paused and sighed. "After Dad died, who else could keep this place running? Who else could make sure everyone is fed, has their sheets changed daily, and is taking their medications? Who? You? You had Abby and Eliot still to care for."

She looked across the expanse of her husband's polished desk at her son. *They're so much alike*, she thought, both happily and sadly.

Kevin continued, "No. There was me. That's who there was to put this place back under control. And the home is out of control again. So now there will be more rules for everything to go back to normal again. I don't want to do it, but I have to."

He turned, flicked on his computer then turned back to his mother. He smiled thinly and said, "Thanks for listening, Mom."

Joanne realized there was no point in saying what she had come into the office to say. Like her husband, her son had made a decision and would to stick to it, no matter what the consequences.

She stood up slowly, and smiled at her son as he opened up a Word document template. "I'm glad I could help."

As she left him composing his new edict for the residents and started down the hallway to her room, she thought, *No matter what happens, it was worth it.*

Entering the elevator, she let out an unladylike guffaw. *I know I shouldn't have done it*, she thought, *but Chuck certainly did look funny after I snuck in to his room and shaved off his eyebrow.*

Twenty One

In the early morning quiet, Marcus strolled along the residential hallway. Only a couple of old folks sneaking back to their rooms, as usual. He didn't want to know, and didn't care, what they were getting up to. He didn't get paid enough for that. Pausing at each door, he slipped a single typed page underneath. When he arrived at Paul's room, he stared ruefully at the paper for a moment before leaning down to slide it under the door. But before the page was entirely underneath, the door opened, and Paul stood there staring down at him.

"Morning, Mister Marcus. Lovely morning for sneaking about," Paul said with a grin.

Marcus stood up and handed Paul the paper. Paul took it without a glance.

Marcus said, "You're up early on this fine morning, Mister Paul."

Paul folded up the paper and put it in his pocket, saying, "You know what they say about early birds and worms."

"I don't know about worms, but they'll have the coffee on in the dining room by now."

"Music to my ears, Mister Marcus."

Paul started down the hallway toward the elevator while Marcus continued in the opposite direction. After a few steps, he stopped and turned around, calling to Paul, "You make sure you read that notice, Mister Paul."

Paul waved without looking back. "The paper is burning a hole in my pocket, Mister Marcus."

Marcus watched him walk onto the elevator, then shook his head. *There hasn't been a guy like Paul at the home in a long time,* he thought, *but I'm not sure if that's good or bad.*

•

A couple of hours later, while sauntering across the lawn, Jim paused. It took Paul a moment to realize Jim had stopped, and then he turned to face his friend.

"We're a team, right, you and me? I've your back, and you've mine, correct? Mutually assured destruction?" Jim said, intently.

"Of course. Semper Fi."

Jim looked at him, warily. "Neither of us were Marines, Paul."

Paul laughed. "Ok, you got me. Scout's honor, then." He raised two fingers to his head in a proper Scouts' salute. "Akela, we'll do our best. We'll dib, dib, dib; we'll dob, dob, dob."

Jim chuckled at the long-forgotten memory of repeating that vow in a cold church hall in his Scouts uniform, then stopped smiling and pointed his polished oak cane accusingly at Paul. "Then why'd you leave me behind when you shaved Chuck's eyebrow?"

Paul raised his cane to counter Jim's and replied, "I didn't."

Jim thrust his cane at Paul, who quickly parried. Wood clanged against stainless steel. The two eyed each other and continued to mock-battle, feinting as quickly as their replacement hips and knees allowed them.

"Come on," Jim said disbelievingly, smoothly deflecting Paul's next parry, "that's precisely the kind of prank you—we—would do. And how'd you grab his key? The man is the most paranoid one in the place about access to his room."

Jim moved forward, pressuring Paul with quick swipes of his cane. Paul backed up, defensively.

"Jim, I swear, as a beloved child of the great state of Montana, I didn't shave his eyebrow. If I had thought of it, I would have shaven both. Besides, I was with you, remember? That's why Chuck is so angry; we both have an ironclad alibi."

"That's why I'm sure it was you. It was too perfect."

Paul smiled and, with a quick double jab, knocked Jim's cane out of his hand. "I surely appreciate the compliment on my nefarious skills, but I'm not a magician. No matter how much I'd like to, I can't be in two places at once."

That said, Paul gently tapped Jim in the center of chest. "Fatal hit."

Jim bowed in defeat and thought for a moment. "I regret accusing you."

Paul waved off the apology. "Nothing to apologize for, Jimbo. If I hadn't known I didn't do it, I would have been sure I did as well."

Paul reached down and picked up Jim's cane, handing it back to his friend with a smile. They strolled a while further, then settled in on a bench in the shade of one of the old cottonwood trees and looked out at the manicured yards.

After a contented moment, Jim spoke up, "Well, then, I've only one other question."

"What's that?" Paul asked.

"If you didn't shave his eyebrow, who did?"

It wasn't until dinner that same night that Paul found out the contents of the note Marcus had given him in the morning. He and Jim were seated with The Bees for a fine dinner of melt-off-the-bone ribs, slaw, and collard greens when one of the women brought up the notice.

"I truly can't believe it," Lillian said, shaking her head. "Do they imagine we're children around here?"

"We're children?" Paul asked, curiously. He did enjoy the banter and furious conversation around the table, even if he could only slip a word in every ten to fifteen minutes. The Bees had a unique language to themselves, and he struggled to understand much of what they were clearly communicating to each other. But they had been kind enough to slow it down when Paul and Jim joined them for meals, which they now did as often as they felt up to it.

Whatever had been between Joanne and Chuck was definitely over, and Chuck now took his meals across the dining room with his gang. Paul suppressed the desire to wave at him each time he sat down beside Joanne at The Bees' table. But the riot act had been read; he wasn't enough of a fool to ignore that. He'd keep the peace as best he could. But damn, it surely was boring around the home without the frisson of the occasional practical joke. During the fun, most everyone in the home had raced to each meal—if only to find out who had been pranked and what had happened to them. But now…

Joanne piped up, "They don't believe we're children now, Lill."

"Of course, they do," Frances said, waving a fork at Joanne. "And 'they' is your son."

Jim sighed. "What pronouncement has Kevin brought down from Mount Sinai this time?"

The table chuckled, but Frances scowled. "Didn't you read the notice? We each received one under our door in the middle of the night. Someone must have been listening at our doors in the wee hours."

"No one's listening at your door, Franny. Besides, if they were, they'd die of boredom."

"Oh, that's not true at all," she said, archly.

As the girls laughed, Paul pulled the folded note out of his pocket. With Jim leaning over, he opened it up, and they read it together. When they finished, Paul and Jim looked at each other, and then Jim rolled his eyes and returned to his meal. Paul crushed the note and tossed it into the middle of the round table.

"Garbage," he said. "They may as well fit us for coffins now and be done with it."

"You're overreacting," Joanne said, weakly. "They're reasonable suggestions."

Lillian scowled across the table at her. "They're suggestions for you; they're edicts for the rest of us."

"Exactly!" Paul said, leaning forward. "Haven't we been through enough in our lives—enough responsible decisions, enough shit—to not need these kinds of rules? I mean, aren't we slightly older than fifteen?"

"Not me," Helen said with a naughty grin.

"You wish," Frances bantered.

The girls laughed, but Paul carried on. "I acknowledge there needs to be rules so we don't wander off in the middle of the night and become lost because we are slowly losing our senses, but none of us are going to do that, are we? Go for a stumble and end up in the river?"

"Wouldn't be a bad way to go," Jim opined.

Paul slumped back in his seat. "Forget it. Just forget it. All of you."

Jim took another bite of his pie and patted Paul on the shoulder. "You're working yourself up over nothing, Paul. It'll blow over, it always does. You'll see. I'd bet you, but gambling became off limits last week. Or was it the week before?"

•

That weekend, Devon came by for a visit—fortunately during visiting hours—another new rule being enforced by Marcus and the other staff. Relatives were actually being turned away at the front door after arriving at the wrong time. Paul had bit his tongue, but was relieved Devon had been able to visit. *Something's better than nothing,* he thought as he took Devon through to the patio where they joined Jim and Joanne at a nicely shaded table.

Any attempts by Paul to find out how his daughter was, or how school was, failed. Devon gave him short, terse answers of no value.

"You sound like my granddaughter," Joanne said with a laugh, cutting the deck of cards she'd been using to play Solitaire.

"And my grandsons, too," Jim piped in. "They're masters of the monosyllabic response. Is it something they teach in school nowadays, or do you have to learn it online?"

Devon shrugged. "Dunno." Then he smiled at them, and said, "Come on, let's play some cards!"

Joanne professionally shuffled the deck, gracefully cut the cards with one hand—much to the amazement of the table—and then dealt cards to each of them, leaving half the deck in the center of the table.

Devon picked up his cards, "What are we playing? Poker? Gramps, can I borrow some money? I'll pay you back, or win it off you." He smiled and sorted his cards, keeping them far away from any prying eyes.

"You don't have to worry about hiding your cards here," Jim said with a sigh. "Everyone has such poor eyesight you could lay them down in front of us and we wouldn't see them."

"Speak for yourself," Paul said. "My eyes are as good as they ever were. Everything else is failing."

Joanne sorted her cards out and said, "All righty. I dealt, so, Paul, you start."

Paul looked intently at his cards. "Fine."

Devon leaned over the table. "What are we playing?"

Paul looked at him, then put on his best poker face and said, "Have you got any 'threes'?"

They stared at Devon while he figured out what game they were playing, and then laughed as his face dropped. "Go Fish?" Everyone nodded. "Could we at least play for money?"

Paul shook his head in mock seriousness. "No way. No gambling on the grounds of Shady Acres."

Devon looked at them for a moment, then said, "You're joking."

More head shaking. "What, are there old folks here with gambling addictions or something?" Devon said, looking around the patio at the other residents.

"The issue is that gambling is controlled in this state," Jim said. Joanne wisely kept herself out of the conversation. She'd found her attempts to defend her son and the rules and regulations of the home had mostly failed to appease whoever argued with her. So, she double-checked the order of the cards in her hand instead of joining in the conversation.

Paul muttered, "The issue is that management doesn't like people having fun here."

"And there is that, also," Jim said.

Devon looked at the three of them and sighed. "Go fish, Gramps."

"Ah, damnit," Paul said slamming his cards down on the table in disgust.

"No swearing," Joanne said with a smile.

"Not yet, anyways, but I'm sure your son is writing up the new rule as we speak," Paul muttered darkly and picked up a card.

The card game moved on at a desultory pace as each of them took turns being in the lead and then, quick enough, slipping down to being last. The conversation meandered about, much like the card game. Joanne delighted in telling Devon childhood stories about her granddaughter, Dawn. Paul had observed Devon paying much more attention to her stories than he would have expected and commented on it, only to receive a studiously neutral reply from him.

"All I'm wondering," Paul said, tiring of Devon's lack of response, "is if you know this Dawn girl or not? You're the same age and at the same school, and you're not giving me a lot of answers here."

"I don't know what you're talking about, Gramps," Devon said, and then suddenly offered to refill everyone's iced tea.

"Nice try, kiddo. You stay seated there."

Paul put down his cards and turned to Jim. "Permission to treat the witness as hostile?"

Jim laughed and looked at Devon. "Son, you going to answer your grandfather's question?"

"What question?" he replied, defensively, looking at his cards instead of making eye contact.

Jim shook his head, chuckled and looked back at Paul. "Now that, my friend, is a hostile witness. Take your best shot."

Paul cracked his knuckles and leaned toward his grandson and said, "Devon. Either you know her, or you don't. A pretty simple question. I know there are a lot of kids at that school of yours. And I'm betting half of them are girls. And you've probably taken a discerning look at all of them. I surely would have at seventeen. But let's see if there's a way to make this a bit easier on you."

Devon looked up warily at his grandfather. Paul leaned back and turned to Joanne and said, with a smile, "Would you happen to have a current photo of your granddaughter on your phone?"

"Of course, I do. Let me find it," Joanne said and pulled her smart phone out of her purse. With the speed of a teenager, she opened up her photo app and flicked through a half dozen screens until she found a particular picture. Meanwhile, Paul stared across the table at Devon, who continued to avoid his gaze.

"You sure you want me to do this, Devon?" Paul said.

"Knock yourself out, old man."

Paul laughed a loud guffaw that Jim joined in on.

"Here," Joanne said. "This is a lovely one of her."

She handed her phone to Paul who looked at the picture on the screen. Jim leaned over, looking at it also. He let out a smooth whistle, "The spitting image of you, Joanne."

Joanne flushed and said, "Have you always been such a charmer, Jim?"

"Alas, no. Something I came upon in my later years."

Paul laughed and turned the phone toward his grandson. "Hey, hostile witness, are you saying you don't know who this is?"

Devon looked up, saw the picture on the phone, and, despite attempting to lock up every muscle in his face, smiled involuntarily. Paul, Joanne, and even Jim saw his flicker of reaction, his instant of acknowledgment, and his heartbeat of attraction. And Devon blushed crimson to make it even easier to spot.

Paul said, with a grin, "Your honor, I rest my case."

Paul handed the phone back to Joanne while Jim leaned over to Devon and whispered, "With a poker face like that, I'd stay away from the card tables, if I were you."

"Thanks for the advice, Jim."

"My pleasure, son. You're lucky I'm retired, or I'd have to charge you for it."

Devon laughed, despite his red face.

"Go Fish!" Devon said with a laugh and Jim grimaced.

Jim picked up a card and added it to his already large hand. "That's what I'd rather be doing," he muttered, sorting his cards while trying to keep them from falling off the table, "instead of losing my shirt here."

Paul asked, "Is the fishing good around here?"

Joanne chuckled, as Jim looked aghast at him. "Is the fishing good? Do the deer and the buffalo roam on your range? Good Lord, did you not learn a single thing about this state or this town before you charged in like a gang of horse thieves?"

"I already knew it was on the East Coast—above Miami, and below Boston. What else is there to know?"

Jim pointed out across the lawn to the river, behind the row of cottonwoods. "That serene river over there pretty much saved the lives of everyone who initially settled this area. They could walk into the shallows and pick up trout with their hands. I've no doubt they were well and truly tired of the taste of smoked trout by the time spring came 'round, but they were alive so that counted for something."

"Ok, so fishing was good here two hundred and fifty years ago. What about now?"

Jim smiled and turned to Joanne. "You reckon your father's spots are fished out?"

"Oh, I doubt it, although I'd have trouble finding most of them now. Been a while since I got to fish."

Paul piped up and looked at both, "You both fish?"

"Fished," Joanne said.

Paul shook his head. "Once a fisherman always a fisherman—woman."

They laughed, and Jim sighed. "I've had some of the finest times in my life alongside a river. Sometimes with my dad, but mostly with my grandfather," Jim laughed at a memory. "When I was ten, on one trip, he taught me how to smoke."

Amazed, Devon asked, "You're kidding, right?"

Jim laughed and shook his head. "Taught me how to roll my own cigarette, light the match with my thumbnail, and how not to throw up while coughing up a lung after my first inhale."

"Sounds gross."

"It was, Devon, it was. I honestly will say I've had no more than a dozen cigarettes in my life since that first one. Cigars on the other hand…"

Devon shook his head. "Did your parents find out?"

"Oh no! My grandfather could keep a secret. He knew my parents would be mad at both of us. The best part of the whole story is this: my grandfather's job? The town doctor!"

Everyone laughed at the irony for a bit and then Paul said, "We should do it again."

Jim looked at him, confused. "You want us to teach Devon how to smoke?"

"Gramps, that's gross," Devon said in disgust.

"Paul, imagine what your daughter will say when she finds out you taught Devon to smoke..." Joanne said, shaking her head.

Paul rolled his eyes skyward. "You overheating or what? I meant fishing! I'm sure, between the two of you, you've equipment stashed away somewhere. All we'd need is a day pass, and we'd be good to go!"

"Like we're going to receive a pass to go fishing, Paul, come on. You read the rules, 'no unaccompanied off-site excursions, and no exceptions.' Sure, it'd be a treat, but we're not going to find anyone to take us, so we're stuck," Jim said with some sadness, before continuing. "And before you ask, there's no fishing in the river from the town down past us to the bay. So, we can't even fish here."

Paul frowned and flicked the edges of his cards. There had to be a way to sneak them out on the river for a day of fishing. And a day of freedom. That was what he wanted most: a day away from the home, out on a river, under a tree, with nothing to do but watch the current going by.

"Yikes, Gramps, I've gotta split. My dinner's in twenty minutes," Devon said, looking at his phone, putting down his cards and hopping up from the table.

He gave Paul a quick hug, and waved to Jim and Joanne before leaving. Paul continued to ponder fishing while Jim and Joanne discussed whether to continue the game or pack it up for the day.

"What do you think, Paul?" Jim said, glancing up from his huge hand of cards.

"Huh? I might be able to figure something out..." Paul said, distractedly.

Joanne looked at him, confused. "Your cards?"

"What? Oh, have you any sevens?"

Twenty Two

That Saturday dawned with one of those perfect late spring days that made a person want to be outside in nature and smile the entire time. Everyone in the dining hall was a notch brighter, the laughter a tad louder, and there were more skips in steps than there had been in weeks. Not large skips, as this was an old folks home, but skips nonetheless.

Paul and Jim's breakfast with The Bees came to an end. The Bees were heading off to commandeer the best swinging chairs outside before anyone else claimed them. As they headed out the patio doors, Joanne turned and started across the room towards the foyer.

"Aren't you joining us, Joanne?" Helen called to her.

"I'd love to, but Ruth needs my help with some curtains at her house. I'll see you for dinner."

Joanne waved and exited the dining hall before any more questions were asked of her. Paul and Jim lingered, people watching over another cup of coffee.

"Chuck's still mad at you," Jim said, with a smile. "Keep your eyes open around him. He's a petty man and won't forget how you embarrassed him and stole his girl."

"I didn't steal anything. Girl or eyebrow," Paul muttered. "And he's welcome to try to start something. I've been to war; there's nothing he'll throw at me I can't knock out of the park."

"That is surely one of the most strained mixings of metaphors I've ever heard in my life."

Paul laughed and finished his coffee. He looked at his watch and then at Jim. "Enough time passed?"

Checking his pocket watch, Jim nodded, put down his cup, and rose from the table. Paul joined him, and they casually made their way across the dining hall and out into the foyer. Marcus looked up from his desk and frowned at the two of them. Paul smiled and sauntered towards the front door, talking to Jim as they walked. "I guess I'll see you at dinner?"

"I guess you will," Jim said back.

Out of the corner of his eye, Paul watched Marcus finish talking on his phone and stand up. As Marcus walked over to intercept them at the front door, Paul noticed Joanne standing outside in the shade of the portico. Marcus arrived in front of the two and said, "Good morning, sirs."

"Good morning, Mister Marcus," Paul said with a smile. "Have you any plans for this lovely day?"

"Keeping an eye on the residents like I do every day, Mister Paul. I can't see why today would be different."

Jim replied, casually, "Consistency is a wonderful thing, is it not?"

Marcus nodded, and the three stood in the foyer for a moment before Kevin stepped out of the hallway to his office and strode across the tile floor toward them. As he arrived and started to speak, Kevin noticed his mother outside, shut his mouth, and carried on past them out the front door.

"I wonder where he's going?" Paul commented.

"I wonder where you're both going," Marcus said.

"Ah, of course. If you check your books, you'll see that my grandson, Devon, is coming by to pick me up for the day. I'll be helping him with a project for school."

"What kind of project?"

Paul shrugged. "I don't know, but I'll be able to tell you when he drops me off this afternoon."

Marcus stared at Paul for a while. Paul stared back. Finally, Marcus crossed to his desk, picked up his tablet, and returned to the two.

"Now, before you ask," Jim said amenably, "I'll let you know my own grandson, Eric, is coming to pick me up. Regrettably, the coincidence ends there, as he is simply delivering me to my son. There are some legal cases he requires assistance with on such a fine day. Alas, the sunshine will be lost on me today."

Marcus flicked around on the tablet until he found the emailed forms for their two separate excursions. Sure enough, both had properly filled and signed forms. Marcus frowned at the two, then looked down to check the forms again and said, "You two sirs will be waiting in the foyer until your rides show up."

"Absolutely, I wouldn't even consider moving farther than that couch over there," Jim said with a smile and started across the foyer to the couch in question. Paul remained where he was, humming lightly to himself.

•

"I didn't know you were going to Ruth's today," Kevin said to his mother, as he joined her outside.

"I suspect that is because I didn't want to bother you with it, Kevin. I'm simply going over to help her with her curtains; she called yesterday and requested my assistance. You know how good a seamstress I am, especially compared to Ruth," Joanne said and laughed.

Not laughing, Kevin held up his tablet and showed her the form she had filled out, "You need to have a signature on this form, mom. You can't simply fill it out and put it on the secretary's desk. It needs to be signed."

"Well dear, could you sign it for me, then?"

"What?" Kevin said, confused.

"I know, I'm confused by these new rules myself. Before, I would simply put my name on the sign-out sheet at Marcus' desk and everyone knew where I was. But now... You're my son, and you're the one who has to sign my form. If not you, then who?"

Kevin looked at her for a moment, and then looked down at the form displayed on the tablet. Damnit, his mother was right. He'd forgotten about her when he'd created the new rules about off-site excursions. He glanced around and saw a few other elderly residents either waiting for someone to pick them up or in the process of climbing into taxis. Inside the foyer, he saw Marcus standing with Paul. Marcus had his tablet and was looking at something.

"Darling?" Joanne said behind him. Turning around, he saw Ruth's car cruising down the long driveway, "Ruth's here. Are you going to sign my form or shall I go back to my room? You'd be able to tell Ruth why I couldn't assist her, wouldn't you?"

Kevin grimaced at the thought of trying to explain to Ruth how his mother wouldn't be able to go with her, so he quickly typed a confirmation on Joanne's form and closed his tablet.

"You need to give me more notice, Mom. What if I wasn't working today? Then what would you have had done? You'd be stuck."

Joanne gave Kevin a kiss on the cheek as Ruth pulled up under the portico. "Of course you're working, darling, it's only Saturday." Then she gestured toward Ruth's car and Kevin stepped over, opened the passenger door, and helped his mother climb inside. Ruth pulled away with a honk of the horn and Joanne waving out the passenger window.

Before Kevin thought any more about his mother, two more vehicles pulled up in front of him. In the first one—a minivan—Paul's grandson sat quietly behind the wheel. He didn't make eye contact with Kevin—he kept looking straight out over the dash, his hands at 10 and 2 on the steering wheel. Frowning, Kevin turned, staring at the driver of the second car. He didn't recognize the teenaged boy behind its wheel. He glanced back and forth between the two cars for a moment then turned, looking into the foyer.

Jim and Paul sauntered out of the home and passed by Kevin, both with smiles on their faces. Marcus came outside and stood beside Kevin as the two old men climbed into the two cars.

"Who's picking up Jim?" Kevin asked of Marcus.

"His grandson."

"Are their forms filled out correctly?"

"Yes, sir," Marcus said. "I double checked them both."

The two watched as the cars cautiously pulled out from the portico and rolled slowly down the driveway.

"Something's up. I don't know what," Kevin said to Marcus, not taking his eyes off the cars.

Beside him, Marcus shrugged. "Yes, sir. Quite possible something's up." Marcus walked back inside, leaving Kevin watching intently as the two cars arrived at the end of the driveway, turned in opposite directions, and drove away.

•

Ruth and Joanne relaxed in Ruth's car in a pull-off underneath a huge shade tree. A gentle breeze through their open windows kept the car cool despite the morning warmth.

Ruth butted out her hand-rolled cigarette and turned to Joanne. "I don't remember you ever doing anything this naughty when were we young."

"Oh, I'm sure I did. You simply don't remember because you were doing something much naughtier at the time."

Ruth laughed. "No doubt, Joannie. And loving every minute of it, I'd bet." She glanced in the rearview mirror and sat up. "How many minivans with Montana plates you figure there are in this town right now?"

Joanne turned around in her seat and watched as the van pulled up behind Ruth's Mercury and shut off its engine. She and Ruth watched as Paul slowly climbed out of the van, waved to them, and then walked around to the driver's side.

"One down, one to go," Ruth said with a grin.

"Speaking of…" Joanne said as Jim's grandson's car came up from the other direction and stopped in front of Ruth's car. Jim exited the passenger's seat as his grandson popped the rear trunk for him. As Jim dug around in the trunk, out of sight, Paul came over to the car and leaned down on the open passenger window.

"Ladies, what a surprise to find you both here," he said with a smile.

"Goodness gracious, Mister Paul, to what do we owe this pleasure?" Joanne said, in her best Southern drawl.

"Well, frankly, Scarlett—" Paul started to say as Jim waved from behind the other car.

"Some assistance from the good gentleman of the plains would be appreciated."

"Hold that thought, Scarlett," Paul said and walked back to assist Jim. Together they returned to Ruth's car with three fishing rods and a couple of coolers.

Ruth handed Paul the keys. He unlocked her trunk and added Jim's fishing equipment to a rod and some folding chairs that lay at the bottom of Ruth's spacious trunk.

Jim shook his head. "Wow, I forgot about trunks like this. You could nearly fit a sheet of plywood in there."

"With room left over for five or six bodies," Paul said with a laugh, and then slammed the trunk with a solid thud, which shook the car.

"What time should we have our rides meet us here?" Paul asked.

Jim looked up at the sky and thought for a moment. "We'd best be back to Shady Acres for dinner; that would be wise. There's another form we were to fill out if we're missing the main meal of the day."

"Really?"

Jim laughed and started walking back to his grandson. "Gotcha. Have Devon back here at five. That will give us lots of time to clean up and return to the home."

Paul nodded and walked back to the driver's side of the minivan.

"You sure I can't come with you?" Devon said, in a near-whine.

"Ah, you don't want to spend your afternoon with a bunch of old fogeys. Meet us here at five to bring me back into the home, understand?"

"You got it, Gramps."

Paul thanked his grandson and turned to join the others in Ruth's car.

"Hey, Gramps," Devon called, and Paul turned around. "You're a bit of a bad-ass, you know?"

Paul winked at him and said, "I'm a lot of a bad-ass, but don't tell your mom."

Twenty Three

A perfect day for fishing. The four of them had Ruth's blankets laid out on the edge of the river, their picnic baskets in the shade under one of the overhanging trees. Before them lay a vista that hadn't changed in hundreds, if not thousands, of years.

The river flowed past them, broad and gentle, a steady current keeping it fresh, swirling eddies along the riverbank underneath huge overhanging trees which must have started as seedlings in the Middle Ages. Both up and down river presented them with a view of nothing but the gentle river and forest. It was as if they'd gotten there in a time machine instead of Ruth's Mercury Marquis.

Paul sat on the blanket, fiddling with one of the other rods and reels Jim's grandson had brought. He took a deep breath and relaxed into setting up the reel. *Over a decade since I've fished a river,* he thought sadly. *I wonder what happened to my equipment?* Then he remembered the huge garage sale Natalie had made him have before they sold the farm and homestead to his next neighbor along the way. They'd been grabbed up for a song, along with everything else. He pushed those thoughts down deep, left Montana, and returned to the river in front of him.

Jim had already settled in on a large flat rock ten feet out into the current, right beside a dark pool along the riverbank. Joanne had joined him with her rod and a fish basket. Ruth had settled herself on the blanket, in the dappled shade, and had begun working on a piece of tatting which looked more like a couple of joined triangles than a doily.

"What kind of lure should I be setting up?" Paul called to Jim.

Jim shushed him with a smile and whispered, loudly, "Try one of those three-inch Curlytail grubs, the gray ones. If we're lucky, the bass will be biting."

As Paul dug around in the tackle box, Ruth lifted her tatting up to study it. Paul looked over and asked, "Kind of a strange doily, isn't it, Ruth?"

She laughed and held it up to her chest. "Bikini top."

"For personal use?"

Ruth laughed even harder and shook her head. "I wish. I make them, and they get sold online to wealthy European women. Either way, I keep tatting, and I make some nice coin, too."

Completely at a loss for words, Paul simply nodded, finished tying the lure to his line, and creaked to his feet. There wasn't any room on the flat rock to join Jim and Joanne, so he moved up the river bank and settled on a section of exposed tree root which had been rubbed smooth by countless other fishermen.

Clearly it was a favorite spot, as there was a rusty tin coffee can half-buried in the dirt behind the root, the bottom of it covered in old cigarette butts and ash. He settled himself and cast his line into the upriver edge of the pool, watching it float down with the slight current.

This is the life, he thought, leaning back against the tree. *Perfect river, perfect day, and, hell, perfect company. I could become pretty happy with this. All of this. It's been a while since I've felt this good.*

Out on the flat rock, Jim and Joanne chatted companionably while occasionally pulling in their lines and throwing them back out into the pool. Joanne would occasionally glance across at Paul leaning against the old tree, eyes shut, his hands gently flicking his rod to keep his lure in motion. Adjusting her hat to cover her face, she let out a long sigh and smiled contentedly.

"Yes, it certainly is that kind of a day," Jim said. "He's an ornery son-of-a-gun from time to time, and he loves breaking any rule he doesn't like, but this is one of his better ideas."

"My son may not like his attitude, but I have to admit he's been an excellent addition to the home," Joanne replied.

Ruth called out to them, "You let me know when you're hungry, and you come over here and set everything while I watch."

"We'll be needing some fish before we're going to be eating," Paul called back.

Ruth rolled her eyes, "Oh Lord, Paul, you're one of those hunter-gatherer types who's going to insist on catching, killing, and eating your food, aren't you?"

"Everything but coffee," Paul replied.

Jim piped in, "And donuts."

•

When Devon returned to the apartment, he found his mom curled up on the couch, a mug of coffee balanced on the arm, pounding away on her laptop. He slipped the car keys back onto the hook by the front door and sauntered into the living room.

"Hey," Natalie said, not looking up from her computer, "where'd you slip off to?"

Devon held up a container of yogurt. "We were out."

He watched as she nodded and returned to her work with a scowl and a grimace. Devon grinned at his half-truth, which hid the lie about sneaking his grandfather out of the home and leaving him on the side of some road with a bunch of other old folks. He grabbed some granola, poured the yogurt over it, and returned to the table and started playing around on his phone while eating.

"Ah damn," Natalie muttered and did some more typing.

"What's the matter?" Devon said, through a mouthful of cereal. "Is it some computer thing you need my help with? Like that time you forgot how to copy & paste?"

"Ha, ha, a good one—but this is far less amusing, so don't joke around."

"Ok, chill..." Devon said and continued eating.

Natalie took a breath and tried to calm down, but failed. "I can't chill. This is about if living in this apartment is financially possible. If we can afford the van, not to mention keep your grandfather in that home. Your aunt has her own troubles and can't send any money."

"Big surprise there. She's probably spending it all on getting a new boyfriend."

Natalie's younger sister, Melanie, was floating around Seattle, looking for a rich computer guy to hook into marriage, but wasn't having any luck. Two divorces hadn't slowed down her sadly flawed plan.

"Damnit, don't joke about everything, Devon. This is serious—"

The buzzing of the apartment intercom interrupted Natalie. Devon grabbed the wall phone and pushed the '6' button to let whoever it was into the building.

"They want us to check who comes inside for security, Devon."

Devon let go of the button and hung up the phone. "It's some pizza guy or someone who forgot their keys, Mom. No big deal."

"But it could be a big deal if it's someone and they want to rob us! Or rob someone else in the building! Come on, consider everyone else around you, instead of only you."

"Jeez, Mom, I buzzed someone in, I didn't murder anyone with an ax..."

"Don't give me that tone. You won't buzz anyone in anymore, understand?"

Devon picked up his now empty cereal bowl and headed into the kitchen. "Understood."

Natalie took a breath and tried to calm herself down. There wasn't any point in being angry at Devon because her finances weren't working out the way she'd expected. That wasn't his fault. And she had been guilty, on occasion, of blindly pushing the enter button if the intercom buzzed.

"Devon," she called after him, as calmly as she could. "I'm sorry I yelled, ok? I'm having trouble with our money. Your father's being a total—he's being difficult, again. And I get stressed, ok?"

Devon leaned through the doorway and looked at her, sullenly. "You know, I am seventeen. I understand shit. You don't have to treat me like a baby."

"Damnit, Devon, I don't treat you like a baby!" Natalie said in exasperation. "Are you going to really help me with our budget, with our finances, with our—"

A knocking on the apartment door interrupted her. She frowned at Devon, and he shrugged his shoulders and sauntered into the hall to answer the door. Closing her laptop—it wasn't like their horrible finances wouldn't still be there in an hour, or in a day—she rose from the couch and called after her son, "Dev, who's at the door?"

Stepping into the hallway, Natalie was startled by a pretty brunette girl standing halfway in the apartment and her son leaning back against the wall across from the open door.

"Oh!" Natalie said, as her anger and frustration with Devon evaporating in an instant. Clearly, Devon was as surprised by this girl's arrival at their door as she was.

"Why don't you invite your friend inside?" Natalie said and stepped back into the living room. After a bit of a pause, Devon and the girl walked into the room.

"Hi, I'm Dawn," the girl said, reaching out her hand. Natalie took her hand and shook it, replying, "I'm Natalie, Devon's mom. I'm sure you guessed that already."

Dawn smiled and nodded. Devon hadn't said anything yet.

Natalie carried on, filling the conversation void, "You two know each other from school?"

Dawn nodded. "I met you in the principal's office last week."

"I was a bit distracted that day, but you do look familiar. Would you like something to drink? Ice tea or pop? Wait, you say soda here instead of pop, right?"

"No, thank you, I came over hoping Devon wanted to come down to the coffee shop to hang out with some people from school," Dawn said as Devon brightened up even more beside her. "I didn't have his phone number, so I sort of came by…"

Devon looked over at Natalie, unable to contain the excitement, but calmed down enough to slowly ask, "Does that work with you, Mom? I'm sure we'd be done by dinner." He turned to Dawn. "Right?"

She nodded. "Absolutely. I can't miss dinner; my dad would kill me."

Natalie smiled, thrilled at her son being happy for once. "That sounds fine to me."

"Ok, great. Then we'll go," Devon said and eased Dawn towards the front door, giving his mother a wide, enthusiastic grin over his shoulder as they walked down the hallway. Natalie leaned against the wall and watched as her son readied himself to go out. As he grabbed his house key and started out the door, she called to him, "You forgot your phone!"

He leaned back in, an embarrassed smile on his face, and rushed down the hall, past her to the kitchen table. "Thanks, Mom," he grabbed his phone, and as he headed back past her, she held up her arm to stop him. With a quick glance to ensure Dawn had left the apartment, Natalie slipped a folded bill into Devon's pocket. "Have fun, ok?"

Devon took out the bill and unfolded the twenty, then looked at her, concerned. "Are you sure we can afford it?"

Taking a deep breath through a heart full of compassion, Natalie nodded and said, "If we can't enjoy coffee with someone we like, we've larger problems."

Devon gave her a quick hug and bolted out the front door with a wave. Natalie stood in the silence for a moment, then crossed the apartment and looked out the living room window down at the street. After a moment, the two teens sauntered down the sidewalk, side-by-side, already deep in conversation.

Everything will work out, Natalie thought to herself. *I may have doubted it before, but I honestly do believe it now.*

Twenty Four

From the depths of Ruth's car's trunk, Paul pulled out an ancient hibachi and a bag of coals. With Jim's help and, when the girls weren't looking, some lighter fluid, they got a nice bed of coals going.

The day had idly drifted away, like leaves floating on the river, and as they realized they were hungry, the fish started biting. So instead of having to head back to reality, they continued their time on the bank of the river. Ruth had enough other food to feed a couple legions of infantry should some stop by for a meal, so they were taking advantage of her forward planning and enjoying a late lunch. As Joanne put out place settings, Jim worked the grill and the four perfect bass they had caught.

"These will be done in no time," Jim said, poking at the fish with a fork.

"Leave them be," Paul said, taking the utensil away from Jim with a smile. "You're going to overcook them."

"You wouldn't say that if you grew up here, Cowboy. We pride ourselves on our ability to cook a perfect fish, no matter what kind of heat source we've got."

Paul laughed and handed back the fork. "Too bad we don't have a good wine to go with these fish."

Jim sighed and said, "True, but I do have a couple of cigars for afterward."

"You're a good man."

"That I am."

Joanne overheard the men and turned to Ruth as she put out the Tupperware containers of coleslaw, potato salad, and cornbread. "Oh, I would certainly enjoy a glass of wine. Ruth, is there any chance you brought something?"

Ruth shook her head and sighed. "I unfortunately forgot, unless you count the '95 Montrachet in the glove box."

Joanne clapped her hands in excitement and started pulling proper wine glasses out of Ruth's picnic basket. She placed them on the blanket and called to Paul, "Since you're not really helping with the cooking, Paul, could you grab something out of the glove box for me?"

Paul scowled while Jim snickered behind him and said, "You go help the womenfolk, Paul."

"You want to be on my bad side, Jimbo?"

Jim stopped smiling and stared back at Paul. No, he did not want to be on Paul's bad side, given the practical jokes Paul had already pulled, and with no idea how many more there were rattling around in that devious head of his. Then Paul grinned, picked up the keys and, using his cane to steady himself, headed up the bank to where they'd parked the car. He called to Joanne as he climbed, "What am I looking for?"

Joanne called after him, "You'll know it when you see it."

Paul shrugged and opened the passenger side of the car and sat down on the seat. He'd forgotten how much of a reach it was to open the glove box in an old car like this. He could have walked inside and stood up to open it. The lid swung down, large enough to carve a roast turkey for Thanksgiving on, and there, nestled within the insurance papers and some outdated maps of adjacent states, lay a dusty bottle of wine. Paul picked it up, glanced at the label, and whistled.

"I sure hope someone's got a corkscrew," he called back to the rest of the group as he climbed out of the car and shut the door behind him.

"What kind of a picnicker would I be if I didn't?" Ruth asked, and pulled one out of her basket. As Paul carefully stepped down the bank to the blanket, Jim turned around and called out, "Attention everyone, these are now perfect!"

With Joanne's help, Jim brought a plateful of grilled fish back to the picnic and settled himself. Soon the wine had been opened, salads and fish passed around, and everyone started eating. Contented silence, except for the babbling of the river, ensued for a quite a while, but finally Paul paused eating, sighed, and looked around, as if for the first time. "This is the best picnic I've ever been on."

The rest nodded in agreement and continued eating. After a while, with their first bites of food finished, the four slid into comfortable conversation and laughter that carried on, with the help of a fine French wine, for the rest of their meal.

•

On the way over to the diner, Devon and Dawn talked mostly about school—teachers, other students they both knew—safe conversation topics. Every couple minutes as they walked along the streets, someone would wave out a car window at Dawn and she'd wave back. He started to make a wise-ass comment about it, before realizing he'd gotten the same attention back home when he ventured into town. Small towns are small towns no matter where they were.

Devon finally said something after another driver honked and waved at her. "Must be tough having everyone in town know who you are."

Dawn shrugged, "I hadn't thought about it, really. Most of them don't really know me, you know? They see me at church, or they know Dad from the home, or they're the parents of school friends. Eleven years of school friends is a lot of parents. But they don't know me."

"It would be hard to get away with anything around here."

"Like what?"

Devon replied, "Like sneaking out after hours. Everywhere you'd go, someone would see you and know who you are. That'd suck. You'd have no freedom to be anonymous."

"Do you sneak out?"

Devon laughed. "You kidding? I'd be grounded so fast—and you heard how those stairs up to my apartment squeak. They'd give me away in a second. I'd have to fly out my bedroom window, except I can't fly and the window squeaks like someone squeezing a cat whenever I open it."

Dawn laughed and continued along the tree-shaded sidewalk.

"Hey," Devon asked after they'd walked a while and he'd thought about it for a bit, "how'd you know where I lived?"

Dawn stopped and looked at him shyly, "I hope you're not mad, but I looked it up on my father's computer at Shady Acres. Your address is in there as the next-of-kin."

"Damn, you're like some cyber-stalker. How cool it that!"

Looking relieved, Dawn continued, now excited, "I would have phoned you but the only number they had was your mom's cell phone, and I couldn't figure out how to explain how I got it."

"No way," Devon said, utterly entranced. "You are totally the coolest girl I've ever met."

Dawn brushed the hair out of her eyes and shrugged. "I suppose Montana girls don't do sneaky things like that."

"Montana girls don't know *how* to do stuff like that!"

They continued walking along the sidewalk and turned onto Main Street a couple of blocks down from the courthouse. As they stopped for the streetlight to change to green, Dawn turned to him and asked, "Am I really the coolest girl you've ever met?"

Devon stared at her deep brown eyes and nodded. Blushing a bit, Dawn smiled slightly, brushed a permanently errant strand of hair back behind her ear, and said, "I guess you'll have to prove you're equally as cool for me."

"I thought I did that in school," Devon stammered.

Dawn stopped to say, "You mean, taking the blame for some stupid jock being a jerk because I didn't join the cheerleading squad this year?"

Devon stammered, "I guess—"

"That was noble, and a bit brave, but not especially cool," she said.

Dawn stared at him until Devon blinked and then smiled, saying, "Buying me a milkshake will be cool enough."

Then the light changed, and she crossed the street. Devon stood on the curb, stunned. He watched Dawn walk away for a moment before running after her, barely dodging a car turning right.

The woman who ran the diner, Marge, greeted Dawn with open arms and a long hug when they stepped through the front door. She shook his hand when Dawn introduced him and said, "So you're Paul's grandson. I see the resemblance! Grab a seat wherever and I'll be right there with some waters and menus."

As he followed Dawn back to a booth, he muttered to himself, "My Gramps's already a regular here… I'm gonna have to ask him about that."

Once they sat down, Devon realized they were in a booth for two. "I thought some others were coming."

Dawn grinned shyly and shook her head. "Nope. I said that so your mom wouldn't make a deal out of it. Or you, either."

Speechless, Devon sat still and listened to his heart pounding in his ears. *A girl who makes the first move,* he thought. *I like this.* Devon felt his pocket to make sure he still had the money. He didn't want this to end up like a bad sitcom episode where the star goes on a date, but doesn't have any money to pay for anything. The cash was there, and he let out a deep breath.

"That's pretty cool," he said, as positively neutrally as he could manage. Then Dawn smiled, and he couldn't help it—he burst out into a huge grin back at her. Their smiling and grinning were interrupted by Marge arriving at the side of the booth with glasses of water and menus.

"Aren't you two cute," she said, quickly dropping everything on the tabletop. "The pie is coconut crème, and the soup is my own special minestrone. I'll be back in a sec, ok?" And then she disappeared in a blur of motion.

"Wow," Devon said, watching Marge race back into the kitchen. "She's non-stop."

Dawn nodded and sipped her water, "She's always like that, and I doubt she'll ever change. But she knows everyone in town—well, everyone who comes in here to eat."

"And if they don't come here to eat?"

"She says, 'Why on God's green earth would I want to know people that downright stupid?'" Dawn said with a laugh. Devon joined her.

Devon slurped at the remains of his chocolate milkshake while looking across the booth at Dawn. She absentmindedly twirled a portion of her long hair between the fingers of her left hand while poking a french fry into a ramekin of ketchup. *How did I luck out and end up here?* he wondered, while trying to drink the remains of his shake without making a loud slurping noise. *Not that I'm arguing, but this is pretty sweet.*

Three hours later, they were finishing up their second milkshakes and the remains of a huge plate of fries, both realizing their time together—their first date—was coming to an end.

"Do you miss your dad?"

Devon was pulled back from his thoughts to look across at Dawn. "Not really. He kinda slipped out of my life when he and mom split up."

"How old were you?"

"Ten." Devon shrugged. "He already worked a lot, but then mom finished her courses and got a better job than him. Then he worked even harder, weekends and evenings. He just wasn't around, even before he moved out."

"Like my dad, always working."

"Yeah, but you see him every day, right?"

Dawn played with a fry. "A little in the morning, and then dinners."

"Wait. I thought you said you had to be home for dinner, or your dad would kill you?" Devon asked, after looking at his phone and being surprised at the time. They'd spent most of the day together! Sweet!

Dawn giggled. "Something else I said to make your mom not worry. Whoa, maybe she's worried that I'm trouble, after meeting me in the principal's office."

Devon started to ask her what she meant—how could she be trouble?—when a loud voice interrupted him, calling out from across the diner, "What the hell, Dawn?"

They both turned and saw a few of the football team exiting a booth at the other end of the room. They were obviously finishing their meals, but had only noticed Dawn as they got up. Devon rolled his eyes and turned back, looking across the table at Dawn instead of at the jocks.

Great, he thought sarcastically, *this is exactly what I need to finish off our first date. Being beaten up by a bunch of jocks in a diner. It was so 1950s. So Archie Comics.* He slouched lower, but watched Dawn's face as she followed their progress towards them. The four linebackers in their pristine letterman's jackets spread out in a line in front of their table, blotting out the sun.

"Don't be a nuisance, Adrian," Dawn said quietly, calmly picking up a fry and eating it. "I didn't want to be a cheerleader this year, that's all."

"But you've been one since grade school. It's your responsibility to the school and the team. You can't be selfish; you have to think about everyone, you know? It's your frickin' job to be a cheerleader."

"And now I don't want to be."

"Yeah, how's that working out? Now no one likes you and you're getting pranked in the cafeteria."

The rest of the jocks laughed behind Adrian. Dawn shrugged and slurped on her empty milkshake. Adrian frowned at her, and then scowled at Devon. "You're the new squirt. Prairie Boy."

The other guys laughed again. *They probably laugh at everything Adrian said,* Devon thought. There'd been those guys hanging around his school's hockey captain back home.

"His name's—"

"Devon. I'm Devon," Devon said and put out his fist for a fist bump. But Adrian left him hanging, so Devon shrugged, lowered his fist, and reached for a fry.

"I don't care who you are, Prairie Boy," more laughs. "But you should leave Dawn alone."

"Really?" Devon said before he could stop himself. "Yikes. It is because she's dangerous? She might date and dump me?"

Adrian shifted around, adjusting his jacket, confused. Devon continued, his confidence building.

"Man, that's good advice. I appreciate it, Adrian. I'll make sure to keep my guard up around her—I don't want to be used and thrown away by some scheming ex-cheerleader."

While Adrian stared down at him, trying to figure out in that thick head of his if Devon had insulted him or not, Devon climbed out of the booth, took Dawn's hand, and together they walked away. When they arrived at the counter, Marge stood behind the till, watching alertly. Devon gave her the twenty, but she pushed it back at him.

"First date's on me. And I should pay you for that move you put on the dumb ox." Before Devon could say anything, Marge pushed the two of them towards the front door of the diner. "Now you two go on and get out of here. I'll slow down those boys for a bit if they even think about following you out."

"Thanks, Marge," Dawn said with a smile, and then pulled Devon out onto the sidewalk. Outside, she quickly slipped around the corner of the building, down the alleyway, and out into a quiet park. Only there did she stop and turn to face Devon, "An excellent move back there, except for dumping all over my virtues."

Defensively, Devon stammered. "I didn't mean it. I wanted him to be confused, really."

Dawn laughed and swatted him on the arm. "I know, you goof, I was just sweating you."

Then she laughed again and skipped over to the swings in the distance. Devon shook his head and, once his heart slowed down, joined her.

"How come the jocks are pissed at you for not being a cheerleader?"

Dawn sighed and swung back and forth a couple times before answering. "That's the way they are. Either you're in or you're out. I used to be in, now I'm not. So now I'm fair game."

"How come you aren't a cheerleader anymore?"

"You always ask this many questions?"

Devon blushed and swung higher. Dawn watched him for a moment before replying. "My parents want to make sure I get into a good college, and cheerleading won't help me as much as Advanced Placement courses and not having a social life."

"That sucks."

"Tell me about it."

"My mom's too busy with her new job to worry about me," Devon admitted.

"Must be nice."

He shrugged, then said, "Most of the time, yeah, I guess it is."

"But not always?"

Devon shook his head, unwilling to say more. Dawn nodded and kicked harder to catch up to him. To the sounds of laughter and challenges, they raced each other higher and higher on the swings, exchanging, for a moment, the pressures of high school for some youthful fun.

•

The empty wine bottle floated on the end of a piece of fishing line in the river beside their picnic site. The sun lit only the top half of the trees on the far bank of the river. Here and there, large and smallmouth bass popped out of the water to feast on the insects hovering at the surface. The four leaned back against the bank, each alone in his or her thoughts, content in the collective silence as only people truly comfortable with each other are.

Relaxing alongside the river, it dawned on Paul that he hadn't felt the need or desire to phone the boys back home in over a week. *That must be a good sign, right?* he thought. *I'm settling in and making new friends.* He smiled to himself. That was exactly what he had said to his children when they started elementary school.

Finally, Jim stirred and pushed the box of chocolates further away from him. "Enough."

Ruth smiled and pulled the box closer, helping herself to another nougat. "Like sex, never enough."

Jim stretched his arms back over his head, and noticed his pocket watch as his untucked shirt slid up. One quick glance at it and he sighed.

"Before I mention what I really should mention," Jim said, as he watched Ruth nibble at the confection, "I'd like to know where in the birth order did y'all come?"

The other three looked at him in bemused confusion.

"Ah, indulge me, please?"

Paul shrugged and said, "I'm the last of seven. Four boys, three girls."

Joanne looked at Paul in a slightly new way and continued, "Last of five. All girls."

"Your poor father," Paul said, and they laughed. "He must have had to wake up before first light to get any time in the bathroom."

"He had a bathroom added to his office at Shady Acres so he could shave there!" Joanne said with a smile.

"And we know where Ruth came in the birth order," Jim quipped, and the three said, simultaneously, "Only!"

Ruth looked offended for a moment, and then laughed. "Another dreamer."

"What about you, Jim? Where'd you come in the pecking order?" Paul asked.

"I was first," Jim said, with a sigh, "that's the responsible one. The one who makes sure everyone is dealt with fairly, the one who becomes a lawyer to ensure everyone is dealt with fairly, and the one who makes sure everything happens exactly when it is supposed to happen. Fairly."

"I thought that's the sixth born," Ruth said jokingly.

Jim slowly shook his head. "Nope, they do whatever they want because their parents are so exhausted from looking after the other five. Nope, I'm here to tell you exactly what number ones get to do. They get to cut the party short and let everyone know to clean up and go home. Especially if they don't want to go home. Three last-born dreamers, I should have guessed. Each of you off in your own world, having fun, none of you minding to the responsibilities."

"What kind of responsibilities are we not minding?" Joanne asked, reaching for a chocolate. "We said we'd be back for dinner, but missing one meal isn't a problem, is it?"

"Oh, like our curfew starting at eight."

"Why, that would only be a problem if it were eight and we were still here," Ruth said.

"What time is it?"

"Seven-thirty."

The other three looked at him for a moment and then collectively sighed.

"Yikes. We're going to be cutting this close," Paul said, worried.

Ruth shook her head. "Looks like the party's over."

Jim nodded. "I'm as guilty for losing track of the time as the rest of you. But what worries me is we're over two hours late for pickup. I wonder why our grandkids didn't call us. We'd better phone and find out where they are."

"And to arrange a new pickup time."

As the girls started cleaning up the picnic, the two men pulled out their cell phones and opened them up. After a few button pushes, they looked at each other, in concern.

"Have you any signal?"

Jim shook his head. Paul scowled and closed his phone, "We'll have to phone from the road."

"Not quite the perfect end to the perfect picnic…"

Twenty Five

Kevin brought home take-out Thai food after receiving a text from Beth that Dawn wouldn't be home for dinner. He came through the kitchen door to a house completely void of the sounds of the newest Taylor Swift-wannabe pop star. Instead, the sounds of Joni Mitchell, Beth's favorite singer-songwriter, filled the dining room. He tossed his phone on the charging table and brought the take-out bag through the kitchen into the dining room. There he was met by candlelight and a bottle of wine in a cooler on the one end of the table with two place settings lying ready.

Beth sat—lounged, actually—at the end of the table with a half empty glass of white wine. She raised it to Kevin and smiled. "Welcome home."

Putting down the bag of food, he leaned down and gave her a long kiss—a kiss much longer than he would have if Dawn were at the table.

"I'm glad to be home. What wine did you pick?" Kevin asked as he started taking the Thai food containers out of the paper bag and placing them on the perfectly arranged trivets on the antique oak table.

Beth took another sip and put down her glass. "I read online that a sweet German wine goes well with Thai food, so I popped over to

Beckworth Falls to that fancy wine store there and bought their best Gewürztraminer. We'll see if the Internet is right."

"I haven't heard of that combination. Are there a lot of Germans living in Thailand?"

Once Kevin opened up the different cartons, they served themselves dinner. Kevin poured himself a glass of the bright, cold wine and topped up Beth's glass before sitting down. Quietly they started eating, commenting only on the quality of the food and the surprising appropriateness of the wine. After a few bites, Beth paused and looked across the table at her husband.

It had been far too long since they had had a meal like this, only the two of them. Even on those nights when Dawn had some extra-curricular activity or hung out with friends, they would make sure the three of them had dinner together. It was an essential part of being a family for Beth after growing up with either her father or mother away working nights—and, sometimes when she was in her teens, both being absent for dinner. But, Beth was realizing, her insistence on having dinner as a family had done its damage on her having dinner alone with her husband. *Funny how you want one thing so badly, but it turns out to ruin another thing you want equally as badly,* she thought while nibbling on a spring roll.

Across the table, Kevin had similar thoughts—only the simpler male version of them. *I know she wants to talk like we did before, when we first started dating and going out,* he thought while serving himself more coconut soup. *But that was twenty years ago. I don't know how to talk like that anymore, to anyone. My damn head is so full of my day; it would take two or three bottles of wine for me to let go enough to have a thought that wasn't work or family related.*

Instead, he said, "The next time you're over in Beckworth Falls, why don't you pick up a case of this wine and I'll put it in the cellar for the next time we have Thai?"

"Sounds like a good idea. If only Dawn liked Thai." The instant Beth mentioned their daughter, she regretted it. They'd spent the whole short time together without talking about Dawn, but now she'd broken that unspoken agreement.

"Who's she out with tonight, anyway?" Kevin asked between bites of pad Thai.

"Some friends from school, she said. They were going to be working on science projects for the afternoon then ordering some pizza," Beth said, holding back her sadness that she'd let the conversation slip over to being about their daughter, instead of potentially being about them.

"I guess that's better than them being out wandering the streets," Kevin replied, realizing how weak his response was.

And with that, their conversation faded, and the two returned to their wine and dinner until Kevin's cell phone rang in the kitchen. Kevin stopped eating and let it ring a couple of times. They both could see he was torn between leaving it and answering it.

"Please leave it," Beth said, realizing the futility of her comment the moment she said it. Kevin was exactly like his father and his grandfather—emotionally attached at the hip to Shady Acres and the residents. Even if he hadn't started out like that, life had conspired to make sure he ended that way.

The phone rang again. With a sigh, Kevin pushed his chair back and stood. Beth reached for her glass of wine and drank what was left in it, surprising them both. She wasn't usually a drinker, but their almost-date-night had triggered more hope than she realized. Kevin wouldn't make eye contact with her as she refilled her glass, and entered the kitchen to answer his phone.

Trying her best not to gulp down the entire glass of wine, Beth sipped at it between nibbles on her chicken satay skewer, taking her time to slather them in spicy peanut sauce. She couldn't hear Kevin's side of the conversation, but she knew Marcus or the other night manager had called about something either deathly urgent or inconsequentially trivial. Either way, Kevin had to take the call and make some decision.

Beth sighed and looked around the dining room. The table, which had come with the house, could seat twelve comfortably, but she couldn't remember the last time they'd actually had that many people sitting around it. Possibly a holiday dinner some years ago, but most holidays now were epic events at Shady Acres that meant Kevin would be working while she and Dawn ate with her family on the other side of town. And those meals were filled with judgments from her parents and her siblings, their spouses, and their children about Kevin's absences from family events. It was easier for her to stay home with Dawn and order in food, which is what they'd done the past couple of holidays, much to her shame.

As she finished off her last skewer, she could hear Kevin wrapping up his phone conversation. He had a skill at talking in a way which made it difficult to hear what he said if you weren't at the other end of the call from him. She'd always been impressed by that—his ability to keep his conversations private—but right this moment, it infuriated her. Maybe it was the German white wine's fault... either way, Beth was infuriated.

She knew, she totally knew, what would happen when Kevin finished the call and came back into the dining room. But she wasn't going to say or do anything to help him out. She took another sip of wine, more of a gulp really, and leaned back in her chair and waited for him to return.

When Kevin came back into the dining room and wouldn't make eye contact with her, Beth knew she had been right. He had to go in. No. He *chose* to go in. But she waited, fuming underneath, but displaying as much calm as she was able to show.

"I have to go in," Kevin said, grabbing up a skewer and pulling off a piece of chicken with his teeth, still not making eye contact.

Beth put her wine glass down hard on the polished tabletop. "Of course, you do," she said bitterly.

Kevin put the empty skewer down on his plate and looked across the table at his wife. "You know I would rather be here. With you."

"Then why are you leaving?"

"Come on, Beth, there's a problem at the home. And that's my job. That's what keeps us in this house, what keeps you from needing a job and going to work."

"But you don't have to go in for everything!"

Kevin grabbed his wine and finished it off in one gulp, completely missing the subtle flavors of plum and pepper, and placed his glass back down on his place mat with as much calm as he could manage. "Yes, I do."

"No, you don't…"

"Beth, I do. It's my job. Since my dad died, it's been my job. I don't have any choice in the matter. I get called, so I go in. If I were a doctor and I had a patient brought into the hospital, you wouldn't flinch at me going in."

"But it's not the same! You have Marcus and a full staff there for the night. It's not like someone needs you to take out their burst appendix. It's probably someone who can't find their Roger Whittaker cassette and can't sleep without it."

She pushed her chair away from the table and started stacking dishes, unable to eat anything else.

"Marcus can't deal with this; it's Mrs. Dirkson. You know how she is when she loses something."

Beth stopped clearing the table and looked at Kevin with disappointment in her eyes. "Yes, I do know about Mrs. Dirkson and her dementia. I know what is going on with every person at the home. But I don't work there, Kevin; you do."

"Yes!" Kevin said, stomping around the end of the table towards the kitchen and his car keys. "I work there, like it or not! Damnit, Beth, I don't have any choice but to go in. She's not going to calm down for Marcus or anyone else but me. I don't want to go in, but I have to."

Beth walked past Kevin with her hands full of empty plates and said, "You don't have to, you want to."

Kevin thought about saying something, but stopped. It wasn't a fight they hadn't had before, although never as bad as this. *The Gewürztraminer could take some of the blame,* he thought. Beth rarely drank this much. He watched as she started loading the dishwasher, scraping plates into the compost bin under the sink. He knew she was right, but picked up his keys and slipped on his suit jacket. "I'll be back as soon as I can," he said softly, while his wife packed uneaten Thai food into Tupperware containers. "Then maybe we could watch a film or something."

Kevin waited for a moment, but Beth didn't reply to him. Instead, she turned her back and retreated into the dining room. *Shit,* he thought, *we nearly had a nice dinner together. Sometimes I hate my job. Despite it being my life, my family's livelihood, and my heritage. Sometimes I really hate it.*

With those thoughts and a couple of glasses of wine jostling in his head, Kevin exited the kitchen door and walked around the house to his car. Through the dining room window, he saw his wife wiping down his great-grandfather's table. The urge to go back inside was huge, but so, too, was the responsibility he had been handed—handed down from father, from grandfather, from great-grandfather. With that weight on his shoulders, Kevin climbed into his car and pulled away from his house.

Twenty Six

"I'm pretty sure your car goes faster than this, Ruth," Paul said tersely from the back seat as they meandered along the road back to town.

Ruth glanced in the rearview mirror. "It does, but I'm not going to wrap us around a tree."

"At this speed, we couldn't even scrape the bark on a tree if we hit it head on."

Jim looked up his cell phone and shook his head. "Still no signal."

Joanne turned around at looked back at the two men. "I'll cover for you at the home."

"No, because you weren't with us today; we weren't even with each other today. Act like you don't know what's going on and you'll be fine. We'll extricate ourselves from any mess your son and Marcus throw at us," Paul said, and checked his phone for a signal. Nothing. He snapped the lid shut, took a deep breath, and looked out the window at the passing scenery. As they rounded a tight curve and passed a cairn on the side of the road, Paul asked, "Was that some Civil War historical point of interest back there, that stone pillar?"

The silence in the car became even quieter. Confused, Paul looked from Jim to the women up front. "What?"

"There was an accident," Jim murmured and looked away. Paul still didn't understand why the silence, but then Joanne sighed deeply and said, without looking away from the front window, "Go ahead, Jim. Tell him."

"I don't have to, Joanne. I can tell him later, if you'd rather."

"Now is as good a time as any," she said.

Ruth looked over at Joanne quickly, concerned for her best friend.

Jim took a breath and turned to face Paul, "This was twenty-four—no, twenty-five—years ago. There'd been lots of complaints about that curve: too sharp, graded wrong, the light is tricky through the trees at certain times of the day, a lot of close calls."

Joanne kept breathing slowly and realized this would be the first time since the crash that she would be hearing someone tell the story.

Jim continued, "It was twilight—the tricky light time of day—in late September, and a group from the home had been out for the afternoon, watching the trees change color."

"Residents of Shady Acres?" Paul said, surprised.

Jim nodded, "There were less strict rules at the home at that time. If residents had cars and licenses, they were permitted to come and go as they pleased. Anyway, for whatever reason, Martin, Kevin's father—"

"My husband," Joanne said, quietly.

"Well, Martin went out looking for them."

"And he found them?"

"No one knows why exactly they stopped the car on the edge of the curve. Maybe they needed a break after all that driving, but the fact was they had stopped their car. And when Martin came around the curve, the sun caught him face on, and he didn't see their car. He hit it at speed."

Paul looked forward at the back of Joanne's head, at a complete loss for words.

"Everyone died," Joanne said. "It was over two hours before they were discovered."

Paul reached forward and placed his hand gently on Joanne's shoulder and gave it a squeeze. Sometimes there are no words. The four spent the next moments quietly remembering friends taken too soon from them. Then Jim's cell phone pinged three times quickly as he received some text messages.

"We have service now," he said. Jim pecked out a message to his grandson, and Paul did the same.

With a soft smile, Joanne turned and glanced at the two men, who looked back at her with concern. "I'm fine. It was a long time ago. All wounds heal. Why, it's barely a scar now, no more new damage to be done. And hearing it doesn't make my day any less wonderful."

The rest of the drive was uneventful, albeit slow because of Ruth's insistence in driving at least ten miles per hour under the speed limit. "We're not racing to put out a fire, and I'm pretty sure neither Joanne nor I are about to give birth, so shut your pie-hole and enjoy the scenery," Ruth had said the last time Paul asked her to speed up.

Jim had laughed, and Paul thought about playing a practical joke on him—but only for a moment.

Then Ruth said, while glancing at the rearview mirror, "Joannie, what car does your son drive?"

"Silver BMW."

"Well, hells bells."

"What?" Joanne asked, looking back. "Oh dear…"

Everyone turned and watched as a silver BMW sedan pulled up behind them, then signaled and started to pass.

"Duck!" Joanne cried out.

The men crouched down, attempting to hide as Kevin accelerated and pulled abreast of Ruth. Jim slid well out of sight, but since Paul was sitting behind Joanne on the passenger side of the car, he would be totally visible if Kevin looked into the rear windows of the Pontiac.

Paul watched as Kevin glanced over, and then realized who was in the front seat of the car he was in the midst of passing. Ruth waved at him with one hand, impatiently gesturing for him to continue. Kevin's mouth dropped open then shut as he shifted gears and pulled ahead of them.

"Did he see us?" Paul said, still crouched down.

"I don't know," Joanne said, watching her son drive off. "I don't believe he did, but he might have."

"He didn't. He was too startled," Ruth said confidently.

Jim and Paul breathed tentative sighs of relief and cautiously sat back up after Joanne assured them her son had gotten far enough ahead to be out of sight.

"Lord, that was close," Jim said, stretching his back. "To tell the truth, it felt a lot like high school for a moment. Except for my lower back and my hip."

"I was caught once with a boy in the back seat," Ruth said. "Luckily, Joanne's dad found us and not my own, or that boy wouldn't have lived to be my second husband."

Everyone laughed, and Ruth made a left turn down the quiet road that led to their meeting place with their grandchildren.

Twenty Seven

When Ruth rolled slowly into the pull off, only one car waited for them.

"Looks like my ride is here," Jim said as they came to a stop. "Where's yours?"

Paul looked up and down the road. No cars in sight either way. Paul shrugged and checked his phone again.

"Devon hasn't replied to my texts. I don't know where he is. But I'll be fine. Y'all head out, but, for goodness sake, make sure you don't pull into Shady Acres at the same time. That would wreck our planning."

Jim asked Ruth for the keys so he could open the trunk. "Why don't you leave it all in there, since we'll be doing this again," she said, leaving her car idling.

With an amenable shrug, Jim waved to the ladies, sauntered over, and climbed into his grandson's car. With a tap on the side of his nose, Jim grinned at everyone as his grandson started up his car and drove off.

"Do you want us to wait with you?" Joanne said, out her open window.

"Ah, I'm good. If Devon doesn't show up, I'll call a cab or something. Maybe I'll jog back," Paul said.

"It'd be faster for you to crawl," Ruth yelled, and Joanne laughed.

"Thanks for the vote of confidence."

Paul leaned down to the passenger window and looked in at Joanne. "That had to be a terrible way to lose your husband. The sudden randomness of it all."

She nodded. "No one could dispute he cared deeply about the residents of Shady Acres. In fact, he mostly called them friends instead of residents or tenants. He was that kind of man."

Paul nodded, imagining that he probably would have liked Martin, given the chance. And a time machine. Then Paul stood up, tapped on the top of the car and stepped back.

"Ok, that should be enough time between Jim and you two."

"See you at breakfast, Paul," Joanne said with a smile, as Ruth rolled out onto the road at her usual leisurely pace. Paul watched them drive off in the opposite direction to Jim's grandson, then stepped back and opened his cell phone. No new messages.

Paul sat down on an old stump and glanced down the empty road. *It was all well and good to be calm and cool with the women and Jim,* he thought, *but if Devon doesn't show up soon, I'll be in a heap of trouble with Kevin, and then no more days out like today. Damn kids, can't trust them to be where they're supposed to be.* Paul paused and realized he was the one three hours late to be picked up, so who was he to complain about not being where he was supposed to be?

After checking his cell phone again and finding no messages, Paul considered calling his daughter but decided against it. No point in stirring it up with her, given what she's going through. *I'll take the heat, no matter which way it comes,* Paul thought.

Paul put his thoughts of Kevin's retribution away and spent the next five minutes reminiscing about their wonderful day on the river until Devon pulled off the road in a skid of gravel and a cloud of dust. Paul coughed and waved the cloud away, then stood up. Devon leaned out the driver's window and blurted, "Sorry Gramps, totally lost track of time and had my phone on silent so your text didn't show up until ten minutes ago, then I had to go home to grab the van and so I booked it over here instead of texting you."

As Devon took a deep breath after finishing his high-speed monologue, Paul shook his head and walked slowly around to the passenger side of the van. "I wasn't worried. I knew you wouldn't let your only living grandparent down." Paul pulled open the van door and stopped suddenly. Instead of an empty seat, a beautiful brunette teenage girl sat there. A teenage girl he recognized. Taking a step back, Paul said, "You're Joanne's granddaughter, right?"

"Yes. Hi, I'm Dawn." Paul shook her hand then pulled the sliding back door open. "Oh, I'll move back there," Dawn said, quickly as Paul slowly climbed inside the back of the van.

"Oh no, the girl gets the shotgun seat. I know the rules."

Devon leaned back through between the front seats. "I know the rules too, parents beat dates."

"Oh, so this is a date?" Paul said, with a smile.

"Uh—"

"A surprise date," Dawn said, shyly.

"The best kind," Paul said and leaned back in his seat. "Home, James, but once through the park. You know how I love the park."

The kids laughed, and then Devon double-checked his mirrors before pulling out onto the road.

Ten minutes of smooth driving and stilted conversation—*it seemed the two teens were completely unable to speak in full sentences with me in the car,* Paul thought. *Or maybe that's the way they always talked.* Must be exhausting keeping up with what's being discussed. Much better to let someone talk too long, but without interruption, than this non-stop ping pong tournament of sentence snippets.

Growing up, it had been different. At the dinner table, once you got the floor, you kept it, knowing no one would interrupt until you were completely done. The down side was listening to his older sister's recitation of every aspect of her day once she took control of the conversation.

As they made their way closer to the home, Paul leaned forward and interrupted some discussion of either a new film or a new song, and said, "Now, Dawn, I need your help with something."

"Oh sure, Mr. Carter, whatevs."

"As far as your wonderful father knows, I spent the afternoon with my grandson, not you."

"How come?" Dawn asked, confused.

"I'm taking a risk telling you this, ok? But I'm going to because I'm willing to trust you. You could get me in trouble and possibly kicked out of Shady Acres if you actually tell your father what you did this afternoon."

"I don't understand. What does it matter where you were or who you were with?"

"Because I snuck off with some friends, including your grandmother."

Shocked silence from the front seat. Paul looked at Devon in the rearview mirror and saw the concern in his eyes. Then Devon said, "It was a surprise, Gramps. She showed up at my house. I wasn't going to say no."

"Of course, you wouldn't! I didn't raise an idiot."

Paul turned to Dawn. "So, you see my problem?"

Dawn nodded and looked at them both. "You told my dad you were with Devon. But you were with my grandmother—"

"Not alone. With friends—"

"And friends. But then I messed everything up by surprising Devon."

"Oh, no! Hanging out, the two of you at Devon's place where no one could see you, that's completely fine. Are you crazy?" Paul said.

Dawn and Devon looked at each other with concern. Paul looked back and forth between the two serious faces. "What? What am I missing here?"

Devon looked back at the road, and Dawn turned around looking at Paul. "We were at the diner."

"Where you were seen by people."

The teens nodded.

"People who know your parents."

Dawn nodded.

"And who might mention seeing you on a date with my grandson when Devon should have been at home working on a project with me."

"I'm really sorry, Mr. Carter."

Paul leaned back in dismay and rubbed his chin, hoping to spur an idea to get them out of their dilemma. "Ok, not a problem."

"Uh, a problem is exactly what it is," Devon said, despairingly. "Especially with Dawn in the van when we drop you off."

To make matters worse, Devon turned, passed the majestic Shady Acres sign, and started down the long driveway. "Should I stop and let her out?"

"Too late for that. Keep driving," Paul said, still thinking furiously. "Ok. Here's what happened. We finished the project really quickly. I stayed at the apartment with Natalie, Devon's mother, my daughter."

Dawn nodded. "Yeah, we met."

Paul gave a nod back then continued, "Exactly. That's when you two met up. As long as we're vague about the times, we should be good."

"That won't hold up under any light, Gramps. What if her dad talks to my mom?"

"I know, but what else have we've got? So, Dawn, are you in? Ready to join our little conspiracy?"

Dawn looked across at Devon, who nodded supportively to her, and then she turned and nodded to Paul.

"Good. Then we've nothing to worry about."

Devon pulled up under the portico, immediately behind Jim's grandson. Before he could open Paul's door, a honk came from behind and Ruth pulled up.

Paul groaned and muttered, "Nothing to worry about except this. All of us arriving back at the exact same moment. Marcus we should be able to deal with. And speak of the devil…"

They watched as Marcus came out of the lobby and opened the large car door for Joanne. As he did, Marcus made eye contact with both Paul and Jim. "Gentlemen, quite the day for coincidences."

"It most certainly is," Jim said, tapping the top of his grandson's car and stepping back as Eric drove off. "You have a quiet afternoon while we were gone, Mister Marcus?"

"Quiet as the eye of a hurricane, Mr. Jim."

Jim smiled and walked under the portico, arriving at the doors in time to hold it open for Joanne. As he did, Jim turned and started to tap the side of his nose, but noticed Dawn in the passenger seat of Devon's van. Instead, Jim rolled his eyes in dismay before following Joanne inside, saying, "Were you able to get Ruth's curtain's finished, Joanne?"

Paul climbed from the van and gave his grandson a quick hug as Marcus, still watching, returned to his desk. Over Devon's shoulder, Paul winked at Dawn, and said, "Hopefully, Dawn, your father has already gone home. That was a bit messy us arriving back at the same time from three different places, but looks like we're going to pull this off."

"I promise I'll stick to the story."

Paul gave her a quick wink. "I'll owe you. Both of you."

"Nice meeting you, Mr. Carter."

"Nice meeting you, too, Dawn," Paul said and strolled inside as Devon hopped in the van and drove off at a calm, respectable pace.

•

From his office, Kevin watched the lobby security camera on his computer. He flicked through to the cameras installed in the portico and watched as his daughter drove off with Paul's grandson. Immediately behind them sat Ruth in her beast of a car. Kevin switched back through the cameras until he found Jim and Paul exiting the elevator and walking, slowly, down the hallway to their rooms.

If I had upgraded the cameras to have audio, Kevin thought angrily, *then I'd know exactly what happened.* At no point did he believe the three were not together, but they were slippery enough to come across like nothing had happened. *Now I'll have to have a chat over tea with my mother and find out what happened,* Kevin decided, as he watched Joanne enter the dining room and cross over to join The Bees. He switched off the camera program, leaving an elaborate spreadsheet open on the monitor.

He stared at it while thoughts bounced around in his head before becoming fed up and quitting out of Excel. Time to go home and have a glass—or two—of wine. And try to dig some answers out of his daughter about why she was consorting with that troublemaker's grandson. As he packed up, he remembered that Beth was angry with him about returning to work. He sighed in frustration.

My wife, my mother, and my daughter—all causing me trouble!

Twenty Eight

Grabbing his briefcase, Kevin left his office and walked out into the foyer. He nodded to Marcus, still at his post, then started towards the front doors. Outside, his car waited—and then it was home to an angry wife and a secretive daughter. That thought slowed his pace considerably as he walked across the parking lot. Hopefully, a bottle of wine would be waiting, too. He unlocked his car with a chirp and put his briefcase in the backseat before settling into the driver's seat.

He put the key in ignition and some old Bon Jovi song blared out of the stereo speakers. Instead of turning it down, Kevin turned it up and sat immersed in the testosterone wailing of guitars and drums. His hands gripped the steering wheel as he let the thundering bass shake the car down to its shocks. And then, with a final wail and scream, the song ended. Kevin turned down the volume before an advertisement for home appliances threatened to burst his eardrums. *I remember liking music,* he thought. *I used to have it on constantly, but now it's one more thing to distract me from what needs to get finished every day.*

He sighed, considered what song he'd like to hear right at that moment-maybe some more Bon Jovi, or Tom Petty-then climbed out of his car, locked it up, and walked back across the parking lot into the home.

Marcus looked up in surprise as Kevin entered the building, "You forget something, Mister Kevin?" he asked, standing up behind his desk.

Kevin nodded, not smiling. "I'm going to go talk to my mother for a moment."

Marcus nodded and sat back down. *No, sir, it can't be pleasant having to go and grill your mother to find out what she had gotten up to today,* Marcus thought as Kevin walked down the hallway toward the dining room.

Kevin already knew his mother was with The Bees, so he cut straight across the dining room to their table without needing to glance around. Everyone looked up and said hello to him, and Kevin smiled back, ever the polite general manager.

"Mom, could I have a quick word with you?"

"Oh, of course, dear," Joanne said, and he helped her up from the table. They strolled outside onto the patio and Joanne sat down on a bench facing the expansive lawn.

"How was your day with Ruth?" he asked, pointedly.

"Oh, quite nice. She's such a good hostess," Joanne replied, airily.

"Yes, it looks like you got some sun today. Sewing those drapes in her backyard, were you?"

Without missing a beat, Joanne smiled and touched her cheek as if to prove to herself she had gotten a bit of sun. "We did take our midday meal on her patio, Kevin. But we didn't drag the sewing machine outside if that's what you're asking." She laughed at her comment.

Kevin sighed in frustration and tried a different approach. "Quite the surprise with Paul and Jim both arriving back at the same time you did, isn't it?"

Joanne frowned. "I didn't see you in the lobby, how did you know we had arrived at the same time?"

"Mom," Kevin snapped, upset his mother caught him apparently spying on her, "were you really with Ruth all day?"

"Darling, of course I was. I wouldn't lie to you, although I'm not sure I appreciate either the tone or the accusation you're implying."

Kevin turned away in exasperation. "I can't be worried about you and who you're hanging out with, Mother! There's too much to keep track of, and still trust you're not getting into trouble!"

"Trouble?" Joanne said with a laugh. "Kevin, I'm eighty years old. I can't get into trouble."

Kevin turned back to her. "I'm not sure I believe that. And what about Dawn with that Carter boy? What's going on there?"

Joanne looked at him in confusion. "What boy are you talking about?"

"Oh, come on. Ruth pulled up right behind them, in that trashy van of theirs. Dawn was in the front seat!"

Joanne stood up slowly. "Kevin, my tea has been delivered, so I am going to go enjoy it before it becomes cold. I suggest you talk to Dawn about what she was doing instead of making up stories. That was always something you got yourself into trouble with as a child."

"I'm not a child anymore, Mom. I have this whole damn place and everyone in it needing looking after. You can't do that if you're a child," he said angrily.

Joanne turned back from the French doors and looked at her angry and frustrated son. "That is true, Kevin. But it doesn't mean those traits simply disappear when you become an adult."

With that comment, Joanne walked back inside to join her friends.

Kevin stood on the patio for a while, staring out at the twilight creeping across the lawn and the trees. The feeling of frustration that had been simmering for a week started to bubble up, threatening to boil over. Keeping everything in control seemed so easy: do the right things and make sure to consider all possible outcomes. But now, everyone seemed to be poking holes in his control.

He took a deep breath and glanced through the patio doors at The Bees chatting away, unconcerned about everything around them. Then he walked around the outside of Shady Acres, unwilling to cross through the dining room and see his mother again today. Once in his car, he kept the radio off and drove home in a stewing silence.

•

"There goes the boss man," Jim said idly as they leaned on their balcony railings and puffed on their cigars. Paul nodded.

"Any interest in heading down for some coffee?"

Jim laughed and patted his belly. "I'm good for the day, possibly the week."

Paul laughed. "I have to admit, you truly aced cooking those fish. Especially using that battered old hibachi of Ruth's. I thought it would collapse into a pile of rust when I dragged it out of her car."

"The quality of the tools matters not to the master chef," Jim proclaimed, and Paul rolled his eyes, shaking his head.

Then Paul paused mid-puff and turned to Jim, "I'm going to ask you a question, ok?"

"As long as the answer is 'The Rock of Gibraltar,' go ahead."

"No, seriously. There's more to the story of how Joanne's husband died, isn't there? Some part you left out. That's why she was so appreciative of how you told me."

Jim sighed a long sigh and took an extended draw on his cigar, then nodded slightly. After a moment to collect his thoughts, Jim said, "The group who were out for the day trip? They were supposed to have a chaperone with them. But he didn't go with them—had other business to do—so let them go off on their own. If he'd been with them, they probably wouldn't have stopped where they stopped, when they stopped. Martin wouldn't have gone looking for them, knowing they had someone responsible with them, and none of what happened would have happened."

Paul thought about everything and shook his head. "Quite the SNAFU."

Jim nodded, looking at Paul. "So you understand, I am telling you this so you don't have to ask Joanne. No need her dwelling on it."

Paul nodded, and Jim continued, "Kevin was in his twenties, home for the summer from business school. That year, he did the job Marcus has now, a little of everything, learning the ropes of how the place ran—not that he wanted to work here, but he was helping out the family, you know?"

"Ok, he worked here for his summer job, so?"

Then Paul's eyes widened, Jim held up his hand to forestall the question and said, "He should have been the chaperone that day. He's the one who skipped out. That's the weight he carries around on his shoulders every moment of every day since he had to quit school and take over the running Shady Acres."

Twenty Nine

Despite a day of uneasy calm at work, Kevin was still late getting home. He arrived just after Dawn. Now, seated around the dining room table, Kevin glanced up from the baked chicken breast with mashed potatoes and spring carrots Beth had made for dinner. *Dry,* he thought, wishing for some gravy—even a thin chicken gravy like his mother made—to moisten up the chicken and potatoes. He sighed and continued eating, chewing in-between sips of a full-bodied Bordeaux Beth had decanted.

Everyone was off in their own thoughts around the table. Kevin mused about the women in his life and how they were conspiring to make his days miserable and utterly confusing. Well, they weren't conspiring together, to the best of his knowledge, although they might as well be.

Across the table, Beth resolutely cut up her chicken—dry because she had to wait until everyone arrived home before putting it on the table—and wished she'd made some gravy. She had tried to fill her days with errands and busyness, but she hadn't enough to do to keep her thoughts off her anger from the previous night and Kevin's never-ending responsibilities at the home. When Dawn was younger, getting her to and from school, after-school activities, and sports kept her on her toes. But now Dawn got herself where she needed to go on her own, leaving Beth feeling rather unnecessary and with lots of time on her hands. The idea of getting some sort of job outside the house had even taken root in her mind. But right now that idea had been pushed aside by her frustration with Kevin.

Maybe making him eat dry chicken is how to get back at him, she thought with a slight smile.

"Mmmm," she said. "This turned out perfect, don't you agree?"

Both Kevin and Dawn nodded, but didn't comment.

"How was your day, Dawn?" she asked and noticed Kevin looking up, attentively.

"Oh, it was fine," Dawn said, not making any eye contact. "No big."

"No big?" Kevin said. "That's good. But how about I ask the same question about yesterday? Driving around with that Carter boy."

"What boy?" Beth asked.

"His last name isn't Carter, Dad. It's Skaarsgard. Like his mom."

"You were hanging out with Devon?" Beth asked, surprised.

Shrugging, Dawn continued eating. Kevin glanced quickly at Beth to try to get her attention, but she ignored him. Instead, Beth said, "And what did you two do?"

"Not much. Devon was doing a project with his grandfather, and after they had finished, we shared a milkshake. Then we drove Paul—his grandfather—back to Shady Acres."

Kevin thought she sounded like she was on the stand in a courtroom, after being coached by the defense lawyers for a week on what to say and how to say it. But before he could formulate a question the front doorbell rang. Everyone shrugged at each other; no one was expecting anybody, so Kevin sighed, rose and headed to the front door to investigate.

"I had no idea you liked someone, Dawn," Beth said under her breath as soon as Kevin stepped out of hearing. "Is he nice?"

Dawn blushed and nodded, "So's his grandfather. He likes Grandma."

"Devon likes Grandma Joanne?"

"Mom! Gross. Devon's grandfather, Paul. He totally likes Grandma. And I'd bet my allowance she likes him too."

"Oh my," Beth said, taking a sip of wine. "That's nothing your father will want to hear."

"Not much he'll be able to do about it," Dawn said with a conspiratorial grin.

When Kevin opened the front door, two primly dressed young Asian women stood in front of him. Both were holding bibles and some pamphlets. Both had large white name-tags with their names engraved in both English and Chinese in black. As soon as he opened the door, Kevin wished he'd checked through the front window before opening it. But a couple of glasses of wine and two testy women in the dining room had messed up his thought processes.

"Yes?" Kevin said, knowing what was coming.

"Good evening, sir. We are coming to your neighborhood because we are your missionaries," the first girl said, stiltedly, with a large yet nervous smile.

"Ah. Ok. Right," Kevin said, wishing he either could have his glass of wine or slam the door in their faces. Neither thought won, so he stood there and let them continue.

"We are here tonight to tell you about Jesus Christ and what his teachings could mean to you."

Enough, Kevin thought, but let them both keep on talking while he pondered what had brought them from the other side of the planet to his doorstep.

Finally, he interrupted the first girl and asked, "How long have you been here, in America? In North Carolina?"

"Oh," the first girl, Sister Xhia, said in surprise. "I have been here for only four weeks. But I will be in America for one and a half years!"

"From where?" Kevin asked. "How did you end up here?"

"Oh. I am from Mainland China. We both are. Our church in Hong Kong has sent us here to be missionaries." She smiled at him.

"Honey, who's at the door?" Beth called from the other end of the house. Kevin turned and called back, "Missionaries. From China." After a moment of silence, Dawn called out, "You're cut off, Dad!" Kevin laughed and resumed his conversation with his missionaries.

"I should return to my dinner table or my wife will be angry at me. I wish you all the best for your time in this country."

"Oh, thank you so much. Would you like to have a pamphlet telling you more about the church of Latter Day—"

Kevin cut her off as he started to shut the heavy front door. "Look, I'm happy you have what you have, and I'm satisfied with what I have to believe in, ok? No need for any pamphlets."

And, with a smile, he shut the front door and locked it. After a moment, Kevin peeked through the windows to the side of the door and watched the two girls walk back down their walkway and continue to his neighbor's, the Mitchelson's. *Good luck there*, he thought. *They're going to react like the racists they are and spray you down with the garden hose.* Shaking his head in amazement, Kevin walked back to join his family in the dining room. And his glass of wine. And his angry wife and his deceitful daughter.

Beth and Dawn stopped talking as Kevin sat down and the three returned to eating their meals in silence. After a moment, Kevin took a gulp of wine and topped up his glass before taking a deep breath. "In case anyone is wondering, those really were Chinese missionaries at the door. Wanting to save me; save us."

"I bet they were persecuted back home, but they escaped, and that's why they're here where they are free to believe whatever they want to believe," Dawn said, her eyes alight with youthful excitement. "Did you grab any of their handouts?"

"You wanted one of their booklets, Dawn? What's next, you're going to go to their temple or church or whatever they call it and start taking classes?" Kevin said, sharply.

"No. I was curious what they had to say. Besides, Pastor Alistair says learning about other religions and beliefs is perfectly fine," she parried back.

"A couple of sessions and they'd have you under their thumb, and then you'd be out with them going door-to-door helping people to find the way, their way."

"Kevin!" Beth said sharply. "That's enough. Just because she's the least bit curious about another religion is no reason to accuse her of wanting to join a cult!"

"Yeah!" Dawn joined in.

Kevin stared at the two, glaring back at him. "I didn't mean she would join a cult; you're putting words in my mouth! I meant that she's not the most discerning about who she considers friends, and she could be drawn into situations where she could end up in a lot of trouble." Then he leaned back in his chair and had a celebratory drink of wine. *Nicely put*, he thought while savoring the Bordeaux. *No way to argue with that logic.*

Beth took a long slow breath, leaned forward on the table, took a sip of her wine, and said, "Do enlighten me, Kevin, on what you're talking about."

"Me, too," Dawn said, with the hurt only a teenaged girl could put into those two words.

"Fine," Kevin said and put down his wine glass. "Our lovely daughter spent the yesterday with that boy who got her into trouble at school. The one who 'claimed' spilling a full cup of soda on a teacher was an 'accident.' The one whose grandfather is the current bane of my existence."

Beth turned to Dawn with a stern face. Dawn braced herself to be caught in the parental crossfire but instead her mother's face softened, and she said, "Is he nice to you?"

"Yeah..."

"Beth!" Kevin barked. "He's trouble! And she shouldn't be seeing him. At all."

"Dad! We're not like dating or anything! God!"

"Good. Then I stopped it before it went too far. There. That's done. We don't need to talk about it again."

He picked up his cutlery and started eating his forgotten dinner. Kevin chewed on the cold, dry chicken while two of the women in his life stared at him. *They're realizing I'm right,* he thought, battling on a particularly tough piece of meat.

Finally, Dawn opened her mouth and said, "You've gotta be kidding! You can't tell me who I'm friends with! I'm seventeen years old! I could run off and join the Army!"

Kevin sighed—outright shock wasn't what he had expected.

"As long as you live in this house, you will live by our rules, young lady."

"Oh. My. God. Do you hear yourself? Did your dad say that same thing to you when you were seventeen? I bet he did! And I bet it was because of some girl, too! You are such a hypocrite!" And with that damning stab, Dawn pushed away from the table and stormed out of the room. Kevin continued chewing while she stomped up every stair, down the upstairs hallway, and slammed the door to her room.

"She'll understand once she calms down," Kevin said, removing a mouthful of chewed up chicken from his mouth and hiding it in his napkin.

"Do you really believe that, Kevin? When your father yelled those exact words at you, did you stop seeing me?"

"That was different..."

Beth looked at him appraisingly. "Again, do you really believe that? What was different? Boy and girl like each other. Parents don't want them to be together. Damnit, we are not the Montagues, and Devon is not a Capulet! They're teenagers. Exactly like we were, or don't you even remember that?"

Beth finished off her wine, left the table a bit unsteadily, and stomped up the stairs, down the hallway, and slammed the door to their bedroom.

Before him the remains of dinner were spread across the table. He reached for the wine bottle, but it was empty. *What the hell is going on with my life?* Kevin wondered. *Doesn't Dawn understand that boy is trouble? Of course she does, and that's why she likes him. Like my mother likes Paul. This is bullshit. And I'm so goddamn tired of it.* He headed into the den to pour himself a tumbler of his good bourbon.

They believe in saying whatever they want, and doing whatever they want, and that I'll lay back and do nothing, he fumed, between sips of Maker's Mark. *But they're wrong. I'm more trouble than they realize, especially when backed into a corner.*

Kevin took a long, hard drink, shuddered as the liquor burned his throat, then returned to the dining room and started clearing the table.

Thirty

By the time he finished his third coffee of the morning, Kevin had the newest rules drawn up and lying on his desk, straight from the printer in the corner of his office. Beth had overturned the edict he had laid down at dinner the previous night by the time he had gotten the kitchen cleaned up.

"No way we are going to ban Dawn from seeing someone because you don't like his grandfather, Kevin. My father wasn't particularly pleased with you when he found out we were together." Beth had said stonily from her side of the couch.

"Your father loved me," Kevin replied.

"Not to begin with. So, let that be a lesson for you about obeying your parent's decisions regarding who you like and who you don't." Then she turned up the television and stopped speaking to him.

Of course he had a say in who his only daughter dated, but, obviously, he should have been a lot more proactive about breaking up Dawn and Devon before they had a chance to become too attached to each other. So he had acquiesced to Beth, despite disagreeing with her—but even that hadn't made anyone happy and this morning's breakfast had been a meal of sullen silence. Clearly, he'd have to be smarter about getting his way and breaking the two up.

"Suzanne," he called out to his receptionist, "could you copy this and have it placed in the rooms and common areas?" He turned back to the spreadsheet on the computer as Suzanne came in and quietly picked up the printed page.

"Thank you, Suzanne," Kevin said tersely, already engrossed in the reams of numbers scrolling across his screen.

•

Suzanne nodded and removed herself from Kevin's office and walked down the hallway to the copier room. As she began to go in, she saw Marcus at the end of the hall and waved for him to join her. Puzzled, he straightened his suit jacket and strolled down to meet her. As soon as he got close enough, she grabbed his arm, pulled him into the copier room and shut the door behind them.

Marcus regarded her with a surprised look. "Damn girl, do I have to tell you again? I'm in a relationship."

Rolling her eyes, Suzanne pushed him away, back against the storage shelves, and said, "For the last time, I didn't know you were with anyone when I made that 'suggestion.'"

Marcus laughed. "All right, all right. So why are we hiding in here like kids then?"

Without a word, Suzanne handed Marcus the page with Kevin's new rules. He took it and started frowning while skimming it, and then he looked up at her in alarm. She nodded and said, "Hot off the presses. I'm supposed to copy it and have it delivered to everyone."

"Well, hell, no one is gonna be happy with any of this."

"Especially us staff," she added, shaking her head in disgust. "How about you go talk to Kevin, convince him to back off on implementing them for a while? Like until he forgets about them, or I retire?"

Marcus wiped his brow and thought about what Suzanne suggested. "He's not gonna listen to me. He's pissed about something, and he's taking it out on everyone else."

"But what? Other than that food fight, I thought the place was running smoothly. The books look good; we're not in money trouble, if that's what he's concerned about."

Waving off her interrupting train of thought, Marcus paced around the tiny room, trying to make sense of events. Suzanne continued, worried, "Oh, his mother will pitch a fit over this."

Stopping suddenly, Marcus turned from staring at a stack of empty file folders and said, "Joanne. Yes, of course. The curfew…" He put the pieces together while Suzanne stared at him, awaiting some explanation, then he said, "He's angry at his mother, and at his daughter, because of yesterday."

Suzanne took the paper back, put it into the copier and typed in the appropriately large number of copies. Punching the start button hard, she turned back to Marcus as the machine whirred and chunked to life.

"What happened yesterday that could be such a big deal?"

While the copier spat out page after page, Marcus explained about the 'coincidental' excursions of Joanne, Paul, and Jim—along with Paul's return with Kevin's daughter in the van. Suzanne shook her head in dismay, "What a mess. I bet he tried to lay down some rules last night and ended up sleeping on the sofa. He certainly didn't look his usual dapper self this morning. So what are we going to do about this?" She pointed at the growing stack of copies in the machine.

Marcus sighed and shook his head. "Not much we can do, except brace ourselves."

"I still believe you could go and talk to him."

Marcus laughed darkly and opened the door to the hallway. "I'm not saying I love my job, but it's the only one I have so there's no way I'm gonna talk to Kevin about this. Maybe once I get my diploma and I'm ready to move on. Catch ya on the flipside, Suzanne."

•

Most everyone in the home had gotten their copy of the new rules by lunch time. The staff weren't making any eye contact and were simply doing their jobs, avoiding being drawn into any conversations about the new rules.

"A complete pile of bull—well, you know exactly what these new rules are a pile of," Paul said in disgust.

The Bees and Jim nodded and continued perusing their menus. Complaining around a meal table wasn't going to change any of the rules.

Then their waitress, Grace, stepped up beside the table and said, quietly, "I'm sorry, but two of you will have to move to a different table."

They looked at each other in confusion, "And why would we want to do that?" Jim asked.

"The new rules. A maximum of five in any group, anytime anywhere."

"Oh, that's ridiculous," Joanne said, picking up her copy and reading through it again.

"Where exactly does it say Paul and I are not allowed to sit with these five lovely ladies, exactly?" Jim demanded. Grace unhappily pointed at the fourth paragraph on Joanne's paper. Jim leaned over, put on his reading glasses and skimmed the words, then leaned back and looked at her. "To be clear to the letter of this law, Paul and I are a group of two, and they are a group of five." Jim smiled lawyerly at their waitress.

Angrily, Grace said, "You're at the same table, that means you're the same group. That's what the rule says, so either split the group up or I will have to make a note in each of your files and call the boss."

Joanne could see that Paul was ready to revolt and chain himself to their table in protest, so she reached over and placed a calming hand on his arm. "We'll figure this out, Paul."

He scowled at her, but released the tension in his shoulders, picked up his coffee cup and took a sip instead of speaking. Joanne smiled at Grace and said gently, "I'm sure there will be some easing in of the rules, won't there? We could promise to eat dinner in the appropriate numbers if you'd like."

"You think I like this? I get paid to serve you food, not be some sort of warden! But that's the rule, so move now. Or the kitchen manager comes out, fires me, and has you written up. Is that what you want? I need this job. So, come on."

In silence, Paul pushed back from the table and stormed over to an empty table for two on the far side of the room. Jim then smiled at the ladies. "Ladies, dining with you was *almost* a pleasure." Grace put their coffee cups on her tray and followed Jim across to join Paul.

"Joanne, someone simply must go and give your son a stern talking to," Hazel said, worried.

"With a strap!" Lillian said, and the women laughed darkly, except for Joanne.

It wasn't possible for Kevin to know they had been together at the river, she thought worriedly. *Other than arriving back at the same time, no one knew...* Then she remembered seeing her granddaughter in front of Paul's grandson's vehicle. Oh no, Paul would have told Dawn not to talk about where they were, wouldn't he? Joanne glanced around the room, but couldn't see Paul or Jim. Instead, she saw Chuck seated with his boys. Feeling guilty for not spending much time with him of late, she gave him a wave that he returned with a smile. *He's a little boy sometimes,* she thought, *and despite how nice he is to me, I believe our time as a couple has come to an end.*

She snickered to herself; she sounded exactly like she had in high school—fickle with her attention to whoever attracted her the most on a near month-to-month basis, if not week-to-week. Not that there was much to any of the dating at that time—some hand holding, some book carrying, a bit of kissing. No getting to any base, thank you very much.

Not until Martin caught her eye in their senior year. Then, despite Martin not being on any sports team or a show off of any sort, Joanne was smitten by his nervous smile to her across the cafeteria. And, much to her and her friends' surprise, they had been inseparable from the moment he had asked her to dance that evening at a school dance. His calm, quiet nature was the perfect balance for her outgoing personality and she still missed him.

Joanne brought herself back to the table and rejoined the conversation on how best to punish Kevin for his latest unreasonable rule. The current favorite suggestion was actually to tar and feather him. Favored by Frances, of course. Joanne bit her tongue, looked at her lunch menu, and let the rest of The Bees carry on planning tortures for her only son.

•

That evening, Paul and Jim stared out at the sun fading behind the trees at the edge of the property from their balconies, cigars in hand.

"Wonder when the barbed wire fences are going to go up…" Jim muttered.

Paul looked over at him appraisingly and then said, "Lord, this isn't going to end well if you're now the cynical one."

Jim laughed sharply "It will end the same way for each of us."

Paul shook his head. "It's official. I have to be the beacon of light around here from now on. You've gone over to that Dark Side Devon keeps on about. Either I join you there, or pull you back to the light."

Jim ignored Paul's ribbing and continued to stare out at the distant trees, a scowl on his face.

"I simply do not see how management believes these random, irrational rules will make anything better around here," Jim said, then took a draw on his cigar. "They are, in essence, tightening up the screws on the lid of the pressure cooker while at the same time turning up the temperature."

"I ain't gonna argue with you; it's a right mess. But hopefully this will get it out of Kevin's system, then the reins will loosen up again."

"Doubt it," Jim said, butting out his cigar before he entered his room without saying good night. Paul watched him leave, then turned back to staring out at the twilight.

As he looked out, Paul thought about everything that had happened since he'd arrived at the home. A hell of a lot of changes, not many of them I have any interest in. It would be so much better to be back on his farm, even if he couldn't work on it, even if he could barely drive himself into town, even if he fell down the front stairs and wasn't found until he was long dead. It would be better than this prison.

He sighed and tried to enjoy his cigar for a time, but realized a cigar without a friend wasn't worth the band he'd peeled off it. So he butted his out, collected the ashes, and, after carefully flushing the evidence down the toilet, sadly climbed into bed with a marginally interesting book about the sinking of the German battleship Bismarck during the Second World War.

Thirty One

The hallway of the high school filled with an explosion of noise and hormonally imbalanced humanity within moments of the bell ringing. Devon managed to flow with the crowds past a long row of classrooms, down a flight of stairs, and to his locker outside the Home Economics room without any drama. *I'm finally one more of the faceless hordes,* Devon thought. *No special treatment anymore, thank God.* He spun his lock, opened his locker and exchanged his last class' textbook for his next class' binder. Then, after double-checking his timetable to make sure he remembered it correctly, he slammed his locker door to find Dawn leaning against the wall.

"Hey!" he said in surprise, "You…"

"Yup, it's me. Happy I'm here?" Dawn said. Devon nodded and, impulsively, leaned in and kissed her quickly, right on the lips. Then he leaned back, suddenly doubting to the core of his being what he had done. Around them, students rushed from one class to the next, oblivious to everything except themselves. Devon looked at Dawn, his face impassive, but his mind frantically attempting to come up with any explanation for his impulsiveness. Then Dawn blushed, leaned forward and kissed him back. It was a quick kiss also, not much more than a peck, but it registered and set up permanent residence in Devon's brain. As Dawn leaned back, he took a deep breath and smiled at her, that sweet, full smile she had liked from the first time she'd seen it. A smile that didn't hide anything. That couldn't hide anything.

"Uh. Happy… Yes. Happy you're here, yes," Devon stammered.

Dawn smiled, and then, for no reason, the smile slid off her face, and she said, "Can we talk? Somewhere other than here?"

"Sure," Devon said, instantly transformed from the blissful excitement of their first kiss to catastrophic panic. "The bottom of the stairwell by the janitor's room is quiet."

She nodded, took his hand, and together they walked down the hall, dodging students until they arrived at the stairwell where they descended to the basement and some relative quiet. Once at the bottom of the stairs, Devon paused, wondering if it would be better to sit down or lean against the wall when Dawn sat down and pulled him down with her. They sat for a moment with the sound of hundreds of feet climbing the stairs to other floors and classes above them, their hips and thighs gently touching. Then Dawn let go of Devon's hand and turned to him. "My dad doesn't want us to be together."

Devon stared at her in confusion. They'd kissed and now this? "Why? I seriously don't understand."

Dawn blew out a breath in frustration and said, "Would you believe it's because of your grandfather?"

"Say what?"

"My dad says you're trouble, like your grandfather. I don't know what he thinks of your mother. Probably that she's trouble, too, or maybe she's the poor woman stuck with both of you. I mean, so what, so my grandma likes your grandfather? What are we like suddenly so puritan that we won't let people over eighty date? That's so totally ridiculous…"

"My gramps is dating your grandmother?"

Dawn shrugged. "I suppose so, the way my dad went off at dinner last night. And then he was totally pissed off I was in the van with you at Shady Acres like you were corrupting me or something."

Devon leaned back, his head spinning. Dawn sighed and leaned back as well. Together, they stared across at the door leading to the maintenance room.

"So, he hates me because he hates my grandfather."

Dawn nodded. "Yeah. My dad's so old sometimes. Paul's way younger than him, in attitude, you know?"

"Jesus, what do we do? This is crazy!" Devon said, standing up in utter impotent frustration. "And it's not my grandfather; your dad hates me because of that bullshit accident. He decided I'm trouble right there in the principal's office, and that was it for him. He isn't going to change his mind about me. We're doomed."

"Devon," Dawn said, gently. "I like you, ok? This is my life and your life. We're not cogs in their lives. We decide to be who we want to be. And do what we want to do."

"But I don't want you being in trouble because of me! And I don't want your dad to take it out on my gramps because he doesn't like me... because I like... really like you."

Dawn stood up, wiped a tear from her eye and stepped up close to Devon. Then she opened her arms and hugged him. He hugged her back, imprinting the experience of her body deep in his memory.

"You're a good guy, Devon," she whispered in his ear. "That's good enough for me."

He leaned back and looked down into her wide, wet eyes through his wide, wet eyes. Then they kissed. And they kissed again, the kiss of star-crossed lovers, the kiss of pop-song teen passion. They kissed until the final bell rang, then once more, before running up the stairs to their separate classes.

•

"So," Chuck said as he stood at the edge of The Bees' table that evening at dinner. "we're back to waving at each other."

"Sorry, Chucky," Helen said with her trademark snarl. "Only allowed five at a table now, so run along to your pups."

"Helen," Joanne said, "that's quite enough."

Helen clucked her tongue and returned to talking to Frances, both darting squinty glances at Chuck. Joanne turned back to Chuck and smiled, hoping to take the edge off Hazel's comments. But he continued looking down at her with a stony face.

"You having 'fun' with Paul, now?"

"I don't know what you mean, Chuck. He's a nice man, and he's new here at the home. One must be polite."

"Bull. I know you've been together, meeting up outside good old Shady Acres."

Damnit, Joanne thought quickly, *he's heard about the fishing trip as well. This place is a sieve…*

"I don't know what you mean."

"You already said that, Joanne. You say that a lot, you know? It wasn't ever a particularly ingenious lie, and it doesn't work now. I know you know exactly what I mean."

"Chuck—" Joanne protested, but Chuck continued, "You go off and fuck around on me with your new beau, and I'm not going to find out? I'm not an idiot!"

The room fell silent. Even the wait staff came out of the kitchen and clustered in the staff area, observing.

"Now, Chuck—"

Chuck waved his hand in her face, silencing her completely. "Don't give me any more words, I've had enough. I'm tired of your words."

"It was a little outing."

"You call it whatever you want. Whatever makes you happy with yourself, you two-timer. You spent high school bouncing from boy to boy, leaving us hanging. Oh, didn't you know we talked about you in the locker room? Oh, we did. Exchanged notes, if you like. Huh, now you're not looking too happy."

In fact, Joanne felt sick to her stomach, but Chuck ignored the distress on her face and the shocked looks of The Bees and continued, "And you know what? I don't care that you're upset. You deserve it."

"How—how did you find out?" Joanne finally said.

"That's what you care about?" Chuck looked down at her in disgust. "Not about me and the feelings I happen to have? Yes, men have feelings! You want to know how I found out? Jesus, you are a piece of work. You witches lording over us from around your steaming kettle, cackling away at our expense."

"Chuck," Joanne said, desperately trying to stop him. "It was only fish—"

"I don't care what you ate! You sneak out and have brunch at the diner together when you were supposed to be here with me! And my daughter saw you there with Paul and Jim, so now you know! There're no secrets in this town, bitch."

And with that, Chuck turned and stormed off through the utterly silent dining room, slamming the door behind him as he left.

Joanne felt the tears start to flow down her face, but brushed away the tissue offered by Frances and let them flow. The heat of Chuck's anger had burnt her badly. She felt the hurt looks of the teenaged boys she'd ever let walk her home on Chuck's face as he had yelled at her. As The Bees tried to comfort her, she rose from the table, struggling with every one of her eighty years and slowly made her way across the still-silent dining room and back to her room. She needed time to be alone.

The sound of her sniffling while alone in the elevator brought back memories of her daughter's pain and sadness after being unceremoniously dumped before junior prom, and how Joanne's attempts to comfort her were futile. Her daughter, Gwen, who now lived out west in Denver and rarely came home, had needed that pain for at least a while, and, despite her mothering instincts of shielding her children from life's pains, Joanne had had to quietly sit on the end of Gwen's bed and let her cry.

Joanne barely made it back into her room and onto her bed before her sniffling turned into unstoppable tears. And cry she did—for herself, for her long-gone husband, for her son trapped in a life beyond her control, and for the future pain and sadness her wonderful granddaughter would inevitably experience. But while she cried, she mostly cried for her own mother, who had passed away over twenty years ago, who wasn't sitting at the end of her bed, silently waiting to comfort her.

Thirty Two

The next morning, Paul sauntered down the hallway toward the elevator trying to work out the tightness and ache in his hip. He'd had a mostly good night's sleep and felt surprisingly refreshed, especially since he had resigned himself to waking up regularly throughout each night. But the price for that refreshing night's sleep was the tightness in his hip from having not moved for the whole night. *If it's not one thing, it's another,* he thought and stretched.

Paul arrived at the end of the hall and pushed the button for the elevator, pondering taking the stairs as he always did, and resigning himself to waiting, as he always did. *No point in causing myself a new bunch of pain climbing down a flight or two of stairs for no particularly good reason,* he thought. It wasn't like there wasn't an elevator for him to use. So Paul waited, glancing over the notice board attached to the wall. No new rules had been added, much to his surprise. Perhaps the clampdown had ended and from now on life would be easier.

Ha, he thought cynically. *Kevin still has a few tricks up his sleeve, and there are still a few more liberties to clamp down on.* At least in the Army, the rules had been created and refined over hundreds of years, there was no disputing them. Rarely were new rules added and even more rarely were old rules removed. Right or wrong, the Army was consistent. And running a farm was the same.

Bob, from across the hall, shuffled up to stand beside him. They greeted each other, then Bob reached forward with his cane and pushed the down button for the elevator.

"Since when do you need a cane?"

Bob rubbed his hip. "I fell out of bed."

"That's a shame."

"Yeah, I was fine until Helen landed on top of me."

"I thought you were dating Marjorie."

"I don't 'date' anyone, Paul. I'm a lone wolf."

Paul snickered, and Bob used his cane to repeatedly push the elevator call button.

"You know pushing it more than once doesn't make any difference, right?" Paul said.

Bob shrugged and hit the button a few more times. He said, "If it makes no difference, I'll keep hitting it then."

And Bob did until the elevator pinged and the doors opened. The two entered and pushed the button for the main floor. Muzak played softly; a bastardization of a Beatles song. Bob sighed and turned toward Paul and said, "Quite the dust up last night."

Paul nodded, distracted by attempting to sort out which song was being butchered through the speakers, then looked at Bob.

"Dust up?"

Bob nodded sagely. "Oh yes. Possibly the most impressive dressing down I have ever seen. And I was a Marine. I've been yelled at by the best."

"That's a shame," Paul said, to keep the conversation going.

Bob shook his head, sadly. "Sounded like she deserved it, not that I know the whole story, but still, you don't dress down a woman, not like that. There are rules, you know?"

Paul nodded. There were rules: no yelling and no hitting. There's a code and, apparently, he and Bob followed the same one. Those rules were sacrosanct.

"What poor woman got that kind of abuse? And who gave it to her?" Paul asked as the elevator arrived on the main floor.

"Joanne Wright. How's that for a surprise? Yup. Chuck really gave it to her—verbally of course—but he sure was worked up about it."

The doors to the elevator opened, and Bob started out. Paul didn't move. He stood in the elevator, still as a statue. Bob turned, looking back at him. "Paul? Hello?"

It took Paul a moment to come back and then he said, "I forgot something. In my room."

Bob shrugged and started down the hallway toward the dining room. Paul paused for a moment, holding the door open. The fight must have happened after he and Jim had left the dining room. Damnit, Kevin's stupid new rule meant he hadn't been there to defend Joanne from Chuck. That cowardly son-of-a-bitch. Paul took a breath and pushed the button for the third floor.

Paul started out when the elevator door opened, only to find Jim standing in front of him.

"Already done with breakfast?"

Paul shook his head and stepped back inside. Jim joined him and the doors shut.

"So," Jim said, "entertaining yourself with riding the elevator up and down?"

Paul shook his head, silently, as the elevator rose to the third floor. Jim looked at him, slightly confused, slightly in need of his morning coffee. When the doors opened on the third floor, Paul stepped out and started down the hallway. Jim leaned out and called to him, "I'll see you for breakfast?"

Paul waved over his head and kept walking. Jim sighed and pushed the button for the main floor. He didn't know what was going on in his friend's head, but he was happy, this time, to be clear of whatever it was. *I'll find out at some point,* Jim thought, as the elevator slowed and stopped to let on residents on the second floor who were utterly confused by Jim already being on the elevator since he lived on the same floor as them. Jim sighed again and leaned against the wall for the rest of the journey, ignoring the pointed stares. *They believe I have been off carousing on three,* he thought. *Now there's going to be rumors setting the woods alight. Lord, this place is as bad as a high school...*

Paul walked down the hallway and stopped outside Chuck's door. He took a deep breath, trying to calm the fury that boiled within. But a half-dozen breaths didn't take the edge off that anger, so Paul stepped forward and pounded on the door. From within he heard Chuck call out, so he stepped back and flexed his fists. Yelling at a woman... Yelling at Joanne... Paul took another deep breath as he heard the lock turn and the door opened. Chuck stood in front of him, a bright yellow Izod golf shirt with the collar flipped up and plaid chinos on.

"What the hell do you want?" Chuck snarled at him.

Paul's calm broke, he grabbed Chuck by the throat and pushed him back into his room, kicking the door shut behind him.

"What the hell!" Chuck gasped, fighting to pull Paul's grip off his throat. Once inside, Paul released Chuck and stepped back. The lunge had done a number on his hip, but he used his anger toward Chuck to push away the pain. Paul watched as Chuck staggered back and sat down on the couch, gasping for a full breath. *Never been under any physical pressure,* Paul thought. He stepped forward wielding his cane up over his head, and leaned down over Chuck. Calling forth the full weight of his Army command days, Paul glared at him, his blue eyes suddenly sharp with menace.

"You crazy fool!" Chuck said, tipping back on the couch to be as far away from Paul and those cold eyes as possible.

"Yeah. I am, I reckon. Crazy because I've nothing to lose. Crazy because I have a code, and my code says you don't yell at women. But you don't have that code, do you? No," Paul said harshly, answering his own question. "No, to you that's acceptable. Make a woman cry, in public; that's what makes you feel like a damn man, right?"

"I don't know what you're talking about…"

"Sure, and I'm going round the world on Christmas Eve delivering presents to little girls and boys. Everyone in the dining room saw and heard you."

Chuck had shuffled himself along the couch to be as far away from Paul as possible and wedged himself into the farthest corner. He held a throw pillow in his lap as protection.

"I'm not here to hurt you, Chuck," Paul said, shaking his head. "But if you ever do anything like that again, to anyone, I will hunt you down and I will hurt you. I may be old now, but I have learned many, many ways to hurt a man in my life, and I would get nothing but joy from trying them out on you. Joanne is off limits. Understand?"

Chuck threw the pillow at Paul, but he knocked it away with his cane and it slid under the coffee table. *That's the full extent of his response,* Paul thought, alternating between fury and sadness. *Pathetic.*

"You got out of going to war, didn't you?" Paul asked him.

Chuck nodded, pouting. "It wasn't my fault I was 4F; I had an ulcer."

Paul thought about ripping Chuck to shreds, but instead turned and walked to the door. Only then did he turn and look back. "Remember what I said, 4F. Joanne is off limits. Or I come back and, next time, we don't talk."

Then Paul left the apartment, letting the door slam behind him. His hip throbbed painfully from pushing Chuck. He leaned back against the wall as a sharp stab radiated down his leg. Damnit, trying to stop violence with violence. Again. Idiots had always riled him up, ever since grade school, and Chuck was no different. But getting into a physical fight at his age? That was reckless and he could have ended up in the hospital. Paul took another breath and considered going back to his room for some painkillers. Instead, he pushed himself off the wall, gave a final scowl at Chuck's closed door, and shuffled down the hallway to go join Jim for breakfast.

•

The rest of The Bees were finishing up their breakfast and heading up to find Joanne while Paul was having his 'chat' with Chuck. They knew she was in her room, but she hadn't answered their telephone calls—either last night or this morning—so it was time for the women to go to her rescue.

"The best thing we could do is go find that asshole and beat on him with our canes until he's broken to pieces," Helen said with a snarl, pounding her cane against the floor of the elevator.

"Lord, Helen, is that a Christian attitude? Is turning the other cheek completely forgotten?" Hazel said, shocked.

"It is today."

Together they tapped gently on Joanne's door. One by one they called out for her to open it and one by one they received no answer from within.

"We should go. Let's leave her be," Hazel said, timidly.

"Forget that! What if she's hurt in there?" Lillian said, turning and pounding on the door loudly. "Listen, Joanne, we don't know if you're dead in there or just sad. So, if you don't come and open this door right now, we will have to go and bring back your wonderful son and his master key. Who would you rather talk to, him or us?"

Lillian leaned back and blew her nose on the hankie hidden in her sleeve. They waited patiently, staring at the closed door before them. After a few minutes, they heard the deadbolt unlock and the door eased open a few inches. None of them could see anything in the gloom within the apartment. Hazel timidly eased the door open, and the four women filed inside. The last one closed the door behind them and, as a group, they entered Joanne's dark living room.

She sat in her comfortable chair, covered with a multicolored afghan, her curly white hair askew. Silently The Bees found seats and waited for Joanne to say something. They waited patiently for quite a while before Helen blew out an exasperated breath and said, "He's a stupid, cruel man, Joannie, who once was charming. Forget him."

The women collectively nodded, most of them had known Chuck since school, the rest only in their time at the home, but they had his number, especially now.

"But he was right," Joanne said, quietly. "I was that kind of girl, back then."

"Oh Lord, we all were," Hazel said, guiltily. "We didn't know any better, any of us."

"And we certainly didn't have any idea that boys thought about anything other than what our parents told us—getting into our skirts."

Joanne shook her head. "No, this is more than that. Honestly, back then I suspected what turmoil I caused and, I'm ashamed to say, I liked the thrill of it. Getting them worked up, that fawning attention…"

Helen stood up and crossed to Joanne, paused, then leaned over and said, "That was over sixty damn years ago. You're making up a story about how you felt when you were sixteen because some lunkhead was hurt. We didn't know anything then about boys and love, and I doubt we know much more about either now," Joanne looked up at her friend, one of her oldest friends, as she continued. "He's upset. Maybe rightfully or maybe not—but if you stay up here, moping in your house robe, you're letting him win. So, let's clean you up and then you'll come downstairs with us, and walk into that dining room as the person you are now—not some flighty, giddy school girl, but as the Queen of The Bees."

Then Helen stood up, crossed her arms and stared at Joanne. One by one the rest of The Bees stood up and joined her, looking down at their friend waiting for her to join them, or tell them to leave.

•

As Jim and Paul walked through the lobby after a mediocre breakfast, they listened in on a crowd of residents berating Marcus about the new rules. Marcus looked under siege, but kept his stern face as impassive as possible. Paul shook his head, and Jim frowned darkly and said, "An ill wind blows here now. We either get out of the way, or we'll be dragged away by it."

"You are quite the beacon of light today, Jim," Paul said with a thin smile, and the two exited the building, crossed the driveway, and walked to a shaded sitting area at the far edge of the property. The adrenalin surge of confronting Chuck was slowly dissipating, but Paul still felt good for getting that anger off his chest. Leave it inside and it will rot you.

Let it go or let it out, he thought, remembering as a teenager how efficiently he could chop firewood when he needed to burn off some anger or frustration. In fact, one fall, he had gotten most of the wood chopped and stacked for winter because some bully had threatened him during a baseball tournament. Instead of throttling the fool right there at second base, he'd kept his cool and watched the same bully strike out at bat and lose the game for his team. Then he'd gone home and turned that anger into four stacked cords of wood.

Once seated, Jim leaned back, wincing until he settled himself into a comfortable position on the wooden bench. He said, "If my body could handle it—which it can't—I'd grab my old pup tent and set up camp over in those woods until this blows over."

Paul nodded, remembering the many times he and his school friends had set out for the weekend with their minimal camping supplies, returning barely in time to clean up and run to school on Monday morning. "Pretty sure there's a rule about no camping on the property."

"Rules about everything now."

They sat in silence, letting the sounds of the forest behind them push away the sounds of the home. After a time, a Mercedes SUV rolled up the drive and stopped under the portico. A well-dressed middle-aged woman entered the building, and then came out with a lady who was clearly her mother. As she started to help her into the passenger seat of the car, Marcus came out with his tablet and spoke to the daughter.

"Uh-oh," Paul said, and Jim looked over at the scene, "someone didn't fill out the right form."

"Forms for everything now," Jim said.

They watched as Marcus made it clear that the woman's mother was not permitted to leave the property, and the woman made it clear she would be taking her mother off property. The poor old woman remained in the middle of the two, buffeted back and forth. Finally, at an impasse, Marcus used his walkie-talkie and shortly Kevin came out of the building, straightening his tie as he crossed to the three.

"Had to call in the heavy guns, Marcus did."

Kevin said a few terse words to the daughter, then took the mother's arm and led her back inside. The woman scowled at Marcus for a moment then stormed around her SUV, climbed in, put it in gear, and floored it—spraying the white crushed stone of the driveway behind her as she drove off. Marcus watched her go, then, in a precise and controlled series of moves, brushed the dust off his lapels, closed his tablet, and slowly walked back inside.

"Wouldn't want to talk to him now," Jim muttered.

Paul whistled in agreement, "Nope. Marcus would cut you to pieces with his eyes. Had a sergeant who could do that. No words, simply those eyes."

"I've been before judges with those eyes. They spoke words— hell, paragraphs—none of which were entered into the court transcript, but clearly understood by everyone in the courtroom."

Paul leaned down and picked up a branch. He picked at the dry bark, peeling it off, but then stopped and threw it back into the bushes behind them.

"Damnit, time for another fishing trip, this tension is killing me."

Jim wiped his brow, sighed and nodded in agreement. "I'm with you, brother."

"Let's get it set up."

Thirty Three

The office fax machine had three filled out excursion forms waiting for Marcus when he arrived the next morning. He took them into the staff room, grabbed a coffee, and then settled in at his desk in the foyer. It was still quiet in the home, only the nocturnal shuffling about quietly. *At least I sleep when I go to bed,* he thought as a couple of women in robes, their hair in curlers, moved slowly through the lobby. He checked who was working the floors, saw it was Janelle and gave her a call. She agreed to come down to ease the two women back to their rooms and into some proper clothes.

After a couple more sips of coffee, Marcus was ready to do some reading on North Carolina Extended Care Guidelines for night school, but the faxes were distracting him. Shutting his textbook, he decided to take a closer look at the faxes. Halfway through the second one, he began to laugh, shaking his head in amazement. By the start of the third, the smile slid off his face as he contemplated the impact of what he held in his hands. A double check of the forms confirmed what he had already suspected—they were completed perfectly, every 'i' dotted, every 't' crossed. But Marcus had to be sure, absolutely sure, because he would be the one who would get reprimanded by Kevin if anything was incorrect, so he grabbed the forms and returned to the main office.

Behind Suzanne's deck, right outside Kevin's office, a row of filing cabinets contained the printed records for the past thirty years of the home. The previous thirty years were in a secure storage two towns over and anything older was kept downtown in the town's museum. Marcus found the cabinet keys in Suzanne's desk drawer, unlocked the first cabinet, and dug through until he found the files he needed. Leaving the cabinet open, he took the files and sat down at Suzanne's desk. After shifting a bit to get comfortable in an unfamiliar chair, he opened the files and double-checked the signatures on the faxes with the authorized person's signatures in the tenant files.

Finding perfect matches to each of the faxes, Marcus frowned— he may have covered for himself, but it didn't mean Kevin wasn't going to be upset when he found out who had requested excursions today. Marcus put everything back in the cabinets, locked them up and returned to his desk and his now cold coffee. Laying the three faxes out on his desk, he studied them like a detective on a cop show. Each signature was legit; each form had been filled out by a different hand with clearly different writing; each—*wait a minute...*

Marcus lined up the three forms on top of each other, and then slid the top two down so he could read the headers printed out by the fax machine. And there it was. Staring back at him. Proof of their collusion. The three forms had been sent, one after the other, from the same phone number. Marcus was surprised Jim hadn't caught that, but he guessed the old guy wasn't as sharp as he had been. It wasn't something most people thought about, that line of information printed at the top of a fax.

Leaning back in his chair, Marcus pondered his discovery. It didn't change whether or not he could deny Joanne, Paul, or Jim their 'individual' outings—their forms were correctly filled out and signed by an authorized person. But it did change what Marcus knew about the three. Whatever doubts he had had the previous week when they left at the same time and coincidentally returned—oh-so-innocently—at the same time, were gone. Clearly, the three were up to something. Again.

Now, he could tell Kevin about his suspicions. Or was it better to keep them to himself? Marcus continued to ponder that while he poured himself another cup of coffee.

•

Two hours later, the home was hopping, within the limits of walkers and canes. Most of the residents were up and either in the dining room or heading there. Despite it being Saturday, Kevin sat in his office, deep in his spreadsheets. Marcus had his list of those residents—including Joanne, Paul and Jim—who had permission to leave the property. At nine o'clock, he turned and looked toward the elevator. The doors opened. Paul and Jim exited and sauntered across the foyer, each looking as innocent as newborn foals. Marcus withheld a smirk and stood up to meet them at the front doors.

"Good morning, Mister Paul. Mister Jim," Marcus said, sweetly.

"And a good morning to you, Mister Marcus," Paul said.

"And where would the two of you gents be off to on this fine day?"

The two looked at each other, then Paul shrugged. "I don't know about my friend here, but I'm going to spend the day with my grandson, another school project he needs help with."

"Hopefully Devon learns to get by on his own before he goes off to university…"

The three laughed heartily at Marcus' joke. Before Jim had a chance to explain what his plans for the day were, they heard a laugh behind them, turned and saw Joanne crossing the foyer with Hazel. Joanne said innocently, "Now where are you boys off to today?"

Marcus had to fight not to laugh out loud as the three played their parts, repeated their lines from their script, each apparently utterly surprised the others were heading out at the same time as they were.

Then Paul looked up at Marcus and said, "Everything in order with our permission forms?"

"Oh yes, they're in perfect order, Paul, Jim, and Joanne. In that exact order, to be precise."

With a final look at each of them, Marcus walked outside, and the three quickly exchanged confused looks about his last pointed comment. Paul finally shrugged his shoulders and followed Marcus, with Jim and Joanne behind him.

•

In his office, Kevin held his office phone to his ear while continuing to type, quietly, on his computer. "So she didn't even tell you where she was going?"

At the other end of the line, Beth replied, "She's probably spending the day with friends, that's what she usually does. I have to say I'm a bit surprised she was up and out before you."

"That's the part that concerns me," Kevin said, then paused. "Hang on a sec."

While Beth waited in their kitchen, Kevin minimized his spreadsheet and brought up the security camera feed. He impatiently switched through the cameras until he found the one looking down at the portico. Idling in front of the door, large as an ocean-going yacht, sat Ruth's old gas-guzzler. Kevin watched as Paul and Jim's grandchildren pulled up and stopped as well.

It was too late for him to run out to talk to his mother, or to spot if Dawn was in Devon's van, so he continued scanning the video feed, looking for any clues. As he watched, Joanne, Paul, and Jim strolled out with Marcus. Then, with innocent waves of goodbye to each other, climbed into their respective cars and were sedately driven off.

"Kevin?" Beth said on the phone. Kevin snapped back from his focus on the computer, fumbled with the receiver then said, "Yes. I'm here. Forget about Dawn. We'll talk to her tonight about what she was doing and how she should be telling us where she is."

"Are you sure?"

"Maybe I'll text her later, see if she can come by and have lunch with me," Kevin said, knowing full well his daughter was either with her grandmother or with that boy. Beth commented that lunch would be nice for the two of them if it worked out, and hung up. Kevin put down the receiver and stared at the screen. After a moment, he switched it over to the camera showing the lobby.

On the video, Marcus walked back inside and sat down at his desk, making a notation on his tablet. Kevin thought for a moment then speed-dialed his phone. When Beth answered he quickly asked the question which had popped into his head, "Did you sign a permission form for my mom to go off today with Ruth?"

On the other end of the line Beth paused, then said, "It might have been a couple of days ago, but yes, I did. Perhaps that's where Dawn is—with Ruth and Joanne?"

"She might be, but I didn't see her in Ruth's car when she was picked up." After mutual assurances that their daughter was surely okay, they both hung up and Kevin returned to his spreadsheets, with only a slight sense of unease still lurking in the back of his mind.

•

"Take your time," Paul said to Devon once they were away from the home. "Ruth doesn't drive more than twenty miles an hour." Devon laughed and then turned left when Paul expected him to go straight. "Where are we going?" he asked.

Devon said, "I gotta pick up something. Won't take more than a minute, then we'll go meet your friends."

Paul frowned, then gave up worrying, leaned back in the seat, and enjoyed being away from the home. *Only five minutes away and already my tension is fading,* he thought with a smile.

After a couple more minutes of driving, Devon pulled up outside the main town library and turned off the engine. Paul looked out the window at the buildings around them, saying, "You going to go and take out a research book or something?"

Devon shook his head, then reached back to push open the sliding door on the passenger side of the van. Paul turned and glanced out his window and saw who—not what—they were picking up. Dawn scampered down the front steps of the library, glanced around like a junior secret agent then dove into the back of the van calling out, "I'm clear! Go! Go!"

She slammed the door shut as Devon accelerated away from the curb, whipping out into traffic and cutting a car off, receiving a loud honking in the process. After they had turned a couple of corners, Dawn leaned forward and grinned at the two in the front seats. "Morning, Mr. Carter!"

"Morning, Dawn. So, what's next? We going to knock over a bank then make a run for the border to Mexico?"

Devon and Dawn laughed at him, and then Devon said worriedly, "Please don't tell Mom that guy honked at me, ok?"

Paul stared at him long enough for him to get concerned before saying, "He didn't hit you, so I didn't see anything. But you owe me now." Devon sighed with relief and nodded in agreement. He turned onto the road leading to the pullout and, in a short five minutes, they had pulled up behind Jim and his grandson, Eric, who looked like a younger, thinner Jim, except for an unruly mop of black curly hair who were parked on the side of the road.

Despite leaving Shady Acres first, Ruth's car arrived last at the pullout on the way to the river.

"They must have had to push it some of the way," Paul muttered as Ruth rolled to a stop directly behind Devon's van. Paul climbed down out of the front seat of the van and stretched, then leaned back inside and said to Dawn, "You've got the front seat now, thanks." Dawn exchanged a quick glance with Devon then exited the van. But instead of climbing into the front seat, Devon came around to stand beside her. Then Paul noticed that Jim's grandson, Eric, had climbed out of his car as well.

"Oh great, you kids going to do some sort of intervention on us? Are we too old to be going fishing by ourselves? Fishing is too dangerous for people of our extended years?" Paul said, starting towards Ruth's car before stopping and turning back to the teenagers, angry. "Well, forget it. You take your intervention and-"

"But Gramps-" Devon started, but Paul raised his hand to stop his grandson from continuing.

He took a breath and calmed himself down.

"It's only our bodies that are a bit past their prime. And don't you think we know that? Ha! We live in these rickety old skins all day long; we know exactly what they can and can't do. Mostly can't now, but that's not the point," he looked at the kids, then at Jim before continuing. "Sitting on a riverbank and fishing might be the only thing left we can do without any assistance, so, whatever you're going to say, forget it, because this is what we're going to do. Help us or not. If not, then Jim and I will figure out another way to get back to Shady Acres on our own. C'mon, Jimbo, there are fish to catch." Then Paul turned and headed towards the massive old Mercury Marquis idling at the end of the pullout. Jim patted his grandson on the shoulder and started after Paul.

"Gramps!" Devon called to him, but Paul waved his hand over his head without turning around.

"I don't want to hear it, Devon. You go have your fun."

"That's what I want to do. That's what we all want. To have some fun."

Paul stopped before climbing into the back seat of Ruth's car and looked across at his grandson, slightly confused. "You don't need my permission to have fun, Devon. Be careful, understand?"

Devon and Dawn blushed at that comment, then Devon stepped forward, took a breath, and said, "We want to come and have fun with you. We want—" Eric stepped forward to stand beside Devon and Dawn. Devon continued, "We want to come fishing."

Paul scowled. "Why didn't you say so?"

"You didn't give me a chance," Devon said with a slight shrug.

Jim and Paul looked at the teenagers before leaning down to talk to Joanne and Ruth inside the car. The kids nervously waited like they'd asked if the Easter Bunny existed and were now wondering if they still got chocolate eggs if the answer was negative. After a heated discussion, Ruth leaned out her window and yelled, "Come get yer asses in the car. The fish are bitin', and we're standing around here!"

The kids grinned widely, grabbed backpacks out of their respective cars and rushed over. After a bit of shifting around, Dawn settled in the front with the ladies and the two boys easily fit in the backseat between Jim and Paul. As Ruth put her car into drive and eased out onto the road, Paul called out, "Good thing you don't have a Prius, Ruth, or we'd have to take three trips to deliver us to the river!"

Thirty Four

"The fish sure as hell aren't gonna bite with all this laughing," Ruth yelled out from her place on the banks of a wider, smoother part of the same river they had fished the week before. Over Jim's protestations and claims of knowing the best spots, they had let Joanne lead and now were thirty miles further up river from town and Jim's fishing spot. After helping Ruth get settled in a shaded spot with an unobstructed view of the fishers and open enough to seat everyone for their meal, they broke out the gear and staked out their preliminary spots with amusement and light-hearted joking.

Getting out of the vehicle seemed to have been the turning point in diffusing the tentative awkwardness of the two generations collected tightly into Ruth's car. Conversation on the drive up had been stumbling—snippets of sentences bumping into each other as the seven attempted some conversational flow. Paul finally gave up and, wondering if bringing the grandkids along would to be the thing to wreck the day, looked out his window at the lush countryside as it swept past at a leisurely twenty miles an hour.

Beside him, Eric chatted with Devon about his job as the stage manager for the upcoming senior musical. Paul rolled his eyes to Jim, on the far side of the backseat and turned back to looking out the window. On the front bench seat, the three girls conversed amiably about random topics, changing the subject much too fast for Paul to keep up with their chatter.

At one point, Jim ahem'ed the car quiet and said, "Everyone, there's one essential fact we simply have to remember. That we are absolutely on time for dinner. We got away with it, barely, last time, and with the new rules at Shady Acres, we won't get any leniency from Kevin or Marcus. Agreed?"

Everyone nodded and Jim continued, "Us eldest," pointing at himself and Eric, "will keep us on track."

Devon piped up, "Hang on, I'm an eldest."

"Me too," Dawn said from the front seat.

Jim shook his head, "You two aren't eldest, you're 'onlys.' We are responsible; you two are—well, the only other only child in the car is Ruth. You come to your own conclusions from that."

Ruth cackled and slapped Dawn on the leg. "And that's why we get to have all the fun, sweetie. They're busy minding the store!"

Now Paul was shuffling out to a flat rock with Devon holding his arm steadily. The current wasn't fast, but the rocks they were walking on were slippery. *The last thing I need is to fall and break the same—or the other—hip,* Paul thought, but then they were on the flat rock and comfortably settled in. As Devon set up their rods and reels and tied on some lures, Paul glanced back towards the shoreline. A few paces downriver from Ruth, Joanne and Dawn were chattering away while settling in on a log by the edge of a quiet pool. Slightly upriver, Jim and Eric were doing the same thing, but near the roots of a huge cottonwood that branched out, shading half the river.

"Thanks for letting us come, Gramps," Devon said and handed Paul a rod.

"As long as you catch more than you eat, you're welcome," Paul said with a grin.

Devon grinned back, sat down to dangle his feet in the cool, clear water and then flung out his line, like his grandfather had taught him when he was just a kid, letting it coast by with the slow current. As everyone settled, the laughter diminished, and the seven started to ease into their day on the river.

The hours slowly passed, with the occasional trip by a grandchild back to Ruth for beverages and snacks. Devon, Dawn, and Eric obviously had planned their inclusion, as their backpacks were full of a wide range of junk food and sodas. Even a couple of Red Bulls and some energy bars. Paul had taken only a tiny bite of one of the energy bars before grimacing and handing it back to Devon, saying, "Forget it. That's what they're gonna feed me before too long when I'm unable to make it down to the dining room. I've seen the meals they give the bedridden. Not for me, not yet."

Devon laughed then happily gulped down the bar in a couple of bites, much to Paul's dismay as the goop tasted like damp sawdust to him.

•

Dawn looked up from struggling with her fishing line as she heard Devon laugh. She smiled as she watched him and his grandfather casually reel in their lures and cast them out in the river, time and time again. Beside her, Joanne sat on the log and watched aimlessly as her line floated on the surface of the pool in front of them.

Dawn asked, "Why aren't we out in the river like them?"

"Because Paul's cocky and figures the fishing he did in Montana will work the same here. But I know better," Joanne said with a smile. "My grandfather taught me that on this river, you look for the dark pools; that's where the bass will be hiding during the heat of the day."

With occasional bits of advice from Joanne, Dawn had finally learned how to fish for herself. Not that it was ever something she wanted to do, now that she thought about it, but after hearing from Devon how their grandparents had snuck off and gone fishing, Dawn had realized it was something she'd like to learn. *And here I am,* she thought, *chillin' with my grandma, fishing. How cool was*—

Her line suddenly sprung taught, and her rod bent towards the water. It was all she could do to keep it from flying out of her hands. She let out a scream and nearly let herself get pulled forward into the river. Joanne reached over quickly and, with a hand on her shoulder, settled her down, "Looks like you've caught one!"

"What do I do now?" Dawn cried out, as Joanne lodged her rod between two logs and came over to sit beside her granddaughter.

"First, relax," Joanne said with a smile. "You're bigger and stronger than that fish. But reel it in before it snags your line on something."

"Ok," Dawn said, taking a breath despite her rod whipping back and forth across the pool as the unseen fish struggled against the hook. "Now what?"

With infinite patience, Joanne taught Dawn how to slowly reel in the line, giving and taking back slack to tire the fish out. Dawn overcame her initial panic and started anticipating the desperate lunges and parries of her quarry, to the positive feedback of her grandmother. Finally, after what had seemed like hours, the fish slowed and weakened, and Joanne scooped it out of the river with a small net. *The white bass looks rather puny out of the water,* Dawn thought, *but I caught my first fish!*

"Not quite *Old Man and the Sea,* but a good-sized catch!" Joanne said and handed her the net after removing the hook and killing the fish with a sharp hit from a heavy stone.

Dawn took the net and stood up, showing it to the others. "My first fish! Ha! We're winning!"

A round of cheers and applause erupted from out on the flat rock and from up river. Dawn grinned and bowed in response, then sat down. Joanne put the fish—her fish!—into a container packed with some ice.

"I did it. I caught a fish!" she said with part amazement and part glee.

Joanne smiled back at her and nodded. "That you did, and you'll remember this moment. And hopefully you'll be there for your child's first catch."

Dawn blushed, slightly embarrassed. "Grandma..."

"I wish Dad were here," Dawn said quietly, as Joanne's words caught up with her. Joanne turned and nodded sadly. "No offense, Grandma, really. I'm so glad you're here, teaching me, it's just—you know..."

Joanne nodded again. "It's not the same, I know. It's the same reason my grandfather taught me, many years ago. My father—you never met him—was a busy man. He worked extremely hard, creating a better life for my siblings and me. And my mother worked even harder, keeping our home running. They barely had time for themselves, much less to come out and teach their children how to fish. Two generations later, nothing's changed. We grandparents," she looked over at Paul and Jim, "get the good jobs—like this—while our children work to make your lives better."

"Well, that sucks all kinda ways, doesn't it?"

Joanne shrugged. "It's been like this for a long, long time, and I doubt it's going to change in the immediate future. And I hope your father—or mother—can be there with you when your kids take this up."

"Can you imagine my mom out here, fishing? Bashing something to death with a rock? I don't think so!" Dawn said with a laugh.

"Good point. Maybe she'd be happier helping out Ruth with the meal," Joanne said, laughing along.

•

Devon looked up from their empty pail and said, "We're behind here. Dawn's already caught one, and she's never fished before. Maybe this is the wrong place to fish, Gramps. We should move."

Paul looked up from the water and replied, "There's nothing wrong with this location, kiddo. I've been fishing since I was way younger than you. And I know this will be the worst thing I could tell you, you being a brilliant teenager who knows everything about everything, but be patient. This is a waiting game, between us and some dumb—but delicious—fish."

"I can be patient, duh. I just don't want to lose."

Before Paul had a chance to reply, two cheers came from up river. Jim and Eric were standing, holding their two catches, arms clasped around each other's shoulders.

"See?" Devon said and sat down, huffily.

Paul laughed and patted him on the back, "Listen, today's about enjoying ourselves, not about some competition. Look at fishing like golf—"

"I don't golf."

"It's a solitary sport. You against the fish. One on one. Mano a Fisho."

Devon groaned at the bad joke, but Paul smiled and continued, "So let's get our lines back in the water, but let's try some different lures this time. I'm willing to admit these aren't working."

"Why not?" Devon asked, shedding his frustration in an instant.

Paul scanned the river, watching the edges for movement, and then dug down into the tackle box at his feet. "We picked lures too large for the time of day. Different bugs are out at different times. Right now, the bigger bugs are staying away from the water. So we do the same thing. We'll try these little buggers instead."

As they cut off their old lures and attached the new ones, Devon said dramatically, "If you want to catch a fish, you've got to think like a fish."

"I should push you in, then you'll be like a fish," Paul said, equally dramatically. Devon snorted and continued tying on his lure. Once he finished, he turned to his grandfather and said, "Ready to catch up to the others?"

"Catch up? We're gonna win this fishing contest!"

Together they cast out their lines and settled in to wait for the bass to bite.

"She seems like a nice girl, that Dawn," Paul said casually, flicking his line to keep his lure moving on the surface.

"Uh-huh," Devon replied, expansively. "Her grandmother seems pretty nice too."

"Yup."

Paul tried again. "You two 'officially' going out, or still 'just' friends?"

"Gramps, you're about as subtle as a tank. I don't know what we are. We've kissed a bit. Probably not as much as you and Joanne, though."

"We haven't done that! We're in our eighties," Paul replied, quickly.

Devon grinned. "But you'd like to. Right?"

Damnit, I'm blushing, Paul thought, *and Devon knows it.* He concentrated on reeling in his line then tossed it back out.

Devon continued, "You're not dead, Gramps. And trust me, I don't want to know if you're sharing a bed, but from what I've heard, there's a lot of hooking up in those homes. So, it's okay if you do."

"Hooking up?" Paul looked over at his grandson.

"Yeah, no commitments. Just, you know, hooking up, like a repeating one-night stand. Friends with benefits."

Paul continued staring at Devon. What exactly was he talking about? Devon looked over and blushed slightly. "Not that I'm doing that with Dawn. Hooking up. I like her a lot, so I wouldn't want to only do that."

"Well, that's good. You're a good kid to do right by her," Paul said, grateful the conversation had shifted away from him and his feelings for Joanne.

"But you. You've nothing to lose, I bet. Dawn says her grandma likes you a lot. I mean, she's risking her son's wrath to be with you and your wingman," Devon said, pointing up the river at Jim. "So, you should go for it."

"Go for it."

"While you're still young."

Paul registered Devon's wiseass comment and flicked him with water. Brushing the water off his face, Devon grinned at him. "I promise I won't tell Mom you have a girlfriend."

Paul scowled, turned back to the river and let a smile slip onto his face. *Joanne likes me*, he thought, giddily. *What a nice feeling. One I haven't felt in a long time.*

Thirty Five

Lillian left the rest of The Bees playing croquet out on the lawn, claiming she was weary and in need of a nap. In truth she simply hated lawn games. *Perfectly good way to ruin an afternoon and a lawn,* she thought as she made her way through the dining room and up to her apartment. To simply relax and watch some television by herself until dinner time would be much nicer than listening to the irritating clacking of wood against wood outside. But before she could have some peace and quiet, Lillian had to drop off a note for Paul quickly. Joanne's birthday was coming up, and she hadn't had the chance to tell Paul in public, as Joanne always seemed to be nearby. So, she'd quickly written up a note to slip under Paul's door, letting him and Jim know about the private surprise party The Bees were going to have in one of their rooms on her special day.

When the elevator opened on the second floor, she headed down the hall towards Paul's room. As she turned the corner, Chuck startled her, as he rushed the other direction.

"Oh!" Lillian said, in shock, but Chuck pushed past her and stormed down the hall the way she'd come, clutching a grocery bag to his chest. "Asshole..." she muttered, turning back as he impatiently hit the elevator button until the doors opened. Then he jumped inside and started hitting the close button inside the elevator. Shaking her head in disgust, Lillian straightened her shawl and carried on to Paul's door.

After retrieving the note from her purse, she leaned over to push it under the door, grabbing the doorknob for support. Suddenly, she felt a crushing pain in the center of her chest and into her left arm. She felt instantly weak, her legs gave out completely, and she crumpled to the floor.

"Oh... oh, no..." she muttered, weakly. She looked up and down the empty hallway, then cried out, feebly, "Help... someone, please..."

•

Kevin watched the ambulance pull away from the portico, his heart still pounding in his chest. He walked back inside to where the cleaning staff who had found Lillian, moments after her heart attack, were nervously waiting. He thanked them again for their quick response. "It could be the difference between her recovering quickly and having to stay in the hospital for quite a while." The two Hispanic women wrung their hands in worry.

Kevin sighed, and told them both to go home for the rest of the day; he'd make sure they were paid for their full shift. After double-checking with him that he really meant what he said, they finally thanked Kevin profusely and headed to the staff area to change. After they had left the foyer, Kevin returned to his office and sat down behind his desk. After double-checking he had locked his office door, Kevin pulled a bottle of bourbon and a glass out of his lower desk drawer and poured himself a shot. He shouldn't be surprised by heart attacks in an old folks' home, but they still shook him up every time.

He could manage fine when a resident passed away in their sleep—it was sad, for the family and the other residents, but death was part of life. Heart attacks seemed to be something different to him. Them and strokes. He took another sip then picked up his desk phone and rung Marcus at his desk.

"Is my mother still out?" he asked once Marcus answered. After Marcus confirmed Joanne's continued absence, Kevin hung up, dug his cell phone out of his suit pocket, and called his mother's cell phone. She'd want to know right away that one of her best friends since childhood had been admitted to the hospital. After two rings, the Verizon automated voice told him the phone he was attempting to contact was out of cellular range.

Frowning, Kevin hung up and had another sip of bourbon. Why would his mother be out of cell range?

After grabbing a breath mint—couldn't let the staff know he drank at his desk—Kevin went out to Marcus.

"Where exactly did my mother say she was going today?"

Marcus pulled out the pile of forms for the day's excursions, flicked through them, and pulled Joanne's out. Kevin took it and glanced at the info. It said she was going to Ruth's to work on valance curtains, whatever they were. Kevin handed the form back to Marcus and opened his cell phone again. He found Ruth's number and pushed dial. After a moment, the same Verizon voice told him the same info—this number was out of cellular range. With a concerned frown, Kevin hung up.

"Did you contact Lillian's son about her condition?"

Marcus nodded. "They're going to go to the hospital immediately."

"Good."

"Can't find your mother?" Marcus asked.

"No. And she'll want to know."

With nothing more to say, Kevin returned to his office and his secret glass of bourbon. As he sipped, he thought about where his mother could be. Clearly, they weren't at Ruth's house, since he'd successfully called her there before. And there were no dead zones downtown, or out at the big-box stores on the highway if they'd decided to go shopping. He was at a loss for where'd they be. He grabbed his phone and hit a speed dial. Maybe now was the time to talk to Dawn and see if she knew what was going on. Two rings later, he slammed down the receiver down and stared at the phone. That same Verizon voice...

One last place to try, and if he heard that Verizon voice this time, he knew he'd been dragged into either *The Twilight Zone* or *The X-Files*. He hit another speed dial, braced himself each time the phone rang on the other end until, finally, Beth answered. "Hello?"

"You're home."

"Kevin? Yes, I'm at home. What's the matter?"

"Lillian had a heart attack."

"Oh, no! How serious was it? How's your mom handling it—that must be quite a fright for her."

"I don't know how Mom's doing, I can't find her."

Beth paused, confused. "What do you mean, you can't find her? She's with Ruth making curtains, I thought."

Kevin quietly took a sip of bourbon then said, "Both of their phones are out of cell range. Dawn's too."

"That's odd..." Beth said.

"Damnit, Beth, if you know where they are—if they're off doing something they're not supposed to, I don't care—but Mom's going to want to know one of her best friends is in the hospital and might not make it!"

"Honey, I don't know where your mom or Dawn are. I promise. Should I drive over to Ruth's and see if they're there?"

"Maybe. Yes. That would be good; I can't leave here, especially right now. The Bees are pretty upset. I had to send home the cleaners who found her."

He could hear Beth gathering up her purse and keys over the phone as she said, "I'll go over right now. I'll call you when I get there. I'm sure it's nothing, and they've put their phones under something that-I don't know—blocks the signal. Or turned them off."

Kevin thanked her, completely distracted and quite frustrated by his mother's disappearance. And where his daughter was. He remembered the first time Dawn had missed her curfew, when she was thirteen. He'd phoned her friend's parents without success looking for her. When she had finally strolled in, two hours late, having forgotten her watch and phone in her room, he hadn't cared that Dawn was safe—just that she'd disobeyed. In hindsight, a month's grounding for one late night might have been too harsh, but she'd never missed her curfew again. He finished his drink, grabbed another couple mints then headed off to check on The Bees before making some more calls.

•

"Aren't you going to put anything on the fish before you cook them?" Eric asked his grandfather as the two squatted beside the old hibachi. Jim poked at the bass on the grill then covered them with the lid.

"These will be most excellent without anything, trust me. If you feel the need to add something, a little butter or olive oil is fine. But nothing else—you'll ruin the taste of the fish," Jim said as he adjusted one of the air vents on the grill before turning back to the rest of the group. "These will be ready in about five minutes. How's everything else?"

With Dawn's help, Ruth and Joanne had set up the rest of the food, including an additional store-made salad the kids had brought.

"Hopefully we have enough for everyone," Ruth said with a smile. "Devon, could you run up to my car and get the wine that's in the glove box?"

"We get wine?" he replied with youthful optimism.

Paul answered for Ruth, "No. We get wine. You get whatever sugary fizzy drink you brought."

Devon laughed and headed up to the car. Eric pulled a six-pack of RC Cola out of the river where it had been keeping cool. Eric handed out cans to the other teens, and when Joanne saw them, she said in amazement, "They still make that? Ruth, we drank that when we were their age!"

"Sometimes with aspirin, if I remember right."

Joanne blushed, and Dawn looked at the two women, confused. "Ew, with aspirin? Why would you do that?"

"The rumor was you'd get drunk," Ruth said with a laugh. "And we believed it. Until we tried it at a sleepover at Lillian's house when her parents were away at a wedding."

"What happened?" Eric asked.

Ruth looked at Joanne, expectantly. "You want to tell them or should I?"

Joanne sighed and waved at her friend to continue. Ruth grinned and said, "Nothing. Not a single thing. We felt like fools." Everyone had a good laugh at that.

As soon as Devon returned, Paul opened the wine and poured glasses for the four adults. By then, Jim had taken the fish off the grill and placed them on a platter that now sat in the middle of the picnic blanket.

Once everyone settled, Dawn raised her can of soda and proposed a toast, "To the neatest day I've had in a long, long time. And to the coolest old people I know!"

As everyone reached around and clinked cans and glasses, Ruth muttered, "Who are you calling old?"

"Me," Joanne said with a laugh. "She's calling *me* old. Because you're way younger than me. A whole six months younger. You could go on tour with the Rolling Stones, you're so young."

Ruth grinned wickedly and said, "Bah, they couldn't keep up with me."

Everyone laughed, and Jim pointed towards the platter of fish. "Come on, get those served up before they get cold! I didn't slave over that grill for nothing."

"Yes, your honor," Eric said and started the platter around the group. Before too long, everyone had a full plate of food and had settled back to enjoy their meal as the sun continued to shine on them and their private stretch of river.

•

Beth climbed back into her car outside Ruth's empty house and dialed Kevin's cell phone. She barely had a chance to tell him of Joanne and Ruth not being at home, and that Ruth's old car wasn't in her driveway before Kevin thanked her tersely and hung up. After closing her phone, Beth sat in her car, her wondering shifting to worry. Once more, she tried to call her daughter, but hung up on the damned Verizon voice again. *Dawn, wherever you are, I hope you're looking after your grandmother*, she thought, then started her car, planning to drive through downtown and see if she could see anyone who might know where the three were.

•

"Suzanne, could you get me Paul Carter and Jim Lyons' files right away, please!" Kevin called through his open office door. Suzanne opened the filing cabinet behind her, grabbed the two files and took them into Kevin. He took them from her without saying anything, and, startled by his uncustomary rudeness, she simply turned and started back to her desk. Kevin glanced up, realized what he had done, and said briskly, "Thank you, Suzanne. Please shut my door as you go."

Still looking away from Kevin, Suzanne nodded and pulled the door shut as she left.

Kevin flicked through the first file until he found Natalie's contact info, then picked up his office phone and placed the call.

"Natalie Skaarsgard, Project Development."

"Natalie, this is Kevin Wright at Shady Acres—" he began before Natalie interrupted him.

"Is it my father? Has something happened?"

"He's fine. I think."

"What does that mean? Don't you know?" Natalie said, impatiently.

"Let me start again," Kevin said, rubbing his hand over his face. "I'm trying to find my mother; there's been an accident here involving one of her friends. And I'm pretty sure Joanne is with your father."

"Okay…" Natalie said, confused.

"My mother isn't here at the home today. She is with another of her friends. But I can't contact them; their cell phones aren't connecting. Do you know where your father is, or could you call and find out where he is and if my mother is with him?"

"I'm sorry, I'm confused. Isn't my father at the home?"

"No. Your son picked Paul up right after breakfast. There is a signed permission form."

"Signed by whom?"

"By you, Natalie."

Natalie sat back in her chair, her mind spinning. Devon had dropped her off at the office because he said he'd do the grocery shopping for the week and needed the van. He hadn't said anything about spending time with her father. It wasn't like Devon to lie to her, and it wasn't like her father to be sneaking off when he wasn't supposed to.

"Hello?" Kevin said on the other end of the phone and Natalie regained her focus. She said, "I'll try calling them right now. Hang on."

Pulling her cell phone out of her purse, Natalie tried Paul's phone only to get a pious AT&T voice telling her the customer was out of service area. She hung up and tried Devon only to get the exact same message. Putting her cell phone down on her desk, she picked up her office phone and said to Kevin, "Both Devon and my father are out of the service area. Where could they be?"

"Together," Kevin said, angrily. "They're all together." Then he hung up on Natalie, leaving her holding her receiver, staring down at her cell phone.

Kevin's next call was even faster as Jim's son said the same thing Natalie had, right down to attempting two phone calls and getting two out of area replies. Kevin thanked him and hung up. Christ! Three residents of the home—his responsibility—gone and no one knew where they were! He could feel his heart pounding in his chest. It was exactly like when—Kevin stifled the gasp before it became audible. It wasn't the same, but it was the same! Except he was the one who let them go without a chaperone, and he was the one who didn't know where they were!

He looked down at the desk drawer containing the bottle of Maker's Mark bourbon. Opening the drawer, he looked down at the bottle for a long moment, noticed his hand trembling on the handle, then slammed the drawer shut. With shaking hands, he locked the drawer and put the key in a misshapen fired clay bowl, made by Dawn for a long ago Father's Day, at the far end of his credenza.

I must do something, Kevin thought worriedly, *but what?* Wait? Wait for what? A phone call from the police? Jesus…

Attempting to be decisive, Kevin picked up his phone and called the hospital to find out Lillian's condition, hoping for some good news to distract him for a while.

Thirty Six

The sun had shifted behind the branches of the trees along the riverbank by the time they finished the freshly baked apple pie Ruth had packed for dessert. Regretfully, everyone helped packing up what little food remained and the teens trudged everything up to Ruth's car. Then, with one last look at the gently flowing river, they silently climbed into the car and started for home.

As they made their way down the road at Ruth's top speed of twenty miles an hour, Joanne leaned over and pushed the cassette into the player custom-installed in the dash. "Look, Dawn, that's 1970s high tech right there."

"A cassette?"

Joanne shrugged with a smile. "It meant we could have our songs with us, instead of waiting for a song we liked to come on the radio. Remember that?"

The men in the back agreed, and Jim said, "We only had one good radio station around here. And one our parents listened to. When you could receive them. In the car was the worst. We'd go park on the hill south of town because that was the best place for the radio signal."

Eric piped in, "Yeah, I'm sure that was the only reason you parked on some far-off hill, Grandad."

Everyone laughed, and Paul said, "Growing up where I did, we didn't have any hills, so I had to climb out my bedroom window onto the roof to get any sort of signal for my transistor radio."

"Must have been tough in the winter." Devon quipped.

"Wise guy," Paul snapped back at Devon with a smile. "You don't know how good you have it."

Joanne and Ruth started singing along with the first song, 'At Last' by Etta James. Immediately, Dawn and Eric joined in with them, much to their amazement. After the song had ended, Joanne turned and asked how they knew the song.

Eric smiled. "Jazz choir, Mrs. Wright."

"As long as you don't expect us to sing along with that Taylor Swift girl," Ruth said with a laugh.

Then the song stopped suddenly. So did the engine. So did the laughter. Ruth struggled with the now-dead power steering and, with Dawn's help, coasted the car to the side of the road to a stop.

"What happened?" Joanne asked.

Ruth shrugged and tried to start her car again. After a couple of attempts, the starter ground down and stopped responding. Ruth banged the steering wheel and then turned to the men in the back seat. "Well, boys, time to prove your worth."

With a shrug, the backseat emptied and the four walked around the front of the car. Paul opened the huge hood, and the four peered inside.

"There's not much we can do here. I figure it's a dead battery, but maybe something worse," Paul said, poking at the battery connections to make sure they were tight. Jim agreed, then said, "Ruth, have you roadside assistance?"

"Why? I've never had a problem with this car."

Paul and Jim looked at each other, then at the boys. The four snickered, hidden from Ruth behind the open hood.

"Ok, someone call a tow truck, they'll be able to help us out. Or at least give us a jump-start," Paul said decisively.

Everyone took out their phones and collectively realized none of them had any signal.

Eric waved his phone around, trying to find a signal, "So this is why you didn't answer last fishing trip."

Jim nodded glumly.

"When did you finally get a signal?"

"Not until the Route 17 bridge."

"Jeez, Grandad, that's gotta be ten miles from here."

Joanne looked over at Ruth, worried. "Uh-oh."

Ruth nodded back at her then turned to Dawn. "Your father's not going to be too happy with us." Dawn checked her phone again and nodded.

•

The patrol car eased up behind the two empty vehicles in the pullout. In the growing twilight, the police officer, with one hand on his revolver, walked up beside the two cars and confirmed they were both empty. Stepping around to the forest side of the cars, he walked along the edge of the road for a hundred yards looking for a trail or any other sign of where the owners had gone. Nothing anywhere, only forest in both directions and on both sides of the road.

Pretty stupid, he thought, *parking in the only fire truck turnaround on this length of the road. I'll have to make a damn report to get the municipal works guys out with a newer, more visible sign.* Angry at his impending paperwork, he triggered his shoulder radio and called in the two vehicles as he walked back to his police car. Dispatch would send out tow trucks while he returned to his patrol.

•

"Maybe I should try walking until I find a signal on my phone," Devon said. "Then I could call Shady Acres and let them know you're going to be late coming back."

Dawn pushed off the bumper she had been leaning on, saying, "You can't do that! My father would totally freak out if he found out I was with you!"

"I wouldn't tell him that, Dawn, only about the car breaking down..."

"They're not supposed to be together either! Oh, this is a total mess! I'm not supposed to be with you at all! Why did you make me come with you today?"

Devon took a step back. "Hey, I didn't make you do anything..."

"Yes, you did! You convinced me to come fishing and now I'm going to be in so much trouble! You know how much my dad doesn't like me being with you, but you totally ignored that! You only care about what you want to do!"

Joanne said, "Dawn, what do you mean you're not allowed to see Devon? You father said that to you?"

Dawn nodded, moments away from tears. Joanne leaned over and rubbed her back. "Don't you worry, I'll talk to my son."

"But what about you? You're not supposed to be sneaking off to go fishing. You're in as much trouble as I am. He's never going to let either of us forget this!"

Joanne started to tell her granddaughter not to worry, but realized Dawn was right. There was a limit to how much she could get away with at Shady Acres, despite being the mother of the current owner and the wife of the former owner. *This is probably going to be bad*, she thought.

Paul and Jim leaned against the front bumper looking out at the empty, darkening road.

"As long as we don't arrive at the same moment, like last time, we should be good. Lost track of time, that kind of thing. We're old, right?" Jim said, frowning. Paul shrugged.

"I could phone and say I'm going to stay at my son's tonight. That dinner started late," Jim continued.

"What does it matter? We have permission to be away from the home, and as long as we're taken back by our grandkids, we'll be fine. They've nothing on us," Paul argued.

"Well, Kevin's not going to let us off the hook. Neither is Marcus," Jim replied tersely.

Paul looked at him and shook his head. "Again, what does it matter? They'll be upset with us; don't matter a lick. We haven't done a thing wrong."

"We don't want them to be angry at us. They'll make our lives miserable, Paul."

"Oh stop being so dramatic. This isn't a courtroom. They're already making our lives miserable; that's why we're out here in the first place! What else are they going to do to us? Send us to our rooms without dinner? We can't let them control us!"

Jim put up his hands, placating. "Whoa! Like it or not, we actually pay them monthly to control our lives, to a certain extent."

"Ah, I don't want to listen to this anymore," Paul said angrily and walked around to the back of the car, looking down the road in the other direction.

Jim watched him stomp off, confused. *No point spending your energy fighting against authority,* Jim thought, *where you end up is tired and dead.* And authority, well, it survives perfectly fine, against all odds. He felt the car shift as Paul leaned against the rear bumper. Jim thought of an appropriate old song so hummed the chorus to himself, 'I fought the law, and the law won.'

Over an hour later, in the lengthening twilight, a pair of headlights appeared. Paul stepped out to flag down the car, but it had already started slowing down. As it rolled to a stop, Devon opened the door and jumped out. "The cavalry has arrived!"

Paul and Devon came around to the front of Ruth's car as an old truck crossed the lane and slowed to a stop directly in front of the open hood. Leaving the old Ford idling, an old man slowly climbed out of the cab and shuffled towards them.

"Thomas?" Jim said and stood up, looking closely at the man in front of him, side lit by the truck's headlights. "Thomas Waxman? Good Lord, is that you?"

Thomas chuckled and chewed on the battered unlit stub of a cigar, which seemed to be a permanent part of his face. "Jim Lyons. As I live and breathe." The two shook hands, and Jim introduced Thomas to everyone milling outside the car. After he had finished, Thomas looked into the engine of Ruth's car and muttered, "Engine trouble? Or is this a surprise party for my birthday and you were waiting for me to show up?"

Ruth said, "Tommy, stop being a wiseass and help us on our way. These young ones have to be home soon."

Thomas laughed and shook his head, then turned to Jim and said, "You'd hope people would change as they get older, but time and time again you're given proof they don't." As Jim chuckled, Thomas headed back to his truck, calling over his shoulder to Ruth, "Keep your panties on, Ruthy. I'll have you on the road again, lickety-split."

"You cantankerous old—" Ruth started, but Joanne rested her hand on Ruth's arm and said, "He's helping us, Ruth. Don't make him mad or we'll have to spend the night out here." Scowling, Ruth kept her mouth shut as Thomas hooked up a pair of jumper cables and her car started again. Amidst much gratitude from everyone, he returned to his truck and pulled up beside Ruth's car, looking down at her from his window. "Good seeing you again, Ruthy," he said with a grin.

With Joanne's hand still gripping her arm, Ruth gave Thomas a thin smile and replied, "Yes, it was, Tommy. And thank you for the assistance. I truly do appreciate your help."

Surprised, Thomas looked into the back seat at Jim who looked as surprised as he did at Ruth's politeness. "Looks like an old dog might learn the occasional new trick."

"Who you calling an old dog, you miserable—" Ruth started to say, but Thomas had laughed and driven off before she could begin. She leaned out her window and yelled after him, but he waved back and continued driving away. Ruth angrily put her car into gear, "Oh, I've a tire iron I'd like to introduce to the back of his head..."

"Ruth! Please. Take us back to the cars." Darkly muttering to herself, Ruth looked back as Thomas' taillights disappeared around a bend, then put her car into gear and pulled out onto the road.

"Why don't you like him? He was so nice to help us," Dawn asked as Ruth accelerated—still ten miles per hour under the speed limit—but Ruth didn't say anything, focused on driving along the empty road in the dark. Receiving no answer, Dawn turned to her grandmother, questioningly.

Joanne sighed and said, "Thomas was Ruth's first husband."

Twenty minutes later, their cell phones binged and trilled and chirped with incoming messages and texts. The teens pulled out their phone and checked.

"We're not that late, so why is my mom looking for me?" Devon wondered.

"Yeah, well my dad and my mom are looking for me, too," Dawn said, still angry at Devon.

"Mine, too," Eric muttered and turned to his grandfather. "Did you hear from Dad?"

Jim shrugged. "My phone doesn't record messages, and I turned off the texting—hate reading on that little screen."

"Me, too," said Paul, nodding in agreement.

"Still, it's totally weird…" Devon said, and the two other teens nodded in worried agreement.

The car was still silent when they arrived at the pullout.

"Uh, where's the van?" Devon said, leaning forward, looking out the front window as they pulled up to where they'd left the vehicles.

Beside him, Eric muttered, "What the hell? Where's my dad's car?"

Everyone except Ruth climbed out and stood in the empty pull out. Devon and Eric started to panic.

"My mom's gonna kill me!"

"My dad's gonna kill me!"

Paul looked down at the gravel. "There's no broken glass, so I don't imagine they were stolen. Probably the police impounded them."

"The police!" the two boys yelled. "Oh, we are so dead…"

Eric turned to Jim. "Is the impound lot open now? Could we go and grab the car so Dad won't know?"

Jim shook his head. "Lot office closes at five. And tomorrow's Sunday, so it won't be open until noon. Noon till three."

"Great," Devon said sarcastically as Eric covered his eyes and rubbed them hard. "Now I'm gonna be grounded for-freaking-ever for some stupid fishing picnic…"

Thirty Seven

"Maybe you should have dropped us off first..." Dawn said, worried, as Ruth turned into the driveway of Shady Acres.

"If you three stay in the car, we'll be okay. You want me to stop and let you climb into the trunk?" Ruth said. The three teens shook their heads quickly. Ruth harrumphed and continued up the drive. Joanne noticed the red and blue flashing lights bouncing off the branches ahead of them. "Police?"

Everyone leaned forward in their seats and watched as the two police cars out front came into view, their top bar lights flashing away in the darkness. "This has nothing to do with us," Paul said, quietly. "Something unrelated."

"You hope," Jim said, just as quietly.

Then they noticed who stood with the policemen at the front doors. Kevin stood tensely, one arm around his wife. Beside them paced Natalie, talking to one of the policemen, while clutching the handle of her purse tightly. Also, Michael was there, Jim's son, along with his wife. Everyone in the car looked at each other, suddenly realizing they were the reason for the police being at the home. They were in trouble. Quite possibly loads of trouble.

Ruth pulled up a distance from the portico and eased to a stop. No one exited the car after she turned the engine off, and after a moment Joanne sighed and said, "Let's get this over with."

She opened her door and climbed out, with her granddaughter following. Behind her, the other four exited. Ruth, wisely, stayed behind the wheel. Joanne leaned back into the car and said, "You go, Ruth. You're not part of this. I'll call you tomorrow if I'm allowed to use the telephone." Joanne smiled weakly and shut the car door. Ruth blew her a kiss and drove off, slowly as always. Joanne turned back to the crowd waiting for them at the front door, steeled herself, and took Dawn's arm.

The six walked around the edge of the portico into the light and an explosion of yelling.

"Where the hell have you been?" was everyone's first question. The teenagers were thoroughly berated by their parents—alerted by the police when the seemingly abandoned cars were towed—and those same parents paused only slightly before berating their own parents for sneaking off.

Finally, the initial fury subsided, the police left after ensuring everyone had arrived safely, and Paul said, "We weren't doing anything wrong. Merely fishing."

"Nothing wrong?" Kevin said, stepping forward into Paul's face. "You call forging documents, claiming to be somewhere other than where you were, and endangering my daughter—you call that doing nothing wrong?"

"Dad—" Dawn tried to say, but her mother gave her a look that shut her mouth. Kevin continued, furious, "Morally culpable, and criminally negligent. Are they better words, Paul?"

"Neither of which pertains to what occurred today, I'll assure you," Jim said, calmly. "Paul is correct, we may have obfuscated slightly, but we merely were fishing. Certainly, the fishing spot in question being out of cell phone range was unfortunate. That was unforeseen. And regrettable."

"Fuck regrettable!" Kevin spat at them. "That's bullshit!" Beth stared at her husband, having never heard words like that out of his mouth. Joanne stared at him, having the same thought.

"What if something had happened? Huh? What if you were in an accident, what if you got—"

Joanne suddenly realized why her son was so upset. A missing group of residents, nighttime, a car broken down on the side of the road. "Oh, Kevin... I'm sure we weren't ever in danger."

"It doesn't matter what you think, Mom! You don't have a say if you're in danger or not. You can't know what's going to happen! You can't! And you had my only daughter with you!"

Beth tried to place her hand on Kevin's arm, but he pushed her away. Everyone else stood in silence, watching Kevin's outburst. Kevin looked like he would start yelling again, but he paused and looked around at everyone staring at him, took a breath, and then said to Joanne, "And you know what, Mom? You may not have thought you were in danger, off having your fun, sneaking out like teenagers, but Lillian—"

Joanne started and looked at her son, concerned. "Lillian? What about Lillian? Is she all right?"

Kevin stared at his mother, disappointment, frustration, and anger clear on his face, "No Mom, she's not all right. She's dead. She had a heart attack, and she died, and she wanted you by her side before she went."

Then Kevin turned and stormed inside Shady Acres, the huge front door swinging shut behind him.

Joanne staggered, but both Beth and Dawn grabbed her arms and steadied her. They walked her over to a bench and sat her down, Joanne in shock at the horrible news and the brutal way her son had told her. Michael, Jim's son, glanced at Natalie and said, quietly, "We should go. I'll drop you two off before we talk to Eric at home."

Eric flinched at the cold way his father had said 'talk.' Natalie nodded and gestured curtly to her son. Devon paused, looking across at

Dawn, trying to find something right to say, but nothing came to him. Besides, she had avoided looking at him since they'd fought beside the stalled car hours ago. Without making eye contact with anyone, Devon climbed into Michael's car and slid into the middle seat, stuck between his mom and Eric. Without a word, Michael started his car and drove off into the darkness.

Paul and Jim stood in the portico, every year of their age heavy on their shoulders. Paul wanted to go to Joanne and comfort her, but she was with Beth and her granddaughter who were doing a much better job of that kind of thing than he ever could. What could he do, offer her a cigar? Paul felt for her; he'd had enough friends die to empathize, but he still didn't know the right thing to say at times like this.

He turned to Jim who met his gaze and sighed deeply. Then the front door opened, and Marcus stepped outside. "You'll be coming with me now, Misters Paul and Jim. I'll be making sure you both end up back in your rooms without any further issues." If Marcus was waiting for some wisecrack from either man, he didn't show any surprise when the two merely nodded and came inside. Marcus looked over at Joanne on the bench, looking frailer and older than he'd ever seen her, and shook his head. Then he let the door shut and followed the men to the elevator.

Paul and Jim walked down the hallway to their rooms in silence, Marcus a few feet behind them. What could be said? Jim gave Paul a tight nod and entered his room. Paul started to unlock his door when Marcus handed Paul a card and said, "Lillian was bringing you this note when she collapsed. Luckily, Maria and Frida found her right away."

"Not that lucky, if she's dead," Paul muttered, looking at the invitation in his hands. Behind him, Marcus sighed then walked back down the corridor. Paul waited until Marcus disappeared around the corner before unlocking his door then pushed it open only to find his foyer covered in shaving cream. Someone—obviously Chuck—must have emptied a couple of pressurized cans through the gap at the bottom of the door. He sighed, stepped through the foam, then over into his bedroom, leaving white footprints across the carpet. Paul folded back his comforter then lay down on his bed, not even removing his shaving cream covered shoes. For once, he had no thoughts of revenge, no plans for retaliation. The war was over.

•

"She's really dead?" Joanne finally said after they had been sitting on the bench for at least five minutes. Beth patted the hand she held and nodded, "Let's talk about it tomorrow."

Joanne turned to her and said, weakly, "Please. I need to know now."

Beth sighed. "She had a heart attack. Outside Paul's room. Luckily, the cleaners found her, and she was rushed to the hospital quickly. But the damage was too extensive. Most of her family arrived in time, and The Bees but—" Beth stopped, not wanting to point out Joanne's absence.

"But not me."

"Grandma, it's not your fault. You couldn't have known," Dawn said, trying to be helpful.

Joanne ignored her and said quietly, "Oh, I should have been there…" Then Joanne started to cry, collapsing onto Beth's shoulder. Sobs wracking her frail form while Dawn held her hand.

Thirty Eight

"I really thought it was going to be worse," Eric said between mouthfuls. Damp and chilled from the day's unseasonably cold weather, Dawn and Eric met at lunch to update each other on their fates over chocolate milk and pepperoni pizza in the cafeteria. "But once my dad started on how irresponsible my Grandad was, I slid through without having too much dumped on me."

"What? Not even grounded?" Dawn asked, in amazement.

Eric shook his head sadly. "Oh no, I'm grounded. A month. And I'm not allowed to be alone with Grandad. Like he's some criminal mastermind."

"Still, not yelled at. Must have been nice. I hope you thanked your parents. My ears are still ringing from the reaming out," Dawn said. "My parents are sure I'm the ringleader. The—" she turned to Eric, "What did you call it? The criminal mastermind."

"You talked to Devon?" Eric said cautiously, vividly remembering how mad Dawn had been at Devon while they waited for Thomas to appear and help them on their way.

Dawn scowled at him, apparently having not forgotten, and then muttered, "Like I care what happens to him, the jerk... It was his dumb idea to go fishing and look what it got us. Grounded forever."

Eric looked up from his pizza, thought about saying something to defend Devon, then decided against it. Instead, he said, "He's grounded for a month, too."

"Our parents must have talked because I'm grounded for a month, too. And no car during that time," Dawn said, picking at the cheese on her now-cold pizza slice. Eric sadly nodded in agreement. "It's so not fair!"

Eric said bye to Dawn and left the cafeteria to make it to his locker then back to the other side of the school for his next class. After getting his textbooks, Eric slammed his locker door to find Devon leaning against the wall, eating from a bag of potato chips.

"Hey," Eric said, "You should talk to Dawn, she's pretty pissed at you."

Devon shrugged the suggestion off, he was pretty mad at her, too, for freaking out—like Ruth's broken car was his fault. "Man, this blows. None of us are really to blame. Sure, we sorta snuck them out of the home—"

"With forged documents," Eric said, sadly.

Devon had to agree with him, but continued, "But the fishing? Come on. They weren't out with us. We were out with them. Our frickin' grandparents. They were the ones in charge. How were we to know they weren't supposed to take us fishing?" Devon leaned back and finished off the rest of his chips.

"That's true, I guess," Eric said. "But I get where our parents are coming from. We could have been in an accident…"

"Sure, and the school could burn down at lunch," Devon said. "Who knows what might happen. If Ruth's old beast of a car hadn't broken down, we probably would have gotten away with it."

"The way to look at this isn't that we 'almost' got away with something," Eric said. "Anyway, I gotta be in class. Talk later."

Devon nodded and watched Eric walk off. *We so would have gotten away with it,* Devon thought as he started off for his next class, *if it wasn't for that old car breaking down, and the cops towing our rides, and Dawn's dad being a total jerk, and...*

•

Paul stared at the painting in the hallway outside Joanne's room. He knew he should go over, knock on the door and find out how she was, but instead he continued to gaze at the depiction of the Battle of Fort Anderson done in the meticulous style of the paintings up and down the hall. When he found himself counting the Confederate flags, he finally mentally slapped himself, turned, and crossed to knock gently on Joanne's door.

"Joanne, it's Paul."

Silence. He knocked again then said, "Let me in, ok? Uh, open the door and I can—hell, I don't know. Make you tea? That's doable. Or toast. If you have a toaster. And butter. And some sort of jam or jelly."

Silence. Paul put his hand on the door, reaching out to Joanne on the other side, and sighed. Then the door unlocked and, startled, he pulled his hand quickly back. The door opened onto the dark hallway. Joanne shuffled back into the gloom and Paul followed, closing the door behind him, cutting off the faint light from the corridor.

"Joanne, how are you doing?" Paul asked as he stumbled against an end table and found a seat on the sofa in the murky living room. He could see enough to know Joanne had settled into her favorite chair, a blanket drawn up to her. She didn't reply to his question. Paul rubbed his hands, a bit of arthritis ache in his knuckles. Savoring, for a moment, the physical pain as a respite to the emotional pain across the room.

"Damnit, I'm no good at this. Never have been. Women and emotions. They're the worst place for a problem solver like me. Tractor won't start? Sure, I'm your man. Give me the right tools and the right parts, I'll have you up and harvesting in no time. A hundred troops who need to take a godforsaken Vietnamese hill? Give me a map and I'll give you a plan," Paul stopped talking, realizing his babbling probably wasn't helping Joanne. "Why can't you have something broken for me to fix?"

After a minute of silence during which Paul seriously considered leaving the apartment, Joanne finally spoke from deep within her armchair. "No way to fix this kind of pain, Paul," she said sadly. "You know that. You doubtlessly had some good-hearted folk try to brighten your spirits after your wife died, and I had many after Martin passed. You know how well that works. So you will have to leave me with this pain, and this guilt. At least for a time."

"But there's nothing to be guilty about…"

The moment Paul spoke, he knew it had been the wrong thing to say. His intention might have been to try help Joanne see how she wasn't responsible, but he could see, now that his eyes had adapted somewhat to the darkness, how his words were heard as the complete opposite of what he said—that she had everything to be guilty about. Sighing deeply, Paul stood from the couch slowly, wincing from a pain in his leg—probably from sitting on a rock in the middle of a river for most of a day, then left the apartment, pulling the door closed behind him quietly. Across the corridor, The Battle of Fort Anderson's gallant soldiers fought on, frozen in time.

"You in there kicking her when she's down?"

Paul turned and saw Chuck scowling at him from the end of the corridor. *Far enough away from me to shuffle to the safety of his room before I grab him*, Paul noticed. *So much for bravery.*

"How about you go find yourself a shallow puddle to lie face down in?" Paul snarled and started walking away from Chuck, towards the elevator. Chuck followed, but keeping the same safe distance behind him.

"Pretty shitty thing you did, keeping Joanne away from her best friend's deathbed. But, not like you care about anyone else, right? You show up here, straight out of the West like some damn Roughrider, and start stirring up shit. Dumbest move Kevin ever made was letting you through the front door. You're nothing but trouble to everyone around you. And, one by one, they're realizing you're only looking out for yourself, and you don't care a lick for any of them."

Paul whirled around and took a quick step back toward Chuck. Chuck stumbled and fell back a half-dozen steps. Letting out a bitter, low laugh, Paul continued towards the elevator, leaving Chuck standing in the middle of the corridor.

"You know what? You've probably shortened Joanne's life. That kind of guilt eats at a person."

"Get lost, Chuck," Paul said, then turned the corner and fell back against the wall, out of sight of Chuck, his breath short in his chest. Was that what Joanne was hurting herself with? *But we had to live our lives, too,* he thought. *And that doesn't mean I don't care about others. I care, a lot. I think.*

The elevator dinged. Paul stood upright and prepared to go inside, but the doors opened, and Jim stepped out. They looked at each other, startled, not expecting to meet then and there.

"How is she?" Jim asked as the elevator doors shut behind him.

Paul shook his head, "She's taking it on herself. Everything Kevin yelled at her last night, plus whatever more she's adding on her own."

Jim sighed. "I see why Kevin's upset, with everything that happened to his father and his personal guilt about it, but that's no reason to be throwing around accusations like he did."

Paul didn't respond, but continued to stew in his thoughts. Jim watched him for a bit before asking, "What's her prognosis?"

Paul rubbed his thinning hair, then pushed it back into position. "Jesus... I don't know. She's sad, sure. Truly sad. What about the rest of The Bees? Have you talked to them?"

"Not yet. Maybe we should."

Paul decisively stepped past Jim and punched the down button. "I saw Chuck lurking around, down the end of the corridor."

"Fantastic, that's exactly what a situation like this needs," Jim said, darkly. "What did he say to you?"

Paul shrugged as the elevator doors opened and he entered. "Nothing really."

Jim followed him inside and pushed the down button. "'Nothing really?' I don't believe you. He blamed you, right? No need to answer," Paul didn't and Jim continued. "Chuck told you no one wants you here. He said you only think of yourself and don't care for others. He was, generally speaking, a little shit."

Paul grudgingly nodded in agreement. It wasn't the first time that had been said to him, but it certainly hurt more than in the past.

The elevator reached the main floor, and the two stepped out into the foyer when the doors opened. Scattered people stopped speaking upon seeing them. Jim steered Paul into the hallway to the dining room. "He's partially right. About you—and about me, if I'd been there to receive his words of wisdom. I know there's blame and guilt for me because I feel it," he shrugged. "Don't have a clue yet what to do about it, other than sit with it, and see what comes."

The dining room quieted down to a low murmur as they made their way across to a table beside The Bees and sat down. Jim ordered coffees from a surly waiter who grudgingly took the order then turned away. Watching him go, Jim said, "Everyone is judging us."

"You blame them?" Hazel said, looking over at the two while wiping another tear away. "Lillian begged for Joanne, but you two had her out on some silly river, being childish."

Paul and Jim looked at each other, guiltily. The waiter arrived with their coffee, nearly tossing the two cups down onto the table and splashing coffee everywhere, then walked off. Neither Paul nor Jim had time to thank him. Paul looked at his coffee suspiciously. "I wonder if these are clean cups…"

Jim stopped his cup right at his mouth, then put it back down on the table and slid it away. "I'm going back to my room for a bit. I'm rather tired."

"I'll walk back with you," Paul said, starting to get up, but Jim waved him back down.

"Sorry Paul, I need some time alone, thanks."

Paul tapped the side of his nose, but Jim only shook his head. Paul settled into his chair and watched his friend wander across the dining room, not making friendly conversation with anyone. Once Jim left, Paul turned towards The Bees, but they had shifted to face away from him, shutting him out completely. Absently sliding his cup around in the spilled coffee on the table, Paul's thoughts stumbled from doubt of his blame to admitting it to himself. Back and forth he went, ignoring the pointed conversations around him. He didn't even react when an old guy seated behind him spat out a mouthful of donut when he discovered the cream filling had been replaced with mayonnaise. Someone had continued playing practical jokes around the home, and Paul didn't even care who it was.

Did he really not care about anyone else and so manipulated those around him into doing what he wanted? Or was he part of a group decision, which happened to come at an unfortunate time? Was everyone around him over-reacting or did they see events for what they really were?

Slowly, while Paul stewed, the dining room emptied until he was the only person left, other than the staff. His coffee long cold, Paul continued to half-heartedly make coffee rings on the table with the cup until one of the wait staff came up and said briskly, "We need to make the room ready for dinner. You'll have to go now."

Paul nodded and slowly stood, eighty years on the planet weighing heavy on his shoulders. He shuffled back to his room, alone in a building full of his angry judging peers.

Thirty Nine

"You understand, we have no choice. This is for the best. For everyone involved," Kevin said sternly from behind his desk. His office was hot, and Natalie felt sweat trickling down her back. She blew her nose again with a soggy tissue and nodded slightly. It was all she could do to keep from breaking down completely. Kevin nodded, knowing he was right.

"We need a couple of signatures from you to ensure everything remains on the up and up." He turned a pile of printed pages around and slid them across the desk to her. Picking up a pen embossed with the name of the home, Natalie printed and signed her name on each of the three forms, then capped the pen and pushed the papers back to Kevin. He took the pages and tapped them back into alignment then put them off to the side of his desk, in front of a framed picture of his mother.

"I assure you, this is necessary. And we will reassess his state and the medications prescribed on a month-to-month basis."

Natalie nodded again, then stood up. "Is there anything else?"

Kevin stood, walked around the desk and opened his office door. "Would you like to go up and see your father? While you're in the building?"

Natalie shook her head. "No, thank you. I... I have to go back to work."

They stepped out of the office and Natalie saw Jim's son Michael sitting in a chair beside the door. He smiled weakly at her, and she tried but failed to smile back.

"Ah, Michael," Kevin said, gesturing to his open office door. "I appreciate you being able to come by on such short notice."

As Michael followed Kevin inside and the door shut behind them, Natalie walked slowly out of the home and, in the privacy of the parking lot, burst into tears.

•

"So what's this about?" Michael said, sitting down in the chair Natalie had left moment before. "Is my father okay?"

"No, he's not," Kevin said, leaning back in his desk chair. "And we have to come up with a way to deal with the trouble he's into. This trouble is dangerous to him and the other residents. This kind of defiant thought has no place here, Michael."

"I understand that, but how is he in trouble? He's eighty-two years old."

"You'd be surprised. Between him and Paul Carter, they've been involved in some dangerous stunts, not to mention sneaking off the property and, well, the fishing trip," Kevin threw up his hands in exasperation. "So here is what we at Shady Acres feel has to happen to ensure a safe and productive environment for the residents and the staff. I just finished speaking with Natalie, and she was in full agreement."

"Full agreement about what?" Michael said, wary.

"Natalie has agreed that her father requires some medication, for a time, to reduce some of his more defiant impulses."

Michael stared across the desk at Kevin, and then said, slowly, "You're going to sedate him? And she agreed?" Kevin nodded and pulled a different set of printed papers to the center of his desk, "I have the forms here, based on the recommendations of our staff physician and psychologist, for a similar treatment for your father."

"Oh, no, that's not going to happen," Michael said, resolutely, "I'll tell you that right now."

Kevin sighed, disappointed, and said, "And may I ask why not?"

"My father made it entirely clear to us when he came to this home he wouldn't be put on any mood-altering drugs. He was adamant about it. No anti-depressants, no anti-anxiety, no mood stabilizers. He said the one part of him which wasn't aging was his brain, and he wasn't going to let anyone mess with it. He made me sign a legal document to that effect."

Michael shrugged, "My hands are literally, legally, tied. There must be another option."

"Only one."

"Good. What is that?"

"You father will have to be moved from the home immediately," Kevin said.

"Excuse me?" Michael said, sitting forward, shocked.

"Being unwilling to follow the recommendations of our medical staff are grounds for revoking your father's contract to reside here. My hands are also legally tied," Kevin leaned back in his chair, nothing more to say.

Michael stared across the desk, his jaw open in both shock and amazement. "All because of a fishing trip…"

Kevin ignored him and continued, "I know there is space available at the Excelsior Convalescence Home. I'm old friends with the manager and could give you a recommendation. I'll give you some time to ponder your choice." He pushed the forms across the desk to Michael and then stood up. "I'm going to find a cup of coffee, you care for one?"

Michael shook his head and picked up the forms. Kevin shrugged and left his office.

•

Marcus knocked on Paul's door an hour later. From within he heard a faint, "Come in if you want, makes no difference to me." Opening the door, Marcus wandered in and found Paul sitting on his bed, staring out the sliding glass door to his balcony.

"I've something for you to take, Mister Paul."

"Don't want it," Paul said indifferently. "Give it to someone else."

"This is special, specifically for you."

Paul turned and looked up at him. In Marcus' right hand he held a bottle of water. In his left, a tiny paper cup with a single pill inside. "That's for me?" Paul asked, staring at the pill. Marcus nodded.

"And if I don't take it?"

"Either I make you take it, or you find a new place to live."

Paul turned away and looked back at the balcony. "Those are some pretty shitty choices, Mister Marcus."

"That they are."

After a long while, Paul sighed deeply and reached out his hand. "Gimme the damn pill."

Forty

Devon caught up to Eric at the bike racks outside the gym when school finished on the Wednesday after the fishing trip disaster.

"Hey, Eric!" Devon called. "I'm going to hang with my Gramps, wanna come?"

Eric rolled his eyes and shook his head. "Nope. Not only am I grounded, but it's straight home after school, for the entire month."

"Wow! That's brutal," Devon said, aghast.

"And no car either."

"Damn..."

Eric pulled his backpack tighter then said, "Yeah, so I gotta go. If you see my Grandad, say hi for me, ok?"

Devon nodded and unlocked his bike while Eric walked off. He started to ride off when he saw Dawn coming out of the school with some friends. Quickly, to avoid confrontation, Devon turned his bike around and rode off in the opposite direction. *No shame in avoidance,* he thought as he biked off the school grounds. *Better to retreat than be defeated.* But despite being angry at her, Devon still missed her like crazy.

Dawn said goodbye to her friends, unlocked her bike—noticing that Devon's bike was already gone—then decided she didn't care where he was. She made her way through the after-school crowd out to the street and climbed onto her bike. Leaving the school grounds, Dawn saw

Eric walking down the sidewalk. She pulled over and coasted along beside him.

"Eric! I'm gonna go see my grandma, want to come?"

Eric explained the rest of his grounding to her like he had to Devon minutes before.

"I'm glad I don't have your dad," Dawn said.

"I'm glad I don't have yours the way he yelled at your grandma. She okay?"

Dawn blushed, embarrassed by her father's anger, "Don't know. That's why I'm going to hang with her."

"All right, well you have fun, say hi for me. And I'm looking forward to more fishing, once we're out of trouble."

"That could be a while…" Dawn said sadly and biked off.

•

Devon sauntered into the foyer as innocently as he could manage and up to Marcus, who sat behind his desk.

"I'm here for my grandfather, Paul Carter."

"I know who you are, Mister Devon. Your grandfather is in the Arbutus Lounge, the end of that corridor. Visiting hours end in thirty minutes, all right? So don't let me find you lingering. You know the rules."

Devon thanked Marcus and started down the hallway. Marcus watched him go, then when he was out of sight, turned back to find Dawn standing in front of him, bike helmet in her hand.

"Oh, Miss Dawn, I didn't see you standing there."

"Totally cool, Marcus. I'm only here to hang with Joanne. She in the dining room with the rest of The Bees?"

Marcus paused before answering, his eye twitching slightly. "I do believe she is up in her room at present. Possibly a bit under the weather."

"Okay, thanks!" Dawn said then ran up the stairs beside the elevator.

Marcus looked down at his tablet, currently open to the medical prescription schedules for the residents, and sighed. *Might be wise for me to head down to the TV room,* he thought, *especially if Devon is anything like his grandfather.*

When Devon pushed open the door into the Magnolia Lounge, he was sure he had entered the wrong room. His grandfather wouldn't be in a room full of easy chairs and couches aimed at an enormous flat screen television mounted on the far wall. Medium density curtains kept the room from being too bright. Other than the sound from a daytime talk show, none of the dozen people scattered around the room were making any noise. Devon scanned the gray faces until he found his grandfather sitting alone to one side, staring blankly at the screen. Devon took another look around, but didn't see Jim or any of The Bees in the room. Crossing over to his grandfather, Devon pulled up a chair and sat down beside him.

"Hey Gramps," he said, whispering loudly, trying to be heard over the high volume of the TV. "Thought I'd come by and say hi."

Paul listlessly said hello, but didn't take his eyes off the flickering screen. Devon frowned and looked around at the faces, arrayed facing the TV. Each of them had the same blank look as his grandfather. Becoming concerned, he turned back to Paul, and gave him a nudge on the shoulder. "You should have heard your daughter yell at me on Sunday night, man... She used some words I couldn't believe she knew. And she's been totally pissed at me all week. And I said I was sorry, like a million times," Devon stopped talked and looked at his grandfather. "Gramps, what's the matter with you?"

Paul turned his head to Devon and slowly said, "Nothing, Devon. I'm just feeling... tired." Then he turned back to the TV.

"Jesus... What did they do to you?" Devon leaned over and checked Paul's hairline, "You didn't have a lobotomy, did you? 'Cause that would be crazy. But you're sure acting like it..."

Suddenly, a melodious 'bing' rang over the home's intercom. The residents in the TV room stirred to faint life as a door opened on one side of the room, and an attendant stepped through holding a tray full of tiny paper cups. With her elbow, she flicked the light switches illuminating the room in harsh fluorescent light. Devon watched speechlessly as the attendant made her rounds, handing out pills and four-ounce cups of juice. She patiently waited as residents swallowed their pill with the juice, and then checked each mouth to ensure their medication had been properly swallowed. Only a couple people didn't take pills out of the entire room. The attendant finally arrived at Paul and said, "All righty Paul, here's your afternoon pill."

"Whoa!" Devon said, blocking the attendant from putting the pill in Paul's outstretched hand. "What the hell is that? He doesn't need any drugs!"

"Son, you need to let me give your grandfather his prescribed medication."

"No way! You've made him a damn zombie! Look at him!" Devon said, rising to his feet and stepping in front of Paul. "I'm not going to let you kill him with that crap!"

The attendant took a step back as Devon puffed out his cheeks and crossed his arms in righteous indignation. They stared at each other for a moment then the attendant glanced over Devon's shoulder, looked back into his eyes, and walked away. Devon rolled his shoulders, proud to have protected his grandfather, then turned around and saw Marcus standing behind Paul's chair.

"Marcus! Did you see what they're doing to him? They've doped him with some drug that makes him... this... a freakin' vegetable!" Devon exclaimed, pointing down at his grandfather, who still stared at the television. Marcus sighed and said, "I know you're angry, but the decision has been made. And, despite what it looks like—"

"Bullshit! This is total bullshit!" Devon snapped and stalked out of the room, leaving Marcus clenching the back of Paul's chair with both his hands. After a couple long, smooth, calming breaths, Marcus let his fingers slowly relax and let go of the chair. *I'm not paid enough to do this kind of work,* he thought. *I'm positive calming down angry teenagers is not part of my job description. And why the hell hadn't Devon been told?* Looking down at the top of Paul's head, Marcus sighed, patted a couple of errant hairs back into place on Paul's head then walked out of the room, gesturing to the attendant to continue with her job dispensing medication.

•

While Devon was discovering the state of his grandfather, Dawn was two floors up sitting with her grandmother in the dark. Despite the beautiful, bright late-spring weather, Joanne was curled up in her bed, a tiny presence under the down comforter. Dawn had made tea and was now perched on the edge of the bed, attempting to engage her grandmother in conversation.

"So I saw Devon today as I left school, but he didn't even talk to me; I actually saw him turn around and rush away! I totally don't get it! Why is he avoiding me now? Ok, I guess I was a bit angry with him on Sunday, but he doesn't understand. My dad is pretty much a terror if he wants to be, and you and me being missing was a pretty bad deal, right?"

Dawn turned and looked over at her grandma, but Joanne continued to be preoccupied with something.

"Grandma, what's the matter? You know it wasn't your fault Lillian had a heart attack. I mean, she was old. Older than you. Not that you're old, but you know what I mean." Dawn looked at Joanne, looking for some reaction but saw nothing.

"Come on, Grandma. Say something to me, please?"

Joanne shifted her eyes slowly to make contact with Dawn and said, quietly and slowly, "I'm sorry dear. I'm quite tired."

"Of course you are, stuck here in this stuffy room! Come on; I'll help you down to the garden, and we'll look at the flowers in the sun!" Dawn said brightly, sure that a change of location would mean a change of mood. She hopped to her feet and gestured for her grandmother's hand.

But Joanne's hand didn't move. Dawn took it in her own and gave a slight tug, then let go quickly. Unconsciously she wiped her hand on her skirt as though she had touched a dead thing. She'd never seen her grandmother like this, so utterly devoid of life. A bit of fear and a few tears welled up in her eyes. *This isn't my grandmother,* she thought. *This is someone else. My grandmother taught me to fish! And told me dirty jokes beside a river!* "Grandma..." she said, plaintively.

But before Joanne could answer, a soft chime rang through the home intercom, followed by a knock on the apartment door. Dawn heard a keycard swipe and the door unlocked and opened. She turned around and saw a friendly attendant come into the bedroom with a tiny paper cup and a bottle of water on a tray.

"Oh, I didn't know you had visitors, Joanne," the woman said, smiling at Dawn and putting down the tray on the bedside table. Dawn smiled back at her weakly as the attendant turned to the curtains and pulled them open, flooding the room with soft afternoon sunlight. Joanne curled up deeper in the comforter. Once the curtains were open, the attendant returned to the bed, picking up the tray and offering the tiny paper cup to Joanne. Indifferently, Joanne held out her hand, received the pill and the opened bottle of water. Dawn watched, confused, as the pill was swallowed and the attendant checked her grandmother's mouth to insure it was gone. Then, with another smile to both, the attendant collected her tray and exited the apartment. Once she left, Dawn turned to her grandmother and impotently watched as Joanne slowly shut her eyes and fell into a deep, medically-induced sleep.

"What are they doing to you here?" Dawn said to her grandmother and herself.

•

Dawn exited the elevator in the front foyer a few minutes later, full of confusion and despair. She'd gotten a couple of steps across the foyer when Devon stormed by her, cursing under his breath, and flung open the front door.

"Devon!" she called after him, but he had already gone outside and the door had shut behind him. As Dawn crossed the foyer, Devon unlocked his bike, tossed it around to face away from the home, hopped on, and rode off as fast as he could. "Devon?" she said, quietly, wondering what had happened to make him so angry. Wiping a tear from her eye, she walked outside, slowly unlocked her own bike and started for home, utterly confused by why her grandmother was on medication and why Devon was so angry.

Forty One

Devon stomped up the stairs to their apartment, steaming mad. After furiously unlocking the front door, he kicked it open, had it bounce off the wall and hit him in the face, making him even angrier. Once he fought his way inside, he kicked the door shut, rattling it in the frame.

Bullshit, he thought as he thudded to his room and flung his school backpack onto his unmade bed. *Total bullshit.* Buzzing with angry energy, Devon charged around the empty apartment, looking for an outlet for the righteous fury building inside him. But he had nothing to help him burn it off. What he wanted was a baseball bat to hit the wall with for an hour, or a pile of old television sets to throw out the apartment window to enjoy them exploding on the sidewalk below. Or something to punch without breaking his hand to pieces.

"Shit!" he muttered, conscious of the old couple that lived in the apartment below them. Still buzzing, Devon stormed into the kitchen and ate a granola bar, despite it being less than an hour before dinner. *I've homework to do, but forget that,* he thought, flopping onto the couch and turning on the television. And that was where he was thirty minutes later when Natalie arrived home from work, a bag of Chinese take-out food in one hand and her briefcase in the other. The moment she opened the front door, she heard the television, grimaced and called out, "No TV was part of your being grounded! Turn it off now." She stood in the hallway and waited. The television stayed on, insolently, until a split second before she began to yell again. Sighing, Natalie kicked off her shoes, flexed her feet to relax them then walked into the living room. "Thank you. How was your day?"

Devon turned to her and hit her with a look of pure anger. Reflexively, Natalie took a step backward.

"Devon?" she stammered, confused and a bit scared.

"What the hell did you do to Gramps? He looks ready to die."

Overwhelmed with guilt and shock, Natalie dropped the paper bag of Chinese food. The smell of chow mein and hot and sour soup filled the apartment. Tears started to trickle from her eyes as Devon continued to glare at her. She felt her toes dampen from the spilled soup leaking out of the bag, but she didn't move.

"I didn't have a choice," she said quietly.

"You always have a choice!" Devon yelled. Natalie shook her head and moved her foot out of the soup.

"No, Devon, you don't. Or if you do have a choice, maybe both of the choices are bad."

Devon was about to fight with her, about to yell and scream and have a fit, like he would when he was little and she didn't buy him a toy in the checkout line at the grocery store. She could see it in his eyes and the way his hands were clenching and unclenching.

"He didn't even want to talk. He only stared at the stupid TV. The TV! Gramps hates TV!"

Natalie felt her heart crack in her chest. "I'm sure you only saw him at a bad time." She said it with as much confidence as she could, but she didn't believe what she said, not for a minute.

"You watch, he'll be dead—dead!—soon, if he stays like that!"

Shit, Natalie thought, *I've made a complete mess out of our lives...*

Then Devon stood up and started pacing in front of their television, his hands still clenching and unclenching at his sides. Natalie took a long breath, attempting to pull her tears and emotions under control. She was the adult, the parent, and she had to be that, if only for a few minutes to help her son.

"Devon," she said, in the same gentle, soothing tone she used with him twelve years ago. "I worry the same way you do about what's happening to your grandfather. He's my father, remember?"

Devon stopped pacing and turned to glare at her. "But I didn't sign the form to make him a vegetable, you did." Then he stomped out of the living room, into his bedroom, slamming the door shut behind him.

Natalie stood holding on to the back of the couch for a long moment while pain and hurt simmered in her, then turned and, grabbing her keys off the counter, left the apartment, stomping in frustration as she went.

•

After firing off a quick text to Devon that she'd gone out—*not that he would read it, in the mood he was currently in,* she thought—Natalie had driven over to Shady Acres, fully intending to go in and see her father. But, when she pulled into the guest parking lot, she couldn't leave her car. She had been able to turn it off and undo her seatbelt, but she couldn't open the car door. *I can't bear him like this, if he's as bad as Devon says,* Natalie thought as she sat there in the late afternoon sun. Sure, Devon's a teenager and naturally prone to exaggeration, but the medication Paul had to take would do exactly what Devon described. Maybe there was another solution. Take her father into their apartment, for the short-term, until Kevin calmed down. Or there must be other places in this town he could go and live. But Shady Acres was the best place in town, the HR people at Enviro-Dyne had assured her of that. She'd been lucky to obtain a spot there for Paul to begin with.

Natalie sat back in her seat and gripped the steering wheel hard, wishing for a cigarette——not that she'd smoked in twenty years, but under pressure the yearning snuck up, surprising her at the worst times.

Looking through the windshield at the portico and the front entrance, Natalie willed herself to get out of her car, go inside and see her father. But she remained seated in her car, crying, until, after the shadows of the tall cottonwoods grew across the parking lot to envelope her, she started up the engine and drove home to an angry son and a full email inbox.

•

From his desk, Marcus watched Natalie drive off. Kevin came out of his office, briefcase in hand, crossed the foyer, waved a terse goodbye to him, and was out the door. Marcus leaned back in his chair and sighed. *Might be wise for me to put a little work in on my resumé this evening,* he thought. *The mood around here is one of imminent catastrophe.*

Forty Two

Kevin was engrossed in a call on his cell phone when he came into the kitchen. Within two minutes—he'd checked—of leaving Shady Acres, one of the attendants had called wondering about the status of two residents who had requested changing apartments for some inexplicable reason. Not that Kevin cared, but the attendant wasn't sure if they were able to, and hadn't bothered to talk to him while he was in his office so now he had to deal with her, and with the two residents who were busy packing in expectation of moving.

"Look, make them both stop packing! Tonight isn't the time to change apartments! Take them to dinner and they'll forget about it till morning and then I'll damn well deal with it!"

Kevin listened for a bit while taking his suit jacket off and squaring his briefcase away in its proper spot. That's when he noticed no dinner cooking on the stove. He checked the time on his phone, frowned, and then interrupted the attendant at the other end. "Stop the packing. Dinner. Bed. Everything else, tomorrow. Understand? Good." He hung up his phone and plugged it in for charging.

Kevin began to call out when he heard someone pouring wine into a glass. Stepping into the dining room, Kevin found his wife sitting in her seat at the table, a half empty bottle of red wine and a now full wine glass in front of her. Confused, he glanced around and confirmed there were no place settings or food of any sort on the table or the sideboard.

"Beth?"

After a long drink of wine, Beth looked up at him, her eyes cold, and said, "Your own mother? How could you possibly do that to her?"

"What are you talking about?" Kevin said, noticing there wasn't a wine glass for him on the dining room table.

"What am I talking about? Are you really going to stand there and ask that?" Beth said, with barely contained anger. When Kevin didn't reply, she continued, slowly and precisely, "Your mother. Your own mother. On medication which makes her a vegetable. Medication approved by you. That is what I am talking about, Kevin."

Kevin pulled back as though slapped, then walked forward angrily, grabbing a wine glass of his own. "She was a danger to herself and our daughter, Beth. I didn't want to put her on that medication, but I had to. Our medical advisor says it's perfectly safe. You weren't there; you don't know what she's like now. She's out of control. Her and those others. Ruth too, if I had my way."

He returned to the table and poured himself a large glass of wine, observing that Beth was drinking a Cabernet Sauvignon out of a white wine glass. "I did exactly what I should have done a while ago. I did exactly what my father would have done."

"Oh, I can't believe your father would medicate his own wife into a near-coma, Kevin. He wasn't that kind of man. No matter what the circumstances."

"You didn't know him the way I did!" Kevin said, slamming his hand down on the table. "I have the files, and I know what he had to do to keep the patients in line! It wasn't all sunshine and rainbows at that place."

Shaking his head, he took another drink. Beth stared at him for a moment and then said, "Did you hear what you said? Just now? The residents of the home. You called them 'patients.' They are not patients,

Kevin, and you are not their doctor. You are the owner and manager of the place they live. And it used to be a good place to live. But you've lost sight of something in the past couple months."

"Oh, and what is that?" Kevin said, angrily. But before Beth could answer, the front door opened then slammed shut. A moment later, Dawn looked into the dining room. She took in the nearly empty bottle of wine, her two angry parents and the lack of dinner. With a look of disgust aimed directly at her father, Dawn turned and stomped up the stairs. After another moment, the door to her bedroom opened and slammed shut.

"What have I lost sight of, Beth? How to do my job? How to keep us living in this house? If they step out of line, I have to get them back in line. That's my responsibility. You may not like it, but that's too bad. If you don't step out of line, you won't have any trouble."

"Are you talking about your residents, or me and Dawn?"

"What?" Kevin said, confused. "What are you talking about?"

"You said if we step out of line, you'll put us back in line."

"No, I didn't. I was talking about Shady Acres."

"I don't believe so. You were talking about this home. We are not your residents nor your patients, Kevin Wright. We are your wife and daughter. We deserve your respect, as do the people who trust you to care for their parents and grandparents." Beth finished off the wine in her glass and put it down on the table. She pushed herself away from the table, slightly unsteadily, then started up the stairs, turning back to say, "And until you realize that, you're sleeping in the den."

Kevin watched with incredulity as his wife stomped up the stairs, and then listened in shock as she stormed along the hall and slammed shut the door to their bedroom.

Forty Three

This room has a funk about it, Jim thought as he sat in a hard wooden chair and looked around. It was his second morning in his new room at the Excelsior Convalescence Home, and he'd forgotten to open the window last night, so now the room had a smell he hadn't noticed before. A combination of old people smells, some dry rot, some damp mattress and—if he hazarded a guess—boiled cabbage. *Am I going to be stuck here for the rest of my days?* Jim wondered. *I certainly hope not.* Kevin would come to his senses; then he'd return to Shady Acres. He already missed Paul and The Bees—and the food.

He hadn't gotten much in the way of a tour of the home after he'd been checked in. Michael had dropped him off and then had had to return to work that fateful day. He was grateful his son had stood up to Kevin and his ridiculous plan to sedate him into good behavior, but, in moments like this, staring at the faded wallpaper in his tiny, smelly room, he wasn't sure sedation wasn't the better option.

With a groan, Jim stood up and used the bathroom. He had his own water closet—a toilet and a sink—but if he wanted a leisurely soak, he had to join the line for the full bath at the end of the hall. Not that he'd be willing to lie naked in that dirty tub. The shower head had been removed, presumably to ensure no one slipped and fell while having a shower. He brushed his thinning hair in the faded mirror over the sink and then left his room.

The day before, he had been shown the grounds—a paved area in the direct sun with a half dozen faded and uncomfortable chairs and benches—the living room for reading, and a grimy common area for those interested in watching TV. Unlike Shady Acres, the television was an ancient model, the old kind that was as deep as it was wide, with a wonky blue tinge that blared away from the corner. It balanced precariously on a battered four-drawer dresser. Jim figured he wouldn't spend a minute in there so powerful was the stench of sweat and urine.

As he walked along the corridor towards the stairs, since there wasn't an elevator at the Excelsior Convalescence Home, he noticed about half the rooms on his floor had latches on the hallway side of their doors. He stopped, turned around and walked back to his door to confirm it, too, had a latch on the hall side. They could lock him in his room if they wanted to. *Pretty sure that's a code violation,* Jim thought, wondering about the residents on the other sides of those locked doors. Not much different from taking a prescription sedative. Except with the sedative, at least you wouldn't really know you were locked in. Shaking his head in dismay, Jim shuffled down the corridor to the top of the stairs and sighed.

Ever since he broke his hip, he'd truly hated stairs. The rest of the time he could walk around, slowly but surely—like the tortoise, he'd arrive there in the end—but stairs were step after step of pain. He'd done well avoiding more than two in a row for the past ten years, but now, to be anywhere other than his new room and its funk, he had to deal with two long flights of wooden stairs.

Standing at the top landing, Jim double-checked he had everything he'd need until he came up to go to bed. Nothing would be worse than arriving down on the main floor and realizing he'd left something behind. No, sir. So he checked again. Glasses, book, extra book, sweater, cigar, lighter, room key, cell phone. Any more stuff and he'd need a personal Sherpa.

With his necessities confirmed, Jim started down the stairs, wincing with each step, always keeping one hand on the railing. But someone had spilled something on the second stair and Jim, focusing on the landing twelve more stairs down—he'd counted—slipped and his bad leg buckled. His grip on the banister quickly weakened until he had no choice but to let go. He crumpled and tumbled down the rest of the flight of stairs, his cane flying away, something breaking with a loud snap halfway down, until Jim came to a stop in a heap against the landing wall.

•

The next morning Devon locked up his bike behind the school, after making sure Dawn wasn't at the bike racks. He still didn't want to talk to her, but he totally wanted to talk to her. Sure, he was angry at what she'd said to him, but that didn't mean he didn't want to go back to the way they were before she'd said what she'd said. Frustrated, Devon fumbled with his lock, missing the combination twice before opening it. After finally securing his bike, he turned around to head inside when Eric rushed up to him, grabbed his arm, and said, "Come with me!" Eric pulled him out of the main flow of students into a quiet corner outside the Home Ec room and let go of his arm. Devon brushed his sleeve off and said, "What the hell, Eric?"

Eric held up his hand to stop him talking and knocked on the door to the Home Ec room. It opened from the inside, and Eric pushed Devon in and followed.

When Devon regained his balance, the first thing he saw was a room full of kitchens. The second thing he saw was Dawn leaning against a stove, her arms crossed, a scowl on her face. She glared at him, then at Eric and said, "You didn't say he would be here!"

Before Eric could reply, Devon said, "And you sure as hell didn't say she would be here!"

Eric locked the classroom door and turned to the two of them. "Well sure, would you have come if I'd told you?" They both scowled some more. Eric shook his head, "I rest my case."

"So," Dawn said, wanting it over with so she could get away from Devon. "What this all about?"

"It's about my Grandad."

"What happened?" they both exclaimed in concern.

Eric shook his head and tried to explain, "He fell last night and broke his arm. He's pretty battered up."

"Oh my God…" Dawn said. "How did he fall?"

"He fell down a flight of stairs. Slipped on something, fell, broke his arm then smashed into the wall at the bottom."

"Why was he going down stairs? There's an elevator at the home," Devon said.

"He isn't at the Shady Acres. They kicked him out."

"Say what?"

Eric paced around the room, angry. "My parents didn't tell me. But they had to find Grandad a new place to live."

"But why?" Dawn asked. Eric turned and glared at her, "Because of your father, Dawn. Because he gave my dad two choices. Either Grandad let himself be kicked out of Shady Acres, or he had to be on some crazy serious medication. My gramps won't take drugs like that. So…"

Dawn's jaw dropped, and she turned to Devon. "My grandmother is on those drugs… I saw her, and she didn't even get out of bed. Oh my God… Eric, I'm so sorry."

Eric shrugged and muttered, "It's not your fault." He clearly wished it could be her fault so he could blame her, but it wasn't, so he couldn't.

"Whoa," Devon said. "My gramps has to be on the same ones. He didn't even care I was visiting him. He stared at the TV the whole time! He hates the TV."

The three slipped into their thoughts for a moment then Eric said, "So what are we going to do?"

"What'll we do?" Devon said. "I'm not welcome at the home now since I 'made a scene' yesterday. Besides, *she* doesn't want anything to do with me." He looked at Dawn, pointedly, during that last comment.

"Well, if you're going to be a jerk about it, I don't want to be around you either," Dawn snapped back at him.

"Yeah, well—"

"Stop it!" Eric yelled and stepped between them. Startled, they stopped and looked at him. Satisfied they weren't going to continue bickering, Eric said, "This isn't about you. Anyway, you have nothing to fight about. God, you were both worried about being in trouble, and you said some shit you now want to take back. Ok. But you were right. We are in trouble. So, now take what you said back and we'll get on with life."

Eric stepped back and glanced back and forth between the two. "Bell's in five minutes and this room will be full of tenth graders baking muffins. Tick, tick, tick."

Dawn looked up from the floor and sighed. "Eric's right. I was worried—scared. I didn't mean what I said. Ok?"

Devon paused, then unlocked his arms and nodded. "Me too. I'm really sorry, too."

Before the two could rush into each other's arms, Eric stepped back in-between them and said, "Finally. Ok. Something needs to be done about what they're doing to our grandparents."

Everyone nodded in agreement.

"But that's gonna mean confronting my father," Dawn said, worried and angry.

"No way we can do that. We're only dumb kids to him. He'll eat us alive," Devon said.

"We need more people. Then there's safety in numbers and he can't blame any of us," Eric added. The three paced around the Home Ec room, each trying to come up with an idea. Eric looked at the clock on the wall and said, "Time's up. The bell's gonna ring. Come on."

Dejected, they filed towards the classroom door.

"We'll figure something out..." Dawn said, hopefully.

"But will it be in time before someone else's grandparent is hurt or drugged or dead?" Eric said.

When Dawn and Eric arrived at the door, Devon was staring at the notice board on the wall. On it were posters for group meetings, an after-school concert by the jazz band, and an upcoming bake sale supporting the Glee Club. The bell rang. They were out of time.

"See you both later?" Dawn asked. Eric nodded and opened the door, letting in the noise of hundreds of students rushing to their first classes. Devon didn't nod, but continued to stare at the bulletin board, a sudden flurry of thoughts percolating in his head. "Devon? You coming?" Dawn said. Devon didn't answer, but after a moment he turned to them and smiled. Actually, more a devious grin than a smile.

"What?" Eric said, confused.

Devon put his arms around the two and led them into the hallway. "I have an idea. I'll tell you both at lunch. My treat!" Hopeful, they walked along with him. Devon suddenly stopped and asked, "The only problem I see is that we'll have to sneak out tonight against our curfews..." The two stopped smiling as Devon started walking again.

Forty Four

When Marcus came in with Paul's afternoon medications, he was staring out the balcony window, or staring at the balcony window. Marcus walked up to him and looked down at what was now a frail old man. He glanced at the pill in the paper cup in his hand. *This is five levels of bullshit*, he thought. *Turn an old man into a drooling turnip because he showed some spunk...*

"You want to take your pill now, Mister Paul?" Marcus asked.

"Whatever," Paul said listlessly after a moment.

Marcus stepped around and kneeled in front on Paul, completely blocking his view. Paul didn't really respond, but slowly shifted his view to the slice of the window he could see over Marcus' shoulder. Marcus looked deep into his eyes then said, "If you want this pill, you tell me. You tell me, right now, and I'll give it to you."

Silence. After a long moment, Marcus stood up, slipped the pill into his jacket pocket, and nodded. "I guess that means you don't want to take these pills anymore. Well, if that's what you want…"

A slight smile slid onto Marcus' face as he left the apartment. He'd always been a rebel at heart, but he'd suppressed that impulse since the day he'd started working at Shady Acres. Now his day had become a tiny bit better.

•

Later that evening, the three teens met up behind Devon's apartment building, well out of view. Devon had two full backpacks and a large travel mug of coffee with two shots of milk, three sugars, and some honey added to it. When Dawn and Eric walked around the corner, he waved them over into the shadows.

"Ok, you're here. Do you have everything?" Devon asked. Eric held up a grocery bag and grinned nervously.

"Are you sure we're allowed to do this? We're not going to be in trouble with the police, right?" Dawn asked, worried.

"No way, you'd do the same thing if you lost your puppy," Devon reassured Dawn. Before she could ask another question, three more people came around the corner and out of the darkness.

"Who's that?" Dawn asked as the three came closer.

Devon grinned and said, "I called in some reinforcements."

Devon and Eric's three cafeteria buddies stepped into the dim light, and everyone said hello in a flurry of fist bumps. He handed a backpack to the guys and said, "Main intersections west of Center Street. We'll do this side of town."

The guys grinned and disappeared back into the darkness. Devon turned to Dawn and Eric saying, "Come on, I haven't much time. I told my mom I've gone to the grocery store!"

Together they headed off up the street, lit only by the streetlights. After a couple of fumbles, they had a routine down. They'd arrive at a residential street corner and Devon would grab a poster from his backpack and hold it up to the telephone pole. Eric would start the packing tape at the bottom then pass the roll to Dawn on the opposite side of the pole. Three times around the pole, firmly attaching the poster from bottom to top. Cut the tape and they were on to the next pole. No one stopped them; no one asked them any questions; no one even slowed down in curiosity. So within an hour, they had emptied Devon's backpack of posters and were out of packing tape. Devon grinned at the two after they taped up the final poster, "If that doesn't change something, I don't know what will."

Dawn had gotten into the excitement of their late night adventure, but now started to worry again. "I hope this doesn't go too badly for my dad…"

"I hope it does," Eric said, angrily. "He's why my dad has a broken arm and two cracked ribs."

"I know, but—"

"Come on," Devon said, glancing at his phone. "I've gotta get home!"

"What about going to the grocery store?"

Devon held up his backpack with a grin, "I filled it with cans from our kitchen when Mom wasn't looking, then said we were out of it all. So now I go back home and put it back on the shelves."

Eric shook his head. "Damn, I'm glad you're not my kid."

They laughed, and Eric trotted off towards home. Dawn and Devon quickly hugged, then she ran off, too. Devon watched her go, and then started home as well.

He was only a couple blocks away from the apartment when he turned a corner and crashed into Adrian, the quarterback jock who threatened him in the diner and who tried to prank Dawn because she quit the cheerleader squad, and knocking him over.

"Prairie Boy! You little shit," Adrian exclaimed, getting back to his feet.

Devon scrambled to his feet and backed up against a lamppost. "Adrian, I'm sorry, I'm really sorry!"

"What the hell you doing running around?"

"I was just—" Devon stepped away from the post and pointed at the poster behind his head. "I was putting these up."

Adrian pushed him out of the way and read the notice.

"What does that even mean?" he said, threateningly.

"Uh, they're doping some of the residents. Including my grandfather. It's really messed up."

Adrian brushed off his letterman's jacket and thought for a moment. Devon braced for the impact of a fist to his face. But Adrian didn't hit him. Instead, he nodded and stepped back.

"So you're stirring up shit."

"Yeah."

"Ok." And he started to walk away.

"Ok?" Devon called after him.

Adrian stopped and looked back at him, "My Granny's at Shady Acres. I don't want that to happen to her. So stir that shit up, big time."

•

Next morning's breakfast was a quiet affair for Kevin as everyone in his house was still angry with him. While he made his breakfast of a toasted bagel with some of his mother's strawberry jam and waited for the coffee to finish brewing, Dawn stormed in, then turned and stormed out again before he could say a word to her. A moment later, he heard the front door slam, and he was alone again. If Beth was awake upstairs in their bedroom, he couldn't hear her.

With a defiant sigh, Kevin took his plate and coffee cup to the kitchen table and consumed them both while skimming the news on his phone. *If I give them time, they'll come around to understanding why what I did was the right thing to do*, he thought, as he read an article on wind farms off the state coast.

After he finished his meal and put his dishes in the dishwasher, he collected his briefcase, phone, and jacket and left his still silent house. With NPR tuned in, he drove out of the driveway and started toward Shady Acres. At the first corner he paused, checking both ways for distracted early morning drivers—usually taking a car full of noisy children to the elementary school at the end of the block. The one that four generations of his family had gone to. The one named after his great-great grandfather. *The good old days*, he thought, *without this ridiculous pressure—two simple rules, do good and obey, and you won't get the strap. The end.*

Kevin began to drive on when he noticed the bright white posters attached to each of the four telephone poles at the intersection. Curious, Kevin checked his mirrors, confirmed no one coming up behind him, put his car in park and walked over to check out the poster. *Probably a lost dog or car*, he figured, *but best to know for sure, in case I see the missing animal.* But when Kevin saw the poster his stomach leaped up into his chest and started pounding. What the hell…?

In huge type, the poster proclaimed:

```
        What is
      going on at
        Shady
         Acres?
     Residents on
         drugs!
        Meeting
        Tonight
    in the Shady Acres
    dining room 8 pm!
```

Kevin looked around in confusion. A meeting tonight at the home? He hadn't announced any meeting. And residents on drugs? What did that mean? Drug dealers at his home? Who the hell put these up and what were they talking about? He looked at the poster again. No information about who had put them up, only that inflammatory question and accusation. *Goddammit*, he thought, *someone else out to make my life miserable.* Grabbing the side of the poster, Kevin tried to yank it off the pole, but succeeded in only tearing a strip across the middle. He tried again and tore off another strip, leaving the poster saying, 'What is Shady drugs! Tonight'.

He tried again to tear the rest of the poster off the pole, but the tough packing tape resisted his attempts to break it. Furious, Kevin ran across the street to the next pole and failed again to remove its poster.

He stopped and nibbled on a cuticle, then yanked his finger away from his mouth and stared at it. He hadn't bitten his nails in years! Not since after his father had died. Shoving his hand down into his pants pocket, Kevin ran across to his idling car, hopped in and drove through the intersection, his mind full of confusion and anger. Slowing to a stop at the next intersection, he glanced to his left to ensure it was safe to go, only to spot the same while poster taped to the pole across the street from him.

"Son of a bitch..." Gunning his car forward Kevin raced to work, realizing every single intersection had posters prominently displayed at them. What the hell is going on?

•

"Wasn't sure you'd be out of bed, Mister Paul," Marcus said when Paul opened his apartment door.

"I wasn't sure I would be, either," Paul replied and gestured for Marcus to follow him inside. With Marcus watching, Paul returned to doing some stretching, groaning as he reached down to the floor.

"Have I been Rip Van Winkle for a hundred years?"

"It will take some time for that to pass."

Paul stretched a bit more then stood up and looked at Marcus. "So why'd the pills stop? Did Kevin change his mind? Or am I being unceremoniously kicked out of here?"

Marcus sighed deeply, thought about making some excuse, but instead decided to tell his truth. "I couldn't do it anymore. There's no reason for you to be taking shit like that." He met Paul's surprised stare calmly for a few moments, then looked at his watch and nodded to himself. "Come on, we have someplace to go."

"Go where?"

Marcus considered the question for a moment, but instead started towards the door, "You'll have to trust me."

Paul studied the large man then nodded and followed. "I owe you that much, Mister Marcus."

"That you do, Mister Paul."

Perplexed, Paul followed Marcus silently through the corridors of Shady Acres and out into the staff parking lot. He started to ask again where they were going when they stopped at a silver four-door Mazda, but Paul kept his tongue and simply climbed into the passenger seat. Marcus slid his bulk behind the wheel, started up the engine, and they drove off to the sound of early Seventies funk.

"Parliament?" Paul asked.

Marcus looked at him, surprised, and then said, "Funkadelic."

"Bootsy Collins. He's all right."

Marcus nodded. "Better than all right."

After ten minutes of driving and most of one Funkadelic song, Marcus pulled into the parking lot of the local hospital. Again, Paul wanted to ask what was going on and again didn't. Instead, he followed Marcus inside and up to the patient wards. Marcus led him along a corridor to a patient room and paused. "I'll let you go inside on your own, Mister Paul. I'll wait right here and take you back."

"Okay..." Paul said, still confused, and pushed the door open.

Marcus leaned back against the wall and let out a deep sigh.

A nurse in green scrubs leaned over a patient, checking something. Behind the bed, on the wall, were flashing and beeping monitors. The nurse turned, looking at him as he moved to the foot of the bed, saying, "He's doing fine. Gave us quite a scare, though. Best to let him sleep, ok?" Then she stepped away from the bed and left the room. With the nurse gone, Paul saw his friend Jim laid out on the bed, a huge purpling bruise on his right shoulder; his right arm in a cast and elevated away from his body. A bandage covered his left eye.

"Oh, my…" Paul started to say then stopped. Instead, he stood at the foot of the bed and stared, attempting to make sense of what he saw, remembering his wife, wasting away in her hospital bed. The smell, the sounds, the hopelessness… Finally, he turned and stepped out into the corridor. Marcus stood up and put his phone away.

"Damnit, what the hell happened to him?" Paul said, shakily.

"He didn't want the meds. So he had to get moved to a different home. He fell down the stairs."

Instead of asking the flurry of questions whirling around in his head, Paul turned and returned to the room. Marcus sighed and leaned back against the wall.

Back in the patient room, Paul pulled up a chair and sat by his friend.

"Why didn't you take the pills?" he asked quietly, knowing he wouldn't receive an answer.

How could a silly little fishing trip turn into such a mess, he wondered. *I wanted to have some innocent fun, to be with friends, doing something I like to do.*

Me, me, me, he heard a voice in his head say; everything is all about you. Paul sat for a moment, looking at Jim's chest rise and fall. *It's been about me*, he thought. *It was my idea, and this is the result. I wonder how the kids are doing… Probably grounded, privileges taken away. Because I wanted to go fishing.*

Paul leaned against the edge of the bed and took his friend's hand, careful of the IV attached to its back. *An old hand, exactly like mine*, he thought. *We're old men, and we shouldn't be taking risks.* Being kicked out of his home and falling down a flight of stairs because he wouldn't take some drugs. *That's not right,* he thought. *I might have persuaded them to do something against the rules, but what they've done to my friend, and to me, is not right.*

With a final gentle grip of his friend's hand, Paul stood slowly up and said, "You'll be back, and I'll have a cigar waiting for you, my friend." Then he left the room without another look.

Again, Marcus stood up from the wall and looked at him. Paul wiped some wetness from his eye and said, "You've taken a risk, bringing me to him. Thank you. And that's hard for me to say." Marcus nodded, slightly. Paul reached out his hand, and Marcus shook it. Then Paul stumbled and Marcus had to ease him down into a plastic chair beside the door.

"How you feeling?"

Paul looked up at the huge man and said, "I'm not sure what I'm feeling. Tired. I'm feeling tired and old. But it's time to go home because I'm not doing too good and need to do some serious thinking."

Marcus sighed and said, "That you do, Mister Paul."

Forty Five

Kevin gave up counting after fifty posters and drove the rest of the way to Shady Acres in a complete fury. Whoever had put up the notices was messing with his livelihood. As the boss—and owner—of Shady Acres, only he could call the kind of meeting that had been announced. After grabbing a cup of coffee, Kevin spent some time going around the home, talking to the staff, watching their responses to discover if any of them had been responsible for the posters. But no one knew anything about the meeting and were as confused as him. His secretary, Suzanne, had taken several calls about the meeting, but, because she didn't know anything about it, had merely denied that a meeting was happening that evening.

"Why would someone say there was a meeting when there isn't a meeting?" she asked Kevin as he entered his office.

"Because whoever they are, they want a scene, so they're going to force me—us—to have a meeting. When the damn dining room is full of people expecting someone to talk to them, then there will be a meeting, whether I like it or not." He shut his office door, then opened it again, and said, "Tell the dining room to keep a couple of staff late this evening, just in case. We have to be on top of this."

Suzanne nodded and picked up her telephone as Kevin shut the door again.

Back in his office and seated at his desk, overly aware of the bottle in the bottom drawer, Kevin called Marcus in from his desk.

"What have you heard about this? Any gossip around here from the residents?"

Marcus shook his head. "No, sir, those who are aware of it are as confused as we are. But they are phoning their kids, and even some grandkids, and telling them to come tonight."

"Damnit," Kevin muttered. "I don't even know what they want. Somebody wants something. But what? Who does this kind of thing?"

Marcus shrugged. "I wonder what it all means."

Kevin waved his hands in the air exasperatedly, saying, "Some garbage about drug trafficking. Like we have drug traffickers here."

"I understood it to be about those few heavily sedated tenants, myself."

Kevin stopped and stared at Marcus. Was that what the meeting was about? Why would anyone be upset about trained professionals administering medications to elderly?

"That's rubbish."

Marcus shrugged again. Kevin's mind raced, considering and discounting options. Could it really be about that? These were standard practices in extended living facilities; he wasn't doing anything wrong. He knew that much. He'd learned that much from his father before the accident and he kept up with the updates and changes as they were announced by three levels of government. Shady Acres ran by the book, guaranteed.

Kevin drank the rest of his now-cold coffee, grimaced, and continued, "We have always treated people right here. My grandfather did, my father did, and I do, too. This kind of bullshit is enough to make me want to shut the damn home down. You imagine I do this because I like it? Dealing with these 'issues?'"

Kevin stopped before saying too much and looked at Marcus. "Let me know if you hear anything concrete, yes? And I expect you to be with me tonight. Seven o'clock, in the dining room. The kitchen staff has been informed."

He dismissed Marcus by turning to his computer and starting to write an email. Marcus paused, nodded, and—keeping his thoughts to himself—left the office.

•

Paul remained in his room for the rest of the afternoon, unaware of the rumors whirling around the home like a forest fire. Still shaken up from finding out about Jim, guilt roiled inside of him. And his system was still fighting back from the effects of the medication he had been on. He had no interest in food, but forced himself to drink a cup of water each hour in an attempt to cleanse his system. But his mind frequently slipped back into cloudiness, and he would have to lie down for a while to regroup.

Jim is right. I'm never taking anything like that ever again, he thought, while lying on his bed staring up at the spinning ceiling. *This is worse than the worst nights of drinking on leave in Saigon.* The spinning finally passed, and he slipped off into an uneasy sleep for a while, only to wake up in a sweat to drink another glass of water and lie back down again.

•

Kevin tried to forestall the mysterious meeting by calling the adult children of some of the tenants to convince them not to come to the meeting, but those who didn't know were suddenly concerned and committed to attending, and those who knew couldn't be dissuaded.

Marcus sat at his desk and watched the residents move around, isolated groups deep in animated conversation. *There's a storm coming,* he thought. *A truly massive storm...*

•

The parking lot was full by six o'clock that evening. Many people had taken advantage of the impending meeting to come early and have dinner with their parent or grandparent. The visitor rules were cancelled for the evening. The unexpected influx had the kitchen and wait staff in overdrive, as everyone wanted to be fed and finished in time for the mysterious meeting. Kevin spent the hour working the room, chatting with residents and their families, but finding a lot of resistance and concern regarding the huge accusation that had been papered around town.

Paul shuffled down the empty hallway and slowly climbed the stairs up to the next floor. The thought of being in the elevator had him feeling sick to his stomach. He made his way down to Joanne's room and knocked on the door. After a long moment, the door opened, and Frances stood in front of him. He frowned in confusion, and asked, "What are you doing here?"

"She needs someone here for her, doesn't she?"

Then Frances stepped aside and gestured toward the bedroom. Paul wandered in, but stopped at the bedroom door. He looked inside as Frances stepped past him and over to the figure nearly buried under a down comforter and a crocheted blanket. Paul frowned and said, "Is she sick? What's the matter with her?"

"Sick?" Frances said, in disgust. "Drugged up to her eyeballs by her son. Because she went fishing with you."

Still unable to comprehend, Paul stammered, "What are you talking about?"

"She's on the same meds you're on. For the same reason you're on them. For the same reason Jim isn't living here anymore. You childish men, playing your silly games and getting women in trouble."

"I-"

Frances waved her hand at him; dismissing whatever he attempted to say, "Keep your yap shut. I've no interest in anything you want to say to me. She's like this because of you."

Paul staggered back and sat down on the couch in the darkened living room, his mind spinning from both the receding drugs and the new accusations.

•

As the wait staff cleared the final dessert dishes off the tables, Kevin, with Marcus' help, dragged the maître d' stand to the front of the room to use as a makeshift podium. As they did, everyone in the room shifted their seats around to face it and him. Standing off to the side of the podium, Kevin scanned the room, expecting someone to stand up and start the meeting. In the room, people started to glance around, unsure what was happening. Something should to be starting, but whatever it was, wasn't. Kevin looked over at Marcus and whispered, "What are your thoughts? They call a meeting, but don't show up?"

"Might be best to be out in front of the situation, Mister Kevin."

Nodding, Kevin stepped up to the podium as the dining room doors opened at the far end of the room and the last few stragglers entered. Amongst them were Natalie and her son Devon; Beth and their daughter, Dawn; and Jim's son, Michael, and grandson, Eric. They clustered against the far wall, as there weren't any empty chairs. Kevin stepped back and said to Marcus, "See if there are some more chairs for the people at the back." Marcus nodded and walked into the kitchen. After a moment, one of the staff pushed a stack of chairs into the room, handed them out, and everyone finally sat down.

Only then did Kevin step up to the podium, take confident hold of each side—as Toastmasters had taught him—and greeted his audience with a confident smile—as Toastmasters had also taught him.

"I'm sure you're wondering why we have gathered here tonight," he paused and glanced around the room, making occasional eye contact before continuing. "I'm wondering the same thing," Kevin chuckled and looked around again, searching for someone to stand up or raise a hand or otherwise make it known they are the one, or ones, who put up the signs. But no one stood up, so Kevin sighed and continued speaking to the group, "Ok, it looks we have a practical joker in town who's really put one over on us. So, whoever you are..." Kevin stepped to the side of the podium and started slowly clapping. After a moment, he stopped and returned to the podium. "Congratulations, you got us. All of us. I'm sorry folks; it looks like we have been the victims of a practical joke."

At the back of the room, Devon glanced furtively at Dawn and Eric. Neither returned his gaze, so he looked back to the front of the room before anyone caught him. Natalie noticed him moving and whispered to him, "This is strange, isn't it?"

•

Devon nodded, but didn't reply. As Kevin talked about how he hoped everyone had a good meal with their family, Devon wondered what he could do to turn the conversation around to the drugging of his grandfather and Joanne, and Jim's accident once he had been kicked out of Shady Acres. But nothing came to mind. If he called out a question, Kevin would know he put up the posters and then Paul would be kicked out of the home, too. The same for Dawn. Eric might be able to get away with saying something, but Devon didn't imagine he would. He looked at his mom, hoping for a moment she might ask a question, but she was busy worrying a fingernail. Nope, she was so concerned about Paul having a place to live so she would stay quiet, fearful of rocking the boat. Exasperated, Devon stood up to leave when a middle-aged man off to the side said loudly, "So what's this about drugs?"

Devon sat back down and leaned forward, trying not to be visibly excited. Was this it? Kevin's smooth patter with the residents in the audience stumbled, and he stopped, a worried look briefly on his face, and then he looked over to the man who had called out. In an attempt to give himself a few more moments, Kevin calmly said, "What do you mean?"

The man, still in his business suit, but with his tie loosened, stood up and looked around the room. "What the poster said, 'Residents on Drugs.' Kevin watched as a few of the adult children of residents nodded in agreement.

"I'm sorry, I don't understand your question, Mr. Isaacson."

"What drugs are they talking about? Have you some medication you're giving to certain patients and not others?"

He pointed at his frail mother, staring off into space from a wheelchair beside him and asked, "Is there something you could give to my mother you haven't told me about?"

Murmurs and whispered discussions rose throughout the room. Devon looked over at Dawn and Eric in confusion.

As the volume in the room rose, Kevin raised his hands and called out, "Please, Mr. Isaacson—Craig—I don't understand. You want more medications for your mother?"

"Look, Wright, if you have something to keep her calm, and keep her from calling my wife and me daily looking for her knitting needles and her cat—who died five years ago—I'd happily pay extra for it."

"You can't mean that!" a middle-aged woman at the front of the room called out, standing up. "That's no way to care for our parents—to drug them into vegetables!"

"Don't you tell me what to do with my mother!" Isaacson retorted, "You don't have to deal with her!" A couple of other parents stood up, calling out in agreement with him.

Natalie watched the spectacle in shock and confusion. The two inner voices she had been tormented by had escaped and were now taking over the room. She shook her head in disbelief and leaned back against the wall, observing the growing anger and raised voices in the room in front of her with unease. Beside her, Devon watched the crowd in front of him become angrier and angrier, as the two sides solidified their positions and refined their arguments.

"You need to get a grip and understand I've a life to live and a family to deal with, without having to worry about what my parents are doing," another man, clearly straight from a construction site with hardhat in hand, shouted to the room. "They're old; they're infirm, and they're both losing their minds. So, what am I going to do, huh? You tell me. Come on, you tell me what I'm supposed to do."

"That's no way to talk about your parents! They brought you into this world, they brought you up; they raised you to be the person you are today. I'm sure they'd both be ashamed of who you've become if they could understand what you're saying," a woman yelled back.

"There! You said it. They don't understand what I'm saying! Jesus, I wish they could, but they don't! They're barely aware they're married most of the time. My mother calls me 'Dad.' She—they—haven't a clue," the man said back, wiping his brow. "What am I supposed to do?"

The woman controlled herself and said, "What you're doing is evil. Contrary to God. He knows it, and you know it, too."

"What God makes my parents lose their minds?" the man asked, visibly shaken. "You tell me, what God makes my mother not know her own son? Her own husband?"

"The Good Lord—"

"Enough!" Kevin yelled from the podium. The room silenced. "Enough," he said, quieter this time. He held the sides of the podium and looked around the gathering in front of him.

"This is not a question of God. This is a question of troublemakers," Kevin paused and looked around the room, his eyes slowing as he scanned past Devon and Eric before continuing. "If you have an apartment, and you're renting it out, but you get some unruly tenants—frat boys, for example—you would punish them if they ruined your property, right?" Nods of agreement met his pause. "Of course you would. You'd withhold their damage deposit, make them pay to have anything broken fixed, and, if they were really troublesome, you could have them evicted. All within your rights as their landlord. You're not going to let them stay in an apartment you own—that you spent your hard-earned money on—and continue to damage it, right?" Again, the audience nodded in agreement with what Kevin said.

Emboldened, he continued, "Right. You have a responsibility to ensure they are not doing damage to your property. Not endangering themselves or anyone else with their recklessness. If that's what they are doing, you have no choice but to do something—am I correct, or am I crazy?"

The audience nodded again. Devon watched, shocked, as Kevin expertly flipped the mood and outrage of the group around to be on his side again. Even The Bees, at their usual table, but without Joanne, seemed to be receptive to Kevin's point. *But what about my grandfather,* he thought, *and Joanne and Jim? They aren't some crazy frat boys running a meth lab in a rental apartment; they're a few old people who don't want to give up and die.*

Up at the front, Kevin realized he had shifted the crowd around to his view, and he could now put the final mortal cuts into the body of this feeble rebellion. "If my residents are disruptive, if they are causing trouble, or creating anxiety and stress for the other residents, my responsibility is to do something. For the betterment of all, I am using my authority to ensure the safety of all."

The vast majority of the crowd in the dining room rose to their feet and applauded. Those defiant ones, including Natalie and the teens at the back of the room, remain seated. Clearly Kevin's speech had taken the protest down at the knees and rendered it mute. Devon leaned back in shock, realizing his plan to bring to light the unfair drugging of his grandfather and Dawn's grandmother, and the ejection of Jim from the home, had failed. But worse, even more old people at the home were going to be medicated into that same netherworld because of him and his friends. Their attempt for justice had backfired and the impact would be far worse than any of them could have possibly imagined. The home would be run in an environment of absolute fear where the smallest infraction would be enough to get a resident sedated, against their will, but with the full backing of management.

At the front of the room, Kevin smiled confidently, knowing he had brilliantly taken a crisis for Shady Acres and turned it into a victory for himself. *Whoever put up those posters must be pretty upset right now,* he smugly thought, as some people gathered around the podium, asking about the medications they could get their aging parents on to make their own lives easier. *These are different times,* Kevin thought, *and new and better medication are part of assisted living now. There's no turning back, no matter what a few dissenters might say.* As he thought this, he realized he was avoiding making eye contact with his wife and daughter. Taking a deep breath, he looked over the heads of the audience at them to do so. And then Kevin saw someone else standing at the back of the room.

Forty Six

Paul had been groggily standing in the hall, outside the dining room, ever since Marcus had woken him from another disturbed sleep and brought him down from his room. As the argument raged on, Paul realized a couple of startling facts: he recognized the typeface used on the poster as one Devon always favored for his school assignments; and, though no one said it, this was really about him, Joanne, and Jim and the fallout from their fishing trip.

He had slipped into the dining room as Kevin finished his closing argument. *He was a smooth talker, with a clear gift for words,* Paul thought, wishing Jim was here to speak in their defense. No matter how skilled Kevin was, Jim would have made their case, perfectly, eloquently, and with no extra words needed. But Jim was still in the hospital and barely conscious. It would have to be up to him to make a stand.

When Kevin looked to the back of the room and made eye contact, Paul knew it was time. Pushing himself off the wall, Paul struggled up to the front of the room, moving slowly through the tables and chairs, still working off the effects of the medications he had been put on.

Kevin warily watched Paul come forward for a moment, and then pre-emptively turned to the audience, "We've had enough talk for one night, so I thank you for your concern, your continued interest in the well-being of your parents, and how Shady Acres is always striving to do right by you and them."

Behind him, Paul heard his daughter call out his name, but he continued until he arrived at the front of the room. Kevin kept talking, his best business smile stuck on his face, winding down the meeting as quickly as he could, "I will write out some of the key points discussed and have it sent out to those on the mailing list. That should help you to make some informed decisions about what we've discussed here."

Kevin remained behind the podium, claiming the authority that came with it as Paul stopped in front of him.

"You should be in bed," Kevin whispered.

Paul scowled back and said firmly, "I should be a lot of things. But being right here, right now, is at the top of my list. So step aside and let one of your residents speak."

Startled by the vehemence in Paul's voice, Kevin stepped back a couple of steps. Paul turned to face the milling crowd, most up on their feet and collecting their hats and coats in preparation to leave.

"I've got something to say," Paul said, weakly. No one noticed, and everyone continued preparing to leave. "Hey!" Paul said, without much more volume. From the back of the room, no one could even hear Paul. Eric and Dawn watched, helplessly, as Paul disappeared from their view by the milling crowd. "Mom, do something!" Dawn said to Beth.

Beth had no idea what to do. A quick glance at Natalie confirmed that neither mother had any idea how to convince the crowd to listen to what Paul wanted to say.

But then, at the back of the dining room, Marcus eased himself in front of the doors, innocently slowing everyone's exit down without being obvious. As the crowd backed up, Natalie impulsively stood up on her chair and yelled loudly, "Someone else wants to speak!"

The crowd slowed and turned around and saw Paul leaning against the podium. A few people sat back down, but most stayed on their feet until Dawn called out, "Everyone, please take your seats for a few more minutes." That was enough to make everyone turn around and quickly sit down again.

Paul looked out at the crowd and cleared his throat. "I've got some words that need to be said."

"Speak up!" someone called from the back.

"I can't," Paul said, with a bit more strength in his voice. "See, I've been on those medications you've been talking about. That chemical straightjacket. I've been on them for a week, so they say. I don't know; I don't really remember anything about that week. Apparently, my grandson nearly got into a fight right in front of me in the TV room—and I don't really remember," Paul paused and rubbed the stubble on his chin. "My throat's really sore; it's been really bad since I stopped taking the medication I had been on last night."

Behind him, Kevin gritted his teeth but kept smiling. *Who decided to stop Paul's meds?* he wondered. Paul continued, "Now, you may imagine putting your mother or your father on these drugs will make your life easier, and that's probably true. But..." Paul's voice caught then got another notch stronger. "It does not make their life easier. I have lived a good many years. I was raised in the dustbowls of Montana in the dirty thirties and I fought in two wars. I have beautiful children and grandchildren, and I've buried one wife and too many friends to count. I have had a great *quantity* of life, yes sir, and now's the time for me to have some *quality* of life."

Paul took a breath, tired from talking more than he'd done in days. He continued,

"This place, this home, is full of amazing people—some of whom I am honored to call friends. But none of us are ready to give up and go softly into the night—that's a quote from Dylan Thomas, for those who wonder about my faculties. We are ready to be put out to pasture, but not ready for the glue factory. I'd like to be with my friends, do a little fishing, and connect with my grandson. Is that too much to ask?"

A couple of people nodded in agreement, but Paul could sense the energy of Kevin's frustration behind him. He had to say more. He had to explain better and he had to do it right now before Kevin regained control of the meeting.

"Listen, I get that we—I—am a bit ornery at times. But imagine how you'd be if you spent your life earning the freedom to do what you want, when you want, only to have that freedom taken away from you. Oh sure, we have illnesses and medical problems which limit what we should be doing, but we're not talking about climbing Mount Everest! We only want some freedom to do what we want."

Paul looked around the room, noticing his daughter wiping tears away from her eyes as she listened. He gave her a smile which she weakly returned, and then continued, "Here's the crazy way I see it: when our children were young, we taught them how to ride a bike. We ran along behind them, hanging on to the back of the seat, not wanting to let go, not wanting them to fall and be hurt. No one wants their child to crash to the ground. So we hang on tight. But what holds them back is us hanging on. You're not riding a bike by yourself if someone is holding it up for you. We had to get over our fears and let go of the bike. And what happened? They crashed a few times, skinned a knee, cried a bit—but after a while, they could ride their bike by themselves."

"Is there a point to this?" someone called out, impatiently. Paul ignored the heckler and continued, "We—me and your mothers and fathers—are the opposite of that little kid. Because we're older, we're now going to need some help. We know how to ride the bike, but now we need some help doing it, now and then. Someone to hold onto the bike for us; to help us stay upright."

Paul paused, looked around the room and saw people making the connection for themselves. "I don't want to be a burden. I absolutely do not want to be a burden. But asking for some help is only asking for help. And after eighty years on the planet, I deserve at least that. But the bottom line is this: just as we learned to trust you to make your way in the world, you'll have to learn to trust us the way we are now and let us live and do what we are capable of doing. That's all we ask."

Paul sighed, complete. Then he stepped from the podium and started back through the room toward Marcus at the doors. Kevin watched him go, then looked over at Beth and Dawn, and was startled to see that they were both crying. Beth held Natalie's hand, and Natalie was also crying. When Paul arrived at the back of the room, he stopped in front of his daughter, leaned down and kissed her on the forehead, then fist bumped Devon.

"I'm so sorry, Daddy," Natalie whispered, but Paul shook his head.

"Nothing to be sorry about, sweetheart. Nothing at all." Then he leaned down to Devon and said quietly, "You need to pick different lettering next time, kiddo. The one you used on the posters was a dead giveaway. You've been using it since fifth grade."

Devon blushed as Paul stood up and left the room, receiving a tight nod from Marcus as he exited.

Back at the front of the room, Kevin announced, once again, the end of the meeting and everyone rose to leave. As the room started towards the now open dining room doors, Kevin stood resolutely at the podium. Despite his calm outward appearance, his head spun. The reaction to Paul's speech wasn't what he had expected. His wife and daughter crying? He did what was right, Kevin knew that, but could doing the right thing not be the right thing to do?

Forty Seven

By the time Kevin put everything back to some semblance of normality at Shady Acres and drove home, it was past nine o'clock. Exhausted, he desperately needed a drink—a large one. And maybe some food—he had only eaten a couple of mouthfuls of a turkey potpie and But when he stepped into the kitchen of his house what awaited him wasn't a tumbler full of ice and bourbon, but two red-eyed women both leaning against the counter with their arms crossed.

"Oh, please..." Kevin muttered, putting down his briefcase, plugging in his phone, and hanging up his suit jacket. "At least let me pour myself a drink before you start."

"Excuse me?" Beth said, standing up. "You will listen to what I've got to say, Kevin Wright, or you turn around and walk right back out that door."

"So, no drink?"

Beth and Dawn shook their heads in unison. Kevin shook his head in dismay and leaned back against the wall, facing them across the kitchen. Despite how tired he felt, he had to make his points quickly before the two wore him down with emotional arguments. So he said, calmly, "I'm within my rights to do what I'm doing at the home. I require sign-off from both the children and from the physicians on staff. I'm not doping the residents, for God's sake. I'm ensuring they don't harm themselves and don't do harm to others. Simple as that."

Dawn and Beth looked at each other and then back at him before Beth spoke, "Simple as that? Like some formula on one of your spreadsheets? If resident does X, then put resident on drug Y? These are real people, Kevin! People who have worked hard all their lives and now deserve some respect from you!"

"They have my respect, but that doesn't mean I'm not going to do what's best for them."

"For them? You're not doing what's best for them, Kevin; you're doing what's best for you. What's best for the bottom line! I bet you've already figured out how to cut back the staff hours if you have more residents doped up."

Kevin looked away quickly, but Beth caught it. "I knew it. I didn't see it before—maybe I didn't want to see it—but I don't like this side of you. Not one bit. You weren't always like this, not when you started working at Shady Acres."

"Of course I was different then!" Kevin said, angrily. "I had both of my parents! I had someone to talk to about how to run the home! But then my father died, and it was on me! And I wanted that? Did I want to suddenly have to deal with two hundred and fifty-seven old people? I can't view each of them as an individual; there're not enough hours in a day. I had to get rid of any personal connection and only look at them as a group."

"As numbers on a sheet?" Dawn asked.

"Yes! As numbers! Income and expenditures. There wasn't any time, and there still isn't, to personalize them. If I do that, then I'm going to be dragged under by the minutia. Don't you understand that?"

Beth could understand, and stared across the kitchen at Kevin.

"If this is the way you are now, then I don't want you in this house. You are not the man I married anymore. You are someone different, and I don't like this new you."

"What are you talking about? This is my house, my home! You're my wife!" Kevin said, angry.

Beth shook her head. "Not right now, I'm not. I'm asking you to leave. Maybe we'll work this out, but not tonight and not here."

She pointed to the back door as Dawn started to cry beside her. Beth put her arm protectively around her daughter, but didn't stop pointing at the door. Kevin began to say something, but stopped and shook his head.

He picked up his phone, briefcase, and jacket, then took a step towards the back door before turning and saying, "You don't understand."

"No, I finally do understand. And it breaks my heart," Beth said before turning and leaving the room with Dawn.

When Kevin returned to Shady Acres, he grabbed a fold-up cot, pillow, and blanket from housekeeping and rolled it into his office. After he had his bed set up, he poured himself a double shot of bourbon and gulped it down. The liquor burned his throat, but didn't even start to take the edge off the confusion and emotional conflict roiling around in his head and heart.

What the hell am I going to do? How do I make them understand that I don't have any choice? Kevin looked at the empty glass in his hand, then at the bottle on his desk. He was pretty sure the answers weren't to be found there, and he was too old to continue looking for answers at the bottom of the bottle. He still had a home to run. That was the problem. No matter what, he still had a home to run. Even if he currently didn't have a house to go home to.

After staring into his glass for five minutes, with no solutions appearing in the remnants of his drink, Kevin gave up, undressed, and crawled into to bed.

Despite the flimsiness of the mattress and differentness of the pillow, he shifted around for only a few minutes before dropping off into a deep, but troubled sleep.

•

The next morning, Marcus arrived at work early, grabbing a large cup of coffee and a freshly baked blueberry muffin before heading back to the office to check the fax machine and collate the requests for permission to leave the property. It was a lot of extra work, but he could usually be done before the home became too busy. The early risers would already be in the dining room with their coffee and toast, and they knew the operation of the kitchen as well as he did.

But when he turned the corner into the office area, Kevin, standing in the middle of the corridor outside his office, staring at the wall, startled him.

"Mister Kevin?"

Kevin turned and Marcus immediately saw he had not changed clothes since yesterday. Marcus walked up beside his boss and offered him the muffin. Kevin shook his head, then changed his mind and pulled a piece off and put it in his mouth absentmindedly.

"The kitchen makes a good muffin," Kevin said.

Marcus nodded and turned, looking where Kevin gazed. The portrait of Joanne.

Marcus began to back away and leave him with his thoughts when Kevin said, "You'd hope it would become easier, but it doesn't."

"No sir, I don't believe it does."

They stood there, looking at the portrait. Finally, Kevin shifted and checked his watch. "You probably have work to do, and I'm wasting your time. I'll see you later, Marcus." Then Kevin turned and walked off down the corridor, straightening his tie as he went. Marcus watched

Kevin leave the building through the staff entrance at the far end of the hall and only then did he turn to continue with the start to his day.

•

Beth and Dawn met with Natalie and Devon on the steps of the church. As the two teens blushed and talked quietly, the two mothers spoke in the warm morning sunlight before going inside.

"Quite the meeting last night…" Natalie said.

Beth wiped away some tears from her eyes and nodded. "What your father said… his words were quite eloquent."

Natalie agreed. "Probably the most words I've ever heard him say at one time. Certainly the most passionate I've seen him in an exceptionally long time."

"I guess that's good…" Beth said, sadly.

Natalie looked at Beth, and frowned. "What's going on, Beth?"

Beth blew her nose on her tissue, then balled it up and took a new one out of her purse. She glanced over and saw the teens were out of hearing and said, quietly, "I told Kevin to leave the house last night after he got home. What he did to your father, and to his own mother… I thought I knew what kind of a man he was, but I don't."

"Understanding men isn't one of my strong suits," Natalie sadly admitted. "But I'm sure he had a good—if flawed—reason for what he did. And he'll change his mind, right?"

"I don't know. He's pretty stubborn."

Natalie sighed, remembering her ex and all the examples of his stubbornness, especially when she finished her courses in project management and got a job in the oil fields that paid better than his running the feed store in town.

"Beth? Do you want to get together for a coffee sometime? Complain about our children's fathers?" Natalie said impulsively.

Beth gently patted her tears away and managed a weak smile. "You know, I'd like that."

Natalie smiled back as one of the church helpers motioned for them to come inside. The two women sat together while the teens slipped into a row at the back. Devon and Dawn held hands, at first cautiously and then with nervous excitement. Devon glanced around the quickly filling church, looking for anyone he knew, hoping to show off who he sat with and who he held hands with. A family noisily taking their seats at the far outside edge of the church caught Devon's attention as the preacher shuffled up to the pulpit and began speaking to the congregation. Devon frowned and leaned over to whisper in Dawn's ear, "Isn't that your dad over there?"

He pointed across the church, and she followed his gaze then nodded.

"Wow, he looks like shit," Devon muttered before returning his attention to the front.

"He is a shit," Dawn whispered angrily before a silver-haired woman in front of them turned and shushed them into silence.

•

Kevin had been sitting at the end of the church pew for hours, hoping for calm, but instead being enveloped in his own fears, confusion, and pain. He'd dozed off at one point, had a short but nightmarish dream, then awoke when someone slammed a door at the back of the church. As helpers arrived to ready the church for today's service, everyone left him alone. Some had been at the home last night for the meeting, and all, he was positive, had heard about it. Kevin remained distracted by his own thoughts, unaware even of the arrival of his wife and daughter until the words of the preacher broke through and brought him back to the present.

"All great spirituality is about letting go," Pastor Alistair intoned from the pulpit, his old hands grasping the sides as Kevin had held the podium the night before. "Here in our church and in churches, temples, and mosques around the world. Let's ponder about those words for a moment. 'Letting Go.'"

Alistair stared out at the congregation, holding the pause to allow those seated to experience the words he said before continuing in his powerful voice that was quite out of place coming from such a frail body.

"Many of us Christians are control freaks—we become totally 'stressed out' when life doesn't go our way… and when strange events happen, when those events don't go the way we planned, we worry so much that we end up actually blocking God's grace in our lives and in the lives of our families—and quite often, the result is the exact opposite of what we originally intended…

"Does this sound familiar? When we block the grace of God through our own stubbornness?"

With faint murmurs of recognition rippling through the church, Alistair continued, "Control over our environment, our circumstances, our family and friends, even our own lives, is a grand illusion—and this is not a modern problem. Absolutely, take control. You make the choices. You call the shots. You don't have to rely on anyone else for your wants, wishes, or well-being. How is that working for us, friends? Has it been a dream come true… or has it been our nightmare? Broken relationships. Broken lives. Lives forever after lived in fear. And guess what? That fear makes us want more control!"

He banged the pulpit with his hand, the loud sound echoing through the church, waking up the few who had dozed off. Kevin flinched, but remained engrossed in the words. Everything said connected with him, unlike any sermon he'd ever sat through. He leaned forward on the back of the pew in front of him and awaited the reverend's next words.

Alistair took a sip of water with a shaky hand then continued, "But, when I choose to give up control, accept the situations I cannot change and trust God with the outcomes, even though my outward circumstances may not change, the way I experience the circumstances changes. When I let go and let God take charge, I have an inner peace that cannot be explained. It is the peace that passes understanding that the Apostle Paul talks about in Philippians. And that allows me to view life in a new light.

"Letting go is not particularly in our DNA. But the words 'let go' mean to abdicate control, to release, to surrender, to give up our sense of possessiveness, and our definitions of 'mine,' and 'not mine.' Let us sing."

Kevin felt the words fall away as the pastor brought the congregation to their feet for the singing of a hymn. He remained seated, the sermon flowing in his head, wrapping around his jumbled thoughts and confusions, picking apart his old fears and stories, then rebuilding them anew.

Forty Eight

That evening, as the sun set behind the huge trees on the western edge of the Shady Acres property, Kevin found Paul sitting on a bench looking out at the river as it flowed slowly past. Walking up slowly, Kevin stood behind the bench and gazed out as well. The crazy whirling in his head which had been non-stop for the past thirty-six hours—since he first spotted the poster for the meeting—had quieted and turned into a nervous excitement. Hope where before there had only been roiling knots of anxiety and stomach churning stress.

"It really is quite pretty," Paul finally said, not looking up.

"Apparently they cleared this view before deciding exactly where to build the main house. What could be seen from the parlor and from the dining room were paramount to Augusta Wright, my great-great-great— maybe one more great-grandmother."

Paul nodded. "She had a good eye."

Kevin stepped around the end of the bench and sat down. They sat in silence for a while, before Paul said, "I know you're trying to do the best for us, but it isn't what we need. In the Army, being an officer is a balance between being too hard and too soft. Either one will harm your men, but finding that balance is the trick."

Paul lapsed back into silence, and the two looked out at the river for a while more before Kevin shifted on the bench and let out a long sigh. Paul glanced at him slightly, but didn't say anything.

"This isn't an easy job," Kevin started, "but my father did it well. He was a good man, and he did a good job because he cared. I didn't really have the chance to learn that from him before... well, before he died. He was a lot like you. Maybe I've been so hard on you because I didn't get to be hard on him. I didn't have time to rebel—besides, he worked hard during my teen years and I could do pretty much whatever I wanted," Kevin shrugged and continued looking out at the river.

After a while, he said, "Maybe we have to rebel, even if we don't want to. Maybe that's the best time to do some rebelling, when you don't want to. So, there you go. I've been rebelling against you."

Kevin laughed at himself and shook his head. "That might be the stupidest thing I've ever said to a resident."

Paul finally looked over at Kevin. "Oh, I doubt that."

Together, they laughed, and then Paul said, "I haven't been making it easy on you either. Probably for the same reasons. I had primed myself to find someone to fight with—to rebel against—and you, Mister Authority, were pretty much perfect."

"We do fight well together, don't we?"

Paul laughed, reached into his coat pocket and pulled out two cigars. Kevin raised his eyebrows in surprise. "You know there's no smoking on the property."

Paul shrugged and handed a cigar to Kevin. Kevin took it and rolled it between his fingers.

"I don't see anyone smoking."

Kevin smiled and nodded. He glanced around for a moment, then stood up and sauntered forward toward the river for a few steps. Paul rose slowly to his feet, stretched to loosen up his back and hip and then wandered down to join him. When Paul arrived beside him, Kevin reached into his pocket and pulled out an old-fashioned Zippo lighter and played with it for a moment. "My dad left me this. He got it from my grandfather, who got it while in Paris on leave during the war. I doubt he ever lit a cigarette with it, my dad. Never smoked."

"Won't hold that against him, I don't think," Paul said.

"No," Kevin said quietly, "I don't think we will."

Paul remained quiet while Kevin played with the lighter for a while, then sighed, put his cigar in his mouth and lit it up. After he had gotten his cigar lit, Kevin passed the lighter to Paul who followed suit.

"I thought you said something about a no smoking rule…" Paul said after a couple of puffs. Kevin continued looking out at the river and said, "No smoking on the property. But presently we are approximately three feet past the property line and are now on the publicly owned foreshore."

Paul grinned, then the two returned to gazing out at the slowly passing river.

•

Weak and groggy, Joanne climbed out of her bed and wandered into her dark living room. Blinking the sleep out of her eyes, she pulled open her curtains and saw the fading light on the grounds and river in the distance. *What time is it?* she wondered. *What day is it?* She rubbed her face a bit and poured herself a glass of water. Surprised at how thirsty she was once it was gone, she poured herself another glass then stepped out onto her balcony. A warm evening breeze full of fragrant honeysuckle replaced the stuffy air of her apartment. She took a couple deep, refreshing breaths, and then glanced out over the lawn to the two people at the water's edge. After squinting for a moment, she gave up, and returned to her bedroom for her glasses.

She let out a weak gasp as she realized who it was she could see.

She watched as Paul and Kevin continued conversing, amiably, while both casually smoked their cigars. *How long have I been asleep,* she wondered, *if I wake up and those two are friends?*

•

Back down at the water's edge, Kevin looked over at Paul and said, "There's going to be some changes around here."

Paul took a puff of his cigar and looked at Kevin, seriously. "Yes, there are." The two nodded at each other and returned to their cigars.

If Marcus noticed the smell of smoke on Kevin's suit when he walked through the foyer an hour later, he didn't mention it. Nor did he comment from behind his desk as Kevin entered the elevator instead of heading out the front doors to the staff parking area. A few moments and a few 'good evenings' to random residents later, Kevin was standing outside Joanne's room. After a couple deep breaths, he sighed and knocked.

"It's open," came his mother's faint voice through the door.

"It's me," Kevin said as he entered and shut the door behind himself. Stepping into the living room, he saw that his mother was out on her porch, clearly enjoying the late afternoon sun. Kevin stepped through the open sliding door and leaned against the railing beside her.

Joanne said, "I see you have a new smoking buddy."

"Mom..."

"I'm just joking," she said. "You always had a hard time with jokes."

"I just don't think a lot of them are very funny."

"Your father was the same way. Always serious, the two of you."

Kevin shrugged. *What do I say to something like that?*

His mother looked out at the river and sighed. "I should have talked to you more... about the accident."

"Mom-"

"And now I'm going to," Joanne turned to her son and took his hand in hers. "Kevin, it wasn't your fault. It was no one's fault what happened. You've been blaming yourself all these years for something that was an accident."

"But I was supposed to be there!" Kevin said, shame and guilt all over his face.

"Yes! You were, but you weren't! Don't you understand?"

"I understand that they died because I wasn't there!"

With tears springing to her eyes, Joanne shook her head and gripped Kevin's hands hard with hers. "No. What you don't understand is if you were in that car, the only thing that would have changed is you would have died along with everyone else! And then I would have been left utterly alone in the world. Despite your father dying that day, my shame is that I am so grateful you are alive because you didn't do what you were supposed to do."

Kevin looked down at his mother. As he held her hands, he felt thirty years of guilt crack apart in his chest. A hundred pounds of bricks slid off his perpetually tight shoulders. With a long sigh, Kevin let go of his mother's hands and pulled her close into a tight hug. He felt his mother hold him back. A long hug. The best hug he'd had since he was a child. Together they stood in a gentle, loving, and forgiving silence, as the sun slid down behind the ancient cottonwoods.

Forty Nine

The changes around Shady Acres were swift and welcomed. In a matter of days, the restrictions that had been put in place were lifted. Immediately, the home became a much happier place again.

Marcus straightened his tie and adjusted his suit jacket as he left his office to meet some prospective residents and their families in the foyer. In one of the largest changes, Marcus had moved from his desk in the foyer into one of the three private offices, and been given a raise with a new title: Assistant Manager. His new responsibilities hadn't been too hard to get a handle on, but his challenge was in not using 'Mister' and 'Miss' when speaking to the residents. But he could happily give that up for his new and improved paycheck.

As he waited in the foyer at his old desk, he listened to the other big change around the home as Beth, Kevin's wife—Shady Acres' new activities director—arranged outings for a couple of the residents. Beth, who had briefly done the job before Dawn was born, worked each morning, and was doing a fantastic job of getting everyone involved and active.

She never should have left that seat, he thought.

Marcus said hello to The Bees, minus Joanne, as they came out of the dining room and settled onto one of the couches at the edge of the foyer. They seemed quite excited about something, but Marcus was distracted as two old guys came in and handed back putters to Beth for her to replace on a rack behind her desk.

"How's the putting green, Mark?" Marcus asked, consciously not saying 'Mister Mark'.

"Terrific!" Mark said, and his buddy, Terry, agreed. "Any thoughts about expanding it into a proper nine-hole course?"

Marcus laughed then had a thought, "What if I talk to a friend who runs the green's crew over at the local course? Maybe we could take you guys over occasionally for a proper nine holes."

The two thought it was an excellent idea and headed off, talking up a storm about golf, while Marcus made a quick note to himself and then sent his friend an email.

"Suit looks good on you."

Marcus turned around and saw Paul coming across the foyer from the elevator. Marcus shrugged and smiled, "I look good in a suit." Paul smiled and checked his watch then looked out the front doors.

Beth noticed his glance from behind the desk, and said, "They're not back yet, Paul."

Paul shrugged, thanked her, and looked at Marcus, "You miss being out here in the middle of the action, Mister Marcus?"

Marcus laughed and shook his head. "You were wearing me out, Paul. I'll leave it to Beth to keep an eye on you."

Before Paul could joke back, the front doors opened, and Chuck and his gang strode in. Paul straightened himself up slightly, putting himself on alert. Marcus recognized the people he had arranged to show around had come in behind Chuck, which meant he'd have to leave Beth to manage any conflict that might arise between Chuck and Paul. "You be good," Marcus whispered to Paul. Paul smiled at him as Marcus walked across to greet the new people—an elderly woman with her daughter— and start their tour.

Paul stepped back from Beth's desk as Chuck came over and tossed a set of car keys onto the surface. Beth smiled and said, "Did you mark down the mileage?"

"I don't see why we have to do that…"

"I'll write it down, Beth," Paul said. "I'm sure Chuck will trust me not to make a mistake."

"I appreciate that, Paul." She handed over the car keys to him. Chuck snarled at Paul and started off before Beth called to him, "Oh! Chuck, this was dropped off for you!"

Chuck turned and walked back over to the desk and took the package: a bright, white cake box with a colorful label from a local bakery tied up with a string.

"It smells delicious," Beth offered.

Chuck gruffly thanked her and stepped over to a table in the middle of the foyer to open the cake box.

"How far will you be going today, Paul?"

"No more than sixty mi—"

Paul was cut off by a loud pop and a startled yell from behind him. He turned around and saw Chuck and his gang barely visible in a cloud of talcum powder that had exploded out of the cake box. Paul then heard shrieks of laughter from across the foyer and saw The Bees hooting on the couch. Chuck tried to wipe his face off, but his attempts only smudged the white powder in even more. Chuck looked around, taking in Paul staring at him in confusion, and then seeing The Bees laughing at him.

Then Helen stood up, straightening the pleats on her dress. The rest of The Bees joined her, and they walked away, staying far from the cloud of still-settling talcum powder. As she walked close to Chuck, she stopped and looked him over. "Got ya, asshole," she said. Then, with a laugh, the women left the foyer.

Beth hadn't moved from her chair, staring, mouth open, at the mess in front of her. Paul tossed the car keys up in the air and caught them.

"Welcome to the front desk, Beth."

Then, with a wide smile on his face, Paul walked out the front door into the morning sun.

Epilogue

The summer sun made the river sparkle, and the trees were bright in as many different shades of green as were imaginable. Along the bank and out on the flat rocks, a dozen people lounged about, most fishing, but some were simply enjoying the peaceful surroundings. It was a scene that could have played out at any time in the past century, even longer. At the top of the bank, four cars were parked—including Ruth's Pontiac and the Prius Paul had signed out from the home.

He and Devon were out on their flat rock, two cans of pop cooling in the still water on the upriver side of the rock, their fishing lines lazily floating down with the current.

"It worked out, didn't it?" Devon asked, breaking the companionable quiet. Paul nodded, glancing over at the others with a smile before replying, "It sure looks like it did. Until it doesn't, and then we'll have to do it again."

"You're quite the optimist, Gramps," Devon said with a laugh.

"Ah, you don't arrive at my age by expecting the best all the time. Occasionally you have to pick a battle and actually fight for something."

Devon nodded and looked over at the shore as well.

Upstream, in their usual spot, Jim, his son Michael, Eric, and Eric's younger brother, Dale, were lounging under the huge overhanging Cottonwood. Jim was explaining to Dale how to tie his lure on correctly while Michael and Eric repeatedly cast out their lines and slowly reeled them back in.

Lighthearted laughter from the women further down the shore caught the men's attention. Jim's daughter-in-law was relaxing on a blanket with Ruth and Natalie, sweating glasses of chilled white wine in their hands. Beside them, Joanne, Beth—who had come out as soon as her morning shift at Shady Acres had ended—and Dawn were chatting away while keeping an eye on their fishing lines. Dawn saw Devon glancing her way, grinned and waved at him, then called out, "We beat you last time, you up for a rematch today?"

Devon laughed and turned to his grandfather. "What do you figure? Three against two."

Paul gave the river a hard scan, and then looked over at where the women were fishing before saying, "Those are the kind of odds I like." He stood up and waved to Jim, and then called, "You want a piece of this challenge?"

Jim conferred with his boys then gave a thumb's up. Paul turned back to the women and said, "We'll take you up on that offer! But what does the winner receive?"

Joanne called out, laughing, "Bragging rights!"

"And loser pays for brunch next week," Dawn added.

"Deal!" Jim called out, and Paul tapped the side of his nose. Jim grinned and returned the gesture.

And, with a whoop from Dale, the games began.

A few hours later, when Paul had carefully waded ashore using his cane and a stout stick Devon had found to grab some snacks, he noticed an additional car further down the road, partially hidden in the shade of the overhanging trees. With a confused frown, he climbed slowly up the bank onto the edge of the road and sauntered down to the car, munching on one of Ruth's homegrown carrots as he walked. As he arrived at the side of the BMW, he saw Kevin sitting in the driver's seat, watching the scene unfold in the river.

"Beautiful day," Paul said, amiably.

"Busy," Kevin replied.

"They get that way, sometimes."

"Seems like all the time."

They watched everyone fishing for a moment then Kevin said, more to himself than to Paul, "I fished with my dad. When I was a kid. This was his favorite spot on the river."

"I know," Paul said, quietly.

Kevin nodded and continued, "I haven't fished in a long time. Good memories turned sour after he died, you know?"

Paul nodded, he knew.

"But," Paul said, after a moment, "never too late to pick up a rod and catch some fish. Not like you've forgotten how to fish. The fish haven't forgotten how to take a lure." A cheer rose from Eric and his family joined in as he pulled in a healthy sized bass. Paul grinned and pointed, "See?"

Kevin nodded but didn't move from his seat. Gently, Paul reached in and turned off the car. Then he opened the door. Kevin didn't move for a long time, and Paul waited patiently beside the car. Then Kevin slowly climbed out. Paul shut the door and handed him back his keys. "Come on. I'm sure your mom will let you borrow her fishing rod."

Kevin slipped off his suit jacket and tie, hung them carefully over the back of his seat, and followed Paul back to the group while rolling up the sleeves on his dress shirt.

"Look who I found," Paul called out when he arrived at the top of the bank.

Kevin gave a tentative wave, then everyone cheered, and Kevin smiled.

THE END

Made in the USA
Columbia, SC
29 October 2017